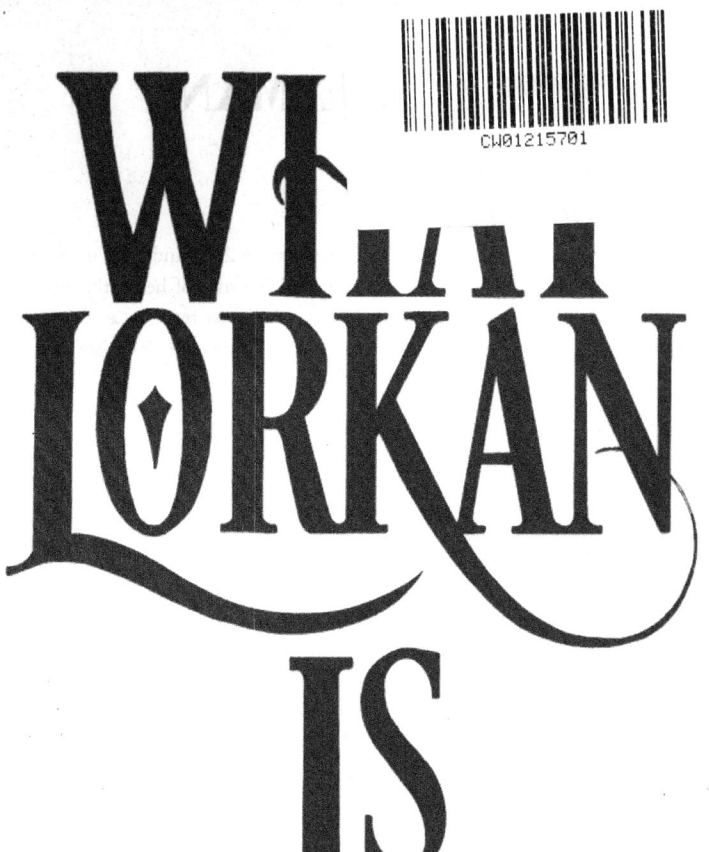

L J R SKYLERMAN

LJR Skylerman was born in 2001 and grew up in rural Norfolk, England. Unsure of her path, she dropped out of sixth form to train as a scuba diver, and wrote her first novel, *What Lorkan Is,* at nineteen years old.

First published online under a different name, the book received over a million reads across several platforms, constant praise, and—after much begging from her online audience—has finally been released in print.

She is currently editing book two, writing book three, and hoping to one day join the Royal Navy. When she's not writing, she is in the sea, at the gym, or wedged between sofa cushions (probably drawing whilst an old film plays on the tele).

For updates and questions regarding her work, connect with LJR Skylerman through:

WEBSITE:
https://AuthorLJRSkylerman.wixsite.com/thebluebloodtrilogy

EMAIL:
AuthorLJRSkylerman@gmail.com

INSTAGRAM:
Author_LJRSkylerman

PINTEREST:
Author_LJRSkylerman

WHAT LORKAN IS

Book one in the
BLUE BLOOD
trilogy

L J R SKYLERMAN

© 2024 LJR Skylerman. All rights reserved.

This book is a work of fiction. Any resemblance to actual persons, living or dead, is purely coincidental. All characters, events, locations, and situations are the product of the author's imagination. No part of this book may be reproduced, distributed, or transmitted in any form or by any means, including photocopying, recording, or other electronic or mechanical methods, without the prior written permission of the author.

All illustrations and cover art in this book were created by the author, LJR Skylerman. These artworks are protected by copyright law and may not be reproduced, distributed, or used in any form without the express written permission of the author. All rights reserved.

All characters, names, and content in this book are the exclusive property of LJR Skylerman. Unauthorised use of these characters and content is strictly prohibited. For information about permission to reproduce selections from this book, please contact the author at:
AuthorLJRSkylerman@gmail.com

Published by Amazon.

First edition: 2024

IBSN: 9798345658321

Dedicated to every single one of my online readers. Without you, this book would not exist.

HYLUNE

The Northern Border

The North

Black Rock

The Three Sisters

◉ Pewet

◉ Gyylthorpe

◉ Kaytsmere

VELÔR

◉ Marsham

◉ L

The Westlands

◉ Barrentel

◉ Nettleheim

◉ Ottersbridge

◉ Oakstone

The Southern Border

CALPURZIA

He sees the word in colours.
Hers is brown.
His is blue, although he doesn't know it yet.
He still thinks it's green.
He has seen her several times, but she has not seen him –
The woman with the mop.
Her uniform is beige and wet and crumpled like a rag dragged over dishes.
Her hair is trapped in a neat bun atop her head, the strands fine as silk, the colour of a hazelnut. She's flecked with freckles like splattered paint—
not that he's ever gotten close enough to see.
Her eyes are brown too.
Brown like the leather spine of a book.
He loves to read.

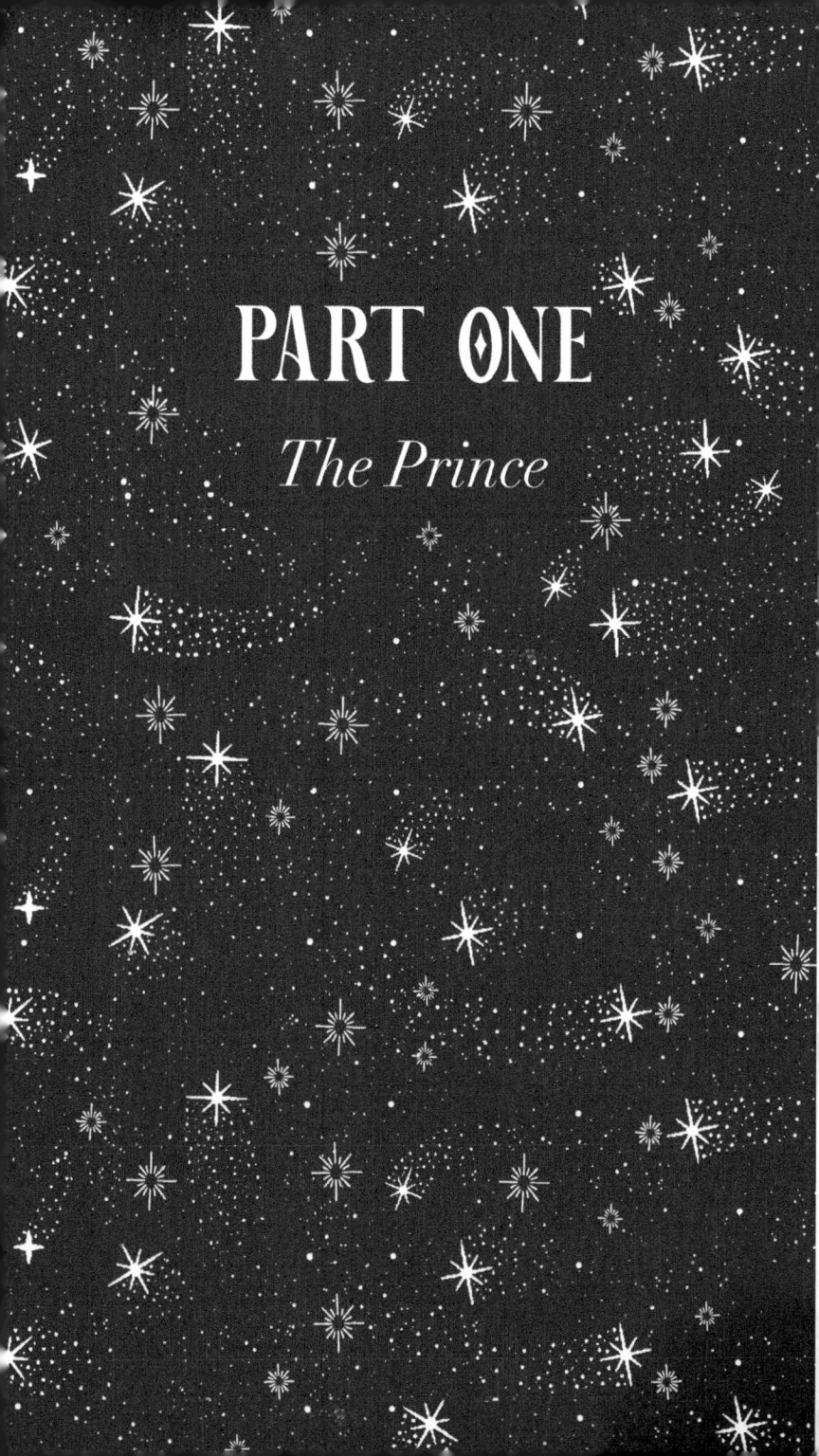

PART ONE

The Prince

PROLOGUE

It has been two weeks since the letter arrived, and it still lies open on the nightstand.

Drawing from the warmth of his wife's arms, Cade takes it as he stands, bringing it with him to the wide windows that look out over his kingdom.

Besides the fishing boat's swinging lanterns and a few wax stick-lit windows, Velôr sleeps.

The thick scent of jasmine seeps from the parchment in his hand, stinging the inside of his nose.

He doesn't know why he picked it up; he doesn't need to read it again.

It simply called to be held, like a newborn babe.

"He is not ready," his queen warns from the mattress. Her hair slides against the silk covers as she braids it. She wears it in a plait to sleep, a thick rope-like twist all the way to the backs of her knees. It's the colour of butter but, earlier, as he'd lain with her, Cade had noticed his wife's first few strands of silvery grey.

He can feel her eyes, sharp on the back of his head, and smiles. "He is a man now."

WHAT LORKAN IS

"You know that is not what I meant."

He turns to his queen. The moonlight falls onto his naked form in planks, pooling in the craters of his scars.

Her hands cease their complicated braiding. There's a concerned furrow between her elegantly plucked brows. It's set up residency there since the letter arrived, etching creases where there were no creases before. Not liking the way the silver moon stains them a sallow, pallid grey, Cade summons light to his palm, and his wife's eyes cringe from his magic as though blinking into the sun.

With a nettled flick of her wrist, she forces him to lower it.

He sighs at the weak, fluttering ember. "Velôr and Calpurzia used to be one, once, did they not?"

Lophia doesn't bid him the courtesy of an answer.

Everyone knows how the stories go.

"Wouldn't it be nice to sew them back together?"

"You'll be darning them with brittle thread." That rift grows deeper across her forehead like a stitch had been pulled too tight. "You know of his secret. What if they found out? The alliance would not be genuine. Discovery would mean war."

Raising a thick, wide hand, Cade strokes his beard absently. It is as coarse as a dog's coat, but to his war-ravaged fingers he feels but a brush. After a moment's contemplation:

"Summon Hectate."

Lophia's shoulders rise and fall in a sigh, but she leans over all the same and pulls the thick cord by the headboard.

They wait, but not for long.

Shrugging on a robe, Cade knots it about his waist. A fine, heavy wolf pelt, the material barely stirs as he crosses the room.

He's lighting the wax sticks on the bedside table as his advisor enters. In the corner of his good eye, he catches Lophia drawing the duvet up to cover her bare breasts.

He inherited Hectate from his father—although, plump and smooth, the man scarcely looks over thirty years old. With an amicable, quiet disposition and mild eyes, Cade knows his wife harbours no bashfulness around the old advisor.

It is his pet she cringes from; a tame amphiptere he wears about his shoulders like a scarf. She has been his companion since Cade was a boy, although he often wonders if it's the same one or a distant descendant.

As King, he has every right to ask, but, for some reason, he doesn't. It would feel like inquiring as to how a friend's fungal infection is clearing up.

A much smaller, more common relative of the dragon, amphiptere are legless, flightless, and carry a spiteful temper. Cade had never known them to make good pets, and, when playing as a child, his mother had warned him to avoid the ones hunting for voles in the long grass.

Those were brown, non-assuming things with ragged scales like the ruffled feathers of a bird.

Hectate's is smooth and slick and silent.

In all his years, Cade had never seen one like it in the wild—not in *his* realm, anyway.

Either way, Hectate appears to love it as one would usually love a woman, and often lifts a doughy hand to caress it as though it were soft female flesh.

He's doing that now, rubbing the wide pad of his thumb over the bridge between the reptile's eyes.

Cade can't tell if she likes it, although he figures if she doesn't she'd simply lash out with those needle-thin teeth.

He would never wish any harm on the plump little man, but, guilty, he finds himself hoping she will strike at him, just once, so he'd have reason to ban him from carrying her around.

As if sensing his distaste, the reptile rearranges its small, neatly folded wings in what must be contempt. The flames from the wax sticks light them up from the inside, illuminating thick blue veins but little muscle. They're composed of transparent, membranous skin stretched over hair-like bones; utterly useless besides the hooked talons that satisfy the occasional itch.

WHAT LORKAN IS

Drawing his eyes away from the reptile, Cade clears his throat. "Something has been on my mind, Hectate."

The man's name is foreign to his ears, for he is one of the few that use it. The common folk have a nickname for him: '*The King's Shadow,*' because, wherever Cade goes, his advisor's satin slippers are scurrying a mere pace behind.

The Shadow goes with him to the window, his amphiptere observing from the lapel of his silk dressing gown with yellow pin-prick pupils.

Through the bay windows, Tawny's city centre spreads out before him like an elaborate quilt; the ribbon-like river Sygg, the patchwork rooftops, the docks lining the coast like trim on a dress.

"On your mind, Sir?" Hectate's rounded stomach is smothering the city centre like an eclipse, and Cade considers ordering him to move.

"Obviously, the Hyluniens would side with the Calpurzians, but..." he eyes the rugged line of the horizon, a wounded pink against the purple night.

Hecatate follows his gaze. It is usually intelligent and vivid but the night has darkened it.

"How would we fare in a war?"

1

THE MAN ON THE STEPS

No one usually disturbs Meren as she sleepily slides a damp mop over the front steps of Aldercliff Palace. No one besides the occasional wren perched triumphantly atop a mountain laurel, its song pouring from its warm little body like smoke from a tiny dragon.

That's her job; to clean the entryway until its smooth surface is polished enough to reflect vague outlines of the clouds. To do so before the first guests arrive—lords with fine leather boots, and ladies with dresses that kiss the ground—she has to rise long before the sun.

She doesn't mind, really. Amongst the repetitive strokes of her mop, she has managed to find a few pebbles of amusement.

She likes watching the little streams of water run off the step she's sponging at and dribble onto the next, then the next, and the next. The gold colour of the staircase shines through the suds, making it look like the base of the great palace is melting.

She likes being awake to witness the dawn chorus. The Royal Gardens circle the base of the palace like a moat of verdant, manicured grass and shrubbery and, from its branches, mistle thrush, blackbirds and warblers declare they've survived the night by bursting into vibrant song.

Most of all, Meren likes the sunrises. Sometimes, as the sun begins to stain the sky a delicate pastel peach, she dares to take a seat on the top step and watch as streaks of pink bloom like spilt paint, slicing the horizon to ribbons.

They're enough to make her forget the tender red skin of her palms, at least for a moment.

Velôr boasts a single, mighty palace; a towering, gargantuan thing of limestone and gold ore, its spires, turrets and towers reaching up towards the heavens like blades piercing the bellies of the clouds. Down below, the servant's quarters weave among its roots like rabbit warrens, the hallways narrow and stuffy with the previous day's breath.

On a good day, the wind will skitter down a chimney, flushing out the tunnels but, this morning, the wax sticks appear to have frozen in time as Meren eases herself from her bed.

She has to do so carefully so as not to wake her sleeping colleagues. Her uniform, starched and crisp, crinkles like parchment as she drags an arm through the sleeve and smooths the long, stiff skirt. She is young; barely halfway through her twenty-second year; yet her knees crackle like nut shells as she stoops to pull on her shoes, her fingers too calloused to mind the prickly cotton of her socks.

Following the wisps of light, she pads towards the mess hall—a low-ceilinged, cave-like stone room–which, at this time of day, is empty besides several bleary-eyed groundskeepers frowning into their porridge.

Too sleepy for conversation, Meren takes a seat in the furthest corner, the light from the brazier overhead glaring at her from the curve of her pewter tankard. It watches her like an eye as, in silence, she shovels down three rounds of sourdough bread, taking sips of water between chunks to loosen the crusts. Saving the pale wedge of hard cheese for last—a childish habit that has prevailed into adulthood—she pops it between her lips as she stands, pressing it against the roof of her mouth.

Sucking now and again at the craggy rind, she fetches her cleaning equipment from the cupboard and, following the trickle of fresh air, makes her way up toward ground level.

Giving the door to the courtyard a hard push with one elbow, the rich, ink-black night floods her nostrils like a wave. Swilling it about her lungs like a fine wine, she finds the air to be cool and sweet, fir sap seeping from the woodlands like tea from a bag. Several stars blink down at her through bundles of cotton ball clouds, the moon's silvery light falling onto her face in a single, limpid beam.

Even on the warmest of days, a slight wind whispers down from the kingdom of Hylune in the north. Miles away, peering from snow-spattered mountains like a falcon from its roost, its melting glaciers feed Velôr's rivers and the well Meren uses to fill her bucket—although she knows the Ice Giants would rather not share if they had the choice.

That frigid water sloshes onto her canvas shoes as she hefts her bucket towards the first step, her mop slung over one shoulder like a bindle.

That step is one of many fat slabs of gold, stacked neatly to form a wide walkway about the palace. It's looped like a ribbon tied elegantly about the base of a cake, and it is there where he stands, silently watching.

He must have been there for some time.

Meren hadn't noticed him approach, although she should have done.

A tall young man who could easily stand level with a shire's shoulder, he's dressed in thin moss-coloured linen; an utterly ineffective shield against the brisk morning air.

And he's King Cade's second-born son—although that thought registers peculiarly late in Meren's mind.

It's not that he doesn't *look* like a prince, he just doesn't look like the sort of prince Meren has heard stories about.

He's the only raven-haired child in a family of blondes.

Most males in the realm are stocky and hardened from manual labour, whereas he is lean and lithe, and, despite the year-round onslaught of vibrant midday sun, his skin remains as stubbornly pale as porcelain.

WHAT LORKAN IS

He looks like he'd be more comfortable living somewhere where the lakes are frozen over all year round.

Glancing sideways at him through the corners of her eyes, Meren's grip tightens on her mop's handle.

Rock doves are fond of roosting on the battlements, their mess soiling the golden path below with stubborn white stains. They turn to chalky dust as they dry, and she had been working them determinedly moments ago. However, aware of the prince's eyes sharp on the back of her head, her movements soon become distracted.

The grounds of the palace are so large that many servants go their entire careers without crossing paths with anyone who owns it.

Rubbing the head of the mop back and forth, smearing the same spot around and around, she wonders whether she should greet him.

Perhaps it is, in fact, rude to address a prince before he's sparked up a conversation first?

He's so tall, his broad shoulders the only giveaway that he hasn't been physically stretched out.

Meren knows she and the prince came into the world only a few seasons apart, yet she feels like a child in his presence, a dirty, sodden urchin losing a battle with a heap of bird mess.

His head tilts curiously to the side, just enough that one wouldn't notice unless they'd been staring at him intently for some time—which, inadvertently, Meren has been doing

She likes the triangle shape of his torso and the masculine point of his nose.

She has pushed the mop into its bucket and slopped it at her feet three times before she makes up her mind that she will have to say something.

The prince's steady, undivided attention is putting her off her work.

And, for some reason, she doesn't want him to feel he's being ignored.

Mind made up about how she is to proceed, Meren pulls away from her task and stands properly, propping herself up with the handle of her mop.

This seems to wake the prince from some kind of stupor, and he blinks as if realising he's being observed. Straightening the long column of his spine politely, he doesn't smile, just fractionally inclines his pointy chin in a nod of greeting.

She wonders if she should curtsy.

Sucking in a lungful of the brisk, early morning air, she clears her throat, her breath condensing before her in a little plume of mist. Before she can summon a sentence to her tongue, the prince hands some words to her:

"Are you cold?"

Meren blinks at them.

Yes, she is cold.

She can barely remember a time when she hasn't been cold, at least a little bit. She has often considered purchasing a coat from the market, but the price tags make her queasy.

Her surprise must be written all over her chill-bitten face because the prince takes a step closer. When he speaks, his voice is soft and quiet like a breeze through branches.

"Let me see your hands."

There's a pause while Meren's brain processes his order. She looks left and then right, checking for a lone guard or solitary stable hand out walking the horses. Someone is bound to scold her for talking to Cade's son, even though *he'd* been the one who had spoken to *her*.

She realises he's still watching her, waiting, and all she's doing is gazing a dazed, vacant look up into his eyes.

They are shockingly green; strangely bright amongst the muted colours of dawn.

Scrambling to stuff the mop handle under one arm, her stomach twists in on itself as she holds out both her hands as if shyly presenting the prince with a gift.

He doesn't touch her, both of his slender arms remaining neatly folded like wings behind his back. He regards the tips of her fingers, his eyes sliding along the crease lines of her exposed palms, the slight scuff of blood seeping from a peeling cuticle.

WHAT LORKAN IS

Feeling strangely naked and wonders if, amongst the morning air, he can smell the tang or carbolic soap she can't seem to pick out from under her nails.

When he is satisfied—or has seen whatever it is he'd wanted to see—he gives another curt little nod.

"Thank you. You may get back to your work."

Her mop held limply under one arm, forgotten, Meren watches with poorly hidden fascination as he carefully skirts around the damp patches she has worked so hard to clean.

Silently, Aldercliff's doors slide closed, engulfing his narrow figure.

2

THE SIXTEENTH FLOOR

The next morning, the sky has cleared into a wide bowl of dusty, gritty little stars—though huddled underground, Meren doesn't know it yet. She has five minutes before she has to fetch the water for her bucket, and she's desperately trying to heat her skin cells in preparation.

She's cradling a bowl of porridge in the mess hall when she's approached by Alfdis, a woman so wrinkled it looks as though she has been thoroughly wrung out.

As head housekeeper, Alfdis is up and about before Meren, or anyone, for that matter, and she won't get to go back to bed until the moon rises once again. Despite this, her steps are just as brisk and energetic as they must have been sixty years ago, and she bustles over like a thin, slightly flustered hen, her pointed shoes clacking like little claws.

Meren's theory is that death simply can't catch up to her.

"Hansen!" Coming to a halt at the bench she perches on, Alfdis assesses it, clearly wondering if it's worth lowering her creaking bones onto the cracked wood.

She decides it isn't, and remains standing.

WHAT LORKAN IS

Even though one of them is seated, Meren can look straight into her thick, wire-framed spectacles. They're pressed so far up the bridge of her hooked nose they're squashing her wiry eyebrows against the glass.

"Goodness, look at you! You're wrapped up like it's winter in Hylune!" She shakes her head. "It's barely autumn!"

"It's still cold," Meren disputes, and Alfdis chuckles.

"In that case, the news I bring will please you. I dare say, your days working out in the elements are over."

Despite towering over her underlings in rank and age, Alfdis is a good-natured, relatable woman if ever there was one, so Meren feels comfortable enough to sputter, shielding her mouthful of porridge with a hot, pink palm:

"What?"

"You, you lucky minx, have been reassigned. You are no longer stationed at the main entrance. Rather than cleaning the steps as you usually do, you are to proceed to the chambers on the Sixteenth Floor and clean those instead," she announces in her usual practical, no-nonsense air—although, there's a puzzled edge to it as if her own instructions confuse her.

Meren blinks. "The Sixteenth floor? Isn't that—?"

"Indeed. Now, before you go parroting rumours and gossip, may I remind you that His Highness is your employer, so it is in your best interest to watch your tongue." She places a fragile hand on her shoulder in a motherly way, and Meren is suddenly overcome by a wave of homesickness.

It distracts her for a moment, and when she comes to, Alfdis' little face is close to her own and muttering, sombre as the dead:

"I need not explain to you what a privilege this is."

Swallowing her mouthful, Meren shakes her head. "I'm to clean a *prince's* chambers? But I'm not a housekeeper!"

"Well, you are now," Again, there's that slight note of uncertainty as if she too is not quite sure how it happened.

"Not to *royalty;* I worked in the kitchen and not even the kitchens upstairs; *our* kitchen," Meren protests. "The only thing that separates me from being a *grounds*keeper is the lack of grass stains on my knees, and a sun hat!"

"Now, now, groundskeeping is honest work," Alfdis chastises, and Meren flushes, smoothing her ruffled feathers.

"I know, I'm sorry. What I mean is, I don't have any training. There are dozens more qualified than me. Katrin was a lady-in-waiting for a time, and Aerin waited on a nobleman in her last house."

Even though Alfdis looks like she agrees wholeheartedly, she shakes her head.

"But his Royal Highness didn't ask for Katrin or Aerin; he asked for you."

Meren's oatmeal is starting to gum up her teeth, the milk growing a thick, lumpy skin.

"But—why?"

Alfdis' little shoulders rise and fall in a bemused shrug below her uniform. The movement tugs her apron askew and she smooths it back down instinctually, ironing out the creases with her hands.

"That, I couldn't tell you. Goodness knows what made The Young Prince decide he suddenly wants his rooms tended to," she frowns. "He hasn't let anyone in there since he grew out of the nursery, you know."

Meren does know, or at least she's heard rumours.

Velôr is ruled by King Cade, whom she has only glanced at once, from a distance, as he left the palace on horseback. The throne was passed down to him from his father and his father before him, their lineage reaching all the way back to the days when The Three Kingdoms were united as one, and the land had not yet felt the piercing blade of its first war.

A courageous warlock—or so it's said—magic and power ooze from him like sweat, collecting in each of his deep furrowing scars.

As a young buck, he met a sorceress in training, said to be unmatched in intelligence, bravery, and beauty.

Every wealthy bachelor in Velôr was in love with her, or so the story goes, and they'll each tell you their own tale of how she broke their heart. Such a perfect woman would be wasted on anyone but a king, and Cade made

WHAT LORKAN IS

Lophia his wife a mere three days after his coronation. The entire kingdom celebrated, merging the two events into a whole week of parades, parties and festivities still fondly reminisced to this day.

The couple was blessed with their firstborn son the next year; a blue-eyed, pink baby boy with hair the colour of the sun, and magic crackling from his fingertips.

They named him Sol and, over time, his chubby child's cheeks widened into the stubble-dusted, angular jawline of a man, his sword of wood and red paint exchanged for a blade of steel and blood.

Each evening, all over the kingdom, by the flickering light of a wax stick, parents regale stories of noble princes, knights and dragons to their children tucked up under covers. Sol is the sort of Prince they imagine, his eyes just as blue, his hair the exact shade of blonde—or so Meren has heard. Whenever a position in Sol's quarters opens up the housemaids scramble over each other like rats to snatch it out of Alfdi's hands.

Cade and Lophia had to wait for The War to end before trying for their second child. Apparently, the pregnancy was a difficult one and went unannounced for five seasons. Finally, when the baby and its mother were strong enough to venture out onto the balcony, the midday sun beating down on their faces, their king unveiled his youngest son for the first time.

It is said a ripple of surprise disturbed the crowd like a rock plopped into a pond. Word quickly spread of this child's skin, pale as snow, and his tufts of jet-black hair. Scribbled over his forehead like a dash of charcoal, it peeked out from under his tiny crown like shadows crawling over the golden metal.

Every set of eyes stared in silence.

Then, finally, someone noticed his eyes; two bright, intelligent, green pebbles watching them from his father's arms.

Just like his mother's.

A cheer exploded like rain from a cloud and, though little Lorkan—so the child was named—began to bawl, the public soon accepted him as their young prince.

As the child matured, it became obvious that he is the polar opposite of his brother not just in looks but in temperament. A boisterous child, Sol became a rambunctious adolescent and, now, sits proudly atop his horse as a fearless man. He branched out while his brother shied away, flinging doors open while his brother bolted his. Sol is his father, his silhouette slotting perfectly into Cade's shadow, approachable, stubborn, a skilled fighter—

No one really knows what Lorkan is.

His nanny would take tea with Alfdis, both women conversing in hushed tones over steaming mugs. In between nibbles of rolled biscuits, she'd express concern over the little prince's introversion.

"It's just not the way, Alfie," she'd fret, distractedly dunking her biscuit into her tea. Giving it a few dips, she'd curse as it crumbled, falling wetly to the bottom of her mug. "The eldest will soon be leaving for Black Castle, you know. Meanwhile, I can't get his little brother's nose out of his books."

"Now, Wilma, dear," Alfdis would soothe, "perhaps he's a late bloomer?"

"Late bloomer or not, he should be out there learning to ride and fight and rule, you know he should. Seven hours straight in a library, I tell you! It's just not the way," she'd repeat, attempting another biscuit. "For the son of a scholar, maybe, but of a king?"

Her concern only doubled when he outgrew the nursery, moving into his own quarters where he proceeded to lock the door to all but himself.

"He spends too much time alone up there, Alfie," Wilma would say. "He comes down for meals, granted, and he loves the gardens, but I can't help wondering what he's *doing*."

"*Doing?* It's none of your business what the Royal Highness is *doing*, Wilma, dear," Alfdis would chastise, hoping that would be the end of it.

But, of course, it wasn't.

Life in the basement of the palace is rather dry of melodrama and mystery. With so little free time, the servants rely heavily on rumours and gossip for entertainment so, naturally, word of The Young Prince's strange habits spread through the stuffy corridors like a common cold. It soon became a tradition to scare new, younger staff with hearsay and theories, each one crawling around like rats for a few weeks after it had been set loose.

Once, in the courtyard, bent over soapy tubs, a scullery maid insisted to Meren that he breeds monsters.

As they worked their uniforms against their washboards, she described rooms teaming with scaly, venomous dragons smuggled down from the mountains, clawing and mouthing the furniture like overgrown cats.

"I think The Youngest Prince was born so sickly," a hall boy once said whilst slicing his way through a heap of onions, "the only way he can survive each night is to pickle youth potions in jars." Blinking tears from his lashes, he continued, even though nobody asked:

"He lures victims to his chambers where he harvests their very being, you know, their…what's it called?"

"Their essence?"

"Yeah. He draws it out their mouth until they're nothing but a raisin-like husk."

And, only last week, Alfdis had to scold a stableboy for frightening the new dishwasher.

"You know how the royal family are the last Velôrians to practise magic?" He'd prompted, elbowing the young girl in the ribs. "Prince Lorkan is a practitioner of a different *sort* of magic."

"*What* sort of magic?"

"Dark sorcery and necromancy. There was a woman called Annexandra who used to work upstairs. One day, out of curiosity, she snuck into Lorkan's rooms—but you know what they say."

"*What* do they say?" She'd nudged him back, already irritated with his antics.

"Curiosity killed the cat."

"That's not the end of the rhyme, though," Meren pointed out, getting a glare from the stableboy. "You're leaving out the part about satisfaction bringing it back."

The girl blinked through her glasses. "Brought what back?"

"The cat."

"Sod the stinking cat! My point was, The Prince's rooms were so saturated with demons and the smell of burnt flesh, that poor Annexandra went crazy."

"Is she okay?"

"Depends how you define okay." He'd shrugged. "She lived if that's what you mean, but her Mother had to quit midwifery to look after her full-time. She has to have her meals spooned into her mouth like a babe."

This had gotten him a sharp rap on the knuckles with a wooden spoon from Alfdis, which Meren thinks he deserved.

She hadn't believed any of it.

The young man on the steps didn't look sickly.

Although pale, his cheeks and nose were tinted a healthy pink from the cold, his movements limber and his eyes bright. His shoulder-length hair, although black as raven feathers, had been carefully slicked back, and reflected the pale light of the morning sun.

And his chambers *can't* be crawling with dragons because his delicate linen shirt was not torn by talons but spotless, ironed, and tucked neatly into the waistband of his trousers.

As for dark magic, Meren had pointed out to the dishwasher that surely someone would have *noticed* if spirits were being summoned to the sixteenth floor.

Her oatmeal forgotten, and suddenly feeling very much awake, she asks:

"How many people will I be working with? And which room am I assigned to?"

"I don't think you understand." Alfdis shakes her head. Her bun doesn't even wobble, the pins holding it firmly in place. "You will be working alone."

Meren's mouth falls open. "But *fifteen* maids are stationed to His Majesty's chambers, and I've counted at least ten women appointed to Prince Sol's, and he's been away for months. If Lorkan's are the same size—"

"It's *His Highness*, to you."

"If *His Highness*'s chambers are the same size, that's a string of over *six* rooms."

WHAT LORKAN IS

During their conversation, Alfdis' hands have been clasping a sheet of parchment, and Meren reaches out to take it.

It's scribbled with a fine, looping cursive that she can't read upside down.

"Are you sure you understood him correctly? Maybe he said one maid *per room*."

Insulted, Alfdis snatches the parchment out of reach and folds it, nettled.

"I'm quite correct, I can assure you. The young Prince is a very private man; perhaps he'll start with one member of staff, then, in time, hire others," she assures, although she sounds doubtful. Shaking it off like harmless raindrops:

"Your shift begins at nine, so I'll collect you at half eight. Now, rest up, we have much to discuss."

∗ ☾ ∗

After trying and failing to go back to sleep, Meren perches on the end of her bed and leafs through a novel by the light of a wax stick.

One by one, her colleagues rise and dress until she's alone, silently buzzing, watching the spindly arm of her clock hack away the minutes.

When half eight rolls around, she hunts about for Alfdis, finding her in her office below a stack of receipts. Having plucked a thick iron key from her key cupboard, she brushes some lint from Meren's shoulder and re-knots her apron in a tight, tidy bow. Licking her finger and using it to slick a strand of her hair back over her head:

"You probably won't encounter His Highness, but it never hurts to look your best."

With her new job and added responsibility, Meren is handed several new rules to learn, and a new set of tools.

The tools include another bucket, but this one acts as more of a basket for her other paraphernalia; new—much nicer—rags, a feather duster, a boar-hair lint brush, and several metal tins of beeswax polish.

The first rule is that no one is to be allowed in The Prince's chambers besides herself. Alfdis made this very clear as she pressed a chunky iron key into Meren's hand with unsmiling solemnity.

The second isn't really a rule, more of a warning:

"Remember, you are not simply scrubbing bird mess and shoe scuffs off some stairs anymore." Her shoes clip-clop importantly on the smooth grey flagstones, and Meren nods attentively, following close to her heel like a dog trailing after its master.

Never having strayed above the basement levels of the palace, the hairs on her arms prickle as they near the great wooden door. She half expects the hefty wedge of keystone to sense she's not meant to be there and drop with a thud onto her head—

But it remains in place, and she steps over the threshold, her hand raising automatically to shield her eyes.

The first dregs of sunlight sluice in through the wide, arched windows, dribbling over statues and running down pillars like a water feature before pooling on the pale marble floor. It reflects the intricate domed ceiling like a still lake, wool rugs set out like gold-tasselled lily pads. They're large, but not large enough to fill the entire space, Meren's shoes scuffing with a squeak on the patches of naked, white stone.

"Pick up your feet, dear," Alfdis chides gently, her voice bouncing about the vast, empty hall.

The palace is constructed in three parts:

Way down below, under tonnes of limestone, sliced gold and carved marble, the basement levels root themselves deep into a hillside; an impossible, shaded maze that's never seen the light of day.

Above, embraced by lush, elaborate gardens, the main body sits squatly, robust and sturdy amongst rhododendrons and mountain laurels. It's made up of just over a hundred exquisitely decorated, cavernous rooms, yet they

WHAT LORKAN IS

usually remain hollow—besides busy maids stoking lonely fires and beating dust from plump cushions. Numerous towers protrude from all angles like pointed stone mushrooms on a log, studded with long, narrow windows and crowned with prickly, tiled spires. Atop each, Velôr's crimson flag writhes among the heavens, occasionally flashing its yellow belly and glinting an embroidered, golden crown.

The Palace is so gargantuan, some have speculated Alfdis is the only person to have lived long enough to explore it all. She seems to have managed, somehow, to memorise it too, because she leads Meren along corridors, upstairs, down hallways and through door after door.

Desperately, Meren tries to do the same, statues and pillars flying past in a blur of gold and icing-sugar white. She etches them hastily onto her mind, labelling prominent landmarks;

The statue of a nude man and his horse,

The huge painting of a pheasant,

The milky-looking room made entirely of quartz,

As they climb their tenth set of stairs, not managing to find her way back to the servant's quarters balloons into a genuine concern. An image skitters through Meren's mind of herself wandering down golden hallways, lost, only to be found two weeks later, dead from starvation.

Maybe The Prince wouldn't notice if she holed up in one of his cupboards, just to save her the trek to and from their respected living spaces?

"You are now the housekeeper of a prince, so you must act as such," Alfdis is saying, breaking Meren's stupor. "If you must address him, he is 'Your Royal Highness' at first, and then 'Sir' after that."

"And will he call me Hansen? Or Meren?"

"He will call you '*Housekeeper*', obviously," Alfdis dismisses the question with a wave of her hand as if it had been a rather unfunny joke.

"Now, his Highness seems to spend much more time in his chambers than the others, so I'd begin your work at nine, if I were you, when he has most likely woken and vacated his rooms for breakfast."

She continues like this, detailing the intricacies of mingling with royalty so fast Meren's brain struggles to mentally scribble most of it down.

The third rule she has to learn is that everything is to be put back exactly as she had found it.

"As you know, the Youngest Prince's chambers have been off-limits to all staff, even cleaners, for as long as we can remember. He's very particular about his belongings being meddled with, so, for all these years, he's been doing his own housekeeping."

Meren ponders this with a mixture of respect and dismay. She supposes, if the mood took him, The Prince could order someone to slide on his socks, tie his laces, and brush out his shoulder-length hair while he reclines on a chaise lounge nibbling plums.

She admires that, instead, he's opted to care for himself.

If he has, indeed, cared for himself. Some ugly little part of her wonders whether she'll try to push his door open only to find it jammed with over a decade's worth of dirty laundry.

"I have a list of things you need to clean and things you are to leave alone." Alfdis, with an expression of someone doing something completely alien to them, finally holds out the piece of white parchment.

It's smooth in Meren's hands.

She's never seen white parchment before; just inexpensive stuff stained a drab yellowish-grey. With curious fingers, she unfurls it, once again laying eyes on the lines of swirling, glistening ink.

Her cheeks flush with every second it takes her to read it.

Her father *had* taught her to read as a child, despite her mother insisting from the next room that literature is for well-to-do people with soft hands and free time. Once she'd got the hang of sounding out the letters, she was delighted and shocked to find pictures materialising like spectres behind her eyes. As she practised, each shaky word linked together to form sentences, which became stories, which she became quite addicted to.

WHAT LORKAN IS

Gobbling through the few novels on her own shelves, she began hunting around for more like a truffle pig, rummaging through chests and relatives' memories for a yarn, a tale or a fable.

As the local washerwoman, everyone knows Mrs Hansen. She's the woman with shoulders to rival any man's, and hands deep red and chapped, as though she's boiled them along with the linen. Her house oozes steam, each room damp with soapy water and strung up with lines and racks, pinafores and aprons dripping inside and out, flapping like the sails of a peculiar, land-bound ship.

Therefore, naturally, everyone also knows of her daughter. A shy wisp of a girl, Mrs Hansen would send Meren door to door with her basket, which clients would fill with their dirty laundry to be taken away, scrubbed and returned.

However, as gossip of her reading habit quickly spread through Holcombe, Meren stopped being known as '*The Washer Woman's Gal*' and soon became '*The Book Beggar*'.

"Ask her," she'd whisper in her mother's ear, her nose buried bashfully in her coarse brown curls. Tugging insistently on her apron, "Please, you said you would!"

"Don't you have enough books at home?" would be the impatient reply. "What about that one Mrs Alcott lent you?"

"I finished that ages ago!"

Mrs Hansen would sigh, hefting her great laundry basket onto her thick shoulder. "I'm sorry, Rosy, dear, I don't suppose you have any books for the gal? She's gone and got herself into reading, of all things."

"Ah, well, at least she hasn't got herself into boys," her client would laugh with a good-natured wink—or something of the like—and disappear into the house to find something with words for Meren to devour.

These would often be paperbacks purchased by the more well-travelled women in her village; romances and mysteries with thin pages and tatty covers. Their spines broken and their pages well-thumbed, they've already passed through the hands of every lonely housewife in Holcombe—and then they passed through Meren's (the more saucy chapters torn out, of course).

However, those books were printed on a press, each letter clearly stamped, all spaced apart and orderly.

This lavish, looping penmanship keeps taking her on unnecessary journeys along elongated, flourishing letters, the tight cursive tangling her up like yarn.

"You can keep the list," Alfdis says, slightly out of breath from climbing another set of stairs.

The sixteenth; Meren had been counting.

"No one else will be needing it. As you can see, you don't need to get up a ladder and do the windows, or wash his clothes. It looks like quite a gentle workload—don't go telling the other girls. They'll be jealous." She gives Meren a friendly nudge in the ribs with her pointy elbow, but she's so short it lands somewhere around the bone of her hip.

The fourth rule is not brought to attention by Alfdis, but written by whoever made the note Meren now tucks safely into her apron pocket.

'Please do not enter the study.'

Rumours surrounding The Youngest Prince bubble up at the back of her brain like lumps in a rug, but she beats them back down.

Alfdis must have noticed her shift in mood but mistakes it for confusion about the layout of the chambers because she clarifies:

"The study is the little room that branches off from the lounge."

※ ☾ ※

Her bucket of cleaning supplies weighing her down on one side, Meren nearly bumps into Alfdis' back as she comes to an abrupt stop.

Expectantly, she waits for an explanation, but receives none.

They've stopped before a huge, carved wooden mural, its glossy varnish tinting the air with wax resin. Hundreds of woodland creatures, plants, and intricate trees have been whittled by hand into the deep, honey-coloured grain, forming a picturesque landscape more tall than it is wide.

Alfdis gestures to it with an air of finality.

Embarrassingly slowly, Meren realises it isn't a mural, but a door.

"This is where I must leave you, I'm afraid." She doesn't look like she wants to. She looks like she wants to hold Meren's wrist and direct her duster herself, just to be sure she's doing it right.

"Leave me?" Meren looks up and down the empty, cavernous hallway, and suddenly feels the urge to reach out and take Alfdis' sleeve. "Aren't you coming in to show me what I have to do?"

"A maid that doesn't know how to clean!" she chuckles, the cavern-like corridor swallowing it whole. "Your mother taught you to keep house, didn't she?"

"Yes."

"So you know what you have to do."

Somberly, she gives her a last going over; straightening her collar and wetting her thumb, using it to wipe a tooth powder stain from the corner of her lip.

Meren watches as her tiny figure disappears, her grey dress drowning among the jungle of white pillars and gold statues.

Suddenly, she feels quite alone.

The door protrudes, slightly raised against the golden wall as if it's too thick for the jamb, the whole thing wide as a tree trunk. She wonders how she'll manage to heft it open at the end of the day and, for a sickly second, imagines she *can't*.

The key Alfdis had given her fits easily into its lock. As she turns it, the mechanism works with a grating of metal, the handle loosening below her hand. Grey, solid and unassuming, it had set her pocket sagging as they'd made their way up sixteen flights of stairs. Slipping it back inside, Meren realises it's a disappointment. She expected the key to a prince's chambers to be much more ornate, maybe even carved from gold—or at least engraved.

Perhaps the one in Lorkan's pocket is.

It takes a few tries to turn the knob, the polished metal slick below her sweaty palm. Despite its size, the slab of wood swings open easily, a panel of sunlight falling silently onto the marble floor.

Feeling as though a small bird is desperately trying to escape her ribcage, she edges inside like a woman stepping onto a rickety bridge—

—and sighs.

His rooms just looked like...rooms.

They're not jammed with unwashed laundry like Meren had feared.

Nor are they scrambling with exotic pets, demons, or giggling swarms of mistresses lounging about in not nearly enough clothes.

They're just rooms, comfortable, lavish rooms, but no different, really, to Meren's own quarters.

His bed is neatly made, his moss-green pyjamas left folded on the pillow.

In the washroom, a pot of toothpowder, a toothbrush, and a bar of soap sit by the sink like a giant, lavender-scented throat lozenge.

His laundry basket fills slowly with silken green shirts, black trousers, their material soft as a shadow. Pairs of shoes lay, kicked off, by the door.

There are scraps of parchment caught between pages in his books and, at his desk, indents freckle his graphite sticks, their bodies pocked by the rocky edges of his teeth.

Yes, The Prince's toothbrush is engraved metal and probably costs more than Meren's shoes.

Yes, his pyjamas are embroidered silk, and his pillows down-stuffed satin.

Yes, his parchment—clean white rather than stained yellow—is probably made from the finest trees grown in his own personal woodland—

—but the general gist of their lives appear to mirror each other.

He's just a person.

Meren finds her way back to the servant's quarters that evening by simply heading downwards and hoping she'll eventually reach somewhere that looks familiar. Having finally made it back down the labyrinthine corridors, she relays this information to the flood of curious peers waiting for her in the mess hall.

WHAT LORKAN IS

Closing the door to the servants' quarters behind her, their collective faces swarm like bees, each one buzzing with questions. Amongst them are faces she's never seen before; chefs from upstairs, housekeepers from the day shift, valets and footmen. However, most of them are faces she knows well; faces from the mirror next to hers when she cleans her teeth, faces munching opposite her at supper—faces that never usually bother to turn in her direction.

For the first time since she'd worked at The Palace, Erik—one of the more popular hall boys—is hurling words at her:

"So, what were they like?"

Meren feels her cheeks colour under the weight of his hazel irises but, before she can open her mouth, someone else is tossing another sentence from her left:

"Is it true he keeps concubines shut up in there? That's what my brother said, that's why no one is allowed in."

A high-cheekboned, slightly pompous chambermaid who has never noticed Meren exists decides to give her input, addressing the room over the top of her head:

"No, there's something *wrong* with him, so the locks are to keep him inside, not other people out."

"Why's she so quiet?" someone else is asking. "Did you see something hideous in there?"

Shaking her head, Meren tries to swat away each rumour as it's thrown at her:

'They're just how you imagine a prince's quarters to be; a bedroom, a lounge—'

'Well, there is one room I'm not allowed in—but it's quiet all the time. Don't you think if someone was stuck inside I'd hear them?'

'There's nothing wrong with him from what I can tell. No, he wasn't there while I was cleaning.'

Nettled on The Prince's behalf, she's tempted to describe, in intimate detail, everything she'd seen in his rooms; to show them that he's just a man —

But the words become clogged in her throat. It would feel wrong to set free descriptions of the space Lorkan has worked so hard to keep private.

And she likes how his secrets sit with her, huddled close to her chest.

As people who never bothered to learn her name try to prize them from her palms, she pushes her way through the sea of aprons, starched shirts and pinafores, vowing to keep them that way; safe from harm, warm and snug in her cradling arms.

WHAT LORKAN IS

3

THE CHARCOAL DOE

Meren wakes the next day brimming with an unexplainable desire to protect Lorkan's privacy, and a vow to repay him for his trust already crossed over her heart.

The Prince has—for some reason—decided to open up his private space to her. Whether he meant to or not, he has given her a leg up to one of the highest rungs of the servant hierarchy, skipping her past at least ten years of labour.

Prodding her key through his lock, she decides she will repay him by tidying as she has never tidied before, both figuratively and literally.

Alfdis' warning about replacing everything in the exact position she'd found it has stuck to Meren's mind like a thistle burr. She isn't quite sure whether the housekeeper had meant it literally, but—due to her recent promise—she decides to take it that way.

It takes her five shifts to find her way around.

Because The Prince receives no guests, the guard room, dressing room, audience chamber, and antechamber appear largely unused. Since there is no one around to ask, Meren decides they only require a light dusting once or twice a week, and perhaps the occasional beating of a rug.

She spends the majority of her time in the bed chamber, sitting room, bathroom, and library, polishing fine tables, fluffing cushions, watering pot plants, and scrubbing the floor, among other things.

Each room boasts a fireplace so large she can stand right inside and thrust a wire brush up the chimney, but the one in the sitting room is the only one ever encrusted with ash.

Sometimes a copper pot will be left on the hearth, soiled with dried food that still smells as wonderful as it must have done when it was bubbling away the evening before. One day, her stomach feeling particularly hollow, Meren had stared at the crusted skin of a stew congealing at the bottom of a pan, half tempted to peel off a strip and pop it in her mouth. It smelt of herbs from the kitchen garden; leaves she had rubbed between finger and thumb and brought to her nose to smell, but never tasted. Disgusted with herself, she brought the pan to the washroom sink and forced the remnants down the plughole.

The Prince's chambers are missing a dining room, and Meren spent three days looking for it only to realise he has somehow disposed of the table and chairs and replaced the whole thing with an extra library.

It took her *ten* days to remember where he liked everything to be kept, and another three to work out a system to keep them there.

Using what was available to her—her fingers already marked into thirds by the creases in her skin, the distance between her ankle and calf, etcetera— Meren found that she could measure the space between objects and the objects adjacent to them.

The left loveseat in the lounge is one calf's length away from the mirror.

There is a hand-and-a-half-length gap between the dresser and the rug.

The end table should be two footsteps from the window.

This method worked so well that, after a day's work, she couldn't really tell she had been in to clean at all. Each day she left the rooms as if she'd never entered, apart from surfaces appearing much shinier and the cushions extra plump.

Meren is thankful for the list of tasks she is *not* required to do because, although her cleaning method is effective, it does double the time it takes to do even simple things like sweeping under desks or wiping down countertops.

Because of the list and the fact that Lorkan seems to be a tidy man by nature, Meren's job mainly involves—besides the obvious dusting and scrubbing—switching things about a bit.

His bed is always made, so she merely has to change the sheets for an identical set. Despite the autumn nights gumming at the window panes, Meren never finds a fur pelt strewn over his mattress, so the task of dragging the huge sheets on and off is made a little easier.

His pyjamas are always folded, so she swaps them for a fresh pair, making sure to bend the material in the exact same way Lorkan had done, spreading tassels and angling sleeves just the way they had been.

The notes on his desk sit patiently in a fairly logical order so, rather than filing them away, she lifts them, rubs a rag over the hardwood surface below, and places them back exactly as they were.

Occasionally, a niggling of self-consciousness will turn her cheeks pink and she'll hope no one in the gardens can see her through the windows. For example, once, she'd been cleaning the lint from under an ottoman that cost more than her family's cottage. To make sure she replaced it—and the book that had been resting on it—exactly where they had been, she teetered on one leg, propping it up with her foot while she dragged a brush back and forth, the book sliding about the seat like a duck on a frozen lake.

But, as she let the ottoman fall back onto the spotless floor, she felt a little swell of pride bloom like a shy flower in her chest.

Even if Lorkan isn't that particular about his armchair facing the door rather than the bed, Meren continues to leave as little trace of her meddling as possible.

She owes that to him, she feels, for rescuing her from the front steps. The work is easy. His chambers are always warm. Each day the sun streams through the tall windows, staining her cheeks with a smattering of freckles. The chapped skin on her hands is turning a feminine pink, and it's much more pleasant to flap out green velvet bedsheets than it is to work a mop over pigeon mess.

Occasionally, Meren does have to flap away a few flecks of loneliness. Clouds drift past the window sill, the door is locked to the outside world, and the air is still beside her own breath. From one room to the next, her lips don't part besides issuing the occasional satisfied sigh as she stands back to admire her work.

However, each of The Prince's belongings is a new and fascinating treasure that, under any other circumstances, she would never be permitted to touch. As she cleans them, Meren enjoys the weight, texture, and quality; the dainty gems set into a looking glass, gold embroidery darned into a green cushion, the carved redwood handle of a shaving knife.

There's a huge cylindrical tube propped up on three spindly legs by the lounge window. It's unbelievably heavy and she doesn't know what it does, but she likes its delicate button-sized dials and the way its shiny, barrel-shaped body warps the reflection of her face.

Whilst flicking a duster over the oil lamp on the bedside table, or edging a rag around the pieces of parchment strewn over his desk, Meren's mind often wanders—without realising it—to the curious subject of The Prince's personality.

His intelligence is a given.

Most wealthy people are clever, Meren understands—they can afford to be educated by tutors, for a start, rather than have their parents shakily recite the alphabet or teach them to count with heaps of seeds or small stones from outside.

Meren also guesses—not a very difficult conclusion to reach, given that he's known for this and *only* this across the realm—that Lorkan is quiet.

WHAT LORKAN IS

His voice was barely a breeze when he'd spoken to her on the steps, and almost all of his possessions point towards his temper being long and his need for socialisation being low. Only a pure-blooded introvert would own as many art supplies, scientific instruments, and novels as Lorkan seems to. His chambers appear to act as a storage space for fat, heavy books about art, history, biology, and countless long-winded stories. They're everywhere, overflowing shelves to such an extent he's started keeping stacks of them piled in corners and along the skirting boards.

And the *art*.

Her walk to the sixteenth floor is saturated in it—if it can be called that.

Murals, paintings and statues line the halls, all with the same sombre, classical style as though carved out of dull stones. Muted, silent people, with eyes cracking below yellowing layers of glaze, they frown down at her from their frames, unsmiling women and stern, bearded older men.

Meren has never tried to draw, besides scraping stick figures into the dirt as a child, or dragging a finger through droplets of condensation. However, if she *were* to attempt a picture of someone, she would try to make them look at least a *little* happy, she thinks.

Once inside The Prince's rooms, the tone shifts somewhat.

Most of these pictures are of scenery rather than people, and Meren could easily guess, with an amused smile, which ones The Prince prefers.

His favourites seemed to be of mountains and forests and towns; detailed, complicated things with so much going on Meren often walks in and can't find her way out for minutes at a time, her mop propped, forgotten, against her hip. These hang within his most-used spaces; in the rare gaps between bookshelves, above fireplaces, and over desks.

There are a few pieces, however, that he's placed behind thick columns of curtain pulled back from windows, or in nooks where the wall bends, hiding them from view. They must have been presents, Meren concluded, half-hearted gifts from people who hadn't tried to know him. They weren't like the vivid, striking paintings he favoured at all, they were more suited to the drab, restrained pictures dotted about the rest of the palace.

In one day, Meren now drowns in more colours, more dabs of oil paint, pale, and more translucent watercolour than she's laid eyes on in a whole lifetime.

It didn't take long for Meren to realise her employer is some kind of artist himself; although she can't find any paintings signed with his name—and she *has* looked.

The first giveaway is was art he keeps.

Even Meren's art-starved mind could tell the paintings Lorkan favours are slightly alive; the artist's own personality unabashedly interlaced with the brush strokes.

The second was the stationary.

It took her exactly ten minutes to discover The Prince's own hand had written the list of duties she still keeps folded in her pocket.

The ink matches the dried black gunk staining his quills, the jar of it sitting on his desk like a glass of liquid night. The parchment is the same as the sheets stacked in heaps, although he has many different types, all with varying grain, colour, and texture.

She came across the third giveaway that The Prince holds some kind of artistic talent when tidying the floors *below* his desks.

The cups and bowls in the cupboard he uses as a scullery are stacked in orderly rows, every bag of dried fruit, nuts and biscuits tied tight with twine.

He's stacked kindling beside each fireplace, the logs carefully placed, their dust swept into the hearth.

His spider plants and climbing ivies never spill so much as a fleck of soil, and his clothes are always folded and stowed neatly in their drawers.

However, his desk is a war zone of bleeding ink and charcoal bruises. He's got hundreds of sticks of it, scattered like fallen twigs, some smooth and waxy, some gritty as dirt. They're lined up in rolls of leather, rattling about in metal tins or, more often than not, accidentally crushed into the rugs underfoot.

WHAT LORKAN IS

Gummy fragments of eraser litter the floors like lint (in fact, The Prince's artistic habits are the only reason Meren has to sweep the floors at all), as do balls of parchment.

Loosely screwed-up, they're strewn around like oversized hailstones as if he's scribbled something, deemed it rubbish, and tossed it over his shoulder.

Seeing as collecting up the parchment isn't on the list of things she is *not* to do, Meren uses her initiative and spends several minutes each day kneeling by the desk in Lorkan's sitting room, plucking up yesterday's discarded drawings.

Plopping them into the wicker basket one by one, they fall with a gentle, dry rustle, charcoal dust shaking free like poppy seeds.

Presently, the afternoon sunlight is dribbling from the windows, pooling around her knees, turning the white parchment a watery gold. Each piece is unique; a streak of black ink on some, a delicately shaded area on another.

For the first two weeks of doing this, Meren managed to stave off the urge to unfurl one.

They must contain art, she had decided, because she couldn't imagine those dusty rods of charcoal could be used for anything else; their nubbed tips too dull for mathematics and too unpredictable for literacy.

The ball by her knee is screwed so tight it's made stripy like a humbug sweet, one side so thick with charcoal it's almost black, the other pristine and unused and white.

She has to know what these patches of hasty scribbles are a part of.

She has to know what one draws when they're surrounded by all the beauty they could ever want.

Before she knows what she's doing, Meren finds herself fervently checking over both her shoulders.

No one is around.

No one is ever around.

Her pulse flurrying in her fingertips, she carefully tweaks the parchment open, bit by bit, wincing each time the delicate material comes close to tearing. Forcing it to reveal its secrets, she finds herself grimacing, the feeling as wrong as forcing a rose to unfurl by pulling apart its petals.

It's a sketch of a deer.

The deer is clearly a doe, everything about it is delicate and slender and feminine, even though it must have been drawn with an angular chunk of charcoal.

The parchment is barely as large as Meren's two hands spread next to each other, but it's captured the texture of the doe's wiry fur, the reflection in its wide soulful eyes.

The shadows carefully warp when met by hills of bone or curves of muscle, pressed on by a slight reduction or increase in pressure.

Meren wants to stuff it into her pocket.

Next to the deer is a spindly tree sprouting twisting, brittle branches.

Meren recognises it but can't place it. She's contemplating this, mentally running through memories of the grounds surrounding the palace—because only a tree on royal property could manage to keep its fruit all autumn without having it pinched.

"Please do not judge my artistic prowess based on that."

Meren starts so violently she nearly rips the drawing in half.

Glancing down, she finds that, thankfully, some deep, primal instinct prevented her from committing such an atrocity.

Obviously, the person who'd spoken was Lorkan. These are his quarters, this is his drawing, and no one else has a key to this room besides Meren and The Prince himself.

She can feel the weight of it in her pocket like a stone.

Meren keeps her head bowed to the paper, frozen like a hare as The Prince steps closer. His footfalls are as light and silent as a cat, so she has no idea how close he is until his toes draw up to her eyeline.

They're bare, a stark contrast against the hardwood floor, light cotton trousers the colour of moss ending just before his bony ankles.

WHAT LORKAN IS

Curiosity overrides Meren's fear of moving, eventually. With difficulty, squinting as though looking into the sun, she manages to climb the sweep of his body.

It's a long climb, and she keeps getting sidetracked, branching off on little detours.

His shirt, darned with embroidered, climbing ivy.

The harsh angle of his collarbone.

The clean-cut of his jawline.

His thin lips, two parallel lines of delicate pink like the inside of a peony.

When she eventually makes it to his eyes, she finds them watching her intently. Not critically, but with a kind of scientific curiosity, as one would watch songbirds fluttering about a feeder, or koi fish in a pond.

Meren moistened her lips. "Why did you throw it away?" The question tumbles out before she can grab hold of it.

Mild surprise blossoms over The Prince's face. Because he has no beard or moustache, she can see it is long and angular and mostly cheekbone. It could be stern if his eyes weren't such a soft green, deep-set below two strong black brows.

"Can't you see what's wrong with it?"

Meren's cheeks heat, and she hastily bends her head to analyse the drawing again, raking her eyes over the quick lines and gentle shading.

As time ticks on, Meren's brow sets into a deeper and deeper furrow.

There's nothing wrong with the picture.

She can't find anything at all; it's a little smudged, but that's clearly been done on purpose to give the indication of colour; soft sweeps and presses of The Prince's fingerprint along the doe's body as if he was soothing it during its creation.

Meren raises her head again. "There's nothing wrong with it."

The faintest hint of a smile twitches the corners of his lips.

Suddenly, she forgets how to breathe.

"Here." The Prince takes another step closer, an elegant stride and, with a rustle of expensive fabric, he's kneeling next to her.

He smells of that scent he keeps in a glass flask on his dresser.

Meren can't put her finger on precisely what it is.

It's rich and dark like the black beans she'd admired at the more expensive end of the market, but it's also earthy and woody; sugary—like leaves after heavy rain.

His entire chambers smell like it at least a little, the sweetness clinging to the fibres in rugs and sofas, and something else, something Meren would later learn to be fresh paint.

So close she could touch him, The Prince doesn't look at her, but at the drawing still clasped tightly in her hands.

She hopes the droplets of sweat quickly beading on her palms won't show through the parchment.

Lorkan holds out one slender hand, his arm extended slightly in the small space between their bodies. He's pointing to the doe's flank.

Meren tries to keep as steady as possible. She's afraid she'll tremble and push the brushes of charcoal into the pad of The Prince's finger.

"You see the shadow here?" He asks. His voice is like honey and she is drowning. It's filling her head and gumming up her jaw.

Swallowing it:

"Yes."

Lorkan's finger moves over to point at the deer's face.

There's a dark patch below its cheek where the sunlight can't reach due to a smooth arch of bone under one of its orb-like eyes.

"Over here, the shadow is coming from the left." Back to the doe's rear leg. "But, over here, it comes from the right."

He turns to Meren, watching her piece this information together. His barely-detectable smile broadens a fraction when understanding lights up the back of her eyes.

"Oh."

"I wasn't paying attention when I drew it. My mind must have wandered and I made the mistake." Lorkan stands again and crosses over to the window.

WHAT LORKAN IS

Meren had polished the big metal tube earlier and it stands, gleaming in the sun, slender and mysterious.

Missing The Prince's proximity, she stands too, edging as close to Lorkan as she dares—which isn't very close.

He doesn't turn around, just stares out the window, his svelte body framed by the blue sky.

It's streaked with cirrus clouds, the city below clear and bright. The land slopes gently towards the harsh, wave-battered coast in the East, and rises steadily towards the mountains in the North, positioning the palace on a slight hill. The city kneeling before it is staggered into several levels, busy cobbled roads running between layers of tiled rooves like arteries.

"But that doesn't ruin the picture," Meren pushes the words from her chest, handing them to him. She feels as though she were a blind woman using a cane to test whether the ground in front of her is safe to walk on. "I couldn't even tell there was something wrong with it until you pointed it out."

Lorkan chuckles, an almost-silent exhalation of air through his pointed nose. He's still smiling, though; if one could call it that.

Meren wishes she could make him laugh properly.

She imagines the corners of his eyes would go all crinkly.

"*I* could tell, though," he says, "so it had to go."

"But it's so beautiful." She steps closer, narrowing the gap between them slightly, and Lorkan notices.

His eyes finally move from the view outside to the floorboards between them as if he's counting how many are left separating his bare feet from Meren's slippers.

"How could you ruin something so precious? Did you at least try to draw it again?" She regrets it as soon as it leaves her tongue and tries to catch it—

But The Prince's mouth has already hardened into a frown. He turns back to the window. "No, because I had things to do. As I am sure, do you."

Meren wants to ask what exactly does a prince *have* to do, but manages to say instead:

"I'm sorry, I didn't mean—"

She doesn't know how to finish that sentence.

Sorry she'd peeked at something he clearly didn't want anyone to see?

Sorry she'd accused him of being heartless enough to destroy beautiful things?

Sorry she'd talked back to him, talking to him *at all,* when someone of her station should have backed silently out of the room as soon as he'd entered?

Probably the only sensible thing she'd done since his arrival, Meren retreats, making a quick grab for her mop as she passes it, its handle leaning, forgotten, against the wall.

She doesn't know if The Prince noticed she was leaving because his broad back is still to her, his pale hands clasped at the small of it; closed off and unapproachable.

Stooped in an awkward sort of half-bow, Meren keeps her eyes glued to the back of his head until she's well into the next room then turns, sprinting for the door.

The heavy wood thuds ominously behind her.

4

THE LETTER

Meren had dropped the drawing of the deer on the dresser by the door, only remembering to do so at the last second.

She flies down three flights of stairs before finally slowing to catch her breath, her bucket having thumped a blue bruise into her thigh. It blooms like spilt ink below her uniform as she sighs, her breath disappearing like a ghost up into the vaulted ceiling. She's never noticed before, but it's painted with stars.

Flopping miserably down the steps to the servant's quarters, Meren wonders if she should tell Alfdis about what had happened in The Prince's chambers. The head housekeeper will want to know why she has been let go so suddenly—and so soon after a promotion, too.

Meren decides that—if Alfdis doesn't find out through some other means—she will take her mistake to the grave. At least that way she stands a chance at leaving with a recommendation.

Although I haven't been fired yet, she reminds herself, her shoes once again scuffing against cool flagstone.

She pulls the door closed, shutting out the glowing gold and white marble as though drawing a curtain on the sun. She has to blink a few times, her eyes adjusting to the flicking dim of the waxsticks.

The Prince never explicitly said *I was let go.*

She gnaws a tear of skin on her lower lip until the tang of metal beads on her tongue. *Probably because I didn't hand around long enough to give him a chance,* she realises with a sensation of a noose looping around her neck.

✴ ☾ ✴

Several people inquire after Meren's listlessness that evening, the others skirting around her, assuming her sallow cheeks and wilted expression are due to some impending sickness.

The next morning, Alfdis still hasn't rapped on her door with a note of dismissal, so she shrugs on her uniform and pins up her hair as she always would; although she doesn't bother to smooth her wrinkled apron, and her bun sags low to her collar.

The mess hall had been next to empty when Meren had to clean the front steps, and it's empty now that she has to clean The Prince's chambers—although for a different reason. She used to have to wake before everyone else, but now they've all feasted and left, the flagstone floor already flecked with crumbs and something sticky she can't identify.

As she approaches cautiously with her tray, Yllva, the servant's cook, glowers at Meren from her hatch in the wall like a bear from a cave.

When Meren first came to the city in search of a job, it was Yllva who originally (and generously, her mother had said), took her on as a servant.

A coarse-looking woman with height and girth trumping most males of the realm, Yllva runs a tight, no-frills operation in the low-ceilinged, perpetually boiling little kitchen flattened under the palace's boot. Never bothering to learn anyone's names, she prefers instead to hurl a barked 'Oi!'

from across the room and, failing to grab someone's attention over the roaring fires and rattling pots, she opts for taking up whichever vegetable is closest to her dinner-plate-sized hands and lobbing it in their general direction.

This ill-treatment might be tolerable—in Meren's eyes at least—if Yllva's culinary skills made up for what she lacks in charm. However, in her kitchen, cleanliness takes priority over quality, and everything that leaves her hatch is tinged with a gritty, burnt outer crust.

Meren's job in her kitchen mainly involved peeling and chopping, but she spent a lot of time scurrying around, mopping up stains before Yllva got wind of them and reacted by concussing the closest individual.

Presently frowning through a curtain of salty steam, she scoops a wad of porridge from her pot and lets it flop into Meren's bowl.

"We're out of egg," she informs her gruffly. "Bread's stale too. Should have got here earlier."

Retracting her tray, Meren finds two slices of rye have been generously prodded into her porridge.

They're end pieces, rough and gnarled on one side like tree bark, but she forces a smile and a polite nod of her head.

News of her promotion had begun as excited, bubbling gossip, but it had soon marinated into ugly green envy, spreading through the servant's quarters like a cough.

Meren knows that, in her own way, Yllva had liked seeing her face pop up at the kitchen hatch each night. Whether she enjoyed the silent company in the early hours of the morning, or simply fed off of her suffering, she isn't sure but—since her promotion—the cook's glower has definitely darkened by a few shades.

Meren would like to tell her she's sorry she got promoted and yes, she knows she doesn't deserve it.

She'd also like to tell her not to bother with bitterness because she'll be back to scrubbing bird mess this evening anyway.

Sure enough, while forcing down her bread, Meren catches sight of a laundry basket bobbing towards her between the tables and benches. It weaves and dips like a sandpiper avoiding the tide, occasionally disappearing to retrieve a dropped sock, and the remaining colour in Meren's cheeks drains like a pulled plug.

Trying to pull a shadow about her like a cloak, her pallid little face pokes out like a depressed spectre.

Alfdis spots it almost immediately and, desperately, she pushes back against the wall in the hope the dusty limestone might swallow her whole.

It doesn't, and the head housekeeper shuffles over, allowing Meren to help her deposit her burden on the flagstones with a relieved sigh. The basket matches her in size, the top of the heap level with her thick glasses, which she pushes up her beak with one finger.

"Thank you, dear. We simply *must* stop hiring staff; the number of bloomers on that washing line! You've never seen the like."

Catching nothing but 'bloomers', Meren rakes the intricate lines of her expression.

Perhaps she'll hear anger in Alfdis' voice for the first time in all her years of service?

Or, maybe, she'll just shake her head in disapproval—which would be *much* worse—as she points her to the door?

"Now, Hansen, this was in my—dear child, whatever is the matter with you? Are you coming down with something?" Sounding troubled, she presses the rocky line of her knuckles to Meren's forehead. "You know the rule—go straight to bed if you feel ill. If sickness spreads, the whole palace could crumble to the ground."

Meren moistens her lips and tries to pull them into a smile. With a stiff wrist, she waves off Alfdis' concerns.

If this is what it's like to be fired, maybe it's not as bad as I feared, she thinks, helping the head housekeeper ease herself down onto the bench.

"I'm fine. I just didn't sleep very well last night." Not a very convincing lie, but Alfdis nods sympathetically all the same.

WHAT LORKAN IS

"You and me both; Their Majesty's anniversary is coming up and it's down to me to plan the feast, but our regular butcher doesn't think he can get enough venison in time so I've had to enlist the help of Paulie, you know, in the market? But I'm not so sure about his—"

"Alfdis," Meren slides the word into her rant as politely as she can.

Her colourless eyes blink a few times. "Oh, yes, sorry, dear, got carried away." Tucking a few strands of cobweb-coloured hair behind her ears as if smoothing her feathers:

"This was left on my desk for you."

"Oh." Meren is the one to blink this time, her gaze following one of Alfdis' bony hands as it draws an envelope from her bodice pocket. She takes it, hoping her cheeks don't look as grey as they feel. "Thank you."

Alfdis wavers, her eyes flicking down curiously to Meren's hands curiously, and guilt nibbles at as she stands—to the best of her ability.

The envelope weighs a ton, even though it's as thin as a few sheets of parchment.

"I guess I should go read it."

Alfdis' shoulders fall in disappointment, but she hitches them back up, shaking it off as if she has no time for such emotions. "Right. Yes. And I better go pair a hundred socks."

※ ☾ ※

Meren knows who the letter is from.

Every day, she skirts a rag around piles of envelopes of the same pearly white, their texture smooth and glossy as a wax stick.

She had wondered, at first, if Alfdis had taken a peek at what was inside, but she couldn't have, because it's still fastened with a dark green wax seal.

It's monogrammed elegantly with a twisting letter 'L', surrounded by a wreath of delicate pin-prick-sized ivy leaves.

The dormitory Meren shares is small but high-ceilinged, with ample space between the narrow single beds lined up along two walls. Each one boasts a modest nightstand at the head and a hefty trunk at the tail, and Meren often finds the room pleasingly empty.

The dormitory is empty now, and she doesn't hesitate to hunt around for an object roughly the same shape as a letter knife. Opting for the toothbrush in her wash kit, she uses it to lightly tear a line along the top of the envelope and pulls its contents free as if gutting a fish.

She doesn't care that it's from a prince, anymore.

How does one spell 'dismissed'?

She's never seen it written down before. She imagines the word full of 's's, hissing from the mouth of a snake.

Before, she would have treated anything The Prince gave her as though it were a butterfly that's landed on her finger—but not this. Not a letter instructing her to pack up what little she owns and find another place of work.

Just because she couldn't keep her mouth shut.

What will her mother say when she turns up on her doorstep?

Meren hasn't visited her childhood home since moving to Tawny, although she'd like to, just to kiss her father on the cheek and bury her face in her mother's apron-covered bosom.

Although Meren grew for a short time and then just seemed to stop, Mrs Hansen is a relatively wide, curvaceous woman with sturdy arms and strong hands that can both console and scold, depending on the occasion.

Meren knows they would scold if she dragged her trunk back to Holcombe and knocked on that stocky brown door.

It's painted brown because Mrs Hansen said brown is a good, humble, dependable colour, and she was right. Each summer the neighbours trudged outside to reapply their bright purple blackberry paint, or their maroon red madder root stain and, each summer Mrs Hansen's brown door muscled on, as brown as it ever was.

WHAT LORKAN IS

Meren Hansen—as were all preceding Hansens—was born and raised in Holcombe, one of the many rural counties smattered across western Velôr.

From above, Holcombe looks like a smudge of mud in winter and a clod of grass in summer, dropped onto the kingdom with a spade. It's split into four hamlets, Meren's being the largest yet somehow least populated. Farmland first and a community last, Rinfield offers few delights besides fat cobs of sweetcorn in autumn, and a single tavern that's slowly slipping sideways into the river.

The third of seven bundled into a dead-end dirt track, Meren's childhood home has sat adamantly stop its slight hill since her grandfather built it from stone and thatch, and it'll be sat there long after all the Hansens are dead and gone—or at least that's what he'd said.

It's Meren's father's birthplace and perhaps, one day, it will be his grave. He'll be given a stone next to his dad's in the back garden, under Mrs Hansen's bodices and chemises fluttering on the clothesline.

Meren imagines growing old behind that brown door, her hair turning as grey as her grandfather's tombstone, and her bread sours in her stomach.

The envelope contains another piece of parchment but it's rough and thick, torn neatly from a sketchbook.

It isn't a letter of dismissal.

It isn't a letter at all.

Reverently, Meren unfurls it, whatever it is, and grains of charcoal flutter into her lap like black snow.

It's another drawing of a doe, identical to the one she had left on Lorkan's dresser—

Apart from the shadow along its flank.

This time it's coming from the left.

A squiggling shadow shines through the parchment along the blank bottom corner, and Meren turns it over.

Inscribed in a delicate hand are the words:

'*I tried again.*'

✶ ☾ ✶

Meren sits for a while, The Prince's drawing spread over her lap.

If she stares at it long enough, the white walls caging the animal blur away until it's stepping with dainty feet across her apron.

Eventually, she slides open the drawer of her bedside table.

It contains very little; a few old-fashioned romantic novels, a bundle of letters from her parents, her own yellowed envelopes and blunted quills. There are a few coppers and reems knocking around that she's been meaning to exchange for wool and darning thread, but she keeps the bulk of her money on her person, strung together on some twine.

She'd like to keep The Prince's drawing in her pocket too, but fears water from her mop bucket might seep through her dress and lick at the soft lines. So, careful not to crinkle the edges, Meren lays the picture inside a paperback and eases the drawer shut.

The drawing may not be on her person, but it is on her mind as she makes the long trek up to the sixteenth floor.

The charcoal deer tiptoes its way about her thoughts as though passing through a thicket of trees, The Prince's message scrawled over her brain in his looping hand:

'I tried again.'

Meren dithers before slotting the key into the door.

The entire way there, she had hoped to find The Prince on the other side so she can thank him—and apologise for speaking out of terms. She'll remember to curtsy this time, and to keep her head lowered respectfully and not to stare at his hair or his pointed face or the green part of his eyes that look like sunbeams filtering through leaves.

However, as Meren steps inside her shoulders sag with relief. Placing her cleaning supplies by the door, she does a quick little check in each room and finds them mercifully empty.

WHAT LORKAN IS

✶ ☾ ✶

The Prince's rooms remain empty for several weeks—at least, they are empty whilst Meren is cleaning.

He returns when her shift ends, she knows because, when she arrives at nine, she finds things have moved slightly.

New balls of discarded parchment litter the expensive rugs like apples—which she *doesn't* open, charcoal sticks worn down to useless, blunted stubs.

She'll find a forgotten mug of tea, the dregs black and drying, the fireplace stacked with ashes.

Ribbons will have burrowed several chapters deeper into his books, and pillows—once plumped—are squashed out of shape where he'd leaned against them.

Sometimes, he'll leave the occasional note atop the dresser telling her not to bother dusting the bookshelves for a few days because they don't need it, or politely asking her to stop trying to get the paint stains out of the red chaise lounge because they really don't bother him.

Sometimes, she wishes *she* could leave *him* a note saying the same thing.

She'd like to tell him he doesn't *need* to clean condensation from the looking glass after a bath—or put away his piles of clean laundry when it's dropped off each morning. He shouldn't sweep stray ashes from the hearth, or replace the oil in the lamps.

That's *her* job.

And he's a prince. His hands shouldn't be stained by washcloths, or splintered by rough broom handles.

At the end of each week, Alfdis hands Meren her wages, which she promptly posts to her parents—for the first time, not feeling so forlorn as she watches them go. It's easier to hand them, packaged up in paper and twine, to the woman behind the post office desk now that her hands aren't raw with the effort of earning them.

There's a new rosiness to her cheeks and a smile to her face that the other maids are growing hideously envious of. They throw sentences at her in the same way devilish children throw small pebbles at pigeons:

'Your prince treating you good?'

'Didn't your prince give you any work today? It's only half four.'

'Are my taxes paying you to waltz around on constitutionals?'

But they shut up quickly whenever Alfdis hurries by.

Of course, cleaning for The Prince isn't as easy as the other servants seem to think.

Meren still has to do *some* work, and the work she has to do is made twice as hard by the method she continues to apply to her tidying; placing things back *exactly* where they had come from, measuring the distance between objects to make sure she does so.

She's doing this—skirting a cloth around a leather-bound notebook on The Prince's bedside table one day—when she feels a presence behind her.

She'd forgotten that he doesn't seem to make a sound as he approaches.

She just *feels* him, his body somewhere close by—although she's not sure exactly where until she raises her head.

Placing the drinks coaster she'd been wiping back down, she turns around and there he is.

He's taller than she remembered. It's not uncommon for Velôrian males to be tall, but Lorkan is *tall*—tall and slender and pale like a willow tree.

Meren's throat tightens, her stomach doubling in on itself, although she isn't sure why.

"What are you doing?" He asks. His voice is silken, *too* silken, a velvety ribbon of syllables slipping around the insides of Meren's ears.

It ties her brain up in a neat bow.

"What?" She chokes out. A Little voice in her head is yelling something about curtseying—or something.

But she doesn't.

WHAT LORKAN IS

A light breeze from the open window teasingly tugs at The Prince's hair like it had done on the front steps.

Autumn is slowly inching its way towards winter, the crisp sunlight catching his lime-green irises, despite the fact that he isn't facing it. It's cresting like a miniature sunrise over one of his broad shoulders, casting Meren's face into shadow.

"You were doing something with your finger," he says, more silky words edged with something.

Meren thinks it might be curiosity.

"While you cleaned my bedside table." He doesn't look angry—although he has no reason to be angry, Meren soothes herself. More amused, actually, the corner of his narrow lips tweaking up into what could be mistaken for a smile.

Subconsciously—and *self-consciously*—Meren smooths imaginary dust from the front of her uniform. "I was measuring."

She should really use more words, but The Prince's ribbon-like voice has become tangled, clogging her vocal cords.

And that s*mile*.

It's not even a smile, it's just a slight shifting of muscles, a *projection* of a smile, like ink shining through parchment.

'I tried again.'

"Measuring?"

"With my hand. To make sure I put everything back in the right place." Her cheeks redden as his smile grows into a smirk; as if he is very much entertained.

Meren holds out a hand to illustrate what she means. "The top of the notebook is a third of my forefinger from the wax-stick holder—" Her anxiety seems to have swung in the opposite direction—like a panicked pendulum—and now she can't shut up.

"—and the stick of charcoal is perpendicular to the bottom of the notebook, with a nail width of space between the—"

One of Lorkan's broad hands cuts her off with a dismissive wave. As big as a dinner plate, his hands are mainly fingers, and his fingers are mainly bone. "I see. May I ask..."

Meren almost blurts, '*You're a prince, you can ask me anything*' but bites her tongue.

"Why?"

"Why?" Meren repeats stupidly, tilting her head.

"Yes. Why measure the distance between things? Why not just..." He reaches over, his forearm almost brushing her elbow.

She feels the back of her neck heat as though she's standing too close to a fire.

The Prince plucks up the leather-bound sketchbook smoothly, then drops it back onto the table.

It falls atop the charcoal stick, and she winces, picturing the dark smudge probably smeared across the rear cover.

"...put things back wherever you like?"

As his right hand withdraws and snakes around to join the other one across the small of his back, Meren lets her spine loosen a fraction.

She licks her lips, her mouth strangely dry. "I heard that...and I *thought* that you don't like your things being moved."

The Prince's smirk widens enough to give her a glimpse at the strong, white edges of his teeth, and then he laughs; a mellow chuckle rippling up from his lungs and filling the air with little waves; like a puddle disturbed by a droplet of rain.

Meren stares at him.

"So you've been...what did you call it?" He's looking at her, his dark eyebrows coming together as he fishes for Meren's word. "'*Measuring*' every single item as you clean around it?"

"Yes." She nearly adds '*Sir*' onto the end of that embarrassed, lonely little syllable, just to give it some company.

A hazy look clouds The Prince's eyes as he suddenly turns pensive.

Meren waits, her hand tapping a nervous rhythm onto her thigh.

His eyes slide over it, then back up to her face and he says, with no particular tone:

"Would you mind coming with me?"

5

THE STUDY

Taking the handle of her mop, Meren bends to heave her wash pail from the floor.

"You won't need those," The Prince says, waving them away with another lazy turn of his wrist.

Confusedly, she places her bucket back onto the marble and stands the mop handle against the wall.

He's already turned around to lead her to wherever he's taking her, his long legs crossing over to the door in several easy strides and, hastily, Meren scurries after his pale ankles as they disappear into the next room.

For some reason, she'd thought they'd leave his chambers. Despite refusing to partake in the rumours surrounding The Youngest Prince, she is a *little* surprised when they don't head towards a laboratory full of half-complete experiments, or a picturesque spot where he likes to treat maidens to wine and a sunset.

As he leads her further *into* his chambers, Meren looks back at the main entrance, puzzled, and, watches as it grows smaller in the distance.

His bare feet are soundless as they wind down the string of rooms.

WHAT LORKAN IS

Over the past weeks, she has passionately cared for each one they pass through, dutifully learning every inch of their skirting boards, crown mouldings and beautiful, cushy furniture.

They look different with their owner in them, though; more alive, each item suddenly becoming interactive rather than an ornamental part of the surroundings.

Meren suddenly feels as though she's got to learn them all over again.

Reaching the very last wall in his chain of rooms, The Prince finally comes to a halt. There's a door sunk into it and, suddenly, Meren understands.

She hasn't cleaned *every* inch of Lorkan's chambers.

They're studded with numerous closets; ornate doors pressed into recesses as though someone has pushed them into the wall with their thumb. Meren would have forgotten *this* door is not a closet, had she not been asked specifically to not open it.

The study.

Although thinking about it, she could have done, if she wanted to, she's now realising:

It's not locked.

She watches as The Prince reaches for the doorknob.

He stops, turning to her. "You know, Alfdis didn't tell me your name."

"Hansen, Your Highness."

He shakes his head. "Not your father's name, I want to know *your* name."

"Oh. It's Meren."

"Meren," he says as if tasting it on his tongue. "Wren like the bird?"

Meren thinks about it. It is entirely possible her parents took one look at their babe's feathery tuft of hair and petite stature and decided to name her after a tiny, brown bird. "I guess so."

"I'm Lorkan, but I guess you knew that."

If she didn't know any better, she could have sworn his sharp cheekbones had gained a slight, pink tint.

With a well-practised hand, he turns the handle to the right and gives it a little push.

As if to add gravitas, or maybe just being a little bit of a showman, he leaves it ajar, the gap so meagre nothing but a thin stream of light can escape.

Meren can tell nothing about the other side besides the fact that it must have a lot of windows.

"I've never let anyone in here," he says quietly—as if giving the room an introduction.

She wants to take the breast of his thin cotton shirt and give him a little shake for being so dramatic. Trying not to lean over to peek through the chink in the door, she gives a small understanding nod.

"Even as a child, I didn't let elders come in to tidy."

"I know."

She remembers last night's game of '*What's On The Sixteenth Floor?*' the staff had started at dinner. Some sickly, sour little part of her brain wonders if they're about to owe each other a few coppers.

"You do?" The Prince actually looks momentarily surprised.

Meren's cheeks heat uncomfortably under his inquisitive gaze.

She could tell him about the things the servants say, but she doesn't. Not because they'd lose their jobs—and maybe their heads—but because she can't bring herself to say them. They'd flick about the room like little hot flames, and she doesn't want to see the look on The Prince's face as they nip at him.

"Yes. Alfdis—the head housekeeper—told me," she says.

The corner of Lorkan's lips twitch into that almost-undetectable-smile he seems to wear quite a lot. "Well, that rule no longer applies."

He gives the heavy door a small nudge, keeping one hand on the handle.

Meren readies herself for a groan of joints or an ominous creak—but the door swung open easily, the hinges smooth and worn.

This room is frequently used? Meren realises.

She's never seen him come in or out of it.

Perhaps he used it a lot in the *past* and then *stopped* when she started working for him.

Or he'd never actually *left*, and had been just on the other side of the wall as she had been cleaning—

He gestures welcomingly with one arm as if to sweep her inside, and she feels herself heat up by a few degrees below her uniform.

Not because he's being gentlemanly and it's making her knees feel like cooked pasta—but because he's treating her like a Lady. A *real* lady, as if her apron is a velvet gown and her starched collar a string of pearls.

She suddenly feels as though she's been caught trying on Queen Lophia's satin slippers.

"By the way, I am familiar with Alfdis," he adds, awakening Meren from her stupor.

He's still standing there, one arm outstretched, his expression expectant.

Even so, Meren hesitates, perhaps waiting for a gust of trapped souls to whizz past her ear, or a giant, carnivorous pet to charge through her legs.

Although, she reminds herself, if there *was* something alive inside, she would have heard it. Each day she'd plumped the settee, dusted the bookshelves, and swept a broom past the door and—each day—it had remained stubbornly silent.

When nothing slips through the jamb besides a pleasing, chalky smell she can't place, Meren takes a tentative step closer and keeps doing so until she's standing on the threshold.

Below her feet, the floor has changed from cold marble to neat slats of hardwood.

"I had to put some panelling down because I kept messing up the marble," The Prince explains sheepishly, noticing her eyes flick to the evenly placed boards below her feat.

It's a studio.

Meren can tell it's an artist's studio, although she has never seen one.

She's seen things close to one; her father's workshop, for one, where he fixes people's broken things for a small fee. His tools are lined up on hooks in the walls, his screws and nails kept in rows of empty pickling jars. His workbench, although pocked with a few slips of his saw, is regularly swept with a goat's hair brush to prevent dust and metal shavings from entering his client's timepieces and sewing machines.

The Prince's tidiness, however, seems to pitter out somewhere between the door and the chair at the back of the lounge.

Bowls and palettes are stacked like dirty dishes, encrusted with dried scabs of colour.

Pots of brushes—and, more often than not, simply *unbound* brushes—litter every flat surface. Their bristles vary in conduction; some matted and caked with dried paint, others fine and full like the tail of a fox.

And other animals, now that Meren thinks about it. A lot of them are indeed soft and fluffy like the brush of a vixen, but there's also a good deal sporting stubby, oily hairs like those of an otter, or long and coarse like the hackles of a badger. There's striped weasel, long bristles from a boar, cuttings of a horse's mane—

Several knives lay about a few small tables, on cabinets, atop the seats of chairs.

Meren would have been alarmed by the sheer number of them, had they not all been dull and wide and innocent; some with curves like a butter knife, and others flat like a cake server. They're stained too, but with paint rather than something more foreboding.

There are spills, spatters, splatters, and scuffs of colour where The Prince must have touched the walls, the desks, the countertops, without knowing he had pigment on his hands, the room littered with very colourful scars.

Some of them are somewhat subdued, neutral tones, like skin and the sky and cloth.

Most of them are bright, ethereal colours Meren has never seen before; the purple heart of an orchid, the piercing yellow of a heron's eye, the plasma blue of the Northern Lights—

She can deduce The Prince's style without looking at the easel standing proudly in the centre of the room.

The easel.

She can't take her eyes off it.

Propped up on three spindly legs, a swatch of Tawny city centre has been snipped out with darning scissors and stretched over a frame.

WHAT LORKAN IS

The swatch has been taken from the market.

The man inside his stall doesn't seem to notice he's been relocated, his smile wide and unbothered as he hands a parchment bag to a customer. He's surrounded by barrels stacked high with beans and seeds; some fine as sand, others as large as a goose egg. Out of sight below the counter, several children are dipping their hands into his produce, enjoying the sensation of the little shells passing through the gaps in their fingers.

If she were to go to the market now, would Meren find an empty square where this stall had been?

And yet, there's a haziness to it. Stepping closer, she finds brush strokes, joining, overlapping, and jostling with one another. They merge like drops in an ocean to form other things too:

A group of stray hens pecking up the spilt beans.

A gaggle of young adults laughing at a whispered joke.

A mother and daughter holding hands, the afternoon sun lighting up their flame-red hair.

Every now and again, Meren finds something she hadn't noticed before; footprints pressed into the gravel paths, weeds managing to sprout in the dust-like mud, hand-written tags prodded into apple pies and heaps of colourful spices.

She has gravitated towards the picture without realising, leaning towards the bright, hopeful brush strokes as though hoping to fall into them.

"They don't look like they knew you were painting them," she says quietly, for a moment forgetting who she is, and who he is, and where they are.

The Prince steps a little closer, away from the door until he's standing a respectful distance from her side. Perhaps amused by her fascination, he's regarding her face through the corners of his eyes. They're crinkled with a smile.

"They probably *didn't* know I was painting them."

Turning to him, surprised, Meren looks the long pillar of his royal body up and down, all parchment-white skin, jet black hair, and eyes like sunshine through a leaf. She pictures him leaning against the trunk of a tree, or sitting cross-legged on the grass surrounded by colours and bristly brushes.

"How can a prince take a seat in a crowded market and without anyone noticing?"

"I didn't."

She wonders if he'll elaborate, but he doesn't.

For a second, she considers prompting him but decides against it. Not because he's a prince, but because she doesn't want to press him. To do so would be forcing a bird's wing to open before it's ready to fly.

There's a while of Meren just staring at the painting, and The Prince just staring at Meren.

After some time, her brow furrows, and he tilts his head at her. He doesn't need to say anything.

"It's beautiful," she assures.

"But?" He takes a step closer, gauging her reaction.

When she doesn't seem to mind his proximity, he doesn't stop, edging nearer until he's in line with Meren's side.

He still isn't looking at the canvas, though.

She shifts her weight onto her other foot, turning her question over in her mind. After a few rotations, she dares to hand it to him.

"Why did you paint it?"

Lorkan tips his head the other way, watching her thoughtfully. "Was I not *supposed* to paint it? I could compensate the people in it; if consent is what troubles you—"

Imagine that; a prince worrying he'd upset his housemaid.

Meren can't help the lower half of her face splitting into a smile. "No, I mean...I know where these stalls are, they're next to a set of steps leading up to a hill with houses on it."

She sneaks a glance at The Prince's face, placing her words down carefully, but less so now.

His gaze is passive and patient, and she replenishes her lungs with oxygen.

It tastes of paint.

"Well, if you would have faced the *other* way, you would have had a view of the palace..."

He nods, if Meren didn't know any better, she would say encouragingly.

"...The grandest building in the kingdom."

"So?"

"So, I just wondered why you didn't paint that, and instead opted for some random villagers selling seeds and vegtables."

The Prince chuckles, and Meren catches it this time, and it makes her forget how to breathe.

"Because The Palace isn't beautiful," he says simply, the long line of his shoulders rising and falling in a shrug. "If I see something beautiful I like to capture it, sort of...freeze it in time so I can look at it whenever I want. I wanted to look at this scene some more."

Meren's forehead furrows. "You think commoners selling things is beautiful?"

The Prince regards her quizzically. "Do you not?"

She ponders this.

Yes, the market is exciting and alive, people bustling around like blood cells through a massive, beating heart—

But it's also loud and crowded; a stifling hot dust cloud during the summer months, and a churned-up pig's trough in the winter.

No, Meren wouldn't call it *beautiful*.

But this version of it? This rectangle in front of her, the way The Prince sees it?

Without her noticing, said prince has crossed the room and is writing something on a scrap of parchment.

Meren glances sideways at him, her eyes tracing the arch of his torso stooped to lean over the countertop.

Placing down his quill, The Prince brings the slip over to her and holds it out.

Although formed from the Velôrian alphabet, the words inscribed in glistening ink are foreign to her eyes.

"I'm showing you this room because I want to add a task to your workload if that is okay."

Meren blinks at him. "Of course."

"It involves leaving The Palace and a short walk. Alfdis won't mind; if she asks you where you're going just tell her you're running an errand for me."

Giving a little nod of her head and hoping her cheeks aren't as red as they feel, Meren takes the list from The Prince's outstretched hand.

The parchment is soft like the underside of a petal.

"These are pigments," he explains, tapping the letters she is still trying to decipher with one long, slender finger. "I use them to make paint. I'd like you to go to the apothecary stall in the centre of the market. Give the man this list, and he'll give you some things in jars and boxes."

Smoothly dipping into his trouser pocket, he draws out several coins and drops them into the centre of her palm.

The metal is cool, despite sitting snugly against his thigh. He's given her a few squares of silver—but there are at least three tiny, thick disks of gold amongst the drab grey, and he must catch her blink at them.

"Some of the pigments are quite rare, like this one," he points to a long name that looks quite beautiful written down, even though Meren doesn't know what it means. "You can tell Frode he can keep the change."

She nods again.

She hopes he's mistaking her lack of words for attentiveness rather than what it actually is; a slight daze. She holds the coins and the note close, as though scared someone will dart from a cupboard and snatch them from her.

Releasing The Prince has started walking to the door, Meren does her best to follow, willing her legs into motion.

"I used to put in orders and wait for them to be delivered, but this will be much faster," he says.

He seems to be able to reach into her brain and pluck out each question before they've left her mouth.

"Instead of starting work here at nine, you can pick up my pigments first and begin at eleven," he says, guiding her through the studio with another sweeping gesture.

She watches as he, once again, leaves it unlocked.

"Just leave them somewhere in the study, I don't mind where. Here." He dips into that pocket again and brings out something else.

Meren reaches for it this time, having assumed he'd forgotten an item he wants her to purchase, but he says instead:

"For your troubles." His fingertips brush her palm as he presses a crescent onto the little mound of money already cupped there.

The sensation bursts on her skin like a raindrop. Her neck heats, her jaw opening and closing several times before she manages to push out:

"Alfdis already pays me."

The Prince's expression falters, and his tongue moistens his narrow lips.

It's pointed and pink like a raspberry.

One of his wide, pale hands reaches up to scratch the back of his neck, the bright green of his eyes avoiding Meren's for the first time since they'd met.

"I don't need it. Take it. And you can have the rest of the day off; I think the lounge is perfectly tidy, for now, thank you."

6

A TRIP TO MARKET

Clutching the money The Prince had given her tight in her pocket, Meren scurries down the narrow corridors of the servant's quarters like a mouse off to stash a wedge of cheese.

Maids, kitchen boys, and people whose job she doesn't even know the name of bustle past her, each one falling into one of two categories: those she definitely knows to be thieves, and those who probably *are* thieves but haven't been caught yet.

She stops before reaching for her dormitory's door handle.

On the day she was to leave to begin her new job as a kitchen maid, Meren's parents had presented her with a bag of tart, round hard candies. Secretly, they had taken on extra work to afford them, her mother's hands pricked with sewing needles and her father's eyes heavy from squinting at cogs and gears through wax stick light.

When Alfdis showed her to her dormitory, she had stashed the candies deep inside the wide trunk at the foot of her bed.

They had been snaffled almost immediately.

WHAT LORKAN IS

Remembering their bitter-sweet taste, her fist wraps about The Prince's coins like a wallet of flesh, tendons and bone.

※ ☾ ※

Her usual seat in the corner of the mess hall beckons to her, but she ignores it, her eyes scraping the crowd for the neatest bun of them all.

Eventually, she locates it, a cold, hard, round little thing tied tight to the head of Alfdis. She's picking at something grey on her plate cautiously with the edge of her knife as Meren slips onto the bench beside her.

"Hello, dear," she greets without lifting her eyes from her tray; as if she suspects the blobs sat atop it to crawl away should she give them a chance. "Sleep better last night? Your eyes look much brighter."

Meren blinks, momentarily confused. Then she remembers her earlier lie and waves off Alfdis' concerns distractedly. "Yes, much better, thank you. I wanted to ask you; Lorkan—"

Alfdis flicks her a warning look—just for a second—and she hastily corrects herself:

"—His Highness. He said he knows you. Is that true?"

Abandoning the grey thing, Alfdis turns her plate around to begin tackling the little heap of something on the other side.

It's grey too but, somehow, *more* grey.

"Yes, I know him," she says. Her lip twitches, and Meren can't tell if it's with a hint of a smile, or a grimace at the way the grey thing is oozing through the prongs of her fork.

She shuffles closer, her grip tightening in her pocket.

The curved edges of the coins wedge themselves into the creases of her hand.

"...And?"

"And what?"

"How do you know him?"

Alfdis gives the grey thing a stir, perhaps trying to comb out the lumps.

Meren hasn't touched her food yet. She went for the vegetables; limp and waterlogged, but at least distinguishable as something that used to be food. Moving closer, she feels her thigh nudge the brittle knot of Alfdis' knee.

"He'd seek me out when he was a young'un; I dare say his nurse didn't do a very good job of keeping an eye on him."

Meren blinks. "He'd come down here?"

"Sometimes to my office, if there weren't many people about. Usually, he'd find me while I was working. He'd play with the bubbles in my pail while I mopped things, or muck about with my typewriter while I did the accounts."

Meren's jaw is still hanging open so far she can nearly feel the rough scrape of the wooden table. Alfdis smiles properly now.

"Hansen, you can't work here as long as I have and not run into your employers."

"What about Sol?" She flushes. "The Eldest Prince, I mean. Did he come down here too?"

"No, no, I've only seen His Highness in passing. The Youngest Prince always came alone. His older brother was often out with his friends, you see, and his parents, well, you can imagine they didn't have much time for games. I suspect he came down here looking for company."

"I thought royalty wasn't allowed down in the servant's quarters," Meren says, finding it hard to picture satin slippers against the uneven flagstones.

Alfdis shakes her head. "No dear, royalty can go wherever they please, it's *us* that are limited to places within our station. Like pawns and queens in chess."

Meren has never played chess before. "Do you still see him now?"

"Yes, for a spot of tea, although not often."

"Why not?"

"Good gracious, all these questions!"

"Why don't you see him much anymore if you practically helped raise him?"

WHAT LORKAN IS

"Were you not listening to my chess analogy?"

The bridge of Meren's forehead creases. "He ignores you because you're below him?"

Alfdis' little tortoise mouth spreads in a little laugh. "No, dear, *I* don't *let* him meet me because he's *above* me."

Meren's forehead is still crumpled. "You deny a prince's summons?" She can tell she's hit a nerve because the wrinkles in Alfdis' lips return as her smile fades.

"I don't refuse him, I make polite excuses; and they're not always excuses, mind; I *am* a very busy woman. He invites me up to one of the drawing rooms, or an empty library, and there are spices in the tea and he gives me cushions for my back. He always gets the best china down from the cabinets, even though I tell him not to." She bristles, and mutters, clearly nettled:

"And he insists on calling me 'Alfie'."

Meren has to swallow a giggle. "What's wrong with that?"

"It's not right, Meren."

There are no windows in the mess hall, but it darkens slightly as if a cloud has moved over to block the sun.

Meren turns to her vegetables, deciding to gnaw through the broad beans first.

Yllva likes to eat them raw, working the ropey pods between her broad teeth. The smell has almost faded from Meren's memory, replaced by the beeswax polish she used to wipe over the palace steps. Now, she rubs it into The Prince's oak countertops tops and twisted, carved bed posts. That brown, allotment smell comes back to her now, though; the steamy whiff of the servant's kitchens.

"What was His Highness like as a child?" she asks, and hopes Alfdis will answer.

If someone were to ask Meren to tell them about Lorkan Aldrin, she's not sure that she'd say very much.

There's something about him that makes her not want to.

"A wonderful young lad," is Alfdis' answer, as if she's reading it off some parchment, and Meren shakes her head.

"No, I mean what was he like? Really?"

Slowly, she chews a round of rye bread, perhaps thoughtfully or perhaps it's just hard to chew.

"He was a little scrap of a thing. Especially next to his brother. Roughly the same age but half the size, The Young Prince was. In width, mind you—he's always been a bean pole." She smiles, almost. "I used to sneak him pies and cakes from the kitchens between meals, but it didn't help much."

"What was he like as a person?"

"I think you already know the answer to that question, don't you?" There's something in Alfdis' tone that makes Meren dip her head to a crack in the table.

She runs the pad of her thumb along the wood, feebly trying to pry some long-forgotten crumb from the centre of it. "No, not really. We haven't spoken much."

Alfdis' eyebrows are plucked so thin they're just a little transparent line.

Meren can't really see them, but she knows one has risen because the housekeeper's forehead suddenly becomes written with wrinkles.

"But you *have* spoken to him?"

Picking at the crumb with her nail:

"*He* spoke to *me*, really. About cleaning. And some things he wants me to pick up from the market for him."

She feels she has to add:

"Nothing like your relationship with him."

The glow has faded behind Alfdis' kind old eyes, that graveness creeping back into the creases of her face, making it look suddenly more ancient than ever, like a knot in a tree trunk.

"Good, because, Meren, The Prince and my paths should never have crossed. The only reason they did was because he was a child that didn't know any better, and I was too young and too sentimental to push him away."

WHAT LORKAN IS

Meren nudges her peas around her plate, their shells pruny like skin soaked in a bath.

"I didn't want to tell you about His Royal Highness because he is just *that*; part of our royal family, the son of our king. Telling you about him would have made him seem...well, like you or me. Common. Working-class. You need to remember that he's not that, Meren, he's second in line to the throne. Do you understand what I'm trying to say to you?"

"I understand."

She'd delivered her warning kindly enough, but Meren suddenly finds herself wanting to leave.

She stands and, for a second, thinks the head housekeeper is going to chastise her for not cleaning her plate. However, by the looks of it, she won't be clearing hers either. Turning to bust her tray, Meren remembers something.

"Alfdis?"

"Hm?"

"If you know Lorkan, why don't you correct people when they make up rumours about him? You could tell them he's actually—well, what he's really like."

"Have *you* told them what he's really like?"

Meren thinks about all the little secrets she keeps safe and warm under her bodice:

The way he keeps his books in colour order rather than alphabetical.

The coins in her pocket.

What he *really* keeps hidden in his study.

And, now, his tea times with the head housekeeper, his royal hands propping her up with cushions and serving her with the best china.

"Why not?" Alfdis asks, slicing a limp mushroom in half.

"It would feel...wrong."

She nods and Meren realises she's answered her own question.

Silently, she sits back down at the older woman's side. Together they struggle through their plates of grey and green.

✷ ☾ ✷

With pleasant sunlight falling in lumps through patches of white, furry clouds, Meren finds herself in much higher spirits as she sets off to run The Prince's errand the next morning. Blowing up from the south for once, the air is surprisingly balmy, the light breeze playing about her ankles and helpfully tugging away the cobwebs of the week.

Dodging between supply carriages, the rear gate finally spits her out into the streets of Tawny; cobbled, uneven, and gradually sloping into the sea.

A chaotic organ of noise, colour and thick, fragrant air, all sweet of The Royal Garden's alyssum and honeysuckle are overpowered by chimney smoke, horse fur, baker's yeast and tanning leather.

Tall, timber-framed terraced buildings create narrow, shaded roads, some so compact lovers can visit one another's bedrooms if they're brave enough to make the leap into each others windows. Gravity takes Meren's hand, tugging her down one and then the next like a raindrop down a gutter.

If she dips through enough alleyways, she will bump into one of the River Sygg's elegant curves. Its silted water slithers through the heart of the city, its fingers branching out across the whole kingdom and into the next; the water running clear and cold from Hylune, and a soupy brown by the time it dribbles into Calpurzia.

Meren had to cross it when travelling to the palace as a teenager, the bullrushes whispering secrets to each other as her cart heaved itself over Norfolk Bridge. Squashed arm to arm with other city-goers, she watched the houseboats chug through the waterlilies below, their engine smoke as foreign a smell to her as the idea of life on the water.

If she follows the squiggling streets even *further*, she'll reach the docks. Whilst working in the kitchens, Yllva would often send Meren to pick up the kippers and cod, prodding her out of bed before sunrise with a thick finger and orders hissed like a steam kettle. She'd stumble down these streets by lamp-light until the sea's salty breath whipped at her hair, the waves crashing into the boats with explosions of frigid spray.

Somewhere between the docks and the river, lies the market.

Meren's hand is still burrowed into the bottom of her pocket, and has been since The Prince placed the money in her care (part from when she had had to go to bed, when she clutched it below her pillow and awoke with red grooves pressed into her skin).

Every now and again, she holds her hand close to her face and unfurls it enough to peek within and count the metal shapes.

Some are familiar.

She's seen silvers before, their four distinct corners cropping up in her life on rare occasions—usually in the hands of more wealthy neighbours eager to show them off.

And, of course, Alfdis pays her in crescents.

Seven a week, one for each day of work, they're shaped like one of the slimmer phases of the moon and made mostly of nickel. To Meren, they're worth a decent amount—although probably not to The Prince, who seems to have dozens knocking about his pockets like lint. Each week, the majority of hers end up jingling in an envelope, posted by mail back to her parents in Holcombe to buy meat for their table and coal to stoke the squat little wood burner.

She has never seen gold coins, let alone *held* one, so she doesn't know what they might be called. Tiny, the size of a blackbird's egg, they're stamped with a miniature crown, the sun glinting off the chipped, pressed metal.

Meren's crescent seems to stick out from the neat little row, fitting jaggedly against the round crowns and square silvers.

For the majority of the night, and then over a shower and breakfast, she has been wondering what to do with it.

Her first choice would be to send it straight to her parents along with her other earnings, but then they'd want to know where she got it. They'd never believe it was a personal gift from the youngest son of Cade himself. They'd assume she's been fired and stooped to pickpocketing like cousin Remi, and Mrs Edmond's lad down the road.

She'd then wondered about writing to them—to tell them about her promotion—but every time Alfdis lends her some parchment and a quill, Meren finds her hand curiously dry of words. Several minutes later, the still-sealed ink pot and blank parchment are handed back to the head housekeeper, her coin still sitting heavily in her pocket.

She has to spend it, or it'll be robbed, she knows. She could buy a decent coat in her size, or some shoes with a nice thick sole; it would be harder for a thieving maid or a light-fingered hall boy to explain to Alfdis how *they'd* suddenly come to be about their person.

Sure enough, the terraced houses and narrow roads open up, spilling into an unpaved field stacked to the brim with brightly coloured stalls, carts, trailers, and wagons. The market must have been here long before the city, each generation of stall owners watching as more buildings crop up about them like weeds. Perhaps real estate owners had tried to get them to move along so a new butchers, or an inn, could be built upon the field, but they'd remained, stubborn, their trodden grass untouched, their stalls sinking resolutely into the mud. There's an old-fashioned, chaotic energy to the place, most merchants seeming to have adopted a bartering system, advertising their goods with snappy slogans thrown into the sea of passers-by.

As Meren passes clothes stalls and cobblers, she isn't sure she wants a new coat anymore, or even a new pair of shoes. The thick soles she'd once craved would echo most horribly on The Prince's marble floors, and the coat would be redundant now that she works inside rather than out.

She turns the extra coin over in one hand, its weight and shape somehow heavier than when it had been nestled amongst the funds for The Prince's pigments.

Perhaps she could purchase her own pigments? Although she wouldn't know what to do with them and, judging by the amount The Prince has given her for *his* colours, this coin alone isn't enough to fund a passion for painting.

WHAT LORKAN IS

Of course, there's always embroidery, and Meren stops at a stall selling colourful yarns and delicate little threads, all wrapped up on spools—but, after mending her uniform until it's bobbly with patches—darning has lost its charm.

Continuing, she passes through a quarter of the market before something makes her stop.

Surrounded by gems and rocks pressed into bracelets and hairpins, two earrings perch atop their own tiny pillow, winking like eyes.

The man behind the stall must catch Meren staring, because he gives a salesperson sort of smile, looking her up and down. "You can have a look at 'em if you promise not to run off with 'em."

Meren nods, and watches as his fingers pluck the little studs off their cushion.

They roll to the middle of her palm, the sun catching the tiny jewel at their centre and lighting them up from the inside.

It's green, just a minuscule dot of coloured glass embedded in simple nickel, but Meren's other hand holds passes her coin to the stall owner readily.

✶ ☾ ✶

Tightly knitted, densely packed, and stuffed with people—like a hole in the dirt filled with ants—finding the apothecary stall amongst the countless others takes a little longer than Meren had anticipated.

She's never visited one before, and doesn't really know what to expect once she does. She pictures a shaded stall with wheels—like those towed by travelling merchants—lined with bottles of dark pickled things, and pox-pocked people pale with fever jostling about, hoping to be cured.

Once Meren *does* locate the correct stall, she finds it to be much larger than the rest, and permanent, almost like a small shed. As she'd suspected, there is a queue, long and winding, squirming all the way down the side.

She joins the end, unable to help listening curiously to the ailments of the patrons served before her, and trying to guess what will be handed over to cure it.

Some people seem to know what they want already, and ask for funny-sounding things she can't even begin to pronounce. She pictures each thing, but most of the time she gets it wrong; assuming something is a herb when it's actually a small vial of liquid, or mistaking a flower for a type of root. So many words buzz about the little medicine stall like flies, each item appearing to come with instructions; '*Mix*', '*Apply*' and '*Rub*'. Meren understands those, but '*Reflux*' and '*Precipitate*' leave her head aching.

As the line of people dwindles and her view of the stall improves, Meren gains images to go with the things each customer is being handed, her understanding of an '*Apothecary*' solidifying into something more workable.

She'd never considered just how many things could be used as medicine. In Holcombe, whenever Meren fell sick, her mother would consult the other women in the village, and together they'd huddle around dried dandelion, madder, and mint leaves, dropping them into stews and teas like a gaggle of witches around a cauldron.

The apothecary stall, however, consists of nothing but shelves, each weighed down by a multitudinous array of glass jars.

Meren's eyes explore them, multicoloured fine powers, bead-like seeds, soil-freckled beans, knobbly, twisted roots, thick pastes. Her gaze reaches a row of fleshy things submerged in yellow liquid and she has to turn away and look at something else.

With the change from her crescent, she had treated herself to a tin of hazelnut biscuits and a dog-eared little novel from a book-merchant's wagon. Since the things in the apothecary's jars had rather turned her stomach, she elects to examine her new book while she waits.

WHAT LORKAN IS

The pages have already been rubbed soft by its previous owner's fingertips, and the font is simple and as easy to digest so, by the time someone nudges her to the front of the queue, she has already gobbled down the first two chapters.

Two men smile at her from behind the till, an older gentleman barely the same height as the worktop he serves people from, and a younger man with straw-blonde hair and a big, friendly face.

The older man's moustache wriggles as he gifts Meren a welcoming smile. He swats his floppy flour-coloured hair away from his thick glasses distractedly as if they're a slightly irritating swarm of bees.

Returning his good-natured demeanour, Meren steps forward shyly and places The Prince's list and coins on the counter.

"Ah, you must be His Highness' housemaid." The little old man's moustache wriggles again as if it's alive, the corners turning up like a caterpillar giving her a cheerful greeting. His voice is bouncy and rounded like a mushroom cap.

Meren can imagine the words jumping from his mouth and hopping around the shelves, knocking various jars and glasses to the floor in their excitement.

She furrows her brow. "Yes. How did you know?" For a second, she wonders whether apothecaries are still, somehow, using magic.

"Don't look so alarmed." The man takes the list in a hand barely larger than Meren's, his magnified eyes sliding over the curves of The Prince's swooping letters. "His Highness told me you'd be picking up his pigments from now on. Thank you for that, by the way; it saves me trudging up all those steps to the palace."

Meren's cheeks heat at her earlier assumption—that he knows who she is because he's some sort of mage—and moistens her lips.

List still in hand, the shop owner, who Meren guesses to be Frode, takes a small wooden box, much like the ones littering The Prince's studio, and begins hunting about under the counter. He reminds her of a mole, or perhaps a water vole, digging a hole underground.

When he surfaces, the box is full of blood-red, chalky lumps.

Meren almost reaches out to touch them.

Frode places a lid on top and fastens it with twine, then fetches another box. Before he can duck back down to retrieve the next pigment, Meren asks quickly:

"Do you pierce ears?" She doesn't know where people usually go to do such a thing, but she figures a medicine man would be as good a place as any.

She had wondered, whilst eyeing the slender needles at the darning stall, whether she could do it herself. She could take one from her own sewing kit, heat it over a wax stick and push it through the lobe; but the world had started to tilt slightly to the left, and she'd had to hold onto the table.

Frode gives Meren another sea lion-bristle-filled smile. "My apprentice can do that for you while I hunt around for the rest of His Highness' supplies." He gestures at the large lad organising a display on the other side of the stall. "Arne is very capable; you'll be in good hands."

At the mention of his name, Arne's straw-coloured head turns in her direction and he waves her over with one hand. It's open and friendly and stained with what appears to be blackberry juice. "You can come around the back, there's a stool to sit on," he says leaving the stall through a little hatch in the side.

Meren goes to him timidly, following his wide shoulders to a patch of trodden grass where a fat, three-legged stool stands waiting, the legs pushed a little into the mud. There's a table, too, dotted with the various equipment a medical man might need while treating or diagnosing a patient.

The apprentice motions to the stool, and Meren takes a seat, tucking her limbs in tight to her body protectively; she fears if she gives her legs too much reign they'll drag her back onto her feet and run for the hills—if they *can* run, that is. Her muscles seem to have turned to whatever that brown stuff was Yllva had served for breakfast.

Meren is contemplating trying to return the earrings and getting her money back when Arne's voice breaks her stupor:

"It doesn't hurt that much, I promise. I've pierced hundreds of ears and only one person has ever cried, but she was just a littl'un so I don't blame her." He'd been smiling as he spoke, the dash of freckles on his cheeks pushed higher up his face, making his eyes into waxing moons.

A little soothed by the surprising softness of his voice, Meren watches attentively as he starts fetching the things he'll need. As he rubs something harsh-smelling over both his hands—to clean them, Meren assumes—he asks:

"Do you have some earrings to fill the holes with?"

She nods, her chest admittedly feeling like it's stuffed with cheese cloth, and holds out her hand. The two green droplets of glass sit daintily in the safety of her palm.

Gently, Arne takes one between his rough forefinger and thumb.

"These are very pretty."

Meren can't tell if he means it, or if he can sense her frayed nerves and is trying to use kindness to matt them back together. "Thank you."

"You want them in the lobes, right?" he clarifies, and she nods, trying not to imagine how they're going to get there.

"I'm going to count to three, but I won't do it on three, it'll be a surprise." He's so close that she can see the little bursts of amber amongst the brown of his eyes. "It'll hurt less that way. Okay?"

"Okay," Meren forces the word from her chest, her tone as wobbly as her muscles.

7

THE COLOUR MAKER

Frode and Arne let Meren stay perched on the little stool for as long as she needs, which turns out to be seventeen queasy minutes.

Arne had been gentle and competent, piercing one ear and then the other, keeping to his word of making each thrust forward with the needle a surprise. It hadn't hurt a huge amount, he'd told the truth about that, it was the thought of what he was doing that made Meren feel as though her blood had been replaced with melted snow. He left her a spotted hand-held looking glass on the table amongst otoscopes, stethoscopes, and thermometers and, feeling strong enough to just about support her own weight, Meren totters over to it like a newborn foal.

The earrings look larger than they'd felt in her hands now that they're poked neatly through her lobes, twinkling like two tiny tea lights. With her somewhat shabby work clothes, she appears far from a *lady;* but not as far as she had been. The healing calluses and cracks in her hands, the stains in her uniform, the drab colours of its fabric, are less noticeable now that the earrings keep grasping her attention and dragging it up to her face.

WHAT LORKAN IS

Feeling solid enough to resume her day, she makes her way to the front of the stall. Frode has finished shuffling about his multitudinous stock for The Prince's pigments and moved on to serving the next person in line. The metaphorical caterpillar below his nose wiggles as he gives Meren a smile and gestures to a neat pile of packages waiting for her.

Most of the pigments seem to be contained within wooden boxes, but a few are encapsulated in glass vials. As slender as Meren's pinkie finger, they boast so much colour they appear to have no colour at all, just a thick, inky blackness.

She pulls a cotton bag from her pocket and Arne helps her transfer the boxes and vials carefully. His almond-shaped eyes sweep over Meren's face as he presents her with the handles of her now-full tote, although she's not sure what he could possibly be looking at.

"They look beautiful," he says and, for a confused moment, Meren wonders if he's talking about her muddy-coloured eyes.

As if sensing her confusion, he lifts a rough hand and points at her ears, and her cheeks heat almost as much as her throbbing lobes.

✳ ☾ ✳

Meren's ears are still smarting slightly as she turns the key in the thick door separating The Prince's chambers from the main part of the palace. The pain has dulled from a sharp twinge to a low, warm ache; much more manageable and, if anything, a little annoying rather than sore.

Before she begins working, Meren tentatively approaches the study, her bag of boxes and vials clutched in one hand. The Prince had given her specific instructions to leave them in this room, but many months of purposely avoiding it have collected into a firm instinct telling her to turn back around.

Wrestling with it, Meren knocks softly before pushing the door open.

The studio is exactly as it had been yesterday.

A curious blend of relief and disappointment confuses her chest. She had been willing it to be that way—

—yet she'd also half hoped to find The Prince inside, perhaps stooped over a new and breathtaking masterpiece.

Alfdis' warning—snoozing in a dusty corner of her mind—stirs. It has holed up and made camp there, an ever-present reminder.

She knows she shouldn't hope to bump into Lorkan.

She should leave him be, for the good of her own feelings; they will undoubtedly be shattered at one point or another, by The Prince himself pushing her curiosity away, disgusted, or by someone else dragging *her* away metaphorically or physically.

Suppose a guard (or, goodness gracious, *Alfdis)* had walked in yesterday, while she'd questioned him about lofty matters of art and paintings as if they were old friends. Meren knows she would have been grabbed roughly by the arm and dragged all the way down to the back door, her belongings and an appalling reference hurled at her feet.

Despite this, despite everything, Meren still hesitates before leaving the studio; her eyes hungry for the painting sat patiently atop the easel. She wants to trace the minuscule, well-practised brush strokes with her finger, feel the rise and fall of its texture, to drink the full, lavish colours in gulps.

The paint is almost dry now. Some parts are still oily and slick, but others have hardened, giving the picture a soft, mellow sort of feel.

She likes it better this way. The Prince must have known the changes each colour would go through and chose which ones to use accordingly.

The view from the windows is tempting too; the staggering height still so alien to Meren's eyes it sets them reeling in her skull. They're open slightly, the breeze rustling loose leaves of parchment, clean and crisp fingers of wind that play with her hair as soon as she pads close enough to let it.

She has to press against the cabinet below the sill to get nearer, her hands finding gaps among the chaos of brushes and paint-stained pots.

WHAT LORKAN IS

The cabinet's doors are closed but Meren can guess what is inside based on the curls of wood prickling the underside of her hands. The Prince must make his frames here, then stretch a reel of canvas over top to paint upon.

She can't imagine him hammering nails and sawing lines of wood —his slender, delicate hands as soft as swan's feathers.

Being the least stained part of the room, Meren sets her cotton bag down amongst the wood shavings and metal thumbtacks and begins unloading her haul. A few of the little boxes and thin vials have shifted during her walk from the market, and she chews her lip. Taking up a box at random, she eases the bow loose to assess the damage.

Tendrils of red air seep from the lid as she peeps inside, the crumbly rocks a little shaken by the multitudinous stairs.

Hoping that doesn't matter, Meren checks the others—although she's not sure why. Most prove to be identical to the chalky lump of red in the first box, just in different colours—mustard-seed-yellow, a crisp orange ochre, eggshell-blue—but a few of the boxes just hold little white rocks and another is just full of coal.

"Pretty, isn't it?" A voice from behind her sounds, and she nearly drops the box she's studying.

It's full of crumbly, cobalt-coloured nuggets, and Meren has to drag her eyes up and away from the addictive depth of its colour.

Somehow, she knows The Prince is referring to the blue lumps—that had very nearly ended up on his hardwood floorboards—rather than the view from the windows.

Her lip twitches; of *course* he'd appreciate the shade of a single colour much more than the obvious–and much more complicated—horizon.

Scrabbling for something to say, she nods her head quickly and moistens her lips.

"I'm sorry, I wasn't expecting you," she says, still clutching the box of blue to her chest, suddenly feeling reluctant to part with it. "I didn't know you needed the pigments so quickly. If I'd have known I wouldn't have—"

The words catch in her throat as The Prince steps closer, having crossed the room in a few lazy, meandering strides as if he—actually—has all the time in the world. He probably *does* have all the time in the world, now that Meren thinks about it. Rushing must be a foreign concept to him.

He's so close now that she can smell that scent he wears, its pine-sap tang sweetness down the back of her throat and prickling her tongue.

Silently, he reaches out and cups her left ear lobe with one large, milk-white hand. It's cool against her burning skin; soothing as ice wrapped in a towel.

Meren fights the urge to lean into it, and he regards her new earrings curiously, angling them gently with the pad of his thumb, watching the light grab and release them.

The colour of his eyes shifts from mossy green to jade as he tilts his head, just like the beads of glass.

"You got your ears pierced."

By this point, Meren isn't surprised that he'd noticed. The back of one of his fingers is against the side of her head as he examines her, and he's probably noticed her pulse flurrying against it as well.

It's beating quick as a bird's.

A lump like the screwed-up balls of parchment surrounding the waste bin forms in her throat and she nods, swallowing around it.

"Do they hurt?" The Prince's lips aren't as thin up close. His cheekbones aren't as sharp either, all his hard angles softening into long, drawn-out curves like the brush strokes in his paintings.

Meren wants to shake her head, but the thought of leaving his grip makes her remain still. Instead, her throat pushes out some words:

"Only a little."

"That's good." He releases her, oxygen flowing back into her lungs like a returning tide. A faint hint of a smile tugs the muscles around one side of his mouth.

She'd been staring at it because it's easier to look at his chin than his eyes.

"Green suits you."

"Thank you." Her voice is higher than she would have liked it to be. She looks down at her hands still grasping the box of blue. She's been gripping it so hard splinters are burrowing into her palms.

When she raises her head again, The Prince is collecting up the little containers and vials stacked on the countertop, spreading his fingers wide to hold them all at once. "I'd like you to help me with something," he says, managing just over half.

He crosses the room to a low, circular table, and Meren watches as, to her surprise, his long legs fold neatly to kneel on the floor. "Would you mind bringing the rest?

☾

The table The Prince sits at is tidier than the rest of the room, although maybe it's simply less crowded.

No, as Meren tentatively steps closer she notices more and more subtle signs of order; most of the bowls have been slotted into each other to create little stacks, the wooden boxes are lined up along one side like soldiers to attention, and the metal instruments are put away in pots rather than scattered like pine needles.

There are also very few paint splatters in this corner of the room. Instead, it resembles the spice stall at the market; fire-work-like eruptions of colourful powers blemish the table and surrounding floorboards, dry and dusty like chalk.

The Prince watches Meren expectantly as she gets closer, and tugs a plush velvet pillow out from below the table. The paleness of his skin contrasts with its colour-freckled material as he offers it to her, giving it a small pat.

He smiles encouragingly when, hesitantly, Meren lowers herself to crouch at his side.

The pillow softens the floor below her knees. Despite being at least a fifteenth of the size, it's more comfortable than her own bed.

Blushing, she opens her mouth to thank him, but The Prince has already taken something smooth and round from the middle of the table.

Meren recognises it as a pestle and mortar.

"Have you used one of these before?" He has set his share of the pigments along his side of the table in a sort of rainbow, leaving a small space in front of himself to work in.

Meren guesses that's what they'll be doing—some sort of work—and places her boxes and vials down one by one. Mimicking him, she connects her row to his, encapsulating them in a ring of colour.

"Yes," she says, liking how this makes his face light up with obvious approval. It encourages her to continue:

"I used to have to grind grain when I worked in the kitchens."

"Which kitchens were you stationed at?"

"Just the servant's quarters."

"Ah, under Yllva's tyrannical rule. You did well to make it out alive."

She stifles a giggle. "You know Yllva?"

"I've heard of her—from Alfdis but, unfortunately, I've never had the pleasure." Placing the pestle and mortar down between them, The Prince plucks up one of the wooden boxes and eases off the lid with his slender fingers.

Inside is the blue Meren had been admiring.

"This will be a little different to crushing grain," he explains, tipping one corner of the box gently until several lumps fall into the mortar. They leave cobalt scuffs on the sides of the box, and, when he taps the underside, the container coughs out a blue cloud.

Curiously, Meren shuffles closer to the table.

"You only have to press the pestle very gently, but for longer, until it's completely smooth. Understand?"

She knows he doesn't mean:

'Did you understand what you have to do?'

WHAT LORKAN IS

He means:

'Have you figured out that this is to be another task added to your list of responsibilities?'

"Okay," Meren says, finding her voice and trying to keep hold of it. Wanting to please him, and excited about playing a part in his craft, she accepts the mortar and pestle eagerly as he transfers it to her hands.

Sitting back a little, he watches as if to see what she'll do with them.

Overly aware of his pale eyes tracking her movements, she—somewhat clumsily—pushes the smooth edge of the pestle into the lumps of blue.

They're softer than she'd expected, the pestle sliding through their malleable shape with ease, and grating roughly against the mortar.

Wincing as if she'd accidentally stood on something dear to The Prince, Meren tries to recall the circular movement Yllva had taught her back in the kitchens. She pictures a hard nut caught below the rounded pestle—

But the blue just clumps up as she squashes it against the mortar, forming sticky wads like pollen.

She nearly throws the whole thing across the room as The Prince reaches across the table.

Gently, his palms slip over to cover the backs of her hands.

His touch is cool like a rockpool.

"Like this," he offers. There's a strength in his grip, a latent power behind the way he starts guiding her movements.

Silently, she lets him.

His way works much better, his hand over Meren's, hers curled around the pestle. He pushes it in wide circles, using the sides of the mortar to scrape the blue pigment continuously all the way around.

"It doesn't need to be crushed like nuts and seeds, it needs to be ground." His mouth is so close to her ear, his breath brushes it like a breeze from the window.

A shiver skitters its way along every disk in her spine.

"It's already a powder, it's just got bunched up into lumps. All we are doing is returning it back to powder again."

After a few more clockwise turns of the mortar, he relinquishes his grip on Meren's hands.

She can feel his eyes still resting on the side of her face as she continues to make those circular movements. It brings a strange sense of serenity, massaging the blue about the round, heavy pot. She supports it with her other hand, like the heavy head of a newborn babe.

She keeps doing this, pushing the crumbs about until they're reduced to half the size, then a quarter, then into nothing but minuscule grains free of clumps, smooth as dust in a desert.

Seemingly pleased with the results, The Prince takes the mortar back and pours the contents into a wooden bowl. Lots of them sit stacked and waiting at the far end of the table, their insides being the only thing in the whole room not stained with colour. There's a basket by his side, which he takes something from.

Meren hadn't paid it much mind, she'd been too distracted by other things —mainly the fact that today, The Prince is wearing a rather low V-neck that frames a hard dash of collarbone—but now that she can see the contents of the basket, she tilts her head in confusion.

It's full of speckled eggs.

"What are those for?" She asks, forgetting herself.

She watches The Prince as he cracks the egg expertly into a second bowl, leaving the sunshine-yellow orb of the yolk in one half of the shell.

He discards it, focusing on the ghostly pale white. As he drags the now-crushed blue pigment over to his workstation, the mortar scrapes on the table with the low growl of rock against wood.

He's smiling, and Meren has a feeling he's finding her ignorance amusing.

"They turn the pigment into paint."

She doesn't need to ask how.

He'd watched the question pop up behind her eyes.

"I mix the white with the pigment, water, and a few oils to create a paste. It dries when I paint it onto the canvas, but the protein and colour remain."

WHAT LORKAN IS

He hasn't asked her to leave yet, so Meren sits by his side as he does this, stirring the mixture until it resembles the stodgy, glistening, gooey substance an artist can use to make art. It's a simple, methodological process, and she can't help an elated light come to her eyes when The Prince says:

"Shall we make another?"

☽

Meren is crushing lumps of a sunbeam-coloured yellow when Lorkan says quietly:

"Your hands are softer now."

For once, he's not looking at her. His focus is lowered to the cobalt blue paint he's still mixing. Now and again, he adds water to it from a glass jar, letting the drops fall like a beetle walking over his fingers. He raises his head to watch her inquisitively, though, when he asks:

"Is working inside suiting you?"

His eye contact makes Meren's heart do a sort of fluttery thing—as though it has suddenly sprouted wings, the tips tickling the insides of her ribs.

"Yes, very much. Thank you...Sir," she adds that last little word, but finds it oddly clunky, its shape foreign in her mouth.

With surprise, she realises she's never used it in these rooms before.

It makes The Prince laugh, the sound rumbling up from his torso.

"'*Lorkan*' is fine. You've seen where I sleep, where I paint, and where I dress each morning; we might as well be on a first-name basis." His cheeks turn a pastel pink, but it might just be a scuff of red pigment. "Unless you'd rather I call you Miss Hansen?"

'*You're a prince, you can call me whatever you like,*' she thinks as she grinds down a particularly stubborn clump of yellow.

"It's okay. I like Meren."

She does like it—when he says it.

The syllables roll nicely off the point of his pink tongue.

8

THE BOOK BORROWER

They sit side by side, Meren crushing up colourful little rocks, and The Prince mixing egg white into the resulting powder. Few words pass across the small space between them. The Prince doesn't say much to Meren, and Meren is too *afraid* to say anything to him—

But the silence lays thick and comfortable like a wool blanket draped over their shoulders, and they wear it happily for several hours.

The Prince points out which colours he would like Meren to prepare, explaining that they'll only make enough for the next few days as the paint will quickly dry and become unworkable. The colours he'll use later remain in their little wooden boxes stacked neatly along the other side of the table.

Back when Meren had been a kitchen maid, she'd internally grumbled to herself whenever Yllva couldn't think of anything better for her to do than slide a knife around hundreds of potatoes, or scrape the grime from every single skillet.

However, kneeling next to The Prince in silence, pushing crumbs of colour against the curved edge of a mortar again and again, Meren can think of few complaints. There's something therapeutic about it; soporific, almost, and she finds drowsiness gripping her several times, especially when the sun begins to set.

It douses the quiet little studio in a soft hue somewhere between yellow and orange, long shadows stretching like sleepy dogs across the floorboards.

Luckily, small things keep nudging her awake; like metaphorical blades, they sharpen Meren's senses:

The rocky, grating grind of the pestle against the mortar.

The cool brush of The Prince's fingers as she transfers it to his hands, like dipping her fingers into a night-chilled lake.

Every time he speaks, she eats up each word he gives her.

He doesn't seem to need to breathe in to push words from his lungs, she realises curiously. They just slip out effortlessly, his tone low and idle as if he's filled with coiled sentences, unravelling each time he opens his mouth. They fill her ears easily, where others would have to pile hundreds of syllables, The Prince needs but a few, and she's happy to sit, digesting them between their short conversations.

Every now and again, he hands her a few facts or instructions about painting, to which she listens attentively.

He inquires about her trip to the market, and whether he had given her enough money for the pigments he needed.

She says she enjoyed it, and yes, he had given her more than enough.

He asks about the health of Frode, to which she replies that he seemed chipper and that she liked his kind eyes.

"Have you ever painted?" he asks after some time.

Meren takes a moment to wonder if drawing shapes in the suds with her mop counts as painting.

She decides that it doesn't.

"No, I don't think I have. Especially not with colours like these." Turning the mortar side to side, she watches the little crumbs of colour tumble about, softer than flour.

WHAT LORKAN IS

"So what do you do for pleasure?" The Prince uncaps a slender glass vial and lets a little of the contents drip into the bowl he's mixing. As lush and green as summer grass, its scent is nutty and sweet like almonds.

Meren thinks about it.

She hasn't had much time for pleasure until recently. Her childhood passion for books seems to have rekindled itself, sparking back to life like a phoenix after years smothered by late nights, early mornings and fatigue.

"I like to read," she offers meekly, and The Prince's face lights up.

"What do you like to read?"

"Oh, anything."

Realising he's waiting for her to go on, she continues tentatively:

"Adventure stories are my favourite. I like reading about places I haven't been, and things I haven't done." She hesitates. "And a little romance isn't unwelcome."

The Prince smiles, watching the thick green oil combine slowly with his pigment; what Meren has silently started calling The Moment Of Truth.

If she has done her job correctly the two ingredients will mix smoothly to form a slick, honey-like paste.

If she has done badly it will mash together in clumps; lumpy like porridge.

"I have lots of books like that. Feel free to borrow some from my collection whenever you like."

Her mouth falls open, a surprised little breath sending a few crumbs of purple periwinkle dashing across the table.

Lorkan's library is perhaps the cleanest of all his rooms, simply because Meren is in love with it. She's drawn her rag over the shelves until they're waxed enough to reflect her wide eyes, pale, little raised eyebrows. She's waxed the floor so often her slippers skid like skates on a frozen pond.

She'd dared to run a finger over a spine, once, the leather soft, each gold-leaf letter bumpy like dragon scales.

"I couldn't."

"You can. Stories are meant to be read, not forgotten. Return them whenever you want."

Beside herself, Meren stammers out a thank you.

In The Prince's bowl, the pigment has accepted the oil, perfect, glossy paint forming like magic.

☀ ☾ ☀

Unnoticed, the sun has dribbled down the sky like a splash of orange juice. Pencilled across the horizon, the ocean turns from a strip of blue to black, the last watery dregs of daylight beading on its surface like oil.

Meren hasn't noticed the view from the window has slowly darkened. Eventually, she squints at the colour she is palpitating, holding it up to her face.

"Is this blue or purple?" she asks vacantly.

The Prince's eyes widen and, suddenly, he snatches the pestle and mortar from her as if they were dangerous.

Her heart leaping into her mouth, colliding with the backs of her teeth, Meren glances at the pigment, half expecting the innocent flecks of dust to burn through it like acid. There's a messy rag on the table for mopping up spills and she grabs it, wiping its stained cotton fervently over her hands.

"I'm so sorry," The Prince stammers just as Meren opens her mouth to ask if she's going to die. His hands are darting about the table, putting lids on things that could dry or spill, stacking empty boxes, collecting up eggshells.

He's not being careful with the box of blue or maybe purple either. Its blemished lid leaves a dark scuff on his fingertips like a bruise, but it disappears amongst the rainbow of countless others.

It finally registers in Meren's mind that he's in the middle of a rather hurried effort to clean up.

"Why?" She asks, finding herself clutching onto the rainbow-coloured rag as he takes it from her.

WHAT LORKAN IS

Disappointedly, she watches as it gets placed with everything else on the far end of the table, out of reach, her eyes already craving the aquamarines, fuchsias and violets.

"I shouldn't have kept you," he mutters, rising to his full height with a graceful, tidy unfurling of limbs; like a dragon arranging its wings before flight.

"Kept me?" Meren repeats dumbly, staring up at him with bemusement from her place on the floor.

Hastily, The Prince extends a slender hand for her to take and, without thinking, Meren accepts it. Effortlessly, he lifts her up, his grip dwarfing her fingers, her legs flooding with pins and needles.

When the flurry of black spots has dispersed from her vision, The Prince is still there, his pale hand clutched in hers like the head of a carved, ivory walking stick.

Colouring, Meren releases him and stutters out a wobbly thank you.

Waving it away:

"It's almost nightfall," his voice is tinted with an edge of surprise as he gestures at the sky.

It closely resembles the blueish purple Meren had been halfway through crushing.

She can just about make it out on the table, forgotten, still all lumpy and grainy and nestled neatly in the curved mortar. Her palm still tingles with the chill of the stone. Or perhaps from The Prince's hand. His skin was as cool as the air dancing through the open window.

"Is it?"

"You didn't notice? It's dark!" The Prince hovers a hand over the small of her back, guiding her from the studio. His strides are brisk and urgent, Meren's legs working hard to keep up. "I'm so sorry, why didn't you say anything?"

Still slightly baffled:

"What should I have said?"

"That your shift ended an hour ago? Or at least asked me how much longer I planned to keep you here. Weren't you ever going to say anything?"

They reach the door and Meren turns back to face him, and shrugs. "It's not my place to say anything."

He winces as if she'd firmly stamped on his toe. "Meren, you *can* say something, I *want* you to say something. I made you sit on the *floor* for—" He struggles through some mental maths before simply deciding:

"—for *too long*. You *could* have *said* something." His usually straight spine is bent at the top like a leaf weighed down by heavy droplets of rain.

"I wasn't on the floor," Meren corrects, trying to flick some of those droplets of guilt away with her words. She wishes the moon would hurry up and lighten the room so The Prince can see the easy happiness this afternoon has scribbled all over her face. "You gave me a pillow."

A tentative smile twitches one corner of his lips, the hard set of his shoulders softening slightly. "That's beside the point. I'll compensate you for your time, of course—" he says, dipping one hand in the pocket of his trousers. He fudges about, bringing out several small coins, then rejecting them, going back into his pocket again.

Meren likes The Prince's trousers. She'd been admiring them earlier; they match his shirt, a breezy, thin material so fine that his skin shows through the fabric at his knees if he kneels, and his spine when he bends over. It turns the fabric from a deep clover shade to a lighter, subtle green like the flesh of a grape. They flare wider around his ankles, draping low over his bare toes, and make a rustling sound as he walks like he's dragging his feet through a pile of leaves.

He finally finds something he deems worthy to present to her for her troubles—a mammoth of a coin, the numbers indicating its value as large as the nail on her pinky finger. He holds it out as if he doesn't think it's nearly enough, but she just pushes it away.

"Assisting you is my *job*. You don't need to pay me extra for doing what I'm employed to do."

WHAT LORKAN IS

He runs his fingers through his hair from his widow's peak to where his crown would sit if he ever wore one—which Meren has yet to see him do. The strands are so dark his face seems to be framed by a hole in the universe; as if someone had cut away at reality leaving nothing but a black void.

What do voids feel like to touch, Meren wonders?

His act of anxiety leaves the void tousled like bird feathers ruffled by a storm.

※ ☾ ※

The Prince pours more apologies over Meren's head as she stands by the door.

Patiently, she waits for a break in his flow to insert a reminder that she'd come with cleaning supplies, and could she please have them back?

Eventually, he figures this out himself because he dashes back inside to fetch them—uttering yet more variations of the word *'Sorry'* that Meren didn't know existed.

As he transfers her mop to her hands, she notices the smooth wedge of his front teeth nibbling at his lower lip.

She clutches her cleaning equipment hard to stop herself from reaching out and freeing it.

"Really, I didn't mind staying late," she repeats. "It's my job, and I don't begin work until late morning anyway."

His features don't truly soften, though, until she shyly soothes:

"It was really no trouble, I enjoyed it."

※ ☾ ※

By the time Meren dumps her cleaning supplies in their cupboard, someone has been around to light the rows of wax sticks lining the otherwise bare walls of the servant's quarters. Their feeble glow lights up Meren's hands, illuminating a plethora of dusty colours staining her skin right up to her elbows.

She pops into the servant's washroom before heading to the mess hall for dinner, and fills a sink. The pigment stains fall away easily, pooling—gritty and brown—to the bottom of the basin. She almost winces as she sponges at them, reluctantly peeling each colour from her skin until she is, once again, plain as parchment.

Hearing footsteps approaching, she pulls the plug and darts into a stall.

As someone next door hunts through her bag for a monthly cloth, Meren holds her forearms protectively to her chest.

Silently, she hopes her slippers aren't visible below the dividers.

If they are, she'll have to explain why she looks like she's been wrestling a rainbow.

* ☾ *

It is raining the next day, although Meren doesn't know what kind until she has climbed the stairs to the servant's courtyard and poked her nose out of the ground like a vole from its hole. The air is sweet with it; a light, humid drizzle falling through bouts of watery autumn sunlight.

Another envelope had been delivered to her over a breakfast of fried egg and mushrooms, written in The Prince's familiar hand:

'Don't bother with my pigments today, the weather is atrocious.'

But Meren had shrugged on an oilskin and headed to the market all the same, fat droplets beading on the wax coating and rolling harmlessly onto the waterlogged cobbles.

WHAT LORKAN IS

On her way to the sixteenth floor, she's so distracted peeking into the mysterious little boxes that she forgets her cleaning supplies, and has to trudge back down three flights of stairs.

She decides to deliver The Prince's pigments to his studio before anything else, the rest of his chambers passing by in a gold and green haze.

Her feet come to a halt as she pushes the door open.

A new canvas is resting on the easel. It's blank beside a few amorphous blobs or colour, bare and blocky like concrete foundation set down before a house is to be built.

Meren stares at it as if she hadn't expected it to be there—then feels silly as she notes the brushes, smears of paint, and messy pallets littering every surface of the room. She's never seen a room better suited for it, yet she averts her eyes as though having accidentally made eye contact with a stranger.

It's not a stranger. Those are *her* colours; paint she and The Prince had mixed only the day before, drying on the flag-like stretch of cotton.

But there are so many doors between it and the rest of the world that she feels as though she's walked in on The Prince whilst changing, or accidentally opened the drawer where he keeps his undergarments.

Turning away respectfully, she begins unloading the boxes of fresh pigments from her tote, trying to picture the colours within.

She likes to turn the boxes in her hands, examining scuffs around the lid, hoping a wisp of colour might escape.

She's doing this when, to her left, something catches her eye.

A brown, leather-bound book.

It's not just brown, there's gold too, thin foil sheets of it forming twisting patterns around the edges like a picture frame.

It's pinning a note to the wood, the white parchment fluttering in the wind from the window. A few droplets of rain have made it through the gap, quivering on the cover like melted glass, and Meren gives the book a wipe with her apron.

Her name is written on the note in ink black as night, then the words:

I thought you'd like this one.

Tentatively, she picks it up.

It's a brick of a thing, well-bound and hefty in her hands. She eases the cover open and finds a hand-drawn illustration of woman astride a horse, and two magical words in bold, strong font. She mutters them under her breath like a spell:

'*Chapter One*'.

※ ☾ ※

Eventually remembering that she has a job to do, Meren drags herself away from the studio and back to her cleaning supplies, leaving The Prince's book on the dresser by the door so she remembers to take it with her.

Not that she will forget.

She wonders if The Prince will ask her to help him make his paints today. He clearly needs them, with a new picture in progress—

But he'd managed without help before, Meren remembers with a sinking feeling. And, yesterday, he'd introduced her to his world—given her a trial run—and it had ended in him frazzled with guilt.

She hadn't accepted his coin either, she remembers, regret flaring in her chest. Perhaps she should have taken it so he felt his debt had been repaid; she could easily have snuck it back and hidden it somewhere in his chambers the next day.

As the hours drip by like the raindrops down the window panes, Meren's worries set hard like concrete.

By three, she is fairly convinced whatever magical thing had happened yesterday will not be happening again.

※ ☾ ※

WHAT LORKAN IS

Meren is stooped over a dressing table in The Prince's bed chamber when he steps up beside her.

She's measuring the space between a bottle of scent and the base of the mirror, using the lines on her fingers to make sure she places a decanter back exactly as it had been before she'd wiped below it.

She knows The Prince is behind her because, suddenly, the musky smell of his cologne isn't just drifting lazily from the stoppered bottle.

A smile graces her lips as she turns to him, finding his pale eyes still on her hands. He must have been watching her because he says, the corner of his lip twitching:

"You *really* don't need to do that, you know."

He never says hello, Meren realises. He just continues where their last conversation had left off, as if they've never been apart.

Meren feels the back of her neck heat below her uniform. "I know."

She remembers him plucking up the sketchbook and tossing it back down, seemingly indifferent to the scuff of charcoal now gracing its rear cover.

She'd found it on his bedside table earlier and tried to remove the mark, to no avail.

He's still staring at her, and feels herself continue, just to fill the silence:

"I just like to try my best. To say thank you. For...everything."

This makes him smile. "Also unnecessary. But thank you. Your efforts have not gone unnoticed. Let it be known I have *tried* to compensate you for the extra work you're putting yourself through." His smile curls into an amused hint of a smirk. "But you seem to be allergic to wages."

The Prince *has* left her extra money, sometimes.

More than sometimes, almost *every* time.

He bundles them in with the money she's to use for his pigments; a little stack of halvings and crescents and, every time, Meren leaves them on the dresser.

"They're not wages," she points out. "They're *bonuses*. Alfdis already pays me, the amount you keep attempting to give me is frankly absurd."

The Prince folds his arms across his chest, arching one dark eyebrow. If he'd done that during their first meeting, Meren would have been certain the gallows waited for her for sure—but now she knows what it means.

It's a challenge.

"You know, most people would have *stolen* something from these rooms by now."

He gestures at the space around them littered with clocks and metal-tipped quills and rings that could so easily be plucked from their shelves and slipped into a pocket.

"Not you, though." His eyes have narrowed to scrutinize Meren's face as if she's a picture that doesn't quite make sense to him. "I leave you coins with the specific intent of *giving* them to you, and you don't so much as look at them."

She turns her attention back to wiping the flecks of dust from between the little trinkets scattered over the desk—

—because she *had,* in fact, looked at them. She'd looked at them and pictured what they could be traded for; a meal of succulent meats, a goose down bed pillow, soft undergarments—all laid out atop the dresser like pieces in a doll's house.

She continues her dutiful cleaning of the desktop, even though doing so means turning her back to The Prince. She almost expects her mother to burst through the door and give her a paddling with some kind of utensil.

The Prince simply sidesteps several paces to the left, angling himself back into her view.

"Why don't you let me give you anything?" He asks. His voice is light, but has a soft edge of rejection; as if he's discussing a bruise he doesn't know the origin of.

"I don't deserve it," Meren replies simply, shrugging her shoulders.

Puzzlingly slowly, her brow furrows at her own nerves.

How quickly one settles into carelessness when given the chance, she muses.

WHAT LORKAN IS

Or, alternatively, how quickly one learns the rhythms and nature of another person.

That is all she's doing, after all. The Prince doesn't act like a prince around her so, she's—for some stupid reason—not treating him like one.

She wishes she would.

She wishes her mouth would remember to tie a 'Sir' onto the ends of her sentence, and her spine would remember to curve itself into a curtsy.

Bemused: *"'Don't deserve it'?* You've been making sure *all* my charcoal sticks point in the same direction. I have a *lot* of charcoal sticks. Even my father's maids don't bother to do likewise."

He likes to use his hands when he talks, Meren has noticed. They'd been folded politely behind his back when they'd first met, but they're not anymore.

She says nothing, and The Prince sighs as though defeated. He can not make Meren take his money, but...

"I would like to repay you for your troubles. What do you want?"

This has the effect he must have been after; Meren's hand pauses halfway through angling a vase so that the little picture of a moon on one side is parallel to the jewellery box to its right.

She has often stared at that box and wondered what's inside. Does The Prince wear jewellery? She's never seen a necklace suspended between his collarbones, or a bracelet adorning his wrists. Meren can't see any holes in his ears—

"I don't want anything."

He doesn't look convinced. "There must be something you want. Please. You think you don't deserve a small bonus for working hard, but look around you. Do you think *I* deserve this for being born into a wealthy family?"

She feels her lips knit together as her eyes can't help gracing the paintings by famous artists, their solid gold frames, the bed linen made of the finest cotton, the chairs carved with such impossible finesse they'd probably constituted one carpenter's entire career...

When Meren doesn't reply—because what is she supposed to say? The Prince repeats:

"Please. I feel guilty. You'll actually be doing me a favour."

Meren hesitates, then turns to him, her fingers tugging at the rag clutched in her right hand. "I'd like—"

He looks at her like he's won something, waving her on encouragingly.

"...I'd like to keep helping you make the paints you need. I enjoyed doing it. I actually bought the next set today, even though you said not to." She flushes, suddenly realising that earlier she'd technically disobeyed an order. "Rain doesn't bother me."

Both of The Prince's eyebrows rise and come together. He looks down at his housekeeper with what can only be described as bafflement. "You want me to thank you for your work..." he spells it out, testing the words on his tongue, "by giving you *more* work?"

Flushing, Meren nods, having to break contact with his piercing eyes because they seem to be able to worm their way right into her head.

She's scared they'll poke about in there and discover that she'd not only enjoyed, but *treasured* those hours spent kneeling next to him, both of them quietly working together to create a little patch of beauty.

She's addicted to them like a drunk to mead.

"Yes. Whenever you need paint I'd be happy to help you make it. It's pretty."

There's a pause, The Prince apparently turning Meren's sentences over in his head, his gaze still roving over her face. He's probably trying to tell whether she's being sincere—if she *had* in fact enjoyed it or if she's just saying what she thinks he'll want to hear.

People probably do that to him a lot, she's realising.

Eventually, he nods like someone agreeing to a business deal. "Okay. But always tell me if you've had enough."

Meren doesn't know how she could ever have enough.

9

JAM

The Prince holds the studio door open, guiding Meren into the cosy little space with a sweeping arm as if combing the entrance for cobwebs he doesn't want getting stuck in her hair.

Eagerly, she helps collect up the new pigments without having to be asked, the colour-tainted boxes staining her apron.

He smiles as he approaches the low round table. "You've taken the book I wanted to lend you."

"Yes, thank you." Her cheeks colour.

Once again he's offering her the plump velvet cushion, the goose down absorbing her knees as she hesitantly lets herself sink into it.

"It's very kind of you to let me borrow it."

"I thought of it just after you left yesterday. I think you're really going to like it. You can take your time with that one, it's best sipped like fine wine."

Meren doesn't point out that she's never tasted wine before.

Settling onto his own cushion, his eyes slide to the window, and she gets the feeling he's marking a dash between the sinking sun and the hard line of the horizon.

Meren *had* been late to dinner yesterday, but there was still plenty of Yllva's stew slowly bubbling away on the stove. According to Alfdis, most of the staff had muttered a meek '*That's enough, thank you*' before she could ladle a second scoop of brown gloop into their bowls.

"I'm happy to help you make all the paint you need," she assures lightly. "I'd prefer to stay here. I don't even mind missing dinner."

She's working a stubborn lump from a powder she thinks might just be finely ground chalk. "Yllva is making—what she calls—offal pottage tonight. Last time she did that, half the servants got sick."

She'd said it to make The Prince laugh—she wanted the corners of his eyes to do that crinkly thing—but it has the opposite effect.

He pauses mid-way through cracking an egg into a bowl, the white tumbling out with the yolk in a gooey, unsupervised globule. "Really?"

"Yes. We think she didn't cook the meat for long enough—or maybe it was just a bad cut."

A claw of remorse drags its way down her spine at The Prince's horrified expression.

"It might not have been her fault," she adds, guiltily. "She does have to feed *all* of us, after all."

"Do you not eat well in the servant's quarters?"

Meren blinks.

On the one hand, The Prince's family funds the culinary services she will be describing.

However, on the other, every lie she tries to summon about Yllva's cooking falls apart before it even reaches her lips.

Just like her pie crust.

"We get what we need. It's different down there to up here; more practical. We get *enough* food, it's just..." Salty memories prickle the back of Meren's tongue, and her taste buds retreat, pulling her expression into a tight grimace.

"Disgusting?" he offers, and she colours.

"Not *disgusting*. Just..."

After some contemplation and various shuffling and re-shuffling of words:

"—not usually very nice."

"And sometimes makes everyone ill," The Prince adds, trying to scoop the yellow orb of egg yolk from the white with a silver spoon.

His brows are still tightly knitted over the ridge of his nose, and Meren wonders if it's in concentration, or the concept of having to live off something other than decadent feasts.

"Can't a better chef be hired?"

Meren doesn't want to say the word 'afford' again—not twice in the same conversation—so she stays quiet.

The Prince seems to know what this means because he drops the subject, and the matter is not picked up again.

Well, not until the next day.

※ ☾ ※

"I brought these."

The Prince joined Meren earlier than usual, catching her just as she was beginning her chores.

Already heading to the studio, he motions for her to follow and, guiltily propping her unused mop up against the wall, she hastily scuttles after him.

She catches up to his side as reaches the study door, and peers at the paper mache box held in one of his moon-coloured hands. Something in her stomach twists. "Did I forget a pigment?"

However, The Prince shakes his head. "These have nothing to do with painting."

Taking a wide china plate from a cupboard, he kneels, placing it on the table. His green eyes turn to Meren expectantly, as if waiting for her to join him.

She does, trying hard to block out the calls from her abandoned mop in the other room.

Since The Prince had started inviting her to his studio, she's noticed several of her tasks are going untended.

It's not a problem, as such; only Meren and The Prince himself ever spend any time in his chambers, so they remain remarkably tidy. Lorkan changes his own bed sheets every Friday, and Meren has a sneaking suspicion he's still wiping down the shower after he uses it—out of habit. However, she can't help feeling the 'house' part of her job title is being neglected, and guilt has started to prod her every time Alfdis hands over her wages.

Silently, The Prince slides the plate in front of her nose.

She's not sure how, but the box atop it smells like the colour pink.

"What is it?"

She'd stacked his new pigments in a neat pile—like a tower of children's building blocks—and he's already easing open lids, exploring.

The one he picks first is a wad of soft, muted grey clay, streaks of rusted iron wriggling through it like veins.

It must have been dug from the malleable soil of Western Velôr, Meren realises. The limestone cliffs protruding from the Eastern coast are pale and hard—jagged, serrated teeth—but the stone in the west is crumbly and creamy with chalk. She imagines it being parcelled up and shipped across the kingdom by river, horse, and foot—just to end up in the little box on The Prince's table.

Meren watches him tip it into the mortar.

It slumps lazily against the porcelain just as the cliffs it came from are slowly breaking away into the sea.

"They're to share."

When she still doesn't move, he dusts off his hands on a rag and—one by one—places the contents onto the plate.

WHAT LORKAN IS

She eyes them sceptically.

"What is it, Sir?"

"Please, call me Lorkan."

"...I shouldn't."

"I'm ordering you to." He's never ordered her to do anything before, and Meren blinks.

"Okay."

He's still looking at her, his eyes ten different dancing, playful shades of green. "Okay...?"

"Okay, Lorkan."

"Thank you. And this is Gateau." He gestures at the plate, now holding ten white little mounds.

Their surface is smooth and solid, like perfect rectangular pebbles.

He looks at her expression and, realising she's still genuinely baffled, he clarifies:

"Cake."

"That's not cake," she points out indignantly. "Cake is yellow and crumbly. Like a sponge."

His mouth twitches as if he doesn't know whether to take pity on her or laugh. "The sponge is inside. Haven't you seen icing before?"

She shakes her head as he takes one of the cakes and places it in her hand. He has to unfurl her fingers first, her palm not accustomed to accepting gifts.

"Try it," he instructs, and her eyes widen. "I *did* say it was to share."

"It shouldn't be," she says, cautiously examining the lump atop her palm, turning it over and inspecting its silky, blemish-less surface. It looks too perfect against the rugged lines of her nails.

"Have it," Lorkan insists. "I don't want all of it." His mouth opens, and Meren gets the sense he's about to say '*There's loads more in the kitchen anyway*' but stops himself.

She imagines them—the royal kitchens—chefs anxiously whipping up steaming pots and sizzling pans, just in case someone gets peckish—or even just bored. In the corner, a heap of unwanted meals grows steadily, the odd scone or apple pie tumbling from the over-stuffed waste bin.

Tentatively, Meren gives the cake an experimental little squeeze.

Its shell-like coating cracks beneath her fingers. Maybe there *is* cake inside. If there isn't, this is like a strange and unusual prank to play on a person, she thinks.

Lorkan must sense her hesitation because he takes one himself, bringing it to his mouth as if to prove it is, indeed, edible. He bites into it, the narrow pink dash of his lips contrasting with the pure white of the so-called icing.

Probably raised to never talk with his mouth full, he swallows before he says, holding out the remaining half of the treat:

"See. Cake."

Meren regards its exposed innards.

Sure enough, there is the promised sponge, yellow and crumbly and all, along with something else, something red and gooey, currently dripping down the side of his thumb.

Her eyes widen, slightly startled, and it makes him laugh; chuckles curling and peeling off his tongue, fluttering about the air like streamers.

Meren is too distracted to notice.

"What's the red stuff?" She figures it's either blood or uncooked, liquidised meat. Her expression must betray her abhorrence, because Lorkan is still trying to bite back his chuckles.

She almost gives his side a playful little shove for finding her horror so amusing.

"It's jam. You must have heard of jam."

"I've *heard* of it, but—" that sentence has five more words on the end of it: *'I've never actually tried it'*

But she snips them off.

"Never mind. Are you sure I can eat this?"

"Of course you can," he assures, sounding puzzled as to why she would possibly think she can't.

WHAT LORKAN IS

His cake gone, he begins lapping up the rouge stream of dribbling, sugary jam. It turns his tongue red, the point of it sliding up his long thumb. His eyes close as he gives a happy little hum.

The room suddenly feels like it's on fire.

Feeling Meren's stare, he turns to her, his brows knitting together. "What? You really can eat it, you know, I'm not going to charge you for it."

Moistening her lips, she dips her warm cheeks down to her cake. She hasn't touched it, yet she already feels as though it's stuck somewhere in her throat. "Thank you. Really. Thank you."

"If you say that one more time, you won't get another piece," Lorkan chides, and she feels the corner of her lip twitch into a smile.

Sheepishly, she brings the cake—warm, from her fingertips—to her lips.

It smells sweet and buttery—that slight tang of jam hidden deep in the porous centre making her mouth suddenly quite moist. Despite her piqued appetite, she only lets her teeth close around its rounded end, slicing off a narrow centimetre. It falls onto her tongue, a fluffy wedge, and she chews it.

A little moaning sound pushes its way up from her ribcage.

If this is cake, what was that brown, spongy brick she'd helped her mother drag from the stove every Winter Festival? That hadn't tasted like this. That had been plain and scratchy, her jaw struggling with the weight of it.

But *this* cake—

She doesn't want to swallow it, her teeth gummed up with syrupy batter. "This is amazing," she exhales through a mouthful.

Lorkan's cheeks have gone pink.

Had Meren not been distractedly taking another bite, she might have noticed. She might also have noticed his gaze has fallen from her eyes to her mouth, and stayed there.

He hasn't reached for another piece—he hasn't actually moved in some time—yet he swallows, watching Meren take another bite, then another.

Humming, she sucks the swirls of jam from her fingers and mutters again, forgetting his earlier threat:

"Thank you."

Lorkan doesn't seem to remember it either because—just as she disappointedly notices her hand is empty—he nudges the plate over to her side of the table.

She looks at it, then back to him, bashfully.

He's still staring at her and, self-consciously, she licks her lips, catching the crumbs dotting her chin like stubble.

"Sorry, it's just...this is the most delicious thing I've ever tasted."

A twinge of guilt nips her side like a stitch as she remembers her mother's baking, her grandma's lovingly nurtured plum tree, and the bag of hard candies her father had hidden in her suitcase.

Their memories feel bland and tart against her spoilt taste buds.

"Don't be sorry. I'm glad you like it." Lorkan clears his throat. His cheekbones are still almost as pink as the jam. "Have as many as you like."

Meren tries not to appear utterly starved as she plucks up another.

∗ ☾ ∗

"If I teach you, would you mind preparing the paste while I paint?" Lorkan asks after a little while of crushing, mixing, and stirring (and occasionally nibbling at the remaining cakes).

He never orders, he asks, he offers, he *invites,* and Meren turns to him, unable to hide her interest.

"It's much easier during the day than by the light of wax sticks."

"You don't mind painting while I'm in the room?"

"No." He pulls the egg carton over to her side of the table. "It'll actually be nice to have some company."

Patiently, he shows her how to turn the powdery pigments into a thick, smooth paste, then how to mix it without catching gritty bubbles of air.

This process repeats itself (much to Meren's silent delight) over the next week, cementing itself into a pleasant routine. Lorkan joins her at the table while they prepare the first few colours then, when he has enough to get started, he stands, stretching the pins and needles from his legs.

She misses his solid, comforting presence beside her, but it's a worthy trade. Intrigued, she watches as he crosses to the easel, palette in hand.

Occasionally, he strays back to the little table to retrieve another colour. He'd spent several days just laying down the foundations of the painting; blocky, amorphous shadows spread out over the canvas. He's stacking them up, and Meren waits patiently for shapes to emerge; for it all to suddenly shift into perspective.

Sometimes—during the hours they spent creating the pigment that goes into them—Meren's lips part to ask Lorkan what the shapes are going to become—

But they always close again, not wanting to puncture the mellow thrill of waiting for the image to develop. Instead, she simply angles herself to— quietly and curiously—watch him.

She does so cautiously, like spying on a rare bird, her heart smouldering with a sense of delicate privilege. She only dares to face him completely when he's particularly absorbed, her hand curled around her pestle coming to a distracted halt.

She decides very quickly that she *likes* to watch him. The moments when he's painting are the only moments when he isn't utterly focused on *her*. She likes him being focused on her—how his eyes make her toes curl in her shoes, and his voice tangles her eardrums in ribbons—

But she also likes those rare few hours when he isn't actually paying any attention to her at all.

He acts differently, then, she's noticed. His joints looser, his shoulders less set.

He rolls up his sleeves, sometimes, if the green shirt (they're always green) he's wearing is particularly baggy. His bare arms are just as pale as the rest of him, all smooth ridges of bone and little hills of muscle.

He tucks his hair behind his ears or—if his hands are stained with paint— gives his head a little flick, huffing a breath through pursed lips.

Meren almost stands up to assist him, some little part of her wishing that was her job; to sit by The Prince as he paints, and sweep his hair away from his eyes.

Something else he does—which is quickly becoming her favourite—is taking a few steps back to absently pluck whatever treat is waiting patiently by her elbow. He munches on it while he squints at the canvas, sometimes leaning back to slouch, hip jutting out. One arm crosses over his flat stomach and the other rests on it, holding his snack to his mouth to lick up the icing, or nibble the corners off a sponge.

Whether he knows she's watching him is a mystery.

If he does, he never comments.

Meren knows painting involves a brush; she's seen enough of them around his chambers; tufts of hair wrapped with a metal band to the end of a slim rod of wood. From this, and from seeing the strokes upon finished pieces, she can deduce that a sweeping motion is required to transfer the paint onto the canvas.

Loading a wide set of bristles with it, Lorkan confirms her suspicions; although he seems to be dabbing rather than dragging; light presses, subtle, soft little strokes like perfectly placed kisses.

He puts them in places that must make complete sense to him, but seem random to Meren; as though he can see the picture on the canvas already, and is just filling bits in—matching up colours—until she can see it too.

She is convinced of this, because he often just stares at it for minutes on end, angling his head, tilting his chin and frowning at the canvas as though trying to figure it out.

He clearly sees something that she can't.

10

THE APOTHECARY'S APPRENTICE

Meren can tell what Lorkan's painting is of, now.

Compared to the one of a bustling marketplace, it's serene and uncomplicated, with a simple elegance just starting to make itself known. The blocky shadows have merged to form the lower half of someone's face, and half of their shirt-covered chest. Their head is propped up on one hand, the other resting comfortably on the table marked by a thick brown streak slicing through the bottom edge of the canvas. A hint of blue just about glows through the first layer of the person's narrow wrist. It's about making paint—well, it will be, once it is complete. It's probably a self-portrait, Meren thinks, of Lorkan's hands stained blue with pigment.

There is an extra heap of money waiting for her on the bureau.

There's the usual pile—sitting atop the daily list of pigments he'd like her to fetch from the market—but now there's a stack of coppers too, shiny and undented as if popped straight from a coin press.

"What's this for?" Meren narrows her eyes at the unassuming stack as if she half expects it to nip at her fingers.

Having insisted on walking her to the door—as he always does—Lorkan lets one shoulder come to lean against the wall. "It's for snacks," he says, and her narrowed eyes move from the money to him. "When you're at the market, if you see something nice, get it, and we can eat it in the studio."

"You don't need to pay me with food," she says, and reaches out a hand, pushing the little stack of coins over to his side of the bureau. "I keep telling you, I *like* helping you make paint."

"I'm not. They're for me; I have low blood sugar so I try to have something to nibble on close at hand."

Meren opens her mouth to call him a liar; he looks as though he photosynthesises rather than eats—he probably doesn't even have blood, he's just filled with that pale sap that oozes out of trees when you snap off a branch. Or ocean water, transparent and sun-dappled.

But that word feels sharp on her tongue like a thistle. She swallows it.

"What's wrong with the palace kitchens?"

Indeed, since introducing Meren to jam, Lorkan had brought other little treats to get them through the long hours in the studio. She had thought them each wonderful in their own sugary, delicate, perfect way, but Lorkan shakes his head.

"Just because they work in the palace that doesn't mean they're *good*. There are nicer things out there, if you can believe it, and I'd like you to find them, let me share them with you and, if it's not too difficult, I'd like you to try and enjoy them."

Grudgingly, Meren plucks the coins off the bureau, and Lorkan looks as if he's won some sort of game. "What kind of food would you like me to buy?" She knows he's going to say:

"I don't mind. Get whatever you feel like."

"You know I shouldn't do that. There must be a law about it, somewhere."

"About what?"

"About using the royal family's riches to please my common-person stomach," she says with a slightly sick feeling. She's not sure if it stems from how worryingly at ease she is becoming around The Prince, or because her mind is running away with all the delicacies that await her curious palate, and it's making her realise how hungry she is.

Before Lorkan can open his mouth:

"Don't you want to choose what your own money is buying?"

He merely waves a nonchalant hand.

The hours they've spent together seem to have mulled him like cider. His voice, once measured, has slackened to a contented drawl, his carefully picked words dropping the formal pleasantries and addressing Meren as if he's known her his whole life. His limbs have no qualms now, leaving the comforting solidness of his body and gesturing as he talks, scratching his chin thoughtfully, stretching up in a relaxed yawn if the mood takes him.

Meren almost feels like nervously pinning them back to his sides, pulling him away from the wall, and ironing his spine back into a formal rod.

Turning her head self-consciously, she checks the door is still closed.

She knows it is, but she can't seem to shoo away that taloned finger of fear running down her neck that someone might be peeping through a crack, watching. Watching The Prince slouch as he talks to her, watching her give him soft little arguments in return.

"I'm really not picky."

* ☾ *

So, Meren's trips to the market have gained a new, delicious responsibility, and her coin strings an extra row of coppers. She turns them over in one hand as she eyes the numerous confectionery stalls, feeling spoilt in every sense of the word.

Despite never having bought from any of them, she already has a firm favourite.

Each day, she purposely takes the route to Frode's that brings her past the row of heavenly-smelling line of baked goods. There's a small man with buzzed hair who looks like he measures the exact length of each wafer before cutting them, a woman who pipes her icing as though carving a delicate statue, and dozens in between; perfect little buns as round as a snowball, crepes folded like delicate origami; serious people with concentrating faces, all their neat biscuits and finger cakes standing to attention in sugar-scented, meticulous rows.

Meren's favourite stall is the messy, disorganised one at the end.

It's run by a woman called Aasta, and Meren has to get up close to see the things she sells. A crowd is always clumped at the front of her stall, a bustling queue of people snaking down and around the side.

It takes a little while for her to get to the front, and she can only tell she's there because of the dusty flour mixed in with the gritty path below her feet. Being careful not to tread on any of the plump sparrows pecking up fallen crumbs, Meren nudges her way forward, having to ease around a gentleman who seems to have only come for a chat.

The treats on this table are like little works of art. Not the kind of art Meren has seen hung up on the palace walls; full of perfect lines and exact proportions. Real art, with little personal touches and mistakes. They're good mistakes, in her mind. Too much caramel seeping out of the millionaire's shortbreads. A disproportionate fudge chip-to-dough ratio in the cookies. Profiteroles like overstuffed pillows, fit to burst with cream.

Aasta, now that Meren is getting a good, clear look at her, closely resembles the food she sells. Every time she's seen her, she's wearing a colourful dress draped over her soft, doughy frame—like icing over a sponge—their patterns like sprinkles and nubs of frosting.

She gives Meren a wide smile in greeting, fetching change for a customer with one hand and neatly wrapping several petit fours in tissue paper with the other.

"Finally come to buy something, ey, pet?" She asks, and Meren tucks a loose strand of hair behind her ear.

Nodding a polite good morning, she holds out the coins Lorkan had given her. "I'd like to, if I can. What can I get with this?"

WHAT LORKAN IS

Aasta gestures at the entire table as though about to pick it all up and give it a hug. "Why, with that, you can buy anything here several times over."

Suddenly, her eyes narrow and, for a second, Meren thinks the baker is going to accuse her of stealing the money—

Instead, she leans over and gives a young boy's knuckles a warning tap with her cake tongs. He retracts his sugar-covered finger guiltily, the beignet he'd poked left with a finger-shaped indent.

Meren has to choke down a laugh at his wounded expression. She would have offered to buy the beignet for him, had he not slunk off into the crowd muttering something about it being worth a try.

"Cheeky bugger," Aasta sighs. "Anyway, what can I get you, missy?"

✳ ☾ ✳

Eventually, Meren settles on two stout wedges of pumpkin cake, and watches as Aasta prizes them off their plate, the buttercream leaving behind two white cloud-like triangles.

"Will you be eating these now?" she asks, and when Meren says she'll have them later, she packages them up in a little paper mache box. She seals it with a stamp and twine—to make sure the air can't get in and dry them out, she says—and Meren places them carefully at the bottom of her tote.

She clutches the handle as she makes her way to Frode's stall. She used to pick up Lorkan's pigments with an interested sense of curiosity but, recently, Frode and Arne seem to have agreed upon something behind her back.

Frode has learnt to expect Meren each morning and, today, he greets her with his usual little wave. He doesn't serve Meren himself, though, anymore. Now, after waving her over, his moustache wriggles as a smile blooms below the bristles and he says:

"You just hand your list to Arne." With a pointy elbow, he gives his apprentice a nudge in the ribs. He's so short it barely reaches the band of Arne's trousers. "He'll fetch you everything you need."

Meren gives him a wobbly smile.

Before this arrangement, she'd take her place at the end of the queue, get out the book Lorkan had lent her, and knock out a few pages while the little mole-like-man tends to the sick, advises the troubled, and mixes up complicated remedies.

Since she's shopping for The Prince, however, Frode must have bumped her up his list of priority customers because, one day, he started skipping her past everyone else to be served by his apprentice. Although meant as a kind gesture, it makes her nervous.

Meren *likes* Arne, he treats her well, but that is precisely the root cause of that pinching feeling in her stomach every time she sees his straw-coloured hair bobbing about over the top of the crowd.

He treats her *too* well; smiling extra wide when he sees her coming, giving her nicknames but never remembering them.

The butcher's boy would do similar things when Yllva had sent her out for cuts of meat. Meren had flushed at first, flattered, but then she'd seen him go through exactly the same routine with the next maid in line, and her cheeks had heated for a whole different reason.

Granted, Arne is a muted, more reserved version of that rowdy blood-stained lad missing three fingers; and Meren hasn't seen him treat anyone else in the same way—

But her insides still wriggle all the same. If anything, his undivided attention unsettles her more than the butcher's boy because it's so sincere. She would rather wait in a queue like the rest of the apothecary's customers if it meant she could do her dealings with the funny mole-like man with the chunky glasses and bushy caterpillar under his nose.

He reminds her of a grandpa, or maybe an elderly uncle, who tells stories that may or may not have happened.

WHAT LORKAN IS

✷ ☾ ✷

Back at the palace, Alfdis stops Meren on her way to the mop cupboard with a letter.

She assumes it's from Lorkan, at first, and hurries over eagerly to accept it—but her name printed on the back isn't in his swirling black penmanship.

As a professional mender, Mr Hansen's words—that had taught Meren to read and write her own—had once been erect and precise, scratched onto parchment with the pointed graphite sticks on his workbench. However, they now sit with his other finer tools, steadily collecting a wispy layer of dust in their tin pots. With every passing year, Meren's father's eyesight has blurred, his vision slowly clouding over like condensation on a window pane. Unsure as a child's, his sentences now droop down one side of the thin yellow parchment, blocky and tentative.

He writes of autumn setting in, the chill aggravating Mrs Hansen's arthritis, her knuckles swelled and chapped. She has been forced to drop another client, her knobbled fingers unable to keep up with the growing heap of dirty laundry dropped at their door.

However, with her extra free time—and through trial and error—she has taken to aiding her husband in his repair work. He has nimble fingers, and she has two working eyes and, together, they have managed to piece together Mr Landford's broken grandfather clock, and Miss Penn's timepiece, both for a decent fee.

He ends the letter by wishing Meren well and, although hopeful, the whole thing dampens her mood like a sudden onset of murky, wet fog. Blinking through it, she folds the letter into quarters as if to somehow trap its despondency inside, and drops it into Lorkan's rubbish bin as she joins him in his studio, making a mental note to accept the next bonus he offers her.

His eyes light up a brilliant green as she greets him, then rove curiously over the bulging tote bag she sets on the low wooden table. Removing his pigments one by one, he explores them first then, seemingly pleased with each colour, he plucks up the boxes stamped with Aasta's hard little wax seal.

"How was your morning?"

"Pleasant. I really like the woman who sold me our cakes. If you don't like it, I can go and fetch something else, she sells all sorts."

"I'm sure that won't be necessary," he assures, plucking the twine bow apart between finger and thumb. Peeling back the lid, his free hand immediately reaches for the green crockery he'd fetched from the cupboard. Transferring his slice to it as though handling some ancient, beautiful treasure:

"Are you *quite* sure you don't have blue blood, Meren? Because you have an eye for luxury."

Meren hasn't gotten into her box yet, her fingernail still prizing up the wax seal. When a shard breaks off, Lorkan eases it out of her hands and takes over, soon having the thick wedge of pumpkin cake standing proudly on a plate. He nudges it over to her side of the table, and her fork hovers over it, one prong absently sinking into the buttercream.

"...Meren?"

"Hm?"

"Are you alright? You're very quiet today. Well, quieter than usual."

"Oh. I'm fine, thank you." Severing off a chunk of sponge, she pops it in her mouth to prove her point—but her eyes close of their own accord, her mind momentarily transported. When she's swallowed and moved hungrily onto her next piece, she realises Lorkan is still looking at her. "...I just got a letter from my parents earlier."

His brows gather over his nose. "Are they well?"

"Yes, thank you. It's just...difficult having ageing parents that live so far away."

"I understand. My parents live under the same roof as me but they're so busy I barely see them, especially recently. Every time I get a look at Mother, she has sprouted more grey hairs."

WHAT LORKAN IS

Meren nods understandingly; she's not set eyes on her parents since New Years Eve. Unable to afford the full trip to the capital, they'd met her halfway at an inland town called Mullberg, and they spent the evening munching fried potatoes and watching the festivities from a wide bridge crossing over the river. Indeed, Mrs Hansen's brown locks have turned silver as the moon in places, her father's already receding past his ears, the fireworks reflecting off his domed head.

"What is your father like?" Meren asks tentatively, her cake already partly demolished. "Not as a king, but as a person?"

Lorkan always looks surprised when she dares to ask a question, but it soon mellows into a pleased smile—as if he's glad she'd been brave enough to do so. He's eating the sponge first, perhaps saving the butter icing, whipped as dandelion fluff, until last.

"It depends who you ask, I think. Father's colleagues would say he's stoic and proud. Mother would say the same but add that he's also a wise man, and not unfeeling."

"And Queen Lophia?"

"Mother is patient and understanding, but I can tell she finds queendom trying, although she hides it well. She often reminds me of a mother hen with too many chicks."

Finishing their cake, Meren and Lorkan slip into an easy chat about parents and childhood, occasionally pausing to hum little awed sounds of delight as they hit unexpected veins of gummy caramel.

She glances sideways at The Prince lapping butter icing from his fingers before daring to do it herself, both of them popping them between their lips like children.

He's dabbing up the crumbs from his plate when he asks, absently:

"Have you had time to start the book I lent you?"

"Yes, it's wonderful!" Meren exclaims, more animated now. "The main character is so brave, I don't think I could ever do half of the things she manages."

Lorkan smiles, his lip shiny with a streak of glossy gold sugar. "I'm sure you could."

Meren fights the urge to lean over and collect it with the pad of her finger. Shaking her head:

"No, I definitely couldn't."

"Well, I'm glad you're enjoying it all the same," he gives in, and she finds herself disappointed. "It always fills me with the overwhelming desire to travel."

"Why don't you?"

"You can't just travel when you're a prince, Meren. I'd have to have a whole convoy of guards, diplomatic advisors, a steward—for some reason. It would be like a circus."

"Oh."

"Have *you* travelled?"

"Only from where I grew up."

"In Holcombe?"

"Yes, that's right." She turns to him, surprised he remembers.

"My brother attended Black Castle for his training, I think that's somewhere in the Westlands too. He's been everywhere," he adds with obvious admiration—and a flicker of something else, something that makes his shoulders sag.

"Even Hylune?"

"No, not Hylune. Or Calpurzia, obviously. I doubt they'd let him in; he looks as Velôrian as they come."

Meren remembers the book she's reading. "Has he ever seen a dragon?"

"Yes, several, but only glimpses."

"How about an ice giant?"

"No, I don't think so. He wants to, though. He was always furious he wasn't born earlier so he could have fought alongside Father in the war."

The space between Meren's brows rucks up in a puzzled frown, and it makes Lorkan's lip twitch, not that she notices. "Why on earth would he want to fight in a war?"

WHAT LORKAN IS

"Much to my father's dismay, I don't know the answer to that question."

"Your father wants you to fight?"

"Yes. It's what princes do."

"Ah. My parents keep bugging me to marry and move back to Holcombe," she says and then stops, losing momentum. "...But I guess that's different."

Lorkan looks at her, his eyes a deep fern green below his dark, creased brows. Stacking their plates and forks in a neat pile he asks gently:

"Do you *want* to get married?"

"Maybe one day, if I met the right person. But I don't want to go back to Holcombe. I like it here."

"I'm glad."

"Why?"

"My studio would feel too quiet."

✳ ☾ ✳

Aasta's cake having been received more than happily by both Lorkan and Meren, it is unanimously agreed that she shall be The Prince's supplier of all things sweet from now on. Meren happily agrees to integrate her stall to her daily rounds of the market, and the routine soon settles comfortably about her like a wool scarf.

She must ensure to visit right after breakfast if she hopes to nab the tastiest treats before a gaggle of hungry workers claim them all for their luncheon. It takes all but three days for Aasta to start greeting her by name, and Meren smiles at her freckles, thinking they look very much like stars.

At first—per Lorkan's instructions—she had chosen the snacks she thought looked good to her. However—eventually and inevitably—she'd sampled everything the stall has to offer, and started bringing back whatever had made Lorkan's sugar-stained mouth turn the most smiley.

Like the treacle tart thicker than a book.

Or the vanilla cake with the fudge filling so gooey they had to hold a plate under it to catch the drips.

They had made The Prince's eyes light up when Meren presented them, then made them slide closed when he bit into them.

Presently, she is trying to decide which will be most likely to make that happen: a tray of pastel pink jelly, dusted cubes, or something spongy and pink and checked like a chess board. She points to the slabs of cake, which Aasta parcels up for her, careful not to squash the little decorations piped onto its top.

She always hands Meren a few coppers in change, which she'd tried to press into Lorkan's palm, but he'd just frowned.

"Thank you, but what am I meant to do with this?"

"That's your change."

When he'd still seemed puzzled she'd added:

"From the cakes."

"I understand that, I just meant why are you giving it to *me?*"

After some persuasion, Meren finally allowed Lorkan to drop them back into her hand, and now, several weeks later, a decent little collection jangles on the end of her coin string. Deciding the amount isn't worth sending home, she's started skipping Yllva's morning culinary delights and taken to purchasing fruit and bread on the way to the Frode's instead.

She has just finished an apple as Arne's hair hoves into view, swaying over the crowd's dark heads like a lone tuft of wheat in a ploughed field.

He gives Meren a smile when he spots her, and motions for her to join him around the side of the building where a half door opens up into the well-trodden outside treatment area.

The pigments Frode sells are still a mystery to Meren as far as understanding their ingredients go, but she has begun to match some of the colours and shades to the words on Lorkan's lists. He'd shown her how to pronounce the more complicated syllables in their names as well, but she still slides his scrap of parchment across the counter to Arne rather than trying to remember them all. She'd tried, but the words felt wrong in her head—as if they were trying to wriggle into a world they don't belong to; silk throw pillows on a straw-filled truckle bed.

Arne's eyes sweep The Prince's list in a well-rehearsed manner. He looks back at Meren as he reaches for the top shelf, though. "Your ears are healing nicely."

She knows the first pigment on the list is something blue and, sure enough, he brings down a large jar of pulverulent, cobalt lumps.

"Have you had any trouble with them?" he asks easily, sounding more like Frode than ever, and Meren can't help her cheeks flushing a little.

She's trying to focus on his hands rather than his eyes, because his eyes make her want to look away.

"No problems, thank you."

She watches him scoop some of the blue crumbly rocks from the jar, and place them into one of the empty boxes on the counter. She's formed a habit of bringing some of the old ones back to reuse, their wood stained, the colours biting deeply into their grain.

"Alfdis told me about someone who lost an ear because they didn't wash it enough, so I've been using carbolic soap every night just to be safe," she says and Arne's face perks up a little.

He always does when Meren utters more than *'Please'* or *'Thank you'* in one go, and it makes her feel worse about his unreciprocated affections.

She has tried saying *fewer* words, limiting her speech as not to seem too interested, but that had just made him think she's shy, and he'd made more of an effort to fill the silences. It was so sweet of him, Meren's eyes sometimes prick at the thought of it.

'Mother would like him,' she finds herself thinking when he lifts something heavy onto an old woman's cart for her, or addresses someone with a polite 'ma'am' or 'sir'.

'And Father would like him too,' she thinks as he patiently hands facts to confused customers, explaining his craft with genuine fondness, asking after their grandmas and pregnant sisters.

Arne inserts the box containing cobalt lumps into Meren's bag, arranging it carefully.

He keeps handing her his affections every now and again, bit by bit. He's been doing it so slowly, so gently, she's barely noticed, and forgets about it sometimes—like a tide gradually rising up a beach, sucking away the sank.

He's doing it now, offering her his affections, and Meren wishes she would just open her palms and accept them.

She tries—tries to appreciate his sandy colours, the curves of his sloping shoulders.

She doesn't really know what it's meant to feel like when she looks at a handsome man.

She *thought* she knew, once. His name was Morgen and he worked as a kitchen boy for some time. He gave her a sort of clenching in the pit of her belly whenever his tawny eyes met hers; a tingling dancing along the column of her spine each time their fingers met reaching for the potato peeler. Morgen had thick hair and a long, thoughtful face but, one time, Meren saw him pick something from his nose and smear it under the table.

At that moment she decided—if she didn't have her parents to support— she wouldn't mind ending up a spinster like Alfdis.

However, those feelings had bubbled up again when she'd started working for Lorkan. The jade of his eyes cut into her in a way that balls her stomach up into a fist and, when his paint-stained fingers brush hers, she can feel the ghost of it for several to tingly minutes afterwards—

But that might be because he is a prince and that makes her nervous, she thinks. It would be unfair to expect simple working men like Arne to fluster her in the same way.

Meren lifts one of the box's lids and holds it out for him to take.

His teeth are round in his smile, his calluses muting the brush of his fingers. He's like a stack of pebbles, her eyes falling from one rounded shape to the next, *plop, plop, plop.*

Lorkan is more like a swift arrow, his appearance taking her hand and leading her in one smooth motion all the way from his head to his toes; sharp shoulders, narrow waist, a stretch of slender leg, pale feet half covered in the green cotton of his trousers.

She wonders, with puzzlement, why her thoughts have once again drifted back to The Prince.

"I was wondering—" Arne says. "There's supposed to be a meteor shower tonight. I was going to go up to Elsie's hill—there's said to be a good view from the east side. I wondered if you would like to join me? I'll bring something to eat, of course—"

Frode is bustling about at the other end of the stall. He spoons some green globules onto a weighing pan. His hands are less wrinkled than her mother's, the joints less knotted. He squints through his glasses to read the scales, and Meren thinks of the lines collecting at the corners of her father's eyes as he does the same, struggling to bring miniature screws and tangles of tiny cogs into focus.

Talk of the meteor shower has been passed around the servant's quarters for a few days, mainly by the maids who have a beau to escort them about town on their Sundays off, and hall boys who do the escorting. Most of the servants have either been invited to Elsie's hill or invited someone and, over breakfast, Meren had realised with an uncomfortable feeling she may be one of the few people spreading out a picnic blanket alone.

She turns back to Arne. He's holding her tote bag out for her to take and she does, her mouth curving with a genuine smile.

"That sounds lovely, thank you. What time should I meet you there?"

11

VELÔR AND CALPURZIA

Arne says he'll pick Meren up at the servant's courtyard just after dinner.

'Pick up' isn't really accurate; he has no mode of transportation to pick her up *with*. He had bashfully specified this, wringing his hands like a sodden dish cloth, and Meren almost giggled.

"I'm from Holcombe, Arne," she assures, placing a hand over his. "I've never met *anyone* that has their own trap. Well, besides farmers. And anyway, the walk will be nice."

✶ ☾ ✶

Lorkan's hair is different.

WHAT LORKAN IS

Usually, Meren has time to give his chambers a light going over before they head to his studio but, today, the door swings open as soon as she inserts the key into the lock.

Surprised, she blinks up at him, his smile falling down onto her face.

He hasn't slicked it back—that's what's different. Usually, he uses a tin of sweet-smelling oil on his dresser, keeping each strand tidily tucked to the curve of his skull like the breast of a magpie. Today, however, it's falling in slight waves about the line of his shoulders like the branches of a willow.

Politely, she averts her eyes. "Should I come back later?"

He tips his head to the side, the movement making the ends of his hair brush his left shoulder. "Why?"

Licking her lips, Meren gestures vaguely. "I thought maybe you hadn't finished getting dressed."

"Well, there's that self-confidence boost I needed."

"No! I didn't mean you don't look—what I meant was, *usually*—"

All at once Lorkan's eyes widen, his hands darting out and clasping about her wrist. She gasps as she's whisked into his chambers with uncharacteristic urgency—as if guiding her in some chaotic waltz. In the same movement, his foot kicks the door shut with a deep thud and she blinks, his green shirt inches from her nose.

It's embroidered with hundreds of golden leaves each the size of her thumb nail.

Lorkan must feel her muscles go taught as a bowstring below his wide palm, because he releases her wrist and takes a hasty step back. "I do apologise, I spotted my mother just down the corridor. I didn't want her catching you being so—" he stops, hunting for the right word, "...informal around me. You'd get into trouble."

"Oh, thank you."

The two dark lines of his eyebrows come together, giving him a wilted appearance. His shoulders sag, setting the little leaves on his shirt dropping. "Even after all the time we've spent together you don't feel at ease enough to call me out when I make you uncomfortable?"

Meren shakes her head so quickly she thinks her hair might tumble out of her tightly bound, mandatory bun. Self-consciously, she tucks a few escaped strands back where they belong. "You didn't make me uncomfortable."

He didn't. For one, *silly* moment, Meren had wondered if he was about to lead her on some great adventure.

Her nerves are still prickling with it.

Lorkan smiles as if relieved, the leaves smattering his chest perking back up. "What were you going to say before I practically assaulted you?"

"You didn't assault me, you stopped me from getting fired."

She'd said it light-heartedly but her smile falters. It's difficult, at times, to keep their secret friendship clutched close to her chest, especially as it's so beautiful; she feels as though she's in possession of a gorgeous rose, but she can't show another living soul because she'd picked it from the royal gardens.

She'd nearly *dropped* her secret several times, by accident; almost let it fall from her grasp and spill, naked and vulnerable on the floor for all to see.

Like yesterday, when she'd sneaked the charcoal drawing of a doe Lorkan had given her from its hiding place.

She became so lost in the muted, monotone world, tracing its delicate lines, lining her digits up with his fuzzy, accidental thumbprints. She didn't notice her roommate poking her head over her shoulder, asking her what she was looking at.

Or when Frode and Arne ask her what exactly it is The Prince does with all the pigments he buys day after day.

Meren had opened her mouth the first time this question had been handed to her—after all, she is his maid. It's only natural that she'd know a little about what goes on in his chambers; there really wouldn't be any harm in briefly describing what sits atop the easel in Lorkan's studio. Frode would probably find it flattering, seeing as it is the arrangement of his pigments she'd be depicting.

But Meren had pulled her jaw back up and merely shrugged.

She knows that if she allows herself to mention Lorkan's picture, she won't be able to stop. She'll start voicing things that aren't her place to ask, like why

WHAT LORKAN IS

is his list of pigments growing shorter by the day, even though it still lacks some of his most prominent features?

And doesn't he ever paint people—not just fleeting strangers, but the people he loves? She knows his style by now, she can recognise his brush strokes, the sweeping curves of them. His own pictures have their places on his walls; the water garden, palace horses, more scenes from Tawny—

Why are there no paintings of his parents, or his brother?

Has he ever painted a lover?

Surly he has friends?

—Although, Meren realises with a hollow feeling, the only friend *she's* managed to make since moving into Aldercliff is Alfdis.

When Meren had to drag herself out of bed before the sun, it was usually just the two of them pottering about. They'd chat sleepily over the first servings of porridge, and help each other heft buckets of water from the well.

Now things are reversed.

When Meren has finished washing Lorkan's brushes and covering his bowls of paint, she is one of the last to take a seat for supper. Alfdis' day, too, reaches its end as the sun sets, so they've become accustomed to sitting amongst the stains left over from dinner, and discussing the day over various stews and roast meats.

Well, actually, most of their conversations are rather one-sided; Alfdis will tell Meren about the various herculean chores she has to do about the palace; organising feasts and ceremonies and such like, while Meren nods and tries not to gag on Yllva's attempts at leverpastej.

Their similar jobs, their direct contact with the royal family, and their shared affections for The Prince has separated them from the other servants, but brought them closer to each other. In Meren's mind, this would make them ideal conversation partners, however, each attempt at discussing her employer is swiftly shut down, and the ones that aren't are bulldozed over by a stern lecture about knowing her place.

Later, Meren would *like* to tell Alfdis about Lorkan's bed-head, if the results wouldn't be imprisonment for treason. Is saying 'The Prince wears his hair ruffled now and for some reason I can't stop staring at it' treason? She would argue no—because it's complimentary—but she's sure the royal court would reach a different verdict.

They'd probably say she should be imprisoned for even *looking* at The Prince's hair, rather than keeping her head respectfully lowered like she's supposed to.

"I was going to say your hair is different." Meren does the little gesturing thing again, pointing vaguely to the loose curls about his now—oddly—flushed face.

A small smile twitches at the corner of Lorkan's lip and he shrugs. "I thought I'd try something new."

"It suits you," she says without thinking.

He blinks, and she tugs the collar of her uniform away from her neck, suddenly feeling as though the room's temperature has risen by several degrees.

It can't have done, the windows showing a swollen sky streaked with approaching rain clouds.

Then she realises something:

"Lophia was here?" Another blush as she hastily corrects herself:

"I mean...Her Majesty was here?"

Lorkan gestures to Meren to follow him, and she does, like a cat waiting for its owner to place down a bowl of scraps. He sighs at the mention of his mother, the sound so etiolated Meren wonders at first whether it had actually been the sound of the studio door sweeping smoothly open.

Of course, it wasn't, the hinges worn smooth. It *was* Lorkan, his shoulders sagging as if some heavy, invisible thumb is trying to press him into the ground like a seed. The weight must be so distracting he doesn't even chastise Meren about using the 'M-word'.

She hands him the bag of pigments she'd picked up from the market; a pitifully small amount due to the painting's apparent near completion.

It doesn't *look* like it's nearly finished.

WHAT LORKAN IS

Well, it does, but not if it's supposed to be a self-portrait. Meren keeps waiting for the day when Lorkan will widen the jaw to give it that manly solidness, thicken the neck and dab on the angular cut of his Adam's apple. So far, he hasn't even applied a hint of black paint about his shoulders.

Maybe he will now that he's settled on which way he'd like to wear it, Meren thinks. She also wonders how he will tackle the task of transforming a blob of indecisive darkness into a convincing representation of strands.

She's been watching the picture form as though it were one of life's fascinating processes; a woman going through pregnancy, or watching an oak grow from an acorn.

She's eager to see it through until the end, until that final, conclusive dab of the brush that will mark its fruition. She'd never raised anything before, but she imagines this is how it must feel to do so.

Turning her attention away from the canvas, she finds Lorkan has already wandered over to the low wooden table, and flopped onto one of the surrounding cushions, his long body folding like a house of cards.

There have been two pillows tucked under the table for a while, now, one for Meren and one for Lorkan.

He'd added another just to put an end to her pestering; she hated the thought that she—a lowly maid—was atop a plump cushion whilst a prince had to kneel on the bare floorboards—

—no matter how many times said prince insisted he doesn't mind.

He may have been brought up as a gentleman but *Meren* was raised a servant. Offering a lady the most comfortable place to sit may be the polite thing to do, but doing all in her power to make her master more comfortable is essentially coded into her DNA.

She didn't let it go and, on day three of her concerned little offers to at least swap the pillow between them in shifts, Lorkan flounced to the other room and returned with a cushion from one of the numerous settees.

"Happy now?" He'd asked, plonking it down, a ghost of an amused smirk playing on his thin lips.

Meren had wanted to say *'No! It's getting all stained!'* But at least his slender legs weren't crushed against the hardwood floor anymore, so she pressed her lips into a smile and gave a nod.

Presently, his head lowered somewhat listlessly, Lorkan removes the last box of pigment from Meren's (now rather colourful) tote bag.

She takes a step closer, fighting the urge to place her hand on his shoulder. "Are you alright?"

He gives her a weak smile. "My mother only enters my chambers when she has important matters to discuss with me."

Something in his voice makes her abdomen curl in on itself. Not in an intense, exhilarating way like it usually does, but in another way, a way that makes Meren unsure whether she'd like to hear the rest.

"Oh."

Has someone found out about their friendship?

Is the kingdom at war?

Is someone he loves in trouble?

That would put Lorkan into such a low mood he might give up on painting altogether—*then* what would Meren do? Go back to methodologically cleaning his rooms? Go back to seeing in black and white? If he no longer chuckles at her timid attempts at jokes, she'll certainly starve.

"Everything is fine, it's just...you are familiar with the rift between Velôr and Calpurzia?"

Her mouth dries. "Obviously, it's as old as time."

"Actually, it's not. The kingdoms were once joined."

Meren lowers herself to kneel at his side. "I thought that was just a story?"

"No, it's true. Its name is long since lost, but it is said at its core were a couple who claimed the land together."

For once, Meren is in no mood for Lorkan's winding velvety sentences. "So?" She could have sworn the corner of his lip quirked upwards.

"There are two versions of the story. One says that, one day, they had an awful argument and vowed never to speak again, and that's why the kingdom broke in two. Others say they were so in love they split the kingdom equally between them so they would each be able to rule their half as they chose."

"I've never heard anyone say any of this," Meren says, her forehead creased.

"People don't like to. Some don't even believe it. My point is, Father has gotten it into his head that the two kingdoms would be better off as once more, and he thinks he's found a way to darn them together."

His words sit before them on the table, and they both stare at them for some time.

"An alliance...with Calpurzia?" Meren spells it out, to give what they're looking at a label, but it doesn't help.

"Yes."

"But—people *hate* Calpurzians almost as much as they hate Hyluniens."

The line of Lorkan's shoulders rises and falls in a shrug. "Father doesn't want them to. He keeps going on about trade and things."

Stunned, Meren wriggles her cushion closer to his, hoping the embroidery doesn't catch on the uneven floorboards. She stops just before her prickly uniform meets the black, linen-covered knots of his knees. "So how's he going to do it?"

Lorkan drags his eyes up to meet hers, one hand fiddling with a loose thread on his left sleeve. He tugs it, several embroidered leaves unravelling as though tugged away by a breath of autumn wind. "It wasn't his idea, he got a letter from the Calpurzian royals. They've suggested an arranged marriage between our two families to unite them."

Meren nods, her mother's voice echoing in her brain; something about matrimony being the smartest career move a person can make.

She imagines it, once it's all done; the wedding bands linked like a chain, acting like a tiny bridge between the two kingdoms. She pictures miniature people crossing over it, pin-sized boats loaded with goods heaving under it. The mental image all runs rather nicely, like cogs in a well-oiled clock.

But then one of the gears gets stuck.

"Isn't His Highness Sol more of a warrior?" she asks.

There's a painting of him on the third floor, his handsome features twisted into a grimace as, with some effort, he drives a sword into the face of some ugly creature.

"The way people describe him, he doesn't seem like the type to settle down."

"Not Sol. Me."

12

TWO INVITATIONS

There's silence. "What?"

"Due to the ever-looming threat of war, my father is trying to broker peace with the Calpurzian kingdom, and Mother asked if I'd agree to an arranged marriage to their princess—"

"No, I understood that, I just meant..." Meren pushes his words away with one hand as if they're a plate of congealed gruel she's refusing to eat. "What did you tell her?"

Lorkan's eyebrows rise so far up his head they nearly brush his widow's peak. "Are you joshing? I said *no*, obviously."

Meren releases a breath she didn't know she'd been holding in. She'd scooted closer to him without realising it, so close her knee is nudging his, and she edges back onto her own pillow, hoping her apron hasn't tugged pills from his nice trousers like a thistle burr.

"I understand that arranged marriages have brought kingdoms together in the past, but I don't want to marry someone I do not love."

He's performing a task he usually enjoys, but he's slumped over his crossed legs as if gravity is trying to claim him. The look in his eyes is unusually vacant, a deep frown pressed into the place his laid-back expression would normally rest.

"Why does the majority of politics involve using lives as pawns?" he muses presently, taking the first box of pigment and tipping the crumbly lumps into the mortar.

Meren gets the sense that his question had been rhetorical. If it wasn't, he'd come to the wrong person for diplomatic advice. She combs her mind for something to say, something that would smooth the worried furrow from his brows, but her net comes up empty.

He continues, addressing the room at large, his movements more animated as despair evolves into agitation:

"Even though the entire system is corrupt, I can't help feeling selfish. I know I *should* sacrifice my happiness for my kingdom, but wouldn't it be more logical to find a solution where *everyone* can be happy?" Lorkan turns to Meren despondently, as if looking to her for reassurance.

She's shocked to find his sharp emerald eyes dulled, their brilliant green now muted and chipped like pastel sea glass.

She struggles, not sure what she should do to comfort him or, more importantly, what she's *allowed* to do. If she had her way, she'd tug him into a hug and mutter various versions of *'It'll all work itself out in the end'* onto his hairline—

But that would not be permitted; legally as well as personally, probably. Meren is pretty sure there's some rule about not laying a hand on members of the royal family. Despite this, how would he react if she did? With a sinking feeling, Meren realises just how much she doesn't know about The Prince.

Is he a hugger?

Does he like playful touches?

Does he greet his loved ones with a friendly kiss on the cheek?

He's touched *her*, occasionally—to show her how to work the pestle, etcetera. But he's never done it out of affection. Never rested a hand on her back as he moved past her, or given a ludic little shove when they'd teased each other.

WHAT LORKAN IS

Despite this, Meren finds herself reaching out and placing her hand over the back of his.

It had been resting on the table, his pale, cool skin contrasting with the rich, deep grain of the wood. His other hand—currently pushing the empty pigment box away from his workspace—grinds to a halt, stilled as if a switch had been flicked; rapids suddenly turning to a quiet little stream. Silently, his gaze falls down to stare at Meren's palm.

Her heart should be in her mouth, she knows. She should be trying to pass it off as a mistake, retreating back to her side of the table with a rushed apology—but she doesn't.

He'd looked so sad, so uncharacteristically deflated, so oddly small.

She gives his hand a comforting little squeeze.

His gaze rises to meet her eyes.

He smiles.

"That's not selfish," her voice is sturdy, almost firm. One by one, she passes him words, pressing them into his hands, closing his fingers around them like they're something to keep safe and close to his heart. "No one can make you do anything you don't want to. And anyway, they're your parents. They don't *want* you to be unhappy; they're probably trying to find an alternative solution as we speak."

The promise tastes bad as it rolls off the tip of her tongue, the bitter hint of a lie prickling her taste buds.

She tries to imagine King Cade, his sword propped, forgotten, against his chair in exchange for a feather quill dwarfed by his thick, scarred fingers. She attempts to picture him surrounded by complicated diplomatic documents and letters, working through the night to keep his youngest son by his side. His last wax stick dribbles and extinguishes itself, but he ignores it, continuing with nothing but the light of the moon—

Although Meren realises, *her* parents had sent her to Tawny when their funds ran low. Who's to say the royal family wouldn't send their child *away* to prevent a war? For a small, horrible second, she wonders if her attempt at comfort had been wildly misjudged—

But Lorkan's smile broadens weakly like rays of sunlight through a cloud. "Thank you. "I don't know about Father, but Mother certainly is."

Meren nods and releases his hand, taking the full mortar and its stubby little pestle. "There, see. Her Majesty probably only suggested an arranged marriage as a last resort."

Lorkan's hand hasn't moved.

He just looks down at the bony ridge of his now exposed knuckles as Meren begins gently crushing the lumps of pigment into a powder.

After all these days, she's good at it now, pressing stubborn clumps of colour against the curved side of the mortar. The movement is comfortable and familiar to her arm, almost instinctual, like stroking a palm over cat's fur.

Rising from his stupor, Lorkan takes a bowl from the pile stacked up on the other side of the table, ready to mix the powder Meren is creating with the other various ingredients that turn it into a spreadable paste.

They've made three colours when something occurs to her.

It's rather embarrassing that it hadn't been her first thought. It hadn't even been her second, third or fourth; it was just an afterthought, a tiny little bud of concern blossoming at the back of her brain. She feels bad for asking it. She doesn't want to invoke any more self-loathing in Lorkan, especially after he'd expressed concern about being selfish—

But she has to know, because anxiety has started tugging the edges of her mind, fraying her nerves.

She clears her throat. "Should we be...concerned about the alliance? I know tensions have always been high between us and Calpurzia, but will they be...you know...angry at you for rejecting their princess?"

Lorkan sighs in a way that suggests he's probably been wondering the same thing. "We don't know. Probably. Maybe. It all depends on how diplomatic Father is."

Meren's face falls. "Oh."

Lorkan makes a single-syllable hum in his chest. "My thoughts exactly."

"Oh, sorry, I didn't mean to imply—" she tries, feeling the back of her neck suffuse with heat, but he shakes his head.

WHAT LORKAN IS

"No, it's okay, you're right. Father isn't exactly known for his diplomatic finesse."

There is a brief, sombre silence while they both mull this realisation over.

"Why can't Sol do it?" Meren asks after some time, being careful not to tread on an invisible line with her scruffy housemaid slippers. The taste of political discussion is odd between her teeth, and she hopes Alfdis won't be able to smell it on her breath later.

"Sol is next in line to *this* throne. Call him old fashioned, but Father would rather—if my brother ever settles down—that his bride has Velôrian blood, should she inherit the kingdom."

"But isn't the Calpurzian queen worried about the same thing? About you inheriting *her* kingdom?"

"I'm younger than the Calpurzian princess, so I guess they hope we'd have children by the time that issue arises."

Something in Meren bunches up into a firm lump. "And...you'd have to move to Calpurzia, wouldn't you?"

"Yes."

"So you'd just get handed over like a..."

"Gift?" He mutters dryly. "That's what I said too."

The word makes her feel slightly sick, something hot and angry straining against the promises to Alfdis she'd made about knowing her place. "Surely we can think of an alternative way to broker peace? If we come up with something, you can tell Our King, and then he can tell—"

Lorkan is smiling at her again, another one of those watery-sun-through-a-rain-cloud smiles, and Meren blushes, pressing her lips together.

"I know, I know. What does a maid know about politics?" She mutters into the mortar as she shoves the pestle about its insides.

"No, it's not that." Lorkan's eyes are on the side of her cheek. "You said 'we'."

She meets his eyes, puzzled. "What's funny about that?"

"It's not funny." He dips his head back to the paint he's stirring, a few loose waves of his hair falling in front of his face, hiding it like a curtain.

Meren wants to reach out and tuck them back behind his ear.

"I'm glad I'm not going through this by myself."

His words bump into Meren's heart like birds flying into a window pane, thick thuds resonating through her chest.

She parts her lips, the whisper of a question leaking from between them:

"You're lonely?"

It confuses her that she hasn't noticed before. Hasn't *felt* it before. She'd just assumed he has other friends. Better, closer, higher-class friends that can relate to his plights. She'd put his solitude down to choice, labelled him a dedicated recluse, but maybe...

Lorkan inclines his shoulders a few inches, up and then down, almost as though he was taking in a deep breath then expelling it. He'd been stirring the bowl he holds with the end of a paintbrush, watching it go around and around, but he meets Meren's eyes.

"Less so, recently."

There's that urge to pull him into a hug, again. She finds her hand twitching, itching to take his narrow waist, the other to burrow in his hair.

Maybe she'd press a kiss to his widow's peak.

Maybe it would feel like touching her lips to the infinite, silky blackness of space itself.

Quickly, she dusts that whim under a metaphorical rug. She should say something, instead—something gentle, reassuring, wise, and comforting—something that would expertly stitch his fraying nerves back together and fill his neglected heart with warmth.

But she doesn't know what.

The words aren't coming.

Not the *right* words.

☾

WHAT LORKAN IS

Meren spends the first hour of their paint-making gnawing the shreds of skin from her bottom lip. After chewing through the prospect of a life without The Prince, then struggling with sympathy for his plight, Meren finally reaches a hard little kernel of empathy for the Calpurzian princess.

She is in a similar position—albeit, for Meren a lot less is at stake.

If Meren can find a reliable, stable man to wed, her parents will be supported right into their old age.

If the princess marries Lorkan, a rift between two warring kingdoms will be filled in.

Although, she realises with a tensing of that muscle by her jaw, the corner the princess has been painted into is much nicer than hers. The princess' future involves beautiful castles, full meals prepared by servants, a gentle, artistic husband by her side and, eventually, a crown atop her head.

Meren's involves wages paid in crescents, enough children to rival a rabbit warren, and a tight little three-roomed lodging to boot.

Eventually, Lorkan drops the subject of diplomacy in exchange for his usual interest in Meren's day, her trip to the market, and the health and happiness of the various people in her life—

But her answers are mostly kept to distracted single syllables.

He must have figured out what's occupying her mind because, after several failed attempts at conversation, he, too becomes unusually withdrawn.

The air so thick with thoughts its consistency resembles that of soup, The Prince and his maid's minds work away silently to themselves as they methodologically pass pastes and pigments and powders back and forth.

Every now and again, an idea pops into Meren's brain space and she sits bolt upright like a startled hare.

She voices it, placing the unformed, desperate little proposal down on the table between them and, together, they pick it apart.

Some are kept; deemed not entirely ludicrous, and stored away for Lorkan to suggest to anyone who will listen. For example: why does the union have to be between people? Why not an actual gift from Velôr to the Calpurzian kingdom? A piece of architecture, or an ancient—probably looted—relic?

However, most of her ideas are so feeble they die before they've even been released; shrivelling up before they've even left her mouth:

Like faking Lorkan's death and simply fleeing the kingdom, never to return.

Sometimes, they think an idea is perfect, indestructible, flawless, only to set it on the table, poke around a bit, and have it shatter like a popped bubble.

Lorkan has been standing at his easel for some time when Meren remembers something else. It seems to have surfaced along with the rest of her contemplations as if she'd pulled one string from a draw and all the rest had come out with it. A pang of guilt makes her face pull into an apologetic grimace as she clears her throat.

"Oh, by the way, I can't stay overtime today."

Lorkan asks a curious little, "Oh?" and she averts her eyes to the pigment she's crushing.

It's as green as a bud on the first day of spring but it's hard to appreciate it, her throat feeling like she's swallowed a large stone. Her voice high and reedy, she mutters:

"I'm meeting someone tonight. For the meteor shower."

She shouldn't be. She should be here, with Lorkan, she thinks, preparing colours for him to dab onto his canvas.

Or brainstorming a way out of that blasted alliance.

Helping him with whatever he needs because—although she knows he shouldn't have—he's become her friend.

He blinks, looking up from dipping his brush into a pale, tanned sort of colour. Some of it has smudged onto his fingertips and, even though the tone is barely that of parchment, it appears dark against his alabaster skin. "You are?"

"Yes. Arne asked me to accompany him."

Lorkan's eyebrows pull together to form one long, dark line across his forehead. "Arne, Frode's apprentice?"

Meren nods.

"I didn't know you felt that way for him."

WHAT LORKAN IS

She opens her mouth to say she doesn't, at least not yet.

She'd like to explain that finding a partner is different for the working class; she has watched the people around her hunt for spouses as though they're picking fallen fruit off the ground, barely inspecting it for worms or bruises before putting it in their basket.

She's been to the weddings that follow quickly—so quickly—after, and thought them bland and formal affairs. The first she'd attended—a friend of her mother—Meren hadn't been able to tell it was a public declaration of love until the actual vows were read. The bride wore a dress cut from a bedsheet, the husband drank too much ale, and he didn't know the names of any of her friends. Despite everything, the guests congratulated them on their union as though they'd managed to dodge a disease.

Weddings in Lorkan's world are no doubt lavish and romantic. He wouldn't understand having to marry as a way to pool money, or bring a child into the world because the family business needs another pair of hands.

"He seems like a nice man, and the meteors are said to be very beautiful."

"When are you meeting him?" Lorkan asks, his words slicing cleanly through Meren's sentence.

He's not looking at her, and he hasn't resumed painting yet, his brush just sort of playing with it in its bowl; dragging swirling patterns into its viscous surface, watching it settle back as it was, and then cutting another line down its centre.

"He's picking me up just after sundown."

Without raising his head, he says:

"You should probably be getting on your way, then."

Meren watches confusedly as he places the paint aside and takes the mortar and pestle from her hands. She looks over at the wide, canvas-like windows.

The evening's sky stretches out across the panes, dusk indeed settling in, but slowly, at its own lazy, leisurely pace. Down in the city, a few chimneys have begun to puff smoke from lit stoves, but not many, the smell of cooked meats and boiling stews not yet wafting through the open window.

Briskly, The Prince helps her up and crosses to the door. Holding it open expectantly, his eyes rest on Meren's with a blank expression she doesn't recognise.

Slightly stunned, she drags herself from her half-ground mortar of green. "I would have stayed if I could," she says, that tooth of guilt sinking into the soft flesh of her heart. "Especially today—"

"Think nothing of it."

She levels with Lorkan outside the studio door, and he closes it, the smooth, cool surface bumping against her shoulder blades. She opens her mouth to make a little surprised sound, but he's already walking away.

She has to pick up her pace to keep in time with his brisk strides, then stops just before he ushers her out of his rooms completely.

"Wait!"

He halts, one pale hand about to curl around the doorknob.

"What pigments do you want me to get tomorrow?"

His shoulders shift and, silently, he turns to the nearest dresser. It's littered with parchment and quills, as are most of the flat surfaces in his chambers, and he plucks up one of the fat white feathers resting amongst the chaos.

When he's noted down tomorrow's pigments, his handwriting unusually slanted and rushed, he hands it to Meren, and she frowns at it.

The list consists of only two colours—the amount he'd need scribbled next to each piteously small. Meren is familiar with the names of each colour by now—the pigments that make them—and she recognises these two immediately.

One is a type of green and the other a delicate pink.

No charcoal-black for his hair.

No white to lighten the portrait's skin tone to his creamy hue.

"Is this all?" she asks, raising her head from the scrap of paper to meet Lorkan's eyes. She can't find them because he's not looking at her.

"Yes. The painting is nearly finished." He doesn't sound nearly as happy about that fact as she thought he would.

WHAT LORKAN IS

When he'd shown her his marketplace piece, he'd seemed bashfully proud, the lightest shade of red touching his cheeks and the tips of his ears at her praise.

Now, though, his voice is flat and as expressionless as his face when he says:

"With the paint we made today, and then this, it will be complete."

Meren opens her mouth but, before she can string them into a sentence, he's saying:

"You really should be going. You'll be late."

13

A DATE WITH ARNE

Meren stands outside The Prince's door, the click of the lock echoing, then fading from the hallway and, eventually, her memory. Prickles of his bad mood still cling to her clothes like angry static and, confusedly, she tries to brush it away.

Like a scribe reeling in past transcripts, she leafs through her previous sentences, searching for...something. Something she's said? Something she's done? She's upset The Prince somehow, that much is clear. If he was angry because she hadn't stayed overtime, that was *his* fault; he'd practically shoved her out the door like she had some kind of plague.

Meren's palms feel empty and too light, the air soft where splintered handles should be. The Prince had been so eager for her to leave, she hadn't managed to grab her cleaning supplies on the way out. Perhaps he'll turn around and see her bucket and mop propped up against the wall? Then the door will open and he'll sheepishly push them into her waiting hands.

She gives him a minute to do so and stands patiently, staring at his door, waiting for it to open. Her eyes slide boredly over the intricate little designs littering its surface; a barn owl with its wide, concave face, a tiny wren perched on the thorny vine of a rose, a narrow, slithering pine martin encircling the door knob...

A fleck of dust passes through a shaft of dying daylight, the corridor silent and lifeless as a tomb.

She'll have to leave her mop and bucket with Lorkan for the night, Meren realises dully. Hopefully, Alfdis doesn't somehow catch wind that she is using The Prince's chambers as her own personal cupboard; the poor woman will never sleep knowing his royal eyes are being sullied by dirty rags and rotting pails.

With a sigh—of puzzlement over the past five minutes, more than anything—Meren begins the long trek to the mess hall. She'll tackle her anxieties over Lorkan's strange behaviour at a later date. For now, she has other things to worry about.

Like the apothecary's apprentice.

Arne had promised to put together a picnic for them both, and Meren hopes she's hungry for it by the time it's presented.

Today, she and Lorkan had worked their way through Aasta's cakes in a matter of minutes. When their hands met with empty space, they'd blinked dully, their brows furrowed as if wondering where everything had gone.

Meren can't remember what they had been. The sweetness about her teeth suggests something with raisins, but she's not sure.

✷ ☾ ✷

As promised, Arne is waiting for Meren as the first slither of moonlight filters down onto the servant's courtyard. Meren has to sift through endless amounts of stars to find its source; that thin crescent of pearly white hanging as if suspended by a string. As they walk, she lets herself revel in the sight of it —as it is—not a soapy reflection on golden steps, or in sneaked peeks between strokes of her mop.

This evening she is not a maid. She doesn't have to sweep or dust or crush anything, she doesn't even have to talk if she doesn't want to.

Arne is not her employer, a prince, a son of the king—he's just a friend.

"Perfect for watching meteorites," he points out, gesturing to the vast expanse of blackness before them, freckled with jewel-like dots; far away suns probably long since deceased (another thing Arne points out).

Meren doesn't think the sky looks like an infinite vacuum. She thinks it more closely resembles a reel of rich velvet material that someone has sprawled over the horizon like a blanket; as if they're trying to hide what lies beyond from view. They've forgotten to remove it, though, and it's gotten dusty; silver pin-pricks of lint turning the secret beautiful.

Her mouth opens to say this to Arne, but it closes again.

He's telling her about *'orbits'* and *'paths'* and logical things like lines and angles.

She'll hold onto it and tell it to Lorkan tomorrow instead—if he's shaken off his strop.

Meren and Arne join the other couples and families already gathered over Elsie's Hill and, after a simple meal of sandwiches and elderflower cordial, they lay back against the reassuring curve of it, their shoulders shielded from the damp grass by a wide jute mat that he's borrowed from his living room.

"I'm sorry I couldn't bring a bit more to eat," he apologises. "I have five mouths to feed back home, not including myself."

"I have to support my parents too," Meren says understandingly, but Arne shakes his head solemnly.

"Actually, I have five sisters. Our parents passed away."

Meren blinks. For some reason, she had imagined Arne's head to be full of quaint, sun-dappled stories entwined with mellow, childish laughter. He looks like someone whose memories are laced with the smell of home-baked pies, warm and golden like a comfortable fire purring away in a hearth.

He doesn't look like that now, though. His eyebrows have wilted into a frown at the sides.

"I'm so sorry."

"Thank you."

"...How did they...? If you don't mind me asking."

"I don't mind. Mum fell ill whilst pregnant, and Dad died as a soldier, so it's just us now."

Respectfully, Meren turns to him on the mat, giving him her full attention—but he nudges her gently back to face the sky.

"You'll miss the shower."

She lets him direct her eyes away from his face, and wonders if he doesn't want her to see him sad. "...Your father worked for Our King?"

"Eventually. During the war, His Majesty managed to push the ice giants right back up into the mountains, and they weren't happy about it. For years afterwards, they kept attacking the villages closest to the borders, trying to claw their way back down south. Dad couldn't stand the thought of those families being driven from their homes, or the thought that the giants might someday reach us, even though we're really far away. He kept saying to my mum, *'What if those were our kids, Mavis?'* He felt a sort of..."

"Responsibility?"

"Yeah. He tried to ignore it for years, but then he saw posters saying the king was getting low on troops and needed volunteers. He left the next day."

A memory flickers in Meren's mind. "I remember those posters. They put them up in my village too. It was the first time most of us had seen a picture of the king. He looked so brave and powerful, Father let me keep the poster on my wall."

"Did your parents fight?"

"No, Father couldn't hurt a fly—even if he wanted to. It's his eyes, you see. And mother's hands wouldn't be able to hold a sword."

"Why not?"

"She has arthritis."

"She needs to take lots of turmeric and ginger," Arne says reflexively, and it makes Meren smile.

"You'll be replacing Frode soon if he's not careful."

"Oh, I wouldn't want that." He hesitates. "I'd actually like to open my own apothecary one day."

"That's a fantastic idea!"

"You think?"

"Of course. I don't see why you couldn't."

"Dad wanted me to be a stonemason like him, making houses and things, so I always felt I should do that." He shifts on the jute rug as if it's tickling, but it can't be; the pile is worn too smooth. "He was so brave, volunteering to protect his kingdom. I feel bad sometimes, hiding behind a counter."

"Your father sound sounds very noble, but there are other ways to help people." Meren turns to him again, but he doesn't tilt her head back to the sky, this time. "You make people better when they're too sick to care for their family, and heal people so they can go back to work. Isn't that helping your kingdom?"

"I guess you're right."

They fall into a content sort of silence, broken only by a group of children chasing each other down the hill, giggling when they land in a heap of limbs at the bottom.

Meren can't imagine this place scarred with streaks of rampant fires and blood, the air writhing with the sounds of battle. If it ever had been, it has healed well, and quickly.

"I've never really heard anyone talk about the war," she muses. "Not in detail."

Arne shakes his head. "A lot of people won't because it makes them sad. dPlus, no one really knows what happened. They just know their warriors come home."

"How could they not know what happened?"

"Because no one that was there says anything about it, and it was so high up in the mountains no one down here saw anything."

Pictures of gnarled monsters ripping through the marketplace with ice blades extinguish themselves before Meren's eyes. "Wait, the mountains? So the Hyluniens didn't actually get into the city?"

"No, our king quelled them long before they even got to the foot of The Three Piques."

She finds a sigh sliding from her lungs, and moves her arms up to cross behind her head.

Arne looks at her as though he thought she was going to touch him, and her cheeks heat.

The sky is still, the meteorites taking their sweet time in arriving.

"Do you get along with your sisters?" Meren asks—because the air is so empty besides the glinting stars.

Her question brings a smile to Arne's lips, and it makes the darkness seem brighter. "Most of the time. But they're also little minxes."

He doesn't *sound* like he thinks they're minxes, Meren thinks fondly.

Angling her head, she can see other couples dotted about their hill, their soft, hushed conversations buzzing about like moths in the gloom. The couples look like cake decorations; sprinkles dusted over the mound of earth and grass. Some are clearly familiar lovers, nestled almost on top of each other. Others are—like Meren and Arne—shyly keeping a respectful foot apart, bashfully averting their gaze to the heavens when they catch each other's eyes.

Meren wonders if they're blushing for the same reason she blushes when Arne looks at her.

She blushes because he hardly knows her, really, and yet, somehow, the little time they've spent together is enough for him to be edging his hand across the mat towards hers.

Enough for him to be telling her, now, about the cottage he resides in, the dog his sisters are so fond of, all of their names and—

She sneaks a look over at his shadow sprawled next to her.

He's saying something about a vegetable patch in the back garden; cucumbers, carrots, potatoes...

He's building a house around her, low little walls paid for by an apothecary's salary, hand-stitched curtains and wood-whittled furniture but, rather than setting her heart aflutter excitedly as it should, the sentences wrap about her middle like rope.

She should be having the same thoughts; wishing it was lighter so she could properly admire his open, freckled face, his soft, fluffy cheeks, wondering what he'll look like in ten, twenty, thirty years, and not being able to wait to find out.

"It's starting," Arne says and, for a second, Meren furrows her brow at him. "The meteor shower. Look." He's gesturing at the sky and she follows the line of his arm, up and up to a tiny light.

It blooms, then slides across the sky like a raindrop down a window. They watch its blazing trail, her lips parted in wonder—

Then it is gone.

Meren turns to Arne, her brow furrowed. Probably guessing what she'd been thinking, he laughs a boyish chuckle, and reaches out. Softly turning her face back to the sky:

"There's more," he says, and Meren settles back onto the mat, tugging her shawl tighter about her shoulders.

The air is bitter, a brisk chill stroking her bare hands and face with each breath of the wind.

Suddenly, the sky comes alive, meteorites blooming, dribbling down the sky then petering out.

Some last but a second, a brief, brilliant blip and then they're gone, others stream across the entire length of the horizon in a graceful arc, their tail trailing like smoke.

At first, they appear sparsely, lighting up the night and then plunging it into darkness with their demise, however, their numbers quickly multiply into a chaotic dance. Like a jar of fireflies, they begin tumbling over one another, sometimes ten at once, cutting the velvet night to shreds.

Meren wonders if Lorkan is watching the shower too, up in the pointed spire of a tower.

He must be so close he could reach out and touch one, their blazing trails scorching his pale fingertips.

WHAT LORKAN IS

✶ ☾ ✶

When the last light has long since died and the night has once more closed in on itself, Arne walks Meren back to Aldercliff, exhilarated recollections of what they'd just witnessed pouring from their grinning faces.

He doesn't ask her for anything she is not willing to give. He simply bids her a verbal, friendly goodnight and the promise that, had his arms not been full with his jute rug and picnic basket, he would politely tip his cap.

Meren gives him a kiss on the cheek anyway, pushing herself up on tiptoes to do so. "Thank you, Arne. I had a wonderful time."

She did.

Her chest is still tingling with the magic of it.

However, even as her lips touch to his fuzzy stubble, the apothecary's apprentice fails to excite her half as much as the meteorites had.

As she pads down into the servant's quarters, that realisation breaks her heart.

✶ ☾ ✶

Meren's eyes droop a little as she tentatively knocks on The Prince's chambers the next morning.

The meteor shower had cut a large chunk out of her sleep and, even though it was worth it, the consequences are quickly making themselves known.

Sleep itself, when eventually achieved, had been fitful and patchy. The meteor shower itself had proven a worthy distraction from the undulating soup of thoughts, worries, and emotions currently sloshing about her skull.

She had stomped them down enough to enjoy her evening, but—once it was all over— they'd once again reared their ugly heads like angry beasts escaped from a cage.

A curious amount of Meren's thoughts had been centred around Lorkan's plights rather than her own.

The idea of him *having* to marry someone bothers her more than she thinks it should and, the more she turned over the *reason* for her emotional involvement, the more distressed she became.

She doesn't want him to marry the Calpurzian princess.

She doesn't want him to marry *any* princess, any prince, any woman, or man.

The mental image of it—vows and kisses and shyly clasped hands—made something tighten around her neck like a noose, a muscle in her jaw feathering as if it's trying to break free.

And something sad wilt and die deep in her chest.

Saving him from a life tied to a woman he barely knows—and certainly doesn't love—wasn't the only thing rampaging its way around Meren's brain late last night.

She couldn't stop contemplating Lorkan's sudden—and somewhat irrational—change of character the evening before. She had replayed their interactions over and over in her head hundreds of times and still couldn't identify what she'd said or done that might have upset him.

Having turned the key in his lock, her hand stops. Instead of nudging it open, she finds it raising to give a timid knock.

Thirty seconds of silence dribble in like sand through a glass.

When she steps inside, her cleaning supplies greet her coldly, her mop still boredly propped against the wall.

Making a mental note to replace the dirty water, she strays to the study to set today's pigments down on the table. It seems to take her longer than usual to trail through the string of rooms, and when she can finally see the study door, it takes her quite a while to reach it.

It's hanging open, a narrow plank of light seeping through the gap.

WHAT LORKAN IS

For the first time, she hesitates, the knowledge that The Prince is just on the other side making her pause. For a moment, she considered doing what servants are supposed to do: silently leaving the pigments on a nearby countertop like an unseen, helpful elf.

She's half a second away from turning around and scuttling back to her mop when the door opens.

The Prince fills its frame, looking down at her.

Well, Lorkan is looking down at her, the glow from the window just about sneaking between his shoulder and the jamb.

He looks more like Lorkan now, that small smile Meren has become so fond of gracing his narrow lips.

It feels good to receive it, and her shoulders visibly loosen.

"Sorry, I didn't hear you come in." He steps aside to let her pass, his usual, welcoming gesture sweeping her into the room.

Hesitantly, she returns his smile.

"My apologies for snapping at you yesterday," he utters. His eyes run away from hers, hiding below his hair. "I'm under a lot of pressure. That's not an excuse, I'm just explaining my actions. Please don't make the mistake of thinking my anger was directed at—or caused by—you."

"It's okay," Meren mutters meekly, and he shakes his head.

"It's not. I shouldn't have treated you that way. I—"

He's saying more things, handing over apologies and pressing them into her palms, but she tosses them away, letting them scatter at their feet.

The easel is empty.

"Where's the picture?" She asks, so preoccupied she doesn't even realise she'd interrupted a prince.

Stepping closer, the air still smells strongly of paint, even with a refreshing breeze sliding through the window. It passes through the empty easel as if they were winter branches and her eyes narrow.

"You didn't do that thing some artists do, did you?"

"What thing?"

"Have a fit of passion and throw the whole thing in the fireplace."

A laugh ghosts her ear, and she turns to come face to face with the light material of Lorkan's shirt. It's plain, besides a line of buttons down the middle; transparent, glassy things like dewdrops on a leaf. The first three are lazily left open.

It makes her mouth go dry, so she looks back at the easel.

It looks strange. Empty. Wrong. Its three spindly little stick legs appear too light without a hefty block of stretched cotton, wooden frame, and slathering of paint to weigh it down. Meren is almost afraid it'll start rising off the ground—catch flight like a crane fly—and escape over the window sill.

"No," Lorkan soothes, clearly registering her distress. His silken tones curl around her nerves, pacifying them like a heavy palm soothing an anxious cat. His words, however, have the opposite effect when he says simply:

"I just wanted to finish it by myself."

Meren blinks up at him, feeling like he's suddenly and forcefully slammed a door in her face—a door that had, for the past few months, been wide and welcomingly open. Trying to iron out the surprise—and disappointment—from her expression, she moistens her lips and turns back to the easel.

"How was the meteor shower?" Lorkan is asking, perhaps to distract her from the hollow, canvas shaped void in the centre of the room.

"Magical."

There is a pause while Meren lets her eyes follow a column of sunlight from the paint-speckled floor to the massive panes of glass on the opposite wall.

The kingdom stretches out across their entire length, the top half of the frame filled with a deep bowl of blue sky, the lower half stuffed with hundreds of rooftops; like a child has spilt all her toy blocks onto a green carpet.

"Did you catch it?" she asks. "You must have a great view from here."

"Yes, it was beautiful," Lorkan says from some way behind her. "It made a nice change of pace. Usually, I just get to looking at planets."

This *does* make Meren spin around to face him.

"You can see other planets? How?"

WHAT LORKAN IS

"With a telescope," he replies simply. He'd given a tiny shrug of the broad line of his shoulders, his buttons lightning up as they shift about.

They're like his eyes, Meren later contemplates; always changing colour; deep pine-needle green one minute, then a silvery sage the next.

She looks blank, so he clarifies:

"The machine in the lounge by the window." The corners of his lips tug into a ghost of a smirk, one dark eyebrow arching. "Didn't you ever take a look through it when you were dusting? Out of curiosity?"

"Look *through* it?" She frowns crossly as Lorkan actually opens his mouth to *laugh* at her, the smooth wedges of his teeth exposed.

"Come on, I'll show you."

14

THE TELESCOPE

Lorkan leads Meren through his rooms, his bare feet soundless as they pad over the hard floor.

It varies widely from room to room—some areas raised, others lowered—sunken down and lined with soft pillows or curving settees. It is impossible to walk in an unwavering line as the crow flies. They have to meander, avoiding pits and platforms, tables, pillars and columns, stacks of books, huge model globes, pot plants—

The floor is swamped in light; it drains in through numerous windows, each room at least waist deep. Every time Meren treads on a patch of it, she can feel the sun's pleasing warmth through the thin material of her slippers.

She stares at Lorkan's airy trousers as she tries to keep up, watching the baggy hem flap loosely about his pale ankles. Her mouth almost opens to ask how his feet never seem to suffer from cold.

Yes, his chambers benefit from a surplus of natural light, but that doesn't change the fact that the majority of his flooring is polished flagstones, heavy gold, or cool slabs of marble. How can he be comfortable going without so much as a slip-on shoe, or a pair of light stockings at least? Affording them is definitely not an issue.

And his clothes.

When they'd first met—what feels like decades ago—he'd only been draped in wide, spacious trousers, and a matching shirt; both made from that green, gauzy material he's so fond of. As he'd politely asked her to extend the raw palms of her hands, his breath hadn't even bloomed in front of his mouth.

Meren is so focused on this that she doesn't notice he's come to a stop.

With a muffled sound, she walks straight into his triangular-shaped back.

He just blinks down at her curiously—as though she's a small butterfly that has just flown into him by accident.

"Hello," he chuckles, the sound a rumbling curl of amusement.

Turning the colour of strawberries, she chokes out a little '*Sorry,*'—

But he ignores it.

He's drawn to a stop where two windows meet at a corner, creating an unbroken, panoramic view of the kingdom.

Nestled between them—as though designed specifically to sit in such a place—stands the golden, barrel-like thing.

She's spent many lonely hours polishing its long, curved body, watching it stretch and warp her reflection. She likes to pull funny faces at it; sticking her tongue out and crossing her eyes as she rubs fingerprints from the little dials.

Now, dully, Meren figures this must be the famed 'telescope'—although, she still has no idea how it works.

Up until now, she didn't even know it could 'work'. The fact that it was always so covered in fingerprints *at all* only puzzled her more.

"We won't be able to see any planets because it's daytime," Lorkan is explaining, and she takes a step closer.

"I thought this was some kind of statue I didn't understand," she muses, watching as Lorkan does something quite strange.

A little stub of metal branches off from the main frame, and he dips his head to the narrow end, resting one eye against it.

Meren would have assumed he'd gone slightly mad, had one of his slender hands not been expertly fiddling with the knobs, turning them one way and then the next, each adjustment minute and delicate and laced with purpose.

As he turns it, part of the machine—for Meren has realised that that's what this thing is—a *machine*—moves slightly. It elongates, just a fraction, the largest part of it inclining a centimetre or two towards the windowpane, then edges back again like the neck of a tortoise retreating into its shell.

"It's not art, technically, but I think it's easily beautiful enough to be, don't you?" Lorkan asks, his face still lowered to the tapered end of the telescope.

Meren nods, then remembers he can't see her.

He's still fiddling with things and squinting into that little stub of metal protruding from the skinny end of the golden tube.

"Yes." It is beautiful, she'd always thought so, even if she didn't understand it.

Is there something *inside* it? Is that what Lorkan is staring at so intently?

"I like the big end," she adds, watching his slim fingers continue to turn various things. "The end full of curved glass. It feels like looking into a giant eye."

Satisfied with whatever he'd been doing, he straightens, his mouth curved into a good-natured smile.

This object is clearly one of his most prized possessions. His passion for it—whatever it is—plainly goes beyond the fact that it's worth a lot of money. As he gestures to it excitedly, Meren realises that he's eager to show it off to her, and listens attentively.

"You're kind of right, it is like a giant eye. But it's not *full* of glass; not in the way you're thinking, anyway." He gives her a knowing look, the edge of a smirk tugging one side of his mouth. "You were picturing it like water in a cup, the glass filling the tube until it almost overflows at this end, right?"

He gestures to the large, curved bud of glass pointing at the horizon, more amused than condescending.

Meren gets the sense he's nudging her along.

WHAT LORKAN IS

She nods, because that's *exactly* how she'd imagined it.

She'd never dared try to move or push the telescope over, but she could easily feel its sturdiness, its mass, as she dragged a rag back and forth over its robust legs. They're not dainty like the easel's, they're planted firmly on the tiled floor, so dense she assumed it *had* to be full of glass.

"It actually has several pieces of glass rather than just one. The whole thing is hollow so light can travel up and down it. This piece takes in the light." Lorkan gestures at the wider end. "It's curved so it can bend it into focus, then it travels down this tube." His extended finger slides along the long length of the telescope's barrel-like body. "Then there's a mirror here." The finger comes to a halt. "Which reflects the light and sends it to the eyepiece."

Meren tilts her head to the side, narrowing her eyes to picture bright lines of light pinging about the inside of the tube, getting stretched and pulled. What confuses her, though, is:

"Why?"

Lorkan's smile grows, like a child about to unwrap a present, or play a particularly devious prank on an unsuspecting peer—or both. One hand rests tenderly at the eyepiece, and Meren knows he's looking forward to letting her look into it; for whatever reason.

"This is how I drew that picture of the deer."

When she still looks sceptical, he steps back, gesturing at the machine as though offering her a chair.

"Take a look. You don't need to adjust anything, just look through the part I was looking through."

Not knowing what he means by '*adjust*' let alone how she would go about doing so, Meren hesitantly moves around to take Lorkan's place.

Awkwardly, she bends over the narrow end of the tube, one eye leaning against the wooden cradle, trying to replicate his earlier stance.

At first, she has one eyebrow raised, still half wondering whether this is all some kind of elaborate ruse; she'd place her eye on that little cup-shaped bit, and then something would happen; she doesn't know what, but it would make Lorkan laugh.

After all, why else would a prince take the time to introduce a member of the help to such a machine if not to amuse himself?

But she'd seen him look through it to no ill effects, and now that she's in the correct position (she assumes it is correct; he hasn't told her otherwise), it feels rather comfortable.

At first, Meren can see nothing.

She knows she is supposed to see *something*, though; something to do with light.

Blinking, she moves her head slightly, bringing it a little further back so she's hovering somewhere above the rim of the cradle rather than plating her eye socket right up against it.

Suddenly, she can see everything.

Well, not everything; she can only see a narrow *part* of everything—but she can see it really well.

Inside the tube, four leaves dance in time with the wind, their shiny underbellies flashing as they catch the sun.

She falls back in shock, taking a few steps away from the telescope. Her jaw opens and closes but no words come; they're all jammed up in her throat, fighting to be the first out of her mouth.

Lorkan is laughing. Unguarded, proper laughs bubbling all the way up from his stomach like beads of air in a glass of mead.

"I don't understand," Meren manages to stammer, her gaze darting from the window to the telescope, and back to the window again.

The sun's rays are falling in the same direction, the wind rolling over the kingdom to the same rhythm as it had tugged at the tree.

There's a silver poplar reaching out over the water garden, its own leaves quivering, falling away, fluttering to balance on the lily pool.

"It was like looking through a miniature window with trees right outside. But the trees aren't right outside, they're all the way over there—"

"You *are* looking at those trees." Lorkan calms his chuckles enough to point along the barrel of the telescope to the poplar tree.

Unaware it's being spied on by a prince and a maid, it continues its dance.

"The telescope makes things you're looking at appear bigger. That's what the glass does when it bends the light."

Meren, still in some kind of shock, just blinks, and Lorkan keeps talking, perhaps scared he's broken her.

"You know when you look through a glass of water, everything on the other side seems larger?"

She nods, managing to break her gaze from the telescope and bring it up to watch his face as, calmly, he dismantles the miracle she'd just witnessed as if it were nothing more than a simple trick to stupefy children.

"The glass does the same thing as the water, just better. So much better, we can see things way off in the distance."

Tentatively, she approaches the eyepiece again, and bends down to it, holding in a breath. She's ready for it this time, so she doesn't leap back—but it still makes her jaw fall open as she stares, wide-eyed.

One of the leaves twists, exposing a map of finger-like veins.

Her hand twitches to reach out and grab it.

"Are you sure it's not magic?" She asks when she's found her voice again, and hears another amused chuckle—from beside her, this time.

"Not magic, just physics."

Lorkan has gotten closer, and Meren continues to stare, awestruck, at the twirling leaves all those yards away.

With the tangy sweetness of his cologne, it's as though she can smell them —the sap from the tree—pollen and bark and fresh air. They might as well be in the water garden right now, taking a stroll amongst the moist mossy grass.

She watches the leaves tossing themselves about in the breeze, finding it strange she can't hear them; as though she has suddenly turned deaf. It makes her long for that familiar susurration of membranes brushing up against each other each, the rattling wind through each twig, like air into lungs.

"This is how you drew the deer? You made it look bigger by looking through this?" She pulls away from the machine, her head admittedly starting to feel like a marble is rolling about inside it.

Lorkan nods, something lighting his pale eyes to a pleasant, pastel green. "Exactly."

"So it can look at other things? Not just this tree?"

This gets another little laugh; as if he finds the idea of a machine designed to focus on one particular piece of foliage very amusing.

Meren's cheeks colour at her incompetence, and she'd like to hide it by ducking back to the telescope.

"Yes, it can look at whatever you point it at and, by turning this dial, you can see things closer or farther away."

"Can we look at the town?"

"Now?"

She blushes again, realising he hadn't meant it literally. "Sorry, is it difficult to do? You made it sound easy."

"No, it's not difficult. It's just, you see the town every day. You can look at anything, the forest, the mountainside, ships on the ocean, whatever you want."

"I know. But can we see the town first? I want to see all the people walking about."

* ☾ *

With a smile, Lorkan re-adjusts the telescope so Meren can peer at the unsuspecting patrons of a stall selling fruit, a barber, and a family taking a morning constitutional.

When she asks to see the other things he'd mentioned, forests and ships, he introduces her to them too.

On the sixteenth time she asks him to rotate and adjust the lens, he gently nudges her out of the way.

"How about I just show you how to operate it, then you can spy on things to your heart's content."

She watches attentively as he shows her how—if she unfastens a clasp on each side of the barrel—the whole thing can swing around on an axis, taking in the mountains to the left, or Kat's Estuary to the right. If she turns the delicate dials on the side, she can take in the entirety of them, stretched out like a mirror or—if she turns the other way—she can burrow right into a rook's nest and watch the ugly, cawing chicks, their eyes black and beady, their heads fluffy and bald.

Making sure not to block her view of the window, Lorkan stands patiently while she explores.

Every now and again, she points at something excitedly and urges him over to have a look.

As she moves aside, he bends to nod interestedly at a woodpecker, a sleeping cat, a man absolutely covered in tattoos—

However, after several uninterrupted minutes of staring fixedly towards the north, he clears his throat, his amused smirk stretched over the telescope's golden body.

"Surely you can't see anything up there?"

Angling the bulging lens as far to the left as it can go, Meren turns the dials, trying to bring one of the mountain's craggy faces into focus. "I'm looking for ice giants," she explains, blushing as the words fog the curved metal inches from her nose. "But it's all just shards of ice and slate."

"Hm, I think if you're hoping to find life, you're looking in the wrong direction."

Agreeing disappointedly, she finds the glistening, snake-like curves of the river Sygg and follows them back down through the base of the mountains. The further south she goes, the more boats she spots, dragged along by the current like leaves in a gutter. Gradually, the riverbanks sprout houses like mushrooms until she's caught in the thick of the city centre. She's about to point a small, sausage-shaped dog out to Lorkan, but something catches her eye.

He must notice her surprise because he asks:

"What's wrong?"

"Nothing's *wrong*, it's just...I think that man has an amphithere."

Bringing the lens into focus, she moves aside so he can bend over the eyepiece.

"Ah, that's father's advisor and his pet. He's always had it. Well, her." Sensing Meren's interest, he relents the eyepiece once more, allowing her to track the man through the crowd.

Moving fast for a short, plump gentleman, he's easy to find, his robes a rich blackcurrant purple and intricately darned, standing out against his pale, hairless head.

Meren suspects his fine clothes are leaving a trail of rosewater scent in his wake, the way people's heads are turning to watch him pass. He clasps a neat stack of envelopes in one of his doughy hands, but what had caught her interest is the other.

With a curled finger, it's caressing the head of a snake-like creature curled around his thick shoulders. The length of a cat and thin as a rope, the dragon doesn't react to his touch besides fractionally angling its head as though enjoying what dregs of heat the afternoon sun provides.

"I've never seen one like that before," she observes, absently.

Indeed, the amphithere's scales are more skin-like than reptilian, and she can't decide whether it's just a sort of wounded pinkish colour, or if she's looking directly at its twisted, blood-filled innards.

"Me neither," Lorkan says, but with much less interest. "Although, we don't get them in the royal gardens."

"Oh, you won't. They like dry grass. They were everywhere where I grew up. They'd hide in the wheat and bite our ankles."

The reflection of Lorkan's eyes widens, their green hue momentarily giving the telescope decorative, emerald studs. "Did it hurt?"

Meren shrugs. "It's like being bitten by a cat."

She can tell by his look that he's never experienced that either. "It's sort of prickly, like a rose bush."

This, he understands.

WHAT LORKAN IS

"Most of them are okay, but some are poisonous. Not to us, but one killed my neighbour's sheepdog."

"That's awful!"

"Yeah. They're small but they have venom to catch mice and things. You have to avoid the colourful ones, the brighter they are, the worse their fangs are, usually. Us kids were taught a rhyme about it."

An amused smile tweaks Lorkan's mouth. "How did it go?"

She pulls away from the telescope just so he can see her eyes roll. "I knew you were going to ask that."

"Of course you did."

With a sigh, Meren dips into a faded memory, and dusts it off. "Black, brown grey, he's okay. Green, pink, blue, no dinner for you. Red, yellow white, you'll lose the fight."

Lorkan raises an eyebrow, puzzled. "No dinner?"

"Because it wouldn't kill you but you'll get sick."

"I see."

Meren turns back to the telescope to see which part of the rhyme the advisor's amphithere slots into, turning the dial to adjust the lens.

Despite standing out from the crowd like a reel of satin amongst burlap, the man manages to disappear by the time the fuzziness pulls into focus.

※ ☾ ※

Time slips sideways, the telescope becoming warm where Meren's hand has sat on the dials, spying on this and that from her vantage point like a hawk from a rooftop.

At some point, Lorkan had strayed from the window and spread himself over a nearby chaise lounge.

Meren only realises he's gone when she finally pulls away from the eyepiece. Feeling as though she's surfacing from a vast time spent underwater, she winces, forcing her spine to straighten out. The vertebrae protest after so long bent her at a right angle, but her grin hasn't left her face. Catching Lorkan's slight smile, her cheeks heat.

"Thank you for letting me use your telescope. I feel like I've explored an entire side of the kingdom whilst swaddled in an invisibility cloak." She narrows her eyes at him. "You don't have one of those too, do you?"

The corner of his lip twitches. "Alas no, I think you'd have to head to Calpurzia for such a thing. And I'm glad you enjoyed it."

"I'm sorry I used it for so long; I fear I rather lost track of time."

"It's quite alright."

"You could have told me to leave it alone if you wanted to."

"Yes, I could have. If I wanted to."

"Surely you were getting bored?"

"Quite the contrary."

He does *seem* quite content; his long legs stretched out before him, one arm lazily bent over the armrest to prop up his pointed chin.

"But I haven't done any work!"

"Oh well."

"It's not '*oh well,*' Lorkan, I get paid to clean—or make paint, now, I guess — not spy on people. You should have stepped in and stopped me."

"But you were having fun."

"I'm not paid to have fun! Goodness, if Alfdis had walked in—"

"Yes, she'd be appalled," he agrees, but the corner of his narrow lip is twitching again.

"You never told me to stop so, really, it's *your* fault."

"Definitely." His eyes twinkle, and her neck heats as she realises he's ruffling her feathers on purpose.

Trying to smooth the annoyed frown between her brows, she sighs. "I should get back to work and do something useful."

He merely shrugs as if it's all the same to him, and stands, stretching his arms up over his head. "Are you *sure* you don't want to play with the telescope some more?"

WHAT LORKAN IS

Momentarily forgetting herself, Meren gives his side a playful little shove.

It takes a fifth of a second for her to realise what she'd done.

A pang of horror skitters its way down her spine.

"Sorry," she utters quickly, taking a hasty step back.

Even though his smile had widened.

And he'd let himself go floppy enough to be pushed, falling pliantly to the left.

And his pale cheekbones had turned slightly pink.

✶ ☾ ✶

The usual ease and familiarity of their friendship back and as strong as ever, Meren had been hoping that, when they returned to the studio, Lorkan would bring out his painting and set it back on the easel where it belongs.

She'd prepare his pigments, and he'd kneel at her side, waiting patiently until the first paints are ready. Then he'd migrate to the easel and start dabbing them on, pausing every now and again to squint and stare, occasionally straying back to take a bite of cake.

However, as Meren sinks into her pillow at the low, paint-stained table—rather than retrieving the painting—Lorkan neatly crosses his legs next to her.

Despite whatever happened yesterday evening, his demeanour is more than amicable, and they pass playful conversations back and forth as usual.

He asks Meren about her day, and tells her about his.

When he catches her eyeing the box, he offers her the last of Aasta's iced buns—even though he knows she'll politely refuse it.

He throws her quips and jokes, trying to pull laughter from her lungs, and grins when he succeeds—

But the easel remains bare, looming like a hollow ghost.

When he used to paint in Meren's presence, Lorkan would narrow his eyes at the colours already on the canvas or smeared across his palette, and mix the new paint accordingly—but not this time. Now, when he accepts the pummelled pigments from her hands, he adjusts its viscosity, transparency and hue from memory.

Meren opens her mouth to ask how he knows how much egg white and oils to add, but closes it again; Lorkan has stared at that same image for so many hours, it's probably etched into the inside of his skull.

Usually, they'll make paint until they have to light the sconces, Lorkan squinting at his colours through the flickering flames. But, as Meren wraps the last bowl of paint in a swatch of waxed oilcloth, they glisten, still saturated with afternoon sun.

It has quickly become obvious that Lorkan had requested Meren's services not because he wants his rooms tended to, but because he wants someone to prepare his pigments. With her help, he doesn't have to put his painting on hold to mash and stir things; she does that quietly in the background, letting him remain focused on the task at hand.

Plus, he seems to like the company.

That is why—now that she's set her pestle and mortar aside hours earlier than usual—Meren doesn't really know how to proceed.

Stretching the cloth tight and tying it with twine, she places the bowl with the rest, her unoccupied hands coming to rest self-consciously on the table.

"Do you want me to catch up on the cleaning I didn't do this morning?" She offers a little awkwardly, and Lorkan turns to her, suddenly thoughtful.

"Not particularly. Do you want to take the rest of the day off? I won't tell Alfdis, so you'll still get a full day's wages."

His generosity doesn't surprise her by now, but these strange new words taste odd as she chews them over.

The autumn's brisk winds seem to have experienced a rare change of heart, choosing to blow a sweet, tepid breeze off the east coast. The clouds are sparse and thin as cobwebs, and Meren looks at the stretch of blue sky laid out across the window—

—then at the man kneeled by her side.

WHAT LORKAN IS

It's cool inside Lorkan's studio, the wooden tables and shelves shaded like a forest of varnished tree trunks, and she realises she loves it as one would usually love sunshine and birdsong. She's become fond of the cold because Lorkan is always cold. He's sensitive and generous and all those other things usually attributed with warmth, but he's not warm, he's cool like a refreshing shower at the end of a sweaty day. He's a cold towel to the forehead during a fever, a chilled drink after a salty meal. He's paddling in a stream and dipping toes in the bitter waves of the ocean.

She'd much rather spend the rest of the day here, with him.

"I don't need a day off."

Lorkan opens his mouth, but she adds before he can argue with her:

"I don't know what I'd do with one. Why don't I just stay here and catch up on some work—you know—as your *housemaid?* I honestly think you keep forgetting that that's what I am." She frowns. "I'm a cleaner that never actually gets around to doing any cleaning."

Her tone makes Lorkan's lip twitch into a smile, but it withers, falling sideways a little. "...It doesn't feel... *right;* watching a woman clean while I just lounge about—"

"But that's my *job*—"

"—so how about I help you?"

15

SOAP TABLETS

It took Lorkan several minutes to explain the concept of '*help*' to Meren, then several minutes more to persuade her to let him actually do it.

"I used to clean every single one of these rooms myself before you came along," he protests indignantly—a curt reminder that he isn't exactly useless.

"I don't mean you don't have the *ability* to help me," Meren spells out, her cheeks heating at the thought that she'd insulted him. "I mean you *shouldn't* help me. A prince doing a *maid's* job? Mopping and dusting and *scrubbing.*" The words feel rough and gritty on her tongue; amorphous blobs of syllables clunking about her mouth. "If Alfdis knew I'd let you do my chores for me she'd—"

"Alfdis won't find out." He shrugs. "And I'm not doing them *for* you, I'm doing them *with* you. I don't understand why you aren't leaping at a paid day off. You should be out there right now, enjoying the sun, reading, going for a walk in the woods or something. That's what I'd be doing."

"Are you trying to get rid of me?" Meren teases, her tone is light with humour, but her heart waiting to sink like a stone.

WHAT LORKAN IS

Lorkan dips his head, prying a wad of dried paint from a crack in the table with his thumb. "Actually, I find your company incredibly desirable."

※ ☾ ※

Meren permits Lorkan to assist her with the cleaning of his rooms on the condition that he doesn't tell Alfdis.

"Or *anyone*, for that matter," she adds, for once leading him through his chambers rather than the other way around.

"Who would I tell?"

"And don't call it 'assisting'. Or 'helping'. It feels wrong. In fact," Meren states as they locate her mop and bucket—still in the same place it has been for a day now. "Don't call it anything. You're not *doing* anything, you're just...following me around and occasionally *choosing* to wipe surfaces, okay?"

"Goodness, even The Royal Guard doesn't have so many rules."

"This isn't funny! If anyone found out you're doing this, I could get fired!"

When he still doesn't wipe that smile from his lips, Meren huffs up at him, a frown furrowed between her brows. "What *are* you finding so entertaining?"

"Oh, I don't know. Perhaps the idea of you—a tiny maid—bossing me—a *prince*—around in my own palace?"

He smirks down at her in a way that makes her cheeks go pink—which makes him smirk more.

"You look like a little bunny rabbit trying to order around a carthorse."

Electing to ignore that, Meren turns back to her heap of supplies, and begins rootling about for something *clean* she can give him—perhaps a fresh tin of beeswax and a nice fresh rag?

"If you want to stop at any time, please do. In fact, you should just stop right now, you go sit somewhere and I'll make you a cup of tea—"

This goes on for some time.

Lorkan regards her silently, that hint of amusement tweaking at his mouth and arching his eyebrows. When Meren eventually finishes lecturing that he is *not* helping her, he gives a light shrug, says 'okay', and plucks the bucket of dirty water off the ground.

Meren makes a little yelping noise as he starts carrying it in the direction of the washroom. "What are you *doing!?*"

"Helping you."

Scampering at his heels, she can't see his face, but she knows it's etched with a grin—all smug and pleased with himself.

With ease, he plonks the bucked down on the lip of the sink, the cracked wood grating against the delicate blue tiles.

Meren winces as the dirty water cascades into the plughole with a gulping sound, a brown droplet splashing onto Lorkan's bare toes.

"Stop making squeaking noises," he chides, turning the tap so that new, crystal clear water starts to pour into the pail.

"I'm sorry it's just...the sink."

"The sink is fine."

"What if you scratched it?"

"It doesn't matter." As if it's second nature, he plucks a round, coin-sized tablet from the basket on the counter and drops it into the tap's roaring stream with a satisfying plop.

'*So that's what they are*', Meren thinks, her mood switching from anguish to curiosity.

Immediately, the tablet begins producing prickly little streams of fizzy bubbles, foaming the water like a head of poorly poured mead.

She'd eyed that tidy heap of chalky capsules every time she'd wiped a rag over the looking glass. The soap in the servant's quarters are simple, chunky bars of sour-smelling detergent; like giant blackcurrant-flavoured throat lozenges. Because of this, Meren had originally been under the impression these white pellets were some kind of sweet—perhaps a breath mint. She *had* wondered why anyone would want mints whilst on the loo, and just assumed it was one of the many parts of royal life she would never understand.

WHAT LORKAN IS

Now, watching the bucket plume with suds, she's pleased she never dared to swipe one and pop it in her mouth.

The bucket takes a while to fill, so Lorkan reaches out a hand and turns the hot tap on as well.

Meren makes made another whimpering noise.

"You're doing it again," he points out.

"I can't help it!" she whines. "You're wasting hot water. I always fill the bucket down the *hall* so I don't—"

Lorkan turns to her at this, raising one black eyebrow as if she'd said something quite mad. "Down the hall?"

Meren mirrors the look exactly. "Don't look at me like that, from where I'm standing, *you're* the mad one. And, yes, I use the servants' utility room; it's where we have lunch delivered, fill our buckets and…you know…" her cheeks redden. "Use the facilities. You *can't* use a prince's washroom as a cleaning station, Lorkan."

"It may have escaped your notice, Meren, but I *am* that prince. And I say why not? It's right here." His furrowed brow deepens with yet more bemusement.

"You're telling me you walk all the way to the other side of the building with a full bucket of water, *even though* there's a perfectly good sink right here?"

"Yes."

"And, the whole time you've worked here, you've *never* used this lavatory?"

"No."

He inclines his wide shoulders simply. "You're an idiot."

The bucket full and rising high with fluffy white foam, Lorkan lifts it from the basin and starts walking back towards her mop still standing to attention in the other room.

He's memorised her routine, Meren realises.

He knows which room she's finished, and which she'll tackle next.

Composing herself, she strides after his bare heels again, her hands planted squarely on her hips.

"*You're* the idiot. What next? You're going to use your own clothes to mop the floors? Polish the windows with your silk duvet?"

Lorkan turns to face her at this, a single, swift rotation of his whole body. He's walking backwards just so he can grin down at her with a smile so cheeky it makes her want to slap it off his face. "Would that annoy you?"

"Yes, it *would* annoy me!"

His pale eyes—now twinkling in a way that makes Meren's insides flop about like a fish out of water—drop to the frothing bucket in his right hand, then back to his housemaid's challenging glower. "...What if I tipped all this water straight onto the floor?"

Her eyes widen.

This is obviously the effect he had been hoping for, because he's grinning like a cat that's learnt to use a tin opener.

It makes Meren nervous.

"What? You can't do that—"

"Why not? It's my room, I do what I want." He sets the bucket down, and she finds her eyes narrowing into another grimace.

She usually keeps her pail atop a rag or a towel to make sure no little bits of gravelly dust etch grooves into the floor.

She swallows. "But—it'll go everywhere."

"That is rather the point."

"I'll have to clean it up."

On its toes, his bare foot walks towards the base of the bucket. "No, I will."

She meets his gaze, *her* stare hardened with challenge, *his* sparkling with mischief.

A little trail of foam has seeped over the brim of the pail and trickled down the side.

Lorkan's toe drags through it as he edges his foot higher, inch by inch, his smirk growing with every centimetre.

Suddenly, he gives it a swift kick.

WHAT LORKAN IS

His lips part with a delighted grin as Meren makes an agonised shrieking noise.

With horror, she watches the water flow smoothly from its container and spread out over the spotless floor. Clumps of soapsuds drift by her feet like clouds, dark patches seeping into her work slippers like rain, turning them a damp, dull brown.

Prickling with rage, she raises her head to Lorkan's smug grin.

She can see most of his teeth, a sharky, white, jagged line.

"*Why* would you do that?!"

"To annoy you, mostly." He gives a nonchalant shrug—but his lip is still twitching with a teasing smile.

He's waiting for something, Meren realises.

Her lips press themselves into a firm line as she looks about her.

Thank the heavens the sofa, the desk, and the bookcase are all propped up on legs. Elegantly carved, expensive legs. At least gold can't rust; can it? But the wooden, mould-prone carpentry, the expensive rugs—a growling sound escapes the gaps between her teeth.

An island of bubbles drifts lazily past her right foot, and she finds herself stooping down and swiping a handful.

Without thinking, she takes aim and hurls it at The Prince.

It isn't a very good throw. Well, it *is*, technically; it had height and range, she'd had a good stance, perfect follow through. It was her aim that had been a little bit off.

She'd wanted the soap suds to land squarely in the centre of Lorkan's stupid, smug face, but it hadn't.

Instead, it hit just above the left side of his temple, some of it streaking all the way along the top of his head as if following the white line of his parting.

Even though Meren had missed her mark, she has achieved her desired result. The wicked smirk has vanished from his mouth and been replaced with a shocked 'O' shape, his eyebrows raised with surprise rather than roguish challenge.

It would have been comical, if the realisation of what she'd done hadn't just started to set like concrete.

All at once, Meren's entire body enters a semi-petrified state, her lips barely parting to utter a meek, weak, little apology.

The Prince doesn't move either.

He's just standing there, his face all full of circles; circular mouth, circular eyes, his eyebrows so arched up his forehead that, if placed them end to end, they'd make a circle too.

The mound of froth on his head drips down his hair and falls onto his shoulder, the gauzy material of his shirt blossoming dark as the moisture infiltrates the airy fabric.

Slowly, his jaw closes, his eyes narrowing, brow pulling itself low and serious like a blind over a stormy view.

He's all lines now.

Harsh angles—dark—like someone has drawn his glower on with a thick stick of charcoal.

Dully, through a haze of terror, Meren realises she might be killed.

The Prince takes a step forward, then another.

Meren urges her feet to back away, but her joints are all gummed up, her knees wooden, her muscles water.

He's so close she can see her own wide eyes reflected in the pearly buttons of his shirt—

—well, she would be able to, if they weren't squeezed tight shut.

She can feel something on her jaw.

Something cold and soft.

Bracing herself, she dares to crack open an eyelid.

Peeking out from below her lashes, she finds Lorkan, bent down to her level, his pale irises following his large, gentle hand as it strokes from one side of her jawbone to the other.

He's scooped the foam from his head and, smirking, is smearing it across her chin.

He's giving her a beard of bubbles.

Meren blinks, her shoulders slackening.

She squints at him, but for a whole different reason, now, watching his eyes slide over her face as he concentrates on his work.

Every now and again, the pads of his cool fingers brush against her skin, and the nerves beneath fire all at once, little bursts of sensation mixed with the smooth dragging motion of soap suds.

When he's satisfied with his work, he straightens, rising back to his full height and grins down at her bemused expression.

She blinks.

He's waiting for her to make the next move.

He's *daring* her to make the next move.

It was several seconds before she *can* move.

She can still hear the rush of her own blood pumping past the drums of her ears, the rapid adrenaline-fuelled thud of her pulse in her chest as her heart throws itself about her rib cage.

The end of her bubble-beard elongates, gravity tugging its scraggly entrails until it breaks in half. The severed piece lands on Meren's slipper with a sodden splat, and she feels the wetness trickle into the cloth.

Her lips curling, she narrows her eyes and reaches out. Using the very ends of her fingers, she snatches up the plump mound of bubbles resting on Lorkan's broad shoulder.

He remains perfectly still as she pulls her hand down over the sharp point of his chin, gifting him with a translucent bubble goatee.

There's a slight indent in one of his clean-shaven cheeks; he's biting the inside of his lip to keep from smiling.

Eagerly, Meren awaits his response. She wonders if he'll take back the beard he'd given her—as ammunition to launch his counterattack—but he doesn't.

Instead, he begins a leisurely walk, both hands behind his back.

Puzzled, she turns to watch him go.

"Surrendering so soon?" Her voice wobbles slightly; left-over nerves resulting from her near brush with the afterlife—

—and because she knows, somehow, that he isn't surrendering.

He's probably doing the exact opposite.

Lorkan's feet actually make a sound, for once, as he crosses the room; wet slaps as he sloshes through the large puddle of lukewarm water now taking up most of the floor. He doesn't reply, just keeps going, then disappears left, back into the washroom.

When he emerges, he does so with a handful of something, and a devilish expression.

"Quite the contrary, Wren, darling."

She realises what he's holding immediately, and what he plans to do with them.

"I'm declaring war."

With that, he tosses the soap tablets into the air like chubby nubs of confetti.

Their eyes follow the white pellets as they rise, run out of momentum, and plummet to the floor, bouncing on the glassy ground with tinkling splashes like hailstones.

Immediately they began to fizz, bubbles oozing from the stone slabs like strange, cloud-like fungi.

Before she has time to react, Lorkan has stooped down to grab the at the nearest bubble-plume and is striding towards her, his hands parting to dump it over the top of her head.

Rubbing the suds from her eyes, she huffs them from her nostrils, which gets a cackle from Lorkan somewhere on the other side of the room.

He's positioned a long, bronze-coloured sofa between them, and Meren's calculating stare dips to it, then to her target, his expression energised and full of taunting provocation.

He's daring her again.

Daring her to risk damaging the priceless piece of furniture between them —he thinks she won't—he thinks he's safe.

Before he has a chance to look surprised, Meren grabs at the bubbles near her feet and flings them in his direction, fear of staining the sofa's velvet cushions sharpens her aim.

WHAT LORKAN IS

She manages to strike the lower half of his face.

With something between a cough and a laugh, he blows a stream of foam from his wide grin. "Oh, you've done it now."

Bending to grab some froth to hurl back at her, he stands to find Meren already in full sprint, her slippers slapping through the puddles.

The marble slick as ice, she skids around a writing desk and ducks behind it with a shriek; of joyful laughter this time.

※ ☾ ※

Soaked, panting—and catching Meren shiver lightly below her damp uniform—Lorkan finally suggests a peace treaty

Their war had nearly ended several minutes ago when their ammunition began to dry up, but he had solved that problem by fetching more water and tablets from the washroom and rejuvenating the growing mass suds with the carelessness and recklessness of a child.

Meren had scolded his actions in an equally mature way; by stretching up to tug the collar of his shirt open so she could drop a half-dissolved soap tabled down the back of his neck.

To this, Lorkan had made a screeching noise as the little bomb fizzed against the base of his spine, then grappled at the hem of his shirt to untuck it before the wedge of detergent could enter the band of his trousers.

Meren giggles tiredly, wringing out the cotton of her apron. Hanging heavily about her waist, it dribbles onto the ground like a heavy rain.

Lorkan's clothes hang wetly off his lithe frame, which—due to his love of thin, gauzy fabric—is making it very difficult for her to look at him without turning the colour of a raspberry. His hair, dripping too, hangs limply around his shoulders, his chest rising and falling, eyes all glowy from the thrill of a chase.

For some reason, she can't stop staring at his mouth as those heavy breaths leave his parted lips.

They spread into a sloppy smile as he calls for a draw, holding out a large hand for her to shake.

Tentatively, she accepts it, their palms meeting with a damp smacking of water; hers small and warm with rushing blood, Lorkan's masculine and cool with—well, he's just always cool, it seems. Tingles radiate from his surprisingly masculine grip—for a painter—and inch their way up her arm.

Although, that may be the soap.

A smile twitches her lip, a memory flowering, tickling the inside of her ribs.

Lorkan notices, looking up from wringing out his own shirt. Untucked and squeezed between his hands, it's risen up to expose a narrow slither of his flat, pale belly. "What is it?"

"You called me '*Wren*', earlier. "And '*Darling*'."

"Oh." His cheekbones dust the slightest shade of pink. "Sorry."

"No, it's okay," she assures, flushing too. "I liked it."

☽

Lorkan is true to his word; after their handshake, he plucks up the mop propped against the wall and starts pushing it about without complaint, wringing the foamy water into the bucket.

He *is* very competent at cleaning, Meren thinks—for a *prince*; rubbing away vague footprints and scuff marks as he goes, so the water doesn't go to waste.

But it's still *wrong*.

Several times, she tries to take the mop from him and take over—

But he simply steps in front of her, blocking her as though it were a game.

WHAT LORKAN IS

He's smiling the whole time, finding her determined attempts amusing; her reaching hands grasping at thin air, her jaw knitted tight shut so she didn't mutter expletives.

A few times, she tries to swipe the handle by ducking under one of his arms—hoping he won't be quick enough—but he's always quick enough.

She swipes *Lorkan* by accident, once, bumping into the solid strength of his torso, which causes her to blush, and him to laugh.

When, eventually, Meren relents and lets him get on with cleaning up his mess, she sets about her own tasks—which mainly involve polishing and dusting the multitudinous array of trinkets littering every flat surface of the room.

At first, she begins her usual lifting-things-and-placing-them-back-exactly-as-they-had-been routine, measuring the distance between objects and their neighbours.

Lorkan notices, and just raises an eyebrow, finding it amusing, at first.

However, when he catches Meren trying to balance a stack of books in one arm whilst wiping under a footstool with the other, he says:

"That really isn't necessary. I told you before, any rumours about me being particular about my belongings are apocryphal. Just leave the books on the floor."

Meren hesitates, the muscles in her arms seizing up with the weight of the heavy volumes. She'd picked them all up at once because she wanted to keep the stack exactly as he'd left them; a few corners jaggedly poking out, the entire thing wobbling off a little to the left like an unsteady building.

"Are you sure?" She asks uncertainly, and Lorkan presses, firmer this time:

"Yes, I'm sure. Just put stuff wherever." He waves a hand at the ground by her feet, and she regards it as if expecting it to come alive and tear the books to shreds.

Lorkan must catch her arm twitch, because a smile plays across his lips. "You'll have to put them down sooner or later, or you'll drop them."

Realising this to be the case—and her arms crumbling like cake—she relents reluctantly, willing her back to stoop and her fingers to let go.

Once the books touch the floor and nothing bad happens, her shoulders slacken.

Lorkan nods, pleased. "Good girl."

Resuming his mopping of the floor, he adds, "You know, you don't need to be doing that at all." He gestures at the rag in her hand that she's pushing about under the footstool. "Everything is clean enough. Sit down, relax, seeing as you insist on staying."

Meren blinks blankly at him.

Seeming to mistake her confused expression for not knowing where she should sit, he inclines his head to a nearby settee, the cushions fat and velvet and inviting.

"Lorkan, I *can't* sit there—and I keep telling you, this is my *job*."

"I'd rather you take a break. I'm a prince, remember? You should do as I say."

He's never pulled that card on her and, even now, he's doing it with that quintessential light, teasing smirk he wears so she knows he's joking.

Mostly.

Meren can feel the back of her neck heating, a faint little twitch tugging at the corners of her lips. "I beg your pardon, Your Highness, but are you *ordering* me to sit down?"

Smoothing his grin expertly, Lorkan straightens his spine and tugs on a domineering stance as if it were a comfortable old cloak.

It suits him; he looks like a king—Meren can't help thinking—the mop held firmly in one hand like a strange wooden staff, a few remaining bubbles dotted over his damp clothes like jewels woven into the fabric.

Not a king of Velôr, though.

Somewhere colder, where skin is pale as snow rather than browned by the sun. Somewhere where intelligence and strategy rule over brawn; where warriors are lean and slender rather than bulky and grizzled from war.

Deepening his silken voice to a darker, velvet tone, The Prince looks down his pointed nose at her as though addressing his subjects.

That little ghost of a smile is still there, hidden below this mask he's pulled on like a fancy dress costume.

"Yes, I command you to sit on this settee—" he thrust the mop-head at it, "—and relax."

His eyes, glinting with the joy of play, sweep over Meren's slightly moist attire.

Tangled in her hair like snowflakes, the foam has melted into slush. and a droplet of it rolls down her cheek and onto the floor.

"And to dry yourself with one of the towels from the washroom."

Her mouth opens to protest—something predictable about a maid using a prince's towels—but Lorkan throws her a stern look, so she shuts it again.

Trailing off to heed his wishes, she gives him a grumpy scowl as she passes.

He just flashes her a smile.

16

BY THE FIREPLACE

Meren has always admired Lorkan's washroom.

She'd been in it many times before but, as she'd explained (much to his bafflement) she'd never used it.

The washroom is not like the rest of the palace; cased in shells of gold or chipped from slabs or marble. It's not green like most of Lorkan's possessions either, but blue, every inch of white plaster pressed with tiny square tiles like the smooth scales of a serpent. Its subtle curves and sloping edges hold a deep sink embedded in the countertop, and the floor slants slightly so water can run into a shiny, ornate little grate.

Despite being one of the few rooms in his chambers that doesn't boast a floor-to-ceiling window, the space somehow remains bright, perhaps through some low-level sort of magic—Meren thinks. There are no windows at *all,* the room nestled snugly between the main hallway outside and the lounge, and several ivies thrive in the darker corners, crawling from ceramic pots, their leaves playing amongst dripping wax sticks, flasks, and bottles of multi-coloured potions and liquids.

WHAT LORKAN IS

Their scents seep through their corks; samphire, juniper, citrus, black pepper, and sea salt, and they stand in bunches, like mushrooms, around the deep, pit-like bath. With a feint trickle, a fountain cascades down one wall and into its plug hole; a thin, wide sheet of water that Meren had—at first—assumed to be a curved piece of glass.

Below Aldercliff, the servants *are* given a room to bathe, but its very existence is due to necessity rather than pleasure. A row of cast iron tubs line one wall and a row of showers protrude from the other, all separated by a slippery wooden privacy panel. The water—heated only in colder months and never enough to produce steam—sluices down several grime-filled channels and into a rusted drain.

Meren aims to spend as little time in the washroom as possible at *any* time of year. Each evening she hops into a cubicle, does what she needs to do, and hops out again before her feet have time to catch some kind of fungal infection from the manky tiles.

She often finds herself wondering why or how Lorkan ever leaves the serene confines of *this* pretty little space. If she had the choice, *she* wouldn't leave; she'd submerge herself in the pond-like tub until the pads of her fingers turn as wrinkly as Alfdis'.

She would summon the piping hot water that bubbles up from the boiler, and chuck in soap tablets until they foam. She'd find a potion that smells of flowers and rub it into her hair until the smell of sweet peonies, musky roses, and succulent blossoms follows her wherever she goes. There's easily enough room for her to swim a minuscule lap or two; she'd cross the entire length in about three strokes, but that's a vast improvement from the tubs in the servant's quarters where she can't even stretch out her legs.

Meren pats her uniform with one of Lorkan's towels (possibly the softest material she's ever felt) but, even when dry, her dress remains the stubborn colour of a puddle on a gravel path.

The skirt is dripping in some places like a raincloud; grey and sombre, the little droplets oozing from the hem and beading on the blue tiles below her feet—almost as if it's crying.

Failing to rid the thick, coarse material of moisture, she relents with a frustrated huff and decides to concentrate on her hair.

Self-consciously checking the door to make sure Lorkan isn't peeking, Meren reaches up and unfastens the tight little bun atop her head.

Her hair falls about her shoulders in a stiff clump and—even after she's combed it through with her fingers—it refuses to forget the shape it's been twisted into since eight this morning.

Matted into a few limp ringlets, she towels it as best she can, and hesitates. It would dry much faster if it were left down.

Lorkan wouldn't mind if she left it down. After all, he'd let her hurl foam at him only minutes earlier (and, whilst cackling, drop a fizzing soap tablet down his shirt in the hope it would end up filling his trousers).

Her fingers reach for the doorknob, but reluctance draws them back.

A maid appearing scruffy before her employer is a more than valid justification for her shyness—

But he's Lorkan. Meren could come to work in her nightdress and he wouldn't even notice, she realises with a smile. Well, he'd *notice*, but he wouldn't *care*, let alone chastise her for lack of professionalism.

Her reflection smiles back at her from the looking glass like a damp, grey ghost.

She understands why he seems to have nicknamed her 'wren'. Her uniform drowns her limbs like a coat, and her fine, brown hair is mousy and—whilst wet—scraggly as bird's feathers. If he were to poke his head around the door, she knows she would yelp as if he'd caught her naked.

Without telling them to, her arms reach up and tie the damp strands safely away.

※ ☾ ※

WHAT LORKAN IS

As Meren leaves the washroom—mostly dry, and her hair now back in its usual conservative bun—she finds Lorkan in the lounge, prodding the fireplace with a long stick.

Raising his head, he smiles welcomingly as she approaches, regarding the flames with interest.

"I don't think I've ever seen any of these fires lit before," she observes, outstretching her cold fingers towards the hearth.

He's perched on the lip of a nearby sofa, which he's pulled up against the fireplace, and Meren dithers, unsure if she's permitted to sit next to him. He answers her unspoken question by giving the plump velvet a little pat.

"I'm not overly fond of heat," he explains with a furrowed brow—as if the reason for this has always bemused him.

"Really?" Meren makes a show of raising her eyebrows in mock surprise, a look utterly saturated with sarcasm.

After all their hours together, The Prince's distaste for high temperatures is not news to her. Even now, he's shifted the sofa so his end is much farther away from the fire than Meren's, and the poker he's using to stimulate the crackling pile of logs must be at least double the length of an ordinary one.

He gives her a sideways smile at her insolence, but doesn't comment. Turning back to the feeble flames:

"I only light them to make food when I can't be bothered to go downstairs; and even then, I wait until the meal has cooled a little before eating it."

Facing him, she can't help the curious edge to her tone as she asks:

"You really hate warmth that much?"

Lorkan looks thoughtful, the fire bright in his pale eyes as he watches their tongues lick the logs, gumming at the charred edges. "Yes. When I was a child, Mother would try to bathe me and I'd cry if she used water warm enough to fog a mirror."

"...When we met, you were dressed as if it were summer in Calpurzia. I figured then that the cold doesn't seem to bother you, but I didn't know that *heat* actually..."

She imagines him as a babe—his tiny, pink face screwed up with tears as Lophia tries to lower him into a tub—and her heart twists in on itself painfully. Softly:

"Does it hurt you?"

He says nothing, and she worries she'd pressed him too hard—

But he's just trying to formulate a reply, thoughts clouding his eyes to a pale, glassy green.

"Yes, sometimes. What's simply hot to you would probably be boiling for me. I'm not sure why. Mother used to say I'm just sensitive, but I've never met anyone else who experiences it. Although," he chuckles but it sounds more brittle than amused. "Being a prince, I don't get to meet many people to compare myself with; mostly sons and daughters of Mother and Father's friends—and staff, obviously," He adds. "But we weren't supposed to talk to them and, when I did, they were too afraid of me to be themselves." The corners of his narrow lips tug into a fond smile. "Apart from Alfdis, of course."

Meren mulls this over as she watches Lorkan jab at the fire, touched that he'd lit it just so she could dry off. She wonders what it must be like, never sprawling on the grass under the summer sun, never pulling gloves over cold hands, and sipping hot soup while frost prickles the window panes.

And she imagines a lonely, raven-haired boy wandering the palace in search of playmates, finding nothing but adult maids and hall boys. They're giggling among themselves, but fall silent as they notice his approach, offering him curtseys and bows instead of light welcomes and friendly pats on the back.

He probably retreated to his chambers to paint their smiling faces instead, capturing their laughter on canvas like a vintner bottling wine.

She remembers the day they'd met; his stroll through the frigid early dawn. He must leave before the sun has time to toast the air and bake the gravel pathways, the night star-pricked and cool.

He's probably just as in love with the cold as most Velôrians are with the warmth.

WHAT LORKAN IS

After a little while, Lorkan squints at the fire critically, as if assessing it, then stands and disappears into another room.

Meren remains, holding out the palms of her hands, the heat tickling her skin.

When he returns, he holds a metal tripod in one hand and a copper kettle in the other. "Tea?"

He approaches the fireplace, but Meren has already pushed herself to her feet. She doesn't want to find out what happens if he gets too close to the flames. She knows he'll try to do it for her; he'll lean right over that bright mass of heat to set the kettle on its stilts; burn himself just so she can have some blasted tea.

More assertive than she's ever been in his presence, she places a hand over Lorkan's on the handle. "I'll do it."

For once, he lets her, handing the responsibility over with a grateful smile. "Thank you."

"How do you cook meals if you can't go near the fireplace?" Kneeling by the hearth, Meren arranges the tripod over the flames, careful to keep her dress away from their nibbling maws.

"I use long sticks with hooks on them," he answers, and she can't tell if he's joking.

When the kettle is settled, its rounded underside already glowing with heat, Meren takes her place on the sofa. It's small, just right for two people, and difficult not to sink back into its squashy embrace and take a quick nap, she thinks sleepily.

Or to lean into the deep dip caused by Lorkan's weight and let her head come to rest on the muscled knot of his shoulder.

That thought makes something occur to her.

"When I touch you," she begins, and his eyes light with sudden attention, "—do I hurt you?"

He turns to her, his brow furrowed. The fire reflects softly off the paleness of his face, his cheekbones casting fluttering shadows over his jaw. "Hurt me? How could you hurt me?"

"Because I'm warm. You're always so cool I wondered if, when I touch you —"

"You don't hurt me," he shakes his head, waving her off with a fond smile.

Meren's shoulders slacken. "Good. But I can stop, if you want, if it's—"

"No, don't." Averting his gaze back to the squat little kettle:

"Don't stop. I like it."

✶ ☾ ✶

While they wait for the water to boil, Lorkan brings out a pretty wooden box that somehow smells of every plant in the world, all at once.

"What sort of tea would you like?" He asks, unlatching the lid.

The box is separated into compartments—peppermint leaves, lemon balm, lavender sprigs, camomile heads—and Meren blinks at them, their confusing smells making her nose twitch. She hunts for the ground-up, brown leaves she's used to watching Yllva pour into the strainer and, when she can't find them, Lorkan offers her the box.

"Or you can pick whatever smells nice and I'll make you your own."

Liking this idea much better, Meren picks a star-shaped herb that smells like liquorice and watches for Lorkan's reaction, hoping she made the right choice.

He smiles as if pleased, and adds a pinch of nutmeg, a roll of cinnamon bark, and a dried seed pod to her outstretched hand.

"These are called cardamom," he explains, sensing her interest.

They smell bitter as they roll about the dip of her palm.

"They only grow in humid, hot forests along the Calpurzian border. We couldn't get them until Father annexed Claridon when I was a child."

"Annexed?"

"Claimed it for himself. It used to be owned by the Calpurzians but it's ours now. Velôr grew by ten thousand hectares last year." He's frowning, and Meren's brows knit over her nose.

"Isn't that a good thing?"

"I guess so."

"You guess so?"

"Well…I can't help thinking about the people that lived there." He catches her expression and continues, "I know, I know; they're *Calpurzians*—but does that make it okay to steal their homes?"

Meren can tell by the troubled slant of his eyebrows that 'yes' might not be the right answer. "…I'm not sure. Do *you* think so?"

"I don't think it's okay to steal *anyone's* home."

"You might be the only person in the kingdom who feels that way."

Lorkan shrugs, taking a sip of his tea. "So be it."

Even though it's barely been twenty-four hours, Meren once again finds herself itching to ask him about the alliance.

It takes longer than that for a message to reach Calpurzia, let alone for diplomats to formulate some kind of alternative act of peace that will satisfy both parties. Plus, they'd probably have to have some kind of meeting in person, Meren supposes, before the wedding can be called off. It will be weeks before any changes to the arrangements can be made—and that is if an attempt at a workaround is being formulated at all.

Despite this, she'd found herself almost opening her mouth at various points in the day, the question, '*By the way, do you still have to marry the Calpurzian princess?*' on the tip of her tongue, even though she knew the answer would most certainly be a sombre *'yes'*.

She jumps as the kettle begins to rattle, protesting as its contents rage against its lid, and she swallows her question once again. Removing it from the heat, she drops her handful of spices into the bubbling water, the steam turning sweet.

It feels wrong *not* to mention the alliance; like they've stuffed something dangerous into the back of a cupboard, mutually agreed to never speak of it again, and are now silently hoping it doesn't escape.

Earlier, Meren and Lorkan had run around his chambers laughing, but that sense of impending doom had still hung over them like a giant wave in the distance, one day to crash down upon their quiet little world and crush it. Meren feels as though someone should point it out, but then, just as the words formulate on her tongue, they wither. Talking about a tsunami won't stop the tsunami. And, in the grand scheme of things, it's only a tsunami to them; to her little insignificant life and Lorkan's love of this quiet place he's built for himself.

When the tea has brewed, Lorkan pours it into two cups, adding a splash of milk and brown sugar until their tannin-stained hue lightens into a creamy beige.

Meren takes a sip and hums as the rich, bittersweet taste seeps between her teeth. "It's amazing, thank you."

"No, thank *you;* you picked the spices."

"I picked *one.*"

Lorkan reclines lazily against the backrest, stirring his tea with a silver spoon. "Do you think tha*t—one day—*you might let me compliment you?"

Meren thinks about it. "Maybe. One day." Returning his smile, she lets her eyes close and takes another sip, the delicately scented steam leaking from her mug. It brushes against her lids and, when she opens them, she finds Lorkan watching her.

He seems to do that a lot, so much so she's almost used to it. He hasn't touched his drink yet, just left it—probably to cool—on the table.

Yesterday, they had been sitting side by side, in comfortable silence, making paint. His engagement had crossed Meren's mind then; the ground suddenly falling away below the pillow she sat on, her whole body tumbling into the hole.

WHAT LORKAN IS

She couldn't imagine—didn't want to imagine—a future in which her days are not filled with colours, the little pigment-freckled table, Aasta's beaming face, Frode, Arne—

Lorkan.

How quickly the heart latches onto pleasant things, and how reluctant it is to let them go.

Meren feels a light prickling sensation in the corners of her eyes and blinks, taking another sip of her tea. It slips over her tongue and down her throat like nectar, warming her from the inside out. She doesn't want to think about the alliance anymore.

Lorkan must be turning the same worries over in his own mind because his shoulders sag when he thinks she isn't looking. Each time a silence stretches long enough for his thoughts to wander, he turns pensive, his teeth worrying his lower lip. They're doing it now, chewing a ragged strip of skin, so Meren decides to talk about something she thinks he'll like, something that's as far away from his life and duties as a prince she can possibly get:

"What pigments do you want me to fetch tomorrow?"

He has picked up his tea now, his finger and thumb dwarfing the china handle. He blows a few cold breaths onto its surface and steam billows over the rim. "I don't think I'll need any," he admits, to the floor rather than her face. "With the pigments you bought today, it'll be finished."

Meren chokes down a giggle; they hadn't actually gotten around to turning those pigments into paint; they'd spent the day trying to drown the other in froth, flooding the lounge, and spying on people through a telescope.

"I shouldn't *really* accept my wages for today; I didn't get much done," she mutters into her cup, her guilt forming little ripples. Then the smile slips sideways from her face.

The painting is finished? Yet they've been into almost every room of Lorkan's quarters and Meren hasn't seen it anywhere. She'd kept a lookout for it just in case he'd simply decided to continue it outside of his studio—for some reason—but to no avail.

He must have *hidden* it—

Although he's never explicitly saying so, Meren can't help getting a sinking feeling he's done so either *because of her,* or to keep it *from* her, or both.

Who else would he hide it from? She is his only visitor, besides Mer Majesty Lophia, on rare occasions, and why would he hide it from his mother?

She wants to inquire about the painting anyway. She'd helped make it, after all, she'd watched it from birth. She knows she doesn't have the right to ask as his maid, but maybe she can as his friend?

And yet she hesitates, prickly memories of yesterday still matted in her mind like a thistle. Lorkan has been so open today, and the air is still thick with their earlier joy. Meren doesn't want to say anything that might cause him to retreat back into his shell. Instead, she asks, trying not to let a taught, hopeful edge creep into her voice:

"Will you paint something else?"

The wide line of his shoulders rises and falls. "I don't have anything I feel like painting."

Meren's heart grows heavy and, as if somehow feeling it, he adds:

"Well, I did have one idea." He watches the swirls of steam flow smoothly from his tea.

Just like them, Meren's hopes begin to rise.

"But I can't. Not anymore."

Encouragingly:

"Of course you can." She sits up a little straighter, relief flushing her veins so quickly she almost feels light-headed.

Perhaps their pigment-making sessions don't have to end after all. And maybe—after today goes so swimmingly—he'll start his new picture while she's in the room, like before; him dabbing at the canvas while she makes his colours.

"You're an amazing artist, you can paint anything."

Lorkan's lip twitches, but he shakes his head. "Thank you, but what I really meant was, the subject is off-limits."

WHAT LORKAN IS

Her brow furrows. "What could possibly be off-limits to a prince?"

This makes him bark an almost bitter, one-syllable laugh. "A surprisingly long list of things."

Meren waits for him to elaborate, but when he doesn't, she prompts: "Well, what was it?"

With an expression that matches his tone:

"You."

L J R SKYLERMAN

PART TWO

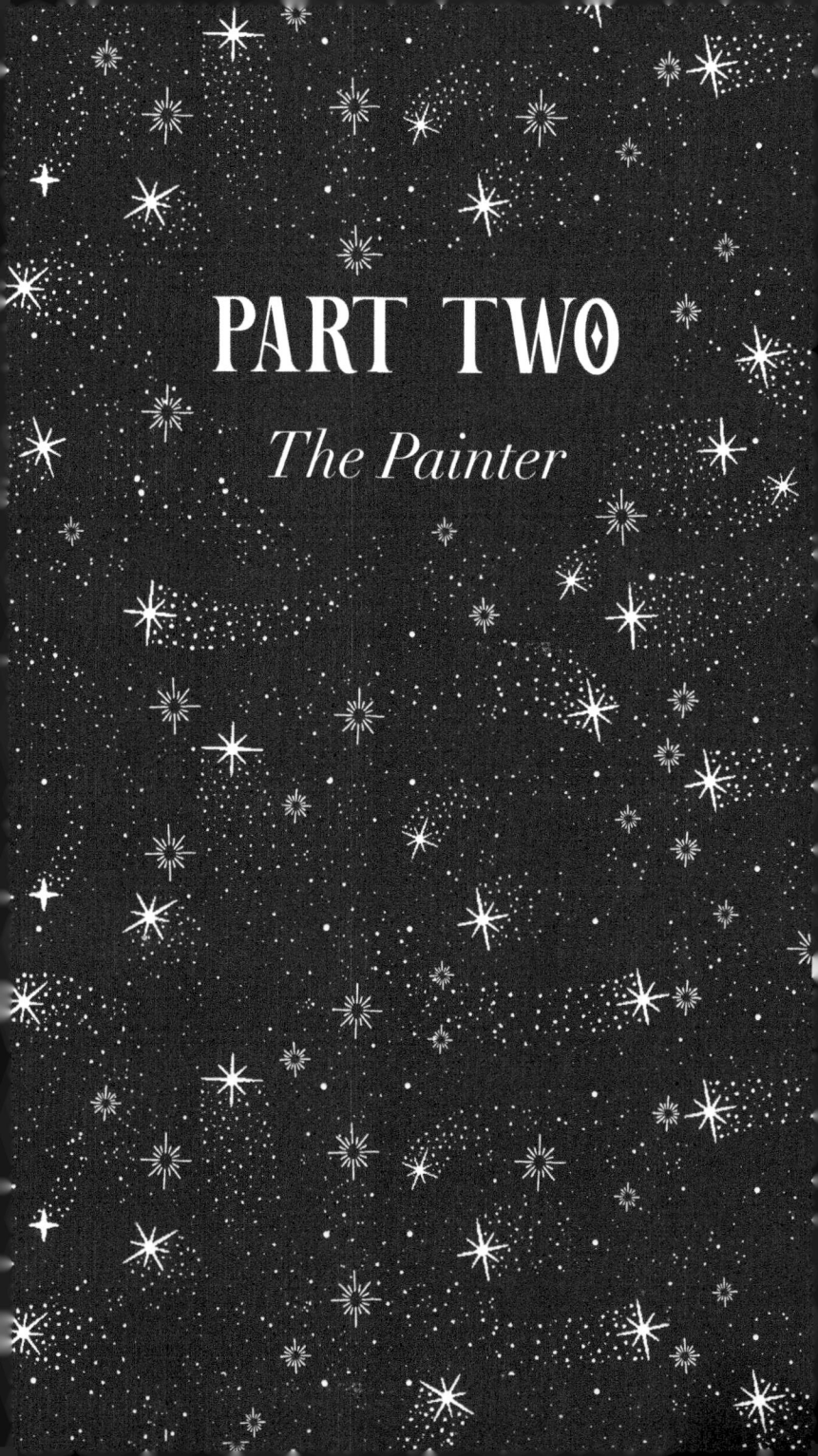

The Painter

17

ARTISTS AND APOTHECARIES

Lorkan's eyes wait for Meren's reaction, green and flickering with the light from the fire.

It takes her a while to react at all, and when she *does,* all she can manage is a weak little:

"What?"

His Adam's apple bobs up and then down the long column of his ivory throat. He repeats, slowly and carefully:

"I wanted to paint you."

Meren turns his words over, examining them with narrowed eyes for malice or some strange, twisted prank—

He doesn't look like he's joking. He's tensed up under the gauzy material of his almost-dry shirt, every one of his lean, powerful muscles taught as a bowstring.

"What's stopping you?" she asks cautiously. Her voice has turned reedy and tight—like she's testing whether a frozen lake is solid enough to walk on.

She returns his stare intently, and he shifts under her gaze, moistening his lips.

"The painting wouldn't be lewd, if that's what you're worried about. It just wouldn't be right, staring for hours on end at you now that you're Arne's —"

"I'm not Arne's anything," Meren says quickly. So quickly, the sentence darting past like a rabbit released from a snare.

She and Lorkan blink at it; her hasty rejection of Arne's sweet, innocent affections. It had come from *Meren's* mouth, yet she has no recollection of thinking it. She'd blurted it out, thrown it up reflexively, her body working of its own volition.

"We only went out once."

Lorkan shakes his head. "He'll obviously ask you out again in the future."

"If he does, I'll turn him down," she confesses, once again watching the statement fly from her mouth and skitter about the air. "I know my parents would have liked him, and he's a really nice man...but I didn't feel anything." With every word, the constricting sensation tight about her chest lessens, giving way to one of deep relief. With the feeling of unfastening a corset and taking a gulp of fresh, cool air, Meren admits guilty:

"Not like that, anyway. Not for Arne. I don't think I ever did."

Lorkan has looked up, his tea forgotten on the table.

Meren can see, now she's up close, that his green eyes are flecked with spatters of gold.

"You didn't?"

"No." A grin twitches her lip and, disgusted, she wipes it off her face with the back of her hand as though it were an unsightly smudge of food. "I went out with him because...dating is different when you're poor, Lorkan. You wouldn't...never mind. But I didn't feel anything. Nothing happened."

A ghost of a smile is pulling at the corner of his mouth, but Meren doesn't see it.

She's dipped her head to stare at her tea, swirling the remaining dregs about the bottom of her cup. Wet sugar and spices form a ring about the bottom, and sour guilt thumbs the pages of her conscience, rubbing them

WHAT LORKAN IS

into scruffy dog ears. Her mouth turning dry, she downs them in a mouthful of sweet, soupy cinnamon and nutmeg.

How can she be so selfish? And what is she doing, boring a prince with the matters of her love life (or lack thereof), she thinks to herself bitterly.

But he doesn't seem bored. Quite the opposite. He's shifted right to the edge of the sofa cushion without her noticing. "Really?"

Meren shakes her head. "No."

No one says anything for some time, their eyes hazing over with their own, separate clouds of thought.

Meren's reverie is significantly shorter than Lorkan's. It consists of one single sentence.

'*I need to stop stringing Arne along.*'

Aromatic steam still leaks steadily from the kettle, and she dithers, wondering if she's permitted to pour herself another cup of tea.

Usually, Lorkan guesses her needs before she can open her mouth:

"*There aren't any more cakes left but, if you're still hungry, I can fetch something from the kitchens.*"

"*Of course you can visit the restroom, you don't need to ask.*"

"*Oh, yes, I forgot the water jug. I'll get some.*"

—but, presently, he's gone almost completely still; besides his pale skin taking the light of the fire and throwing it back. He looks like a statue, Meren contemplates. If he *were* a statue, he'd be one of the few in the palace made of alabaster rather than gold.

Her fingers are curling hesitantly around the kettle's dainty handle when her brain finally digests his earlier words. She almost drops it.

"You wanted to paint me?"

Lorkan lifts his head, his attention settling back on her astonished little face.

His attention is a powerful force. Sometimes, when he looks at her, she feels as though he can see right into her psyche. He probably can. He probably meanders through her thoughts just for the fun of it; plucking up and inspecting daydreams and memories as if they're trinkets on a shelf, set there for his own personal amusement.

Quietly:

"I *still* want to paint you. I'd love to—if you'd let me—and if you're sure I won't get a jealous apothecary apprentice breaking into the palace to punch me in the nose." A nervous chuckle emanates from his chest, but Meren makes a guess it's from shyness more than at what he'd said.

She returns his laugh uneasily. "Arne wouldn't do that."

At least, she can't *imagine* him doing that.

If he *did*, he might have to stand on a chair to reach Lorkan's face, she thinks with a blush.

"And, as I said, he'd have no reason to because we're not...you know—"

She can't bring herself to say '*lovers*', or even '*sweethearts*'; she doesn't want to imagine Arne's fuzzy chin pressing kisses to her neck, and she gets the feeling Lorkan doesn't either. Wrestling with various words, she sighs.

"—we're just friends."

Lorkan sips his tea. It makes it difficult for Meren to see his expression, and she feels that's exactly why he's doing it.

"I don't understand though." The corner of her mouth tugging into a bashful smile, she edges a little closer to him, curiously. "Why would you want to paint... *me?* You could paint anyone in the kingdom—in *any* kingdom, if you wanted to."

"I don't want to paint *anyone,* I want to paint *you.*"

Her lungs push up a sound; something between a baffled scoff and a laugh. "But *why?*" She gestures to her still-sodden uniform the colour of a gravestone, her mousy hair that looks like she's been attacked by a thundercloud, and her long, pointy nose she's always rather disliked. "You said you paint what you find beautiful."

Lorkan gives her a long look.

The back of Meren's neck turns so red she expects steam to start seeping from her damp collar. "Thank you," She stutters, clasping her cup in both hands. Tentatively:

WHAT LORKAN IS

"...Will you want me to pose or something?"

✶ ☾ ✶

It is decided that they'll begin the painting tomorrow.

Lorkan writes Meren a list of the pigments he'll need for her to pick up at the market, his handwriting returning to its bold, decadent loops.

She watches him print the names of each colour fondly, as though they're old friends he's adding to a party guest list. He seems to know exactly what he wants; he must have at least a rough image of the painting in his mind already. That realisation makes something skitter along Meren's bones; knowing she walks through his thoughts, that he's arranged her body, draping her over the furniture of his mind—

"Those colours are so bright," she muses, trying to picture the bold yellows and rich greens somehow becoming the drab beige of her clothes. "Are they for the background?"

The corner of Lorkan's lip ghosts with a hint of something as he folds the parchment neatly, and hands it to her. "Something like that."

Meren looks forward to her trip to the market the next morning. For a short while, she'd thought she wouldn't have a reason to go there for some time. After all, how long would it have taken Lorkan to conceive another painting if she had not agreed to sit for him? A week? A month? With the ocean of worries currently thrashing about his head, he may not have felt that tickle of artistic inspiration again for many moons.

Now he has something to paint, something to do, some kind of *goal,* and it suits him. The promise of a new project—a new purpose—has already rejuvenated his mood considerably and, when he bids Meren good night, he does so with a broad, unbridled smile.

Unlike their farewell yesterday, it makes her chest flutter as though her ribs have sprouted tiny, feathered wings, and she has to try hard not to break into a joyful little skip as she makes her way to the servant's quarters.

* ☾ *

A wind has picked up, stirring up the autumn leaves, although it's impossible to tell from deep below the palace. The mess hall has steadily emptied since six o'clock, leaving only a handful of late diners still remaining. Several sconces have already burnt themselves out, so they huddle in pockets of light, the flagstones littered with crumbs, the tables sticky with gravy stains.

As has become their habit, Alfdis had perched next to Meren and—in their own pool of slowly-fading light—they chat happily, picking their way around their plates.

As she spoons down what Yllva had claimed to be bread and butter pudding, Meren tries her best to wrangle in her thoughts and pay attention to Alfdis' story.

It has something to do with guest towels, and she had to gnaw at the fleshy inside of her cheek to keep herself from bursting out with:

'I have much more exciting news, Alfdis! Lorkan wants to paint me! Me! He thinks I'm pretty!'

The realisation has settled in now, even if his motive still bemuse her:

He's going to paint her.

The *Prince* Of Velôr is going to paint Meren, a lowly maid—and he thinks she's *beautiful*.

She'll pose for him whilst his eyes, those serene, clover-coloured eyes, trace her body, her face, and immortalise everything he sees in paint and oil and canvas.

WHAT LORKAN IS

She could never tell he found her pretty; he gazes at *everything* as though he's eating it up with his eyes. She'd seen him staring at her like that—with dedicated, interested intensity—and thought nothing of it. It's the same stare he gives fudge cake, the novels on his shelves, the view from his telescope, and every pigment he's dabbed on with a brush—

But now she knows what that look means—that he's *admiring* her—and, from now on, it will make her blush every time she catches him at it.

Absently, Meren prods a wrinkled raisin about her dish.

When Lorkan had said—well, *implied*—that he finds her beautiful…what kind of beautiful had he meant?

Beautiful like a mountain capped with snow?

Beautiful like his sister or mother; familiar and warm and comforting?

Or beautiful like a woman?

Beautiful as in he'd like to slowly ease her clothes from her body? To relish her shape, her curves, the tone of her skin?

Meren chokes on her pudding, and Alfdis has to give her a hefty slap on the back.

✶ ☾ ✶

Meren manages to keep her jaw firmly clamped about the painting, Lorkan, and his admiration, all throughout dinner. She finds sleep difficult to achieve, then hard to maintain, excitement and anticipation fizzing away to itself like baking soda in every corner of her brain. Despite this, she isn't tired when she throws off the covers the next morning, and she walks to the market in high spirits.

However, when she catches sight of a familiar blonde mop of hair bobbing about over the crowd, her good mood is snuffed out like a flame suffocated between finger and thumb. She'd been so wrapped up in the comfy shawl of Lorkan's admiration that her earlier promise had utterly slipped her mind.

Unable to wait, Meren breaks her usual routine and pushes her way towards the apothecary's stall, dodging between bag-laden shoppers and hollering, insistent merchants until Arne's eyes lock with hers among the chaos.

As usual, his cheeks dimple as she offers him a tentative smile and slides Lorkan's list across the counter. His hand is warm as he hands over the first wooden box, his skin softly bronzed, his wide fingers calloused by homely responsibility.

She can easily picture him chopping wood in autumn, re-tiling the roof in summer, and digging over an allotment in spring. Everything about him is bright, the corners of his eyes and mouth crinkled like the first curled leaf of September.

But, slowly, Meren is realising isn't drawn to summer days filled with sweltering planks of sunlight. Not anymore, at least. Now she prefers the playful nip of winter, the cheeky, frosty wind that chases her ankles and whips up her scarf.

Most Velôrian men are grizzled and thickened with mead, like stocky, bristly bears; but she isn't interested in that, she knows that now. She'd rather the slender, svelte build of a philosopher, or a writer...

Or an artist.

While Arne gently scoops powders, dried roots, and berries into each box, Meren tries to form some kind of sentence.

Failing, she sighs in the hope that it will ease some of the tension coiled up in her torso like a pile of writhing snakes—

But it just makes Arne ask if she's alright—which makes the snakes coil tighter.

By the time he's fastening the final piece of string about the last box, she still hasn't thought of something to say to him.

She hasn't thought of something to say by the time he's helping her slot them into her tote bag either, or when he presses the bag's handles into one of her hands.

WHAT LORKAN IS

He drops another smile into the other, but something strange happens when she returns it:

He reaches up one broad hand and scratches behind his neck.

"Meren, I want to talk to you about something." His voice is edged with something and she blinks up at him. His lips have pressed themselves into a line, his pale eyebrows pulled close over the bridge of his nose.

'Cade help me,' she thinks as she forces her shoulders into a casual shrug. *'He's about to ask me out again, and here I am about to break up with him because a prince wants to paint my portrait'.*

Why does her time with Lorkan make perfect sense in his chambers—she wonders frustratedly—but as soon as she enters the real world, it appears mellow and fanciful as a dream?

Arne gestures for her to follow him around to the back of the stall, and she does, the half-door setting the shelves of glass bottles tinkling. He hops heavily down onto the trodden dirt, and Meren stops before the three-legged stool where he'd pierced her ears what seems like years ago.

"What is it, Arne?" Frantically, she tries to squish together an excuse that won't twist his large, friendly features into a hurt frown.

'I'm moving to a new town—?'

Terrible, how would she buy Lorkan's paints? In *disguise?*

'Someone else proposed to me—?'

No, he'd expect to see a ring, and he'd want to know what her fictional fiancé has that he doesn't.

'My father forbids me from seeing you?'

But she knows he wouldn't, no one would. Mr Hansen would admire Arne's adept, careful way with tools, and he'd love his easy disposition.

She's is a little short of breath by the time he turns to her, his expression almost sombre.

He's laced his thick fingers together, his gaze not lining up with hers. He scratches behind his neck once more, probably setting the freckled skin below his shirt collar streaked with red nail marks. "I just wanted to say...I had a really nice time the other night."

"So did I," she assures, although it comes out more forced than cheerful.

Wincing, she dares a glance at Arne's face for signs of hurt, but she needn't have worried; he seems preoccupied with his own plight. She's puzzled to find he looks like a Frode when he's about to deliver a troubling diagnosis, his fingers loosening and tightening as though he's trying to keep hold of a bird.

"You're kind and funny and clever," he continues. "But..."

"Yes?" The tension getting to her now, she almost wants to take his shoulders—thick and curved like two knots of mooring rope—and give him a good shake.

"There's someone else." Cringing, he manages to drag his eyes up from her shoes to her face.

"Someone else?"

"Yes. He comes by to get medicine for his mother, and we've met in the evenings a few times before—as friends. But I think...well, with your permission, I'd like to ask if he wants to be a bit more than that."

When Meren just stares at him, he continues, pouring out everything in one great breath:

"I *really* like you, I do, but, after we went out, you didn't ask to see me again, and you didn't seem to want to...you know, kiss me or anything. You didn't even take my hand." He sucks in another quick lungful of air. "But Bazyll does—at least, he did until I mentioned I took you to Elsie's Hill. But you *didn't* that's my point, so I thought maybe...you wouldn't mind..."

Meren reaches out, pressing the pads of her fingers to his mouth, silencing him.

He'd squeezed his eyes shut as if in anticipation of a hefty slap—

But peeks out from under his lids at her gentle touch.

She's smiling.

His lips are coarse and chapped under her hand.

She retracts it, and he blinks down at her. "It's okay."

Hesitantly, "It is?"

Meren nods, and his spine loosens, so much so that he seems to shrink by an inch. "Yes. I like you a lot too but...not like that. Sorry."

"Don't be sorry," Arne's mouth turns up into a tentative smile. "You're really not upset?"

Shaking her head, "Not at all, really, I promise. Thank you for the meteor shower. We should do more things like that, just…not as sweethearts. As friends."

"I'd like that." Beaming, he extends a hand, all smooth wedges of teeth and splatters of freckles; like he'd been on a very muddy walk.

It's the most handsome Meren has ever found him.

Firmly, she accepts his rough palm and gives it a good shake, and they stand a little awkwardly, scuffing their shoes against the patchy grass.

Eventually, she gives him a teasing nudge with the point of her elbow:

"So, Arne. Tell me about this Bazyll guy."

18

THE WISDOM OF A BAKER

It's much easier talking to Arne now that Meren knows he doesn't expect anything from her, she muses gratefully as she basks in the warmth of his excited smile.

On her request, he's stringing together a poetic description of Bazyll Sharpe; a lanky young man with hair the colour of embers and a spirit to match. He sounds much more suited to Arne's sunny, extroverted disposition, and Meren wishes their relationship all the best.

Bidding the apothecaries a good day—having to raise her voice so Frode can hear her from the back—Meren heads in the direction of Aasta's stall feeling positively chipper.

Her tote bag bumps her leg with each step, jagged and bulging with boxes and vials and, curiously, she wonders what Lorkan can possibly have in mind for them all. His chambers *do* boast an array of greens that could rival any forest—for that is what many of these pigments are—but few are as rich and full as those that Arne dished out into their little containers.

Perhaps he intends to use them not in the foreground, but as a base layer, Meren ponders. If so, the painting will turn out to be quite dark, she thinks, remembering a lump of mossy powder Arne had nudged from its scoop. She places it down as a foundation layer—as she's seen Lorkan do—and imagines painting over it with regular colours—skin tones and the grey of her pinafore—

But, no matter how many coats she piles onto the make-believe picture, the green manages to seep through, turning everything…green, staining the canvas with a sickly tinge, as if mould is nibbling through the paint.

※ ☾ ※

Midday breaks around Meren as she drifts through the stalls, the sky ripening to a pleasant forget-me-not blue. She lets the natural ebb-and-flow of the crowd nudge her along like she's afloat on a lazy, winding river, and peers interestedly at the products for sale as she passes them.

Some are sold from sheds, others marquees and, sometimes, just kitchen tables clearly taken from home. No matter the quality of someone's stall, however, the playing field is levelled by geographical location; no spot is better or worse, no one area hogs all the foot traffic. Rich and poor sell their goods side by side; one moment, Meren is browsing a heap of home-grown vegetables flecked with soil and fat caterpillars, the next, she finds herself face to face with a glass case of gold rings, pressed with grainy little diamonds like raisins in a bun.

Her coin string feeling disappointingly light, she drags her eyes from something glinting and green and lets the crowd sweep her away once more.

She can smell the sickly mixture of sugar, dough, and cinnamon from the other side of the market, and it grows steadily thicker as she nears the cake stalls. It leads the way like the needle of a compass, until she's wading through it, the air foggy with flour.

Meren has to make it through what she's calling '*The Fresh Bread District*' before she reaches Aasta's stall. With well-practised ease, she dodges sticky mixtures tossed from hand to hand, and ducks below elbows vigorously whipping things in bowls. The baker's portable ovens puff away, and she steps around them too, sweet-smelling heat pouring forth like water as their doors swing open, flooding the stalls and raising the temperature to that of a humid summer's eve. They've managed to funnel their smoke through gaps in the canopy of awnings using a network of makeshift chimneys and pipes, and they rattle fit to burst, others gasping out whistles and sighs.

Having purchased a hot white roll to nibble while she waits, Meren finds herself deposited at the end of a familiar queue.

One by one, they shuffle forward like pilgrims taking turns bowing before a shrine until, finally, it's her turn to be plonked into Aasta's glowing, inviting aura.

She can't help smiling as the baker tosses a welcoming grin in her direction.

Aasta is just like that, Meren has noticed; *everyone* starts smiling when they see her. They can't help revelling in her warmth, sunning themselves in her pleasant disposition. Her attention is soft and addicting like the smell of dinner on the stove, or a jumper that fits just right.

Meren waits patiently for her to finish serving a customer, and begins eyeing the teetering layers of sponge, blackberry tarts, and gooseberry-filled dough.

Without realising, she's been taking more time to choose since talk of Lorkan's engagement. Wishing she still had some bread left, she nibbles the inside of her cheek, her spare hand threading her coins up and down their string like an abacus.

"What will it be, honey?" Aasta's kindly tone finds her deep in her pit of worries and pulls her up to the surface by the armpits.

Her voice is curled with a distinct accent, although Meren can't place it. It's clipped with short, rounded syllables, and would sound gruff on a man but, coming from her cupid's bow, it borders more on motherly.

Unable to drag her eyes away from something oozing toffee, Meren's teeth fiddle with a tear of skin that just can't seem to find time to heal. "I'm not sure yet."

"Well, what does he like?" Aasta asks, her plush fingers digging around her till for some change.

Meren blinks up at her eyes, deep set and bright below thick, dark lashes. "What makes you think they aren't for me?"

She gives her a knowing look, the left side of her mouth twitching with the edge of a smirk. One of her oval eyebrows raises in a challenge. "Well, *are* they for you?"

"Yes!" Meren insists, then hesitates, realising she's spent the last few minutes imagining what sound Lorkan might make as he bites into that toffee thing. The back of her neck heats under her starched bodice. "Well... sort of. How could you tell?"

Counting out a few coppers, Aasta drops them into the hand of the man to Meren's left and waves him on his way.

Although large as a bull, he stammers out a meek thank you, his cheeks pink below his prickly beard.

Meren has never seen so many people look so smitten before she became a regular at Aasta's stall.

Everyone is in love with Aasta.

"You always take so long to choose," she shrugs simply. "Every day, I watch your eyes flick over each of my cakes like you're shopping for King Cade himself."

'*Almost,*' Meren thinks.

"Perhaps I'm just really picky about what I want," she tries, and Aasta shakes her head.

"No, I know that look. You buy what you think *he'll* like, not what *you* like. You wouldn't take half as long if it was for you."

"You keep saying *'he'*," Meren points out, although she'd be lying if she claimed not to be impressed.

Who knew a homely baker could also possess the astute observational skills of a law enforcement officer? She probably could have been one, in another life. Or a midwife. Yes, Meren can easily imagine her rounded shoulders stooped like protective angel wings, welcoming a newborn babe into the world, her smooth, doughy hands swaddling him up warm and cosy like an apple strudel.

"I could have been buying for my mother or sister or—"

Her bun bouncing from side to side in its little net, Aasta shakes her head again. "Nope, they're for a man—and a very special man, by that look in your eyes. You were thinking about him a moment ago, I could tell." The flour-dusted pad of her finger taps the side of her curved nose, leaving a smudge.

Indignantly, Meren opens her mouth to tell her she's wrong, but closes it again. Self-consciously, she smoothes some invisible creases in her pinafore just to check it's still there, feeling suddenly naked.

"Are you a witch?" She asks, only half-joking, and Aasta's plump lips spread in a loud laugh.

"No, deary, I've just been in this business for a long time—since I was a young'un, actually. This was me mum's stall. Plus, I have five daughters; they think they're being all secretive and cunning, hiding their crushes from me, but I know. I always know."

"I don't *have* a crush," Meren snaps, and the little old woman Aasta is serving jumps, almost dropping her honey cake. Her cheeks colour. "Sorry. It's just, I *don't.*"

So what if Lorkan is the most breath-taking male she's ever seen? What does it matter that he's gentle and patient and intelligent and funny and generous and—

An image flashes hot and sweet in Meren's mind of The Prince, his wide hands the colour of rainbows, his eyes a tangle of ivy, the way they crinkle at the side when he smiles, his *smile*—

Oh dear.

A soft chuckle yanks Meren back into reality. "What?"

WHAT LORKAN IS

Aasta gives her that wise, knowing look, and a smile that suggests she'd watched every single thought that had just passed through her head.

"You were thinking about him again."

※ ☾ ※

Aasta has served four customers by the time Meren eventually—feeling somewhere between humiliated and troubled—picks out two thick wedges of toffee cake. She hadn't managed to reach this conclusion on her own; Aasta had intervened after six minutes of blank staring, her eyes glazed over.

Meren wasn't thinking about cake; the glacé cherries and smooth marzipan had merged into a fuzzy, fog-like haze of reds and whites. Her mind was far off in some *other* distant realm of thought, turning over her life decisions and glaring at them critically.

'A prince*, of all people,'* she cursed herself as Aasta attempted to coax her decision along. *'If he ever finds out, he'll fire me on the spot for misconduct.'* Her stomach coils in on itself uncomfortably. *'Or laugh at me.'*

For some reason, the idea of Lorkan cackling at her affections cut into her heart more than losing her job ever could.

What finally brings Meren out of her introspection is Aasta saying, slipping a wide, flat knife between the plate and the dessert's spongy underside:

"Here, take this one. It's nice and filling. Lonely people always like my toffee cake."

Opening her tote bag, Meren's brows furrow, suddenly paying attention. "How'd you know he's lonely?"

"Everything you buy him is comfort food, poor lad. Is he very shy?"

She blinks again at the baker's uncanny powers, but recovers quicker this time. Finding freedom in the anonymity, she nods, unable to help a small smile grace her lips.

Lorkan interests her like a rare bird or a wildflower, but she has no one to pour her endearment to. She feels as though she's stumbled across an endangered creature, but can't tell the world because people might hunt it for sport.

"Yes." The light returning to her face, she passes the little stack of coins over the counter, warmed by so long gripped embarrassedly in her palm. "He's not really a people person."

"But he likes you, though," Aasta points out, making something in Meren's chest flutter.

Cheeks turning pink again, she mutters shy as a child:

"I hope so."

Aasta presses some change into her hand, giving her one of her signature smiles, the freckles on her cheeks merging into a galaxy as they fall into her dimples.

"Of course he does. Here's your change, pet. Now you go give him a big hug from me, okay? We have to look out for the quiet ones; they're often ignored for so long they forget they're special."

✳ ☾ ✳

Lorkan greets Meren as soon as her tentative knock resonates about the empty corridor. He invites her inside with a wide smile, which makes her shoulders loosen in relief; every time The Prince smiles nowadays—with his uncertain future hanging over him like a cloud—she sees it as some kind of blessing.

They spend a couple of hours preparing the pigments Meren bought, sitting at the low little table in the studio. Although there hadn't actually been any kind of hiatus between his paintings, Meren revels in the plush, colour-stained pillows, the pigment-dusted surfaces, and the sharp, tang of paint as though she's missed them for weeks.

WHAT LORKAN IS

Velôr's alliance with Calpurzia forgotten for now, they crush chalky lumps, mix oils, and pass bowls and light conversation back and forth between sips of tea. As usual, Lorkan asks after the health of Alfdis and Frode, then, after Arne. He doesn't raise his head from the paint he's stirring, but his tone shifts in a way only few would notice.

Which Meren does.

"He's fine," she shrugs, Arne's name feeling clunky and strange in Lorkan's presence; as though she's telling her husband she ran into an ex while she was out.

When he says nothing, she dumps some words into the uncomfortable hole of silence just to fill it:

"I finally got up the courage to tell him I just like him as a friend, which took a weight off my mind. I didn't like to think I was stringing him along."

This does make him look up, his piercing eyes boring into the side of Meren's face.

Only for a second, though.

He soon directs them back down to his paint, dragging his brush around and around.

"Did he take the news well?"

Meren can't help smiling at the memory; he'd look so endearingly bashful. "Yes, actually, better than I'd thought he would. He's found someone new already. He's called Bazyll."

Lorkan nods slowly then asks, as if treading carefully:

"And you are...okay with that?"

"Of course." She must have sounded convincingly indifferent because he relaxes next to her, and seems rather cheerful for the next half an hour.

When elevenses roll around, Meren begins freeing Aasta's cakes from their prettily-packaged prison. She always seals each box with twine and a stamp of hot wax, and she enjoys the process of catching the underside with her nail and peeling it off. It looks like a candy itself, soft and shiny and the colour of maple syrup. She's kept each one, just because it feels wrong to throw them away.

As they eat, Lorkan continues to ask after characters Meren has told him about; an elderly cheesemonger who always wishes her good morning. The girl she sometimes bumps into at Frode's, buying daily medicine for her sick brother. Lorkan has also become somewhat invested in Aasta; seeing as she makes the snacks he's now so fond of.

"I'm glad she's well," he nods, pleased. "If I were to go one day without her cakes I suspect I'd wither and die."

"The Palace chefs will whip you up a whole baker's cart at the snap of a finger," Meren points out, trying to intercept a stream of toffee dribbling off her plate and into the table's grooves. It's sticky and prickly with shards of sea salt.

He shakes his head. "They're not like Aasta's. Aasta's desserts are... uncomplicated."

"You mean peasant food?"

His cheekbones dust the lightest shade of pink. "If that's what you want to call it, yes—but I mean it as the highest compliment," he insists, and Meren believes him.

He squishes a lump of sponge under his fork, watching it ooze toffee like a tree bleeds sap. "It's just different to what Father's chefs make. They use the most expensive ingredients they can buy, just because they can. Butter, eggs, milk, all are for common people—the way they see it—" he adds, catching Meren's expression. "Instead, they use fats from beans, and milk tree nuts—"

"They *what?*"

"Use milk from nuts. Wait here, I'll show you."

Before she can ask where he's going, he's unfolded his long legs and disappeared into the lounge. When he returns, he offers her a thin, dry, yellow slice of something flopped limply on a glass plate.

"Here. It's almond cake—or so they say. Try it."

Meren frowns at him, unamused. "I'm not going to eat a washroom sponge, Lorkan."

He shrugs and brings the so-called cake to his mouth.

WHAT LORKAN IS

Meren doesn't have time to stop him sinking the white wedges of his teeth into it.

She watches in horror as he chews as if working a tough bread crust then, after some time, swallows.

Leaving the rest untouched, he returns to Aasta's cake with relish.

There's that happy little moan sound she'd hoped for.

Dipping her head, she moistens her lips, pretending to concentrate on dissevering a neat lump from her own sponge.

"So," he asks, eventually, "what did you eat where you grew up?"

Lorkan seems to be intrigued by anything that happens beyond Aldercliff's defensive walls. Imperfections, blemishes, entropy and flaws seem to fascinate him in a simple, innocent kind of way. He's curiously drawn to things that aren't good enough, things that are cheap and inelegant and disgusting—and the more Meren learns about his life as a prince, the more this begins to make sense to her.

So she strings together yarns for his amusement, describing things she's seen with long, decadent sentences.

His world is so untarnished and symmetrical; surely his head must ache after so long squinting through the glare of gold?

So she focuses on the things that are ugly. Things that are difficult, simple and dirty; things that are out of his reach.

Like street food; meat on sticks sliding toward oily fingers, fish and potatoes served in greasy, parchment cones,

The games the children are playing in the roads, their knees scuffed with blood and their faces scuffed with mud.

She describes a woman pricking a dragon onto a man's shoulder with a needle; his grimaces, the twitches of his eye, the beads of blood swirling with blue ink.

The Prince can not simply walk through the centre of the crowded marketplace unnoticed. Children would stop playing to gawp. Sellers would cease shouting praise for their products and, instead, bend themselves into a bow. All idle chat would silence, mothers would dab stains off their son's cheeks, and fathers would comb out their beards. All eyes would lower respectfully to the ground as though he's a reaper, come to harvest his next soul.

So Meren tells him about things she'd heard that made her smile.

Women telling stories about their useless husbands, and husbands showing off about their wonderful wives.

Snotty-nosed toddlers putting up a fuss about nothing in particular, siblings arguing over bites of a toffee apple.

Arguments. Shouting. Swears he didn't know existed; the sound of knuckles against cheekbones.

These things interest Lorkan the most; the gross, nitty-gritty things that are strange and wrong and leave a vile taste in most people's mouths.

So she tells him of the man who'll swallow a sword for a copper, and the tales scarred sailors haul to shore like the fish in their nets.

She describes watching one of them fillet a cod, the dexterity of his knives, the flash of scales, the colour pouring onto the floor, the stumps of his missing fingers.

She tells him about the accident she'd seen as a girl; two carts colliding, the noise of it; breath knocked out of animals, wood crumpling like parchment. She tells him about the bodies they'd dragged from the mess, alive, barley, indigo eyelids, crimson skin, twisted monsters.

The prince can't leave Aldercliff's grounds without guards; to be alone, he must settle for the royal gardens, caged in by high walls, everything perfect and manicured, not a leaf out of place, not a rock where a rock should not be.

So Meren describes the precise shade of the crabgrass and how it's starting to creep up through the gravel pathways, the crunch underfoot of mud and stones, how little bits of it get into her shoes no matter how careful she is.

She tells him of the smell of chimneys, vegetables, horses, flowers, meat, people, all packed in together, sweet, sharp, pungent, and so bitter with sweat.

Throughout it all, he listens.

He listens when she tells him about her past in Holcombe.

WHAT LORKAN IS

He listens when she tells him about her present in Tawny.

He eats up her words with hungry, childish interest because she's from another universe, even though it's only several yards from his front door.

✸ ☾ ✸

When the paint has been made and is standing to attention in a row of delicate bowls, Meren eyes them, her fingers compulsively picking a wad of pigment out from under her nail.

The idea of a prince painting her portrait had seemed appealing in theory but, now that the time has come, she's realising it's quite daunting in practice.

Despite their leafy hue, his eyes are startlingly intense and sharp at the best of times. How will it feel to have that intensity, that attention, trained on her for so long? Especially now, after Meren's revealing chat with Aasta. She expects his gaze to meet hers and burn right through her like a flame through parchment.

She swallows, moistening her lips, and Lorkan watches her tongue run across them.

"What's the matter?" He asks gently, his voice bringing her out of her stupor like a gentle guiding hand.

"Nothing."

"I don't have to paint you if you don't want me to."

"No, I want you to," she assures quickly. "I want you to because otherwise you'll have nothing to paint, and I *like* it when you paint; I like making it, and watching you use it."

A smile grazes his lip, flattered. "Then what's wrong?"

"I just…I feel like you're looking at my tense shoulders and wondering how you'll smooth out the knots with a paintbrush. Or my bony hands and wondering how you'll ever manage to make them look soft and feminine. Or, you're looking at all these rich greens and chestnut browns and thinking of dropping them in the bin."

"Why would I do that?"

"Because look at me," she gives a self-conscious chuckle. "You could just use a single shade of beige."

"I wasn't thinking that. Any of it."

"Oh." Meren blushes.

He's still regarding her steadily, and it makes her shift about on her cushion, avoiding his face as if he's as bright as the sun. When he doesn't say anything else, she tries to puff up her chest, sucking in a lungful of air.

It tastes of paint and pine wood and the bottles he keeps by the bath.

"So..." Gesturing about the room, "Where do you want me?"

A smirk tugs at the corner of Lorkan's lip, and colour flushes from the tips of Meren's ears, right down to her collarbones.

"I-I mean, for the painting," she corrects hastily.

"Really? I'm crushed," he quips, his voice a velvet curl of amusement, and she gives his side a light jab with her pointed elbow.

Suddenly he's not a prince.

He's just her friend, who wants to do some art.

"I meant *where do you want me to pose?*"

Pensively, he runs a cloth along his mixing brush, carefully easing the olive-coloured paint from the hog hair bristles. "I'm actually not sure yet. I've been mulling that over all day."

"I assumed you had a painting in mind."

His angular face has turned absent again, probably picturing each room, placing Meren somewhere and adjusting her limbs, gently raising her chin and directing her to sit up straighter, or lay down.

Something stirs deep within her stomach, and she has to avert her eyes again.

"I knew I wanted to paint *you*—I just don't know where, or how."

"What's with all the greens, then?" She gestures to the rows of bowls; ferns, jades, hazels—

WHAT LORKAN IS

Lorkan blinks as if remembering something. "Oh yes." A small, sheepish smile twitches his mouth up at one end. "I have something else to show you."

19

LORKAN'S GIFT

Curiously, Meren follows close at Lorkan's heels.

She has to walk fast to keep up with them and, eventually, he glances over one broad shoulder, his dark brows furrowed.

She smiles gratefully as he slows his elegant strides to accommodate her much shorter legs. Watching the nubbed point of her canvas slippers, she's careful not to kick his pale shins—

—which is difficult because he's slowed even more.

When he eventually draws to a sluggish halt, a question rises in Meren's lungs, but it catches in her throat.

One of his large, deliberate hands has reached back and taken her wrist.

Gently, he tugs her closer until she's level with his side. "You don't need to walk behind me."

A sideways smile.

A blush.

Releasing her arm, he sets into another walk.

WHAT LORKAN IS

✶ ☾ ✶

It feels wrong to walk in line with a member of the royal family, Meren thinks, like slamming a door in a Queen's face, or asking a King to fetch her some water. Part of her wants to drop back behind him and scurry along with her head bowed—

But there had been a tautness to his voice, a pleading edge that reminded Meren of something he'd told her; something about people seeing him as a prince instead of a person.

Smiling shyly, she matches his steps, his green trousers flapping in time with her uniform, their feet lining up and falling into a comfortable tempo; his bare and as pale as the marble they tread on, Meren's tucked into her brown slippers and much, much smaller.

Her excitement bubbles away, boiling over into apprehension as she realises —embarrassingly slowly—that Lorkan is leading her to his bedroom. What could he possibly want to show her in here?

Well, she could think of one thing. Several things—

But he's not that kind of prince.

He's not that kind of man.

Is he?

If he is, would she mind?

Not even in the secure fortress of her thoughts, or the dark, shaded area at the back of her consciousness had Meren admitted to herself that she has a primal kind of fascination with Lorkan's long, sinewy body. Some secret part of her can't help but wonder whether the parts of him she hasn't seen are as magnificent as the parts she has; sleek, silken, inky hair, jutting ridges and hills of bone, supple muscles sliding below ethereal moon-beam skin—

Her cheeks tint and Lorkan pushes the door open, motioning for her to follow him inside.

The door jamb passes her eyeline like teeth edging a gaping mouth, and she swallows, her mind running away with mental images of—

Of things that are not going to happen.

Lorkan is waiting for her by the bed, fully clothed and smiling a smile.

But not that kind of smile.

It's bashful. Expectant.

A dress has been spread out over the bed.

It's green. Green like gazing into the woods at night, dark and endless. Green like evergreen trees. That's the shade, Meren realises vaguely, the waxy hue of pine needles, thick leaves immune to frost and snow. The bodice and skirt are pricked all over with tiny leaves and stars, darned with glinting, gold thread.

Meren has never been to one of Aldercliff's palace balls, but she'd heard of them. With the other maids, she's peeked from the servant's courtyard as the guests arrived in horse and chariot, filing into the main entrance in a line like decorations on a cake. Each woman had worn a dress like this. Meren had imagined them flouncing deftly about The Great Hall, the light rustling swish of expensive fabric, the trail of floral perfume, the stupefied male gazes in their wake.

She swallows, looking from Lorkan's patient, waiting eyes, then back to the dress sprawled like a goddess across the bed.

The neckline hangs in a low rectangle, delicately exposing skin only to teasingly hide it behind a soft, opaque mesh. It flows all the way up to a modest, slender collar, and Meren's hand twitches to reach out and touch it; a glass beaded cuff or, perhaps, the delicate, membranous tulle—

But she withdraws it. She imagines her fingers, calloused and stinging with carbolic soap, reaching out and, like a leaf stroked by the hand of death, the material withers and dies before her eyes.

Sluggishly, the pieces click together.

The painting.

The green pigments.

Her voice wobbles. "...You want me to wear this?"

Lorkan's broad shoulders rise and fall in a shrug. He's propped his long, lean body up against one of the four bedposts.

"I don't mind if you do or don't," he says, sounding like he's telling the truth. "You'll look radiant in the painting either way."

A shy heat suffuses Meren's cheeks.

"I just thought you might want to wear something a little more...you, seeing as I'm about to immortalise your likeness."

"Thank you. I did think...well, I didn't want to be trapped on a canvas as a maid forever. Not that being your maid isn't—"

His lip twitching with amusement, he watches her flounder until she gives in with a defeated sigh.

"Being painted in this...even *ten minutes* spent in this dress..." But something makes her bite her lower lip. "Lorkan...who does this belong to? It's not your mother's. I've seen her statues and these aren't her measurements."

His past lovers dance through Meren's mind on long, shapely legs, swishing their waist-length hair the colour of the sun, feminine and sensual with skin soft as a rose petal, and the fluttering lashes of a doe.

This dress must have belonged to a woman Lorkan has...entertained. Or, *she'd* entertained *him*, just like Meren had thought he wanted *her* to do only moments ago. Does he have a whole wardrobe of clothes discarded by former sweethearts? Women so wealthy, so elite, they can afford to just throw away, forget about, leave behind a dress like this?

"It's yours."

"What?"

"I had it made for you. It should fit, but if it doesn't we can have it altered—"

"You *bought* this?" Meren would have shrieked it if her throat wasn't doing a strange tightening thing. "*You* bought *this?* For *me?* That's *absurd*, it's—"

A dream? Surely this is some kind of fantasy. She must have been pushing a mop about on the steps in the brittle winter dawn, slipped on the slick soap, and now she's lying, concussed on the stairs, vividly hallucinating. Perhaps a nobleman is carefully stepping over her limp body as they speak, being careful not to sully his nice shoes?

"Yes. Is that okay? I know I should have asked what you like, but I knew you'd be too humble to pick so you'd just choose whatever's cheapest."

"Lorkan, I wouldn't have let you buy this *at all!* I'm a *servant*. I can't wear clothes like this!" She gestures at it, barking a bitter, cackling laugh. "Can you imagine if someone walked in and saw me parading around in this?"

He waves a dismissive hand. "No one will know." His words are low and silky but, suddenly, the dark lines of his eyebrows pull into a frown. Something awfully close to worry flashes over his expression, his cool completely disappearing:

"You don't like it?"

Meren's mouth opens and closes several times before it manages to push out anything resembling a sentence. She turns to him, his hooded eyes now uneasy, watching her, disquieted, waiting. She wants to touch him, to take some part of him—mainly to hold herself upright.

"Don't be stupid," She almost laughs, the sound coming out as a watery little giggle. "How could anyone *not* like it?"

His chest deflates as if he's been holding in a breath, his smile returning tentatively.

She finds a surprisingly firm knot of muscle as she places a hand on his arm and gives a comforting squeeze. "Lorkan, I absolutely love it. I'm *in* love with it."

Obviously relieved, "Are you sure you're content with green? I guessed you liked it because of your earrings, although I went for gold accents rather than silver because its warmer."

Meren is too distracted to ask or even wonder why he sees her as warm. She still hasn't let go of his arm, and does so hesitantly—because her knees seem to be made from Aasta's toffee cake. Reaching out, she lightly runs the pad of one finger along a chain of tiny, embroidered oak leaves, each the size of a ladybird.

"I would have bought gold earrings if I could have afforded them," she mutters absently as the silky bumps pass under her skin. She can feel Lorkan's gaze on the side of her face, the quiet curve of his smile.

WHAT LORKAN IS

Straightening back up, she shakes her head. "You shouldn't have done this. You shouldn't have wasted all that money on me."

"Yes, it was a waste to buy you *another* dress," he replies tartly. "You've got so many after all. It'll probably just get stuffed to the back of your wardrobe and forgotten about."

Meren moistens her lips, and his features suddenly soften.

"I'm sorry. I didn't mean—"

"No, it's okay," she waves him off. "I was just realising you're right. I don't even have a wardrobe, so if I did accept it I'd have nowhere to store it. Something like this doesn't fit into my life, Lorkan." She turns to him, expecting to find confusion and irritation at her ungratefulness.

Instead, his pale eyes have turned to a tender pastel as he regards her almost sadly.

"I can't accept this. You wouldn't understand; this is just a casual outfit for the women in your world, something to lounge around in. For me...well, put it this way: even if I'd saved up every copper I've ever earned, I still wouldn't be able to afford the material to *make* this dress."

Without warning, beads of water are pricking the corners of her eyes, although she's not sure why. She's not really *sad*, she's just...everything. She's happy and upset and afraid. She's so full of *things* that *something* has to escape, and that something is tears.

They bead hot and humiliated on her lashes.

"Wren, darling." Lorkan has stepped closer without her realising; she'd been too busy trying to blink away that stinging sensation to notice him raise a large, gentle hand.

Full of latent strength, he cups her face and, carefully, brushes a tear from her cheek with his thumb.

"I wouldn't have gotten it for you if I'd known I'd have to watch you cry."

She sniffs.

One of her cheeks burns hot with an embarrassed flush, the other cooled by the spread of his palm. Her jawline slots snugly into it, the bone softly cradled as though he's holding an eggshell.

"Sorry," she mumbles, desperately willing herself not to let another tear dribble from her lid. It collects, swelling until she blinks, the little damp trail of it cold against her skin.

Lorkan wipes that one away too.

He's so close she can feel his breath. If she closed her eyes, she might have guessed he'd left a window open; a subtle breeze brushing her skin like feathers.

He shakes his head. "Don't apologise, you've done nothing wrong. You don't have to keep the dress if it makes you feel sad."

"It doesn't," Meren insists, not because she wants to keep it (even though she *does)* but because she doesn't want Lorkan to think he's upset her. "You remembered I love the colour green. You had this *made* for me, your *housekeeper*, just to make me feel beautiful. That's so thoughtful of you, I don't think...well, no one's ever treated me as nicely as you have."

Lorkan beams bashfully, retracting his hand now that her tears had given away to a weak smile.

She misses his touch, the reassuring firmness of it, his strength shifting below his skin. There's a power within him, held back and restrained in a way that reminds Meren she's a woman.

"I'm glad you like it." He turns to the dress still laid out neatly over the bed.

It lacks creases, every inch of it unwrinkled, the fabric like verdant rolling hills.

He must have spent time smoothing it out earlier, so it looks perfect for when he introduces it to its owner. She pictures him like a nervous boy about to give his first sweetheart a posy.

"I'd really like you to keep it," he says, waking her from her stupor. He's watching her, his eyes on her damp cheek. He must know she loves it, it must be written all over her face because he's smiling. "It's a gift, it's designed for you, it won't fit anyone else—or suit anyone else."

WHAT LORKAN IS

"I can't believe you had it made from memory," she muses in quiet awe, her eyes sliding down its whole length, the pinched waist, the curve of the shoulder. It's her exact shape; a green, star-speckled shadow.

"The dressmaker was very patient with me." His cheekbones dust with pink again. "I can keep it here for you if you like. You can change into it when you arrive each morning and change back into your uniform before you go down to the servant's quarters."

Meren doesn't have the heart to ask, *'What happens to it if you move to Calpurzia?'*

Instead, she pushes that thought from her mind, turning back to meet Lorkan's gaze. "I shouldn't..." she mutters, mainly to herself—he seemed so hurt when he thought she didn't like it.

Almost shaking, she reaches out and takes the gown in her hands, lifting it from the duvet.

It's heavy in her arms, the pleated skirt falling, a wave of plush, elegant velvet; as though midway through a dance.

"If it makes you feel better," he adds "you can think of it as payment for posing for me. You'll have to sit still for a long time, are you sure you're okay with that? We will take breaks, of course—"

Still in a state of disbelief, Meren shakes her head, batting away his concerns with a laugh. "I've been working since I could clutch a dishcloth; that sounds like a dream. And, anyway, I didn't agree to be your muse for the finished product—although it will be breathtaking," she adds, which gets a flattered smile. "I like the colours, and the sound your brush makes as you dab the canvas...and our conversations." Without thinking, she pushes herself up onto her tiptoes and presses a chaste kiss to his cheek. "Thank you. For this. All of it."

Lorkan waves her off, that smile still there, and something different, something new; a tint of red on both cheeks. Red, proper red, red like the scarlet sheen of a tomato—although, it's gone so quickly Meren puts it down to a trick of the light. All sorts of colours get reflected off of Lorkan's alabaster skin. He's like a china cup next to a stained glass window.

"You are quite welcome." He rubs the rough collar of her servant's uniform between finger and thumb. "I never knew how you put up with these scratchy uniforms, anyway. I would have given it to you sooner but I didn't think Arne would be very happy with me. And..." His thin lips turn up into a sheepish smile, so out of place on his angular face. That redness is back as he adds:

"...I like our conversations too."

* ☾ *

In Lorkan's washroom, Meren can barely keep from hurling her uniform into a disorganised heap as she drags it up and over her head.

She'd hung her new dress on the door, next to one of his silky dressing gowns, and admired it as she unlaced her apron, the crisp, hardened cotton scraping and scratching.

When she's finally standing in nothing but her undergarments, she pauses, chewing her bottom lip between her teeth.

Her simple white briefs she sees no issue with, but her thick underbodice...

It protrudes like an ill-fitting bed sheet, squaring off her waist into a non-discernible box—

But she can't keep the bodice *on*. She pictures it sprouting from the gold neckline like a weed, lumps and bumps of coarse fabric bulging like molehills.

She knows Lorkan wouldn't mind either way. He could easily use a little artistic license to remove the bumps and creases from the painting, and Meren doubts he'd laugh at her for being shy.

She *is* shy, she realises, her fingers hesitating at the tie.

She thinks of her mother's sleeves, only rolled up to submerge clothes in a wash tub, and Alfdis' starched collar, tickling the underside of her chin even on the hottest days, the servant's quarters baking like a vast brick oven. Even

WHAT LORKAN IS

Aasta, with her alluring curves, keeps them shrouded in several layers of ironed, shapeless cotton, stifling every feminine jiggle and shake as she kneads her dough.

* ☾ *

After a lot of contemplation, Meren's under bodice joins her discarded uniform on the little blue tiles.

20

THE MUSE

With almost glacial slowness, Meren eases the dress over her hips and up onto her shoulders. It's not that she doesn't trust the obviously high-end material, it's that she doesn't trust *herself* not to jam her leg through the skirt, or her jagged nails not to shred one of the mesh sleeves. Thus, she climbs into it like a lizard shedding its skin but in reverse; a lot of awkward shimmying and uncoordinated peeling.

When she's finally settled in, she dares a tentative peek at the looking glass.

There's a woman inside, draped in green and gold.

She'd be scrawny if she were swamped in linen and wool, but she's not, she's wrapped in velvet and tulle, and stitched all over with stars. She turns her neck, long and elegant, at the same time Meren does and, when she blinks, the woman blinks back.

Shocked, Meren takes a step closer to the sink.

That's *her* bony chest rising and falling with quickened breaths, *her* wide eyes, *her* lips parted in an awestruck little circle. That's *her* waist, the dress clinging subtly to curves she didn't know she had. It's as though it's doing it on purpose, she thinks amusedly; as though it's taken a good long look at her and is saying, *'Yes, we'll emphasise this bit here'* and *'That area is gorgeous, let's pay attention to that'.*

She swallows and tastes something new and strange; something that must be the sweet tang of vanity.

After several selfish moments simply gawking at herself, Meren eventually begins the tricky business of lacing it up. She'd known it would be difficult as soon as she'd set eyes on the complex strings of ribbon, weaved and knotted into a labyrinthine pattern; a trellis tangled in roses.

Clumsily, she manages a few knots, looping the ribbons into what she can only assume are the right holes. They keep slipping from her fingers with snickering whispers of silk until she's sure they're teasing her graceless attempts on purpose, and the looking glass is no help; throwing her reflection back the wrong way just for the fun of it, confusing her fumbling fingers.

After several admirable minutes of stubbornness, Meren deems the feat impossible with a frustrated frown.

'So this is why upper-class women have ladies maids to dress them,' she realises with a defeated, silent sigh. *She* doesn't have anyone to help her untangle what is now a tight bunch of ribbons because she's an imposter, only *pretending* to be part of this world—

Well, there is one person.

* ☾ *

Humiliated, Meren uses both hands to clutch the back of the dress together as though it's an open wound, and bashfully nudges the door open with her foot.

The skirt's gold-trimmed hem flutters playfully about her ankles as she pads across the cold marble, an uncomfortable heat scorching the tips of her ears.

She had removed her slippers to climb into the dress and opted to leave them off. Gowns like this are designed to make the owner appear to *sweep*, not step, she reasoned, and her clumpy canvas shoes would erase its efforts. She doesn't own any flat, dainty pumps, but she isn't opposed to going barefoot; the chilled floor is helping to cool her red cheeks, the reassuring weight of Aldercliff keeping her steady as she approaches a long, green divan.

Lorkan is waiting there for her, sprawled leisurely across the cushions, a book spread neatly in one hand.

Despite her almost soundless approach, his ears prick as she scurries towards him.

He turns his head and, with a papery thud, his book falls, forgotten, onto the floor.

Meren sheepishly comes to a stop before him, gripping the back of her dress, and he clears his throat, pushing himself up off the divan.

"Beautiful," he mutters.

Her skin prickles under the weight of his attention, and she dips her head. She has all of it—his attention.

It falls to her waist, lingering a second before he catches himself, his cheekbones dusting pink.

It sends something skittering up the column of Meren's spine.

He may be a prince, but he's also just a man.

"Thank you," she stutters, two simple words and yet, with his eyes scorching into her like they are, unblinking, she screws up both of them.

"Is it comfortable?" He's moved his hands to rest behind his back; as though he's observing a priceless artefact in a museum and wants the guards to know he doesn't plan on touching it.

He hasn't asked whether it fits well, Meren realises with a curl of amusement.

He doesn't need to.

"It's perfect," she beams. "It's the most heavenly thing I've ever worn but... the back. I can't do it on my own." Turning, she presents it to him shyly, both hands still anxiously clamping the fabric together. "Could you?"

WHAT LORKAN IS

Taking a breath, she forces her fingers to let go, exposing a long, wide column of bare skin. It stretches from that dip between her shoulder blades to the very small of her back, naked beside the occasional mole, and that scar she got as a child from falling out of a tree.

Who was the last person to see her shoulder blades, she wonders? The two slight dimples pressed softly into the base of her spine? Her mother, probably; back when she was a babe in a wash tub, having her skin scrubbed with a coarse old sponge.

"I'm not sure I'll be much help," Lorkan chuckles bashfully, but he moves up behind her all the same.

"I assume it's just like undoing it but in the other opposite way," Meren suggests helpfully with a shrug in her voice. She can feel him rather than hear him, the broad line of his shoulders stooped as he takes the two ribbons gently.

Slowly, he begins at the base of the bodice, patiently easing them from her knots and re-threading them with his own.

"I haven't had much experience with undoing dresses either."

In her mind, Meren is sweeping imaginary palms over the thick velvet, observing the weight and brush of the heavy skirt, the airy, crinkly sleeves delicate as frost—

—but, suddenly, she's paying attention.

Surely wealthy women don't summon their ladies-maid to the bedroom when they have male company? Plus, she wonders, why get a faceless servant to strip you of your clothes when you could have Lorkan's dexterous, competent fingers easing off each garment?

Hoping he can't see the blush trickling down the back of her neck:

"I think it went in a sort of criss-cross pattern. You could try to follow any progress I've made, but I think it's just a big clump." She laughs, a little one-syllable bubble from her chest, just to ease some of that tension that's pooling in her abdomen.

Now that she thinks about it—which feels odd after so long of trying *not* to think about it—Meren has never actually *seen* one of The Prince's many supposed lovers. Not once has he asked her to leave his company early because he's going to be entertaining a lady friend. She's never had to pluck a discarded chemise from his bedroom floor or scrub pink cheek tint powder from the bathroom sink. She's never stumbled across a stray earring, lip-stained tumbler, or found a long, silken hair that *isn't* black as night or her own wispy, wren-feather brown.

Her reverie is broken by several words tumbling onto her shoulder:

"You didn't do as bad a job as you think." Lorkan seems to have figured out what he's doing and picked up a quick, graceful rhythm, his fingers looping and threading, arranging the ribbons as the dressmaker had intended. "You did well managing to get it this far."

Every now and again, he brushes her skin—the back of a cool finger, a gentle thumb—and it doesn't help Meren's efforts to banish the thoughts flooding into her brain like sweet honey.

It's a strange experience, someone—a man—a *prince*—*Lorkan* dressing her. He's probably thinking the same thing because he muses absently:

"I feel like your maid."

She flushes, her self-consciousness swelling with every second of his time she's taking up. "I'll practice tying it when I'm not wearing it, then, one day, I should be able to do it myself."

Quietly:

"You don't have to."

Meren can't see his face, but she knows him well enough to guess the dashes of his cheekbones are flushed pink.

※ ☾ ※

Even if Meren did manage to learn how to tie the dress herself, she wouldn't want to make use of the skill. Lorkan—despite his lack of practice—proved to be more than competent, doing a better job at entwining the silky strands than she would ever be able to manage.

WHAT LORKAN IS

She had braced herself for him to tug the ribbons tight, to shrink the circumference of her waist like a corset—but his nimble knotting and threading reached midway up her back and she realised that moment would never come. He's left the material loose and roomy and continued to do so, fitting it *to* her rather than trying to fit her to *it*.

"Beautiful," he mutters again, his fingers carefully knotting the final bow. He takes a step back and Meren turns another awed pirouette, watching her skirt flare about her ankles in a rainbow of green and gold, a joyful grin splitting her face in two.

Lorkan waits patiently for her to finish her twirling, watching her with quiet amusement as she turns her body this way and that. He's propping up his pointed chin with one hand, the corners of his lips ghosting with a smile below the curl of his fingers, and Meren eventually notices, blushing.

Mistaking his posture for boredom, she lets her skirt settle back about her legs and clears her throat. "So, have you decided where you'd like me to pose?"

He sighs pensively, the arm crossed over his narrow middle rising and falling. "I still don't how I want the painting to be, yet. When I paint, I tend to wait for a scene to present itself, rather than hunting about for it."

Meren listens attentively, her curiosity hungry for anything he can teach her about the magical process that is art.

"I know I *want* to paint you, but not *how*. When I drew that deer through the telescope I knew I wanted to capture its likeness, but I had to wait an hour and a half before it took the pose I eventually sketched it in."

She pictures Lorkan stooped over the vast machine in the other room, waiting patiently for inspiration to hit whilst the arms of the clock hacked away at time like miniature hammers. "That's okay, you don't have to think of something right away."

"Actually, I do because one day I might not be able to finish it."

When she looks puzzled, he mutters bitterly:

"I can't paint you if I'm shipped off to Calpurzia."

"You're not even engaged yet," Meren corrects and he shakes his head.

"Wren, I *will* be engaged one day. Maybe not for a while, or even to the Calpurzian princess, but one day a prince must be wed. We have to start the painting as soon as possible, in case we can't begin it at all."

Meren chews the inside of her cheek thoughtfully. "Do you really...*have* to marry?"

He turns to her, and she shrinks under his stare.

"I just...when I was growing up, I thought you royals were gods—"

"Thought?" He teases, and she rolls her eyes

"What I mean is, I can't believe someone can tell *you*—of all people— what to do."

"Really? You do it all the time."

"Lorkan, I'm being *serious*."

A sad smile twists his mouth. "I know but, as princes, Sol and I have to obey our king and queen just like you—although my parents don't actually *order* me to do anything, per se. They prefer persistent nudging. Like this whole thing with the alliance; Father has this way of using guilt to eat away at my conscience. I'll turn down the Calpurzian's proposal at first, but after a few weeks of *His Majesty* going on about the blood of future wars staining my hands..."

"Yes, Meren sighs. "I did think you were worrying about that. Your forehead goes all frowny when you think I'm not looking."

He presses his lips together. "I didn't know you'd noticed."

"Of course I noticed." Tenderly—as tenderly as she dares—she places a hand on his arm. "Nothing has been decided yet. For now, why don't we find somewhere for me to sit, you can paint, and I'll nibble those shortbreads I know you keep in the pantry."

A smile ghosts the lower half of his face.

"And don't worry about finishing it, just paint it because you *like* to paint."

Her brow furrows, pensive. "Could we try to...create inspiration somehow?"

"Create it?"

"Yeah. Maybe we can *spark* an epiphany? I could pose in each room and we can see what looks good?"

* ☾ *

Meren spends the next few hours letting Lorkan arrange her in various rooms, on various pieces of furniture, in various positions—although, the positions weren't actually that varied; he seems to favour the more relaxed poses, whether for Meren's benefit or because that's the atmosphere he's aiming for, she isn't sure.

She feels comfortable with all of them, and believes she could easily hold each for as many hours as he may need. Plus, they are tasteful, and she silently thanked the heavens for this; not that she *had* expected The Prince to ask her to spread herself lewdly over a chaise lounge.

The clock strikes two, and they still haven't found a pose or location that pleases them—and, by this point, it really is '*them*' and '*they*'.

Lorkan seems as interested in Meren's input as he is his own, if not more so. Right at the beginning, when he'd suggested she try lounging on a divan, she'd shyly proposed resting one arm along the backrest; to give the whole thing a smooth, sweeping feel. He had replied with a smile:

"I don't know whether to be proud of you for thinking of it, or concerned for myself because I didn't."

From then on, Meren holds nothing back and even begins taking the initiative, learning from Lorkan what might look good and what might not—what would make a pose work with her surroundings and what would set a specific mood.

"How about I face this way, so my profile contrasts with the curtain?" She asks, demonstrating, and he nods, his previously critical expression giving way to a pleased smile as though a few pieces are finally slotting into place.

It's always a *few* pieces, never all of them.

He'd liked the soft light in the lounge, but seemed unhappy when Meren perched on the empty settees, or tucked herself into the cramped armchairs.

He'd liked the green of the wool rug spread before the fire, but not the position; her legs bent awkwardly below her body, one hand propping her up —

She tries to hold each titbit in her mind—posing where she thinks he might like her to pose, in places he might like to paint—but there are so many, that they spill through her fingers like marbles.

She doesn't mind.

Lorkan reminds her again and again that it's not her fault. Every time he sighs and shakes his head, he reminds her it's the *room's* fault, the *lighting's* fault, his *own* fault.

21

MANNERS

Lorkan sighs as they, once again, circle back to the lounge, declaring it time to take a break.

Earlier, Meren had left her packed lunch on an end table by the window, and he must have noticed her gaze gravitating towards the little parcel, lingering hungrily as if her eyes could eat through the cloth.

"We don't have to do this," he says after permitting her to move.

He'd set her sitting in an armchair, framed by two towering bookcases, and had been staring at her intently for about thirty-two seconds.

He'd done that for a few of the more promising poses, and she'd quickly realised the amount of time he asks her to hold a stance is a good indication of how appealing he finds it. Not because he's analysing it—he's not taking in the colours, tones and the general aura of the scene. It's more like he's...waiting for something to happen.

At first, she'd thought he was waiting for *her* to do something—although she wasn't sure what. But then she realised what he's *actually* doing is waiting for that bolt of inspiration to hit, and is just giving it enough time to arrive.

Thirty-two seconds of waiting isn't bad—this pose must have potential. But there had been *one*—on a blue divan back in the study—where he'd asked her to hold her position for *forty-eight* seconds.

Meren hops happily from the armchair's plush grip, extending her arms over her head until she feels a few joints give a satisfying click. "Do what?"

"The painting. If you're bored—"

"I'm not bored." As has become their habit, she retrieves the crockery Lorkan keeps in the cabinet by the door.

They're green and made of some sort of glass—or perhaps, more likely, crystal—giving them a misty, sea foam sort of transparent look.

They remind Meren of his irises.

"Honestly, I enjoy it."

"Are you sure? I keep feeling as though I'm bossing you around," he says, leaning over Meren to reach into the cupboard he uses as a larder. He pulls out some cured meats, two honey cakes, a loaf of manchet bread, and a truckle of cheese. "Will you want any meat? It's venison today."

"Yes, please. Oh, and I bought some sloe preserve at the market."

"Delicious, thank you."

There's a rustling of parchment and the clink of knives scooping out jars as they exchange lunch items like children in a playground:

He decorates her sandwich with meat and cheddar from the palace kitchens, and she slathers preserve and drops strawberries onto his fancy bread.

"By the way, you're not bossing me around, I'm enjoying being a muse. Art is something I never thought I'd witness first-hand, let play an active part in."

Taking his loaded plate to a chaise lounge, Lorkan flops neatly onto its plush pillows, tucking his legs up below him as though folding a pair of wings. "Isn't it the working class that makes most of Velôr's furniture, buildings, and instruments?"

Briefly, Meren wonders about pushing one of the plump armchairs over for herself, but the window seat looks more appealing.

WHAT LORKAN IS

Set back into a niche in the wall, a row of plump cushions have been arranged across the stone sill, their fabric sun-washed and warm. Through the glass, dandelion-fluff clouds cast thin shadows over woodlands, fields, rooftops and, eventually, the sea, mottling it like the scales of a fish.

Settling her back against the pane, Meren tries not to focus on the dizzying height. Instead, she watches the kittiwakes playing amongst Aldercliff's towers, their wings bowed, and capped with black as though dipped in ink.

"I would have thought your family has a few tile makers, blacksmiths or wood carvers here and there." Lorkan muses. "Are they not artists?"

"My family is in the *lower* working class. We don't really make things, we fix what is broken. Mother washes and sews the village's torn clothes for a few crescents, and Father repairs what is brought to him; timepieces and fishing rods and things with little gears and screws."

Lorkan uses the end of his finger to wipe up a smear of fruit preserve, popping it in his mouth with a hum.

It makes all of Meren's atoms vibrate.

"I think fixing things counts as art. There's something beautiful about having enough patience and compassion to mend, rather than simply replace."

※ ☾ ※

Lorkan and Meren often emerge from the studio to luncheon in another room, just for a change of scenery, their pigment-stained hands giving their fingers a chalky taste as they lick up stray bread crumbs and scuffs of butter.

Before, whilst caged in her uniform, Meren preferred to crouch by the plain, practical wooden table with her sack of rye bread and raisins. Though her dress snagged the embroidery of the cushion she sat on, it hardly stood out amongst the paint stains and wood shavings already marring the fabric. She felt more at home with the splintering brushes and rainbow-streaked rags, blending in with the walls, floors and furniture, all an unassuming shade of brown.

However, now, with her dress flowing like an emerald waterfall from her spot by the window and a decadent feast on her lap, she realises she doesn't feel so out of place among the emerald silks, heavy curtains and carved oakwood.

Using one of Lorkan's silver forks, she pops a cube of cheese between her teeth.

"Besides the studio," she asks after swallowing her cheddar, "which room do you think you use most?"

Her curiosity in Lorkan's life has—until very recently—gone unsatisfied.

He's made it clear she can ask him questions right from the beginning, but she's still not sure whether that had been some kind of test. There's always a sharp look in his eyes, as though cogs are turning quietly, right at the back of his mind.

She's seen that look in the cats that hang around the kitchens, hoping for scraps. She thinks they're just lounging, fast asleep on the front step, but then their ear will twitch and she'll realise they'd been alert and aware all along, never really dreaming at all.

Lorkan looks pensive as he contemplates his answer, probably sifting through multitudinous memories, all somewhat identical.

Life can't be very varied for a prince, Meren thinks—especially not the *youngest* prince. At least Sol's days are stuffed with training for when he will one day inherit the throne.

"Probably this one. I like the lighting so I often read in here." He smiles. "You're actually in my favourite seat."

"Do you want to swap?" Meren offers, although she doesn't bother to stand because she knows he'll reply with—

"No, I'm quite happy here, thank you."

A smirk twitches her lip. "I knew you'd say that."

This makes him smile. "I was thinking about what you said earlier, about having no contact with art. I think you're wrong."

"Oh?" Meren raises a challenging eyebrow.

"Aasta's cakes," he states proudly. "They're art. The ingredients are simple but she's managed to make them into something special. For instance, how do they stay so moist, even when we leave them in a box for several hours?"

She would like to say something clever—she has worked in a kitchen, after all, so should have picked up a few tricks. However, Yllva had never once made a cake that *didn't* feel like grains of sand—at least while Meren was working under her—so the only trick she learnt was how to peel a potato in under five seconds. Instead, lowering her voice, she says seriously:

"I think she's a witch."

Lorkan laughs, and it fills the air between them like sunlight. "What gives you that idea?"

"Think about it; even the palace chefs couldn't keep that lemon cake moist, and all you did was bring it from downstairs. Plus..." her eyes narrow "...she knows things."

"Everyone knows things," he points out, and she shakes her head.

"Yes, but Aasta knows *more* things. She put her uncanny detective abilities down to raising five daughters, but I bet she has some kind of magic stirring about in her veins as well." She thinks for a moment, tapping her chin with her delicate, silver fork.

"Perhaps elven? That would explain the allure she seems to hold over almost everyone she meets. I've never met an elf, but I've heard some of them are more beautiful than the sun."

When Lorkan doesn't look convinced, she adds, "She *could* be a witch. After all, a few people in *your* family are sorcerers."

Humouring her, he cocks one eyebrow. It gives him a smouldering, mischievous sort of look, and Meren likes it very much—although it does make something inside her tingle most peculiarly.

"Fair point. So, what sort of magic does she specialise in? Baking? And—how did you put it? Knowing things? That would make her a seer *and* an alchemist."

Meren uses her fork to waggle it in his direction—the way she's seen her mother do with a wooden spoon countless times. "If you'd met her, you'd know what I'm talking about. She knows about you, you know."

"Of course she knows about me," Lorkan says simply, leaning back in his seat. "*Everyone* knows about me because—must I once again remind you? I am the youngest son of *King Cade*."

"No, she knows about *you*. To quote her, you're *'lonely'*, and *'quiet'*—"

"I'm not *actually* so lonely anymore."

"I see you're not quibbling *'quiet'*."

"I'm a recluse, Meren, people call me *'quiet'* more than they do my actual name," he deepens his voice, trying to mimic his father's rumbling, grating tone:

"*'Oh, that's my second born, he's a little quiet, but he's a good lad.'*"

"No, I mean, Aasta doesn't know I work for *you,* specifically."

"Well, then, it seems *knowing things* isn't one of her powers, after all."

"She *does* know things!" Meren persists, frustratedly. "She knows the money I use for the cakes isn't mine, and that I'm sharing them with a man. A man who she says is quiet and shy and not a people person."

She leaves out the part where Aasta implied she's kind of in love with him. And the part about him liking her back.

A smirk twitches his lip. "Who is this *man* you've been sharing my cakes with? I want a word with him."

"*Lorkan.*"

"Okay, okay, she is *right*, but that doesn't mean she's a *witch*."

Recognising defeat, Meren lets her shoulder blades fall back against the glass. "You *look* like a witch." She prods teasingly, but his head tilts to the side.

"In what way?"

Surprised, she ceases dragging her fork about her plate to collect the last scuffs of preserves.

He's watching her with an expression she doesn't recognise and, even though she can't read it, she knows immediately that she doesn't like it.

"I didn't *mean* it. I just meant your hair," she gestures at it, all loose waves the colour of night. "And your eyes. I feel like you can see into my head sometimes; as if you're reading my thoughts as they pop up."

This makes him laugh, and Meren can see his tongue.

The jam has stained it purple.

Relaxing back into his seat, "Rest assured, Wren, darling, I can do many things, but reading minds is not one of them."

"Are you sure?" She wonders about lapping the last few smudges of her own preserves from her plate, but thinks better of it. Placing the crockery down on the table:

"Maybe you just haven't figured out how?"

"A valid point. I'll make an attempt."

A smile tweaks her lip as Lorkan makes a show of trying to look thoughtful, his eyes scouring her temples like they're seeking a weak spot to burrow into.

If she didn't know he was playing with her, she would have been tempted to shield her face with her hands, just in case he somehow manages to pinch a thought from her skull—

But then his lips spread into a victorious smirk.

"You were thinking about licking your plate."

Blinking, her breath catches in her throat, and Lorkan must catch it because his grin doubles, exposing his teeth.

"Don't look so horrified, I'm joshing. It doesn't take a psychic to know you enjoy quality food."

He's finished his lunch by now, and draws the plate to his mouth, dragging his own pointed tongue across it. He's stretched his narrow legs out lazily along the length of the chaise lounge, reclining and, still trying to soothe her bristled nerves, Meren lets out a nervous, relieved little laugh.

"For a prince, you have a piteously small compilation of manners."

Through a smirk:

"For a commoner, you seem to have a surplus of them."

"I must have gotten your share."

"I wish you hadn't."

Her eyes narrow. "Are you saying I'm uptight?"

"No, no, no." He smiles—that same smile he wore just before he tipped that bucket of water all over the floor. "Not uptight, no. *Prim*, yes."

"That's unfair, you forget that if I'm anything other than *prim* I'll get fired."

"Not now, you won't, so why don't you relax?" Casually, he gestures to his own more-than-comfortable posture—which is mostly legs, covered in black linen and crossed at his bony ankles. His invitation had been a silken drawl—all hooded eyes and an amused, curling grin—but there's a challenging edge to his tone, as if he doesn't think she'll do it.

Meren feels herself prickle.

He can just *lay* there, all sprawled out like a cat soaking up the sun, *without* a nagging little voice in his head (that sounds oddly like Alfdis) making him feel as though he's doing something heinous and evil.

She crosses her arms. "Force of habit."

"A*nd* because you're prim. It's in your bones."

"It is *not*."

"It is. You're terrified of doing something wrong."

"Only because I'll get—"

"Fired, yes, you mentioned, but I think it's more than that. You're afraid of upsetting everyone. Alfdis, me, your parents—" He shifts onto his front, crossing his arms neatly over the armrest and setting his pointy chin on them. "You don't do what you want."

"What do you mean?"

"I mean you *want* to do things, but you don't *let* yourself do them because you're scared of how other people will react." He says it so simply, laying out her entire personality stark and bare before her, so easily, so effortlessly.

Her gaze hardens. "I don't have to care what anyone else thinks. I can be spontaneous."

Irritatingly dismissive, he waves a hand. "No, you can't."

"Yes, I can."

WHAT LORKAN IS

"Lick the plate, then. Let your hair down. Curse and raise your voice and make lewd jokes and slouch when you sit."

Meren's lips pinch themselves into a tight little knot, Lorkan's only spreading wider. "But I don't *want* to do those things."

"Yes you do," he states frankly, examining the back of one of his hands. They're smudged with charcoal and he tries to rub it away disinterestedly, his tendons slipping smoothly below his skin. "But you're too scared to."

Huffing, Meren's shoulders bunch up by her ears.

He thinks she's...*boring?* Scared? Scared of what he—what *anyone* thinks? When he looks at her does he see a quaking, snivelling servant so eager to please she's forgotten to develop a personality?

"I am *not*." Vehemently, she shoves herself deeper into the window seat, her spine curving in a lazy, compressed arc. Her dress flaring like green fire, she kicks her legs out to take up all the space she's been told a woman should never invade and, before Lorkan has a chance to look startled, both of her hands reach towards her head.

His eyes widen, and they watch as her fingers grab the pins holding her bun tight in place.

In a few quick movements she's yanked them free, her hair falling about her shoulders in a disorganised cascade of brown strands.

Mouth pursed, she drops them onto the table with a metallic clink.

There's silence.

Then Lorkan smiles. "That's it."

※ ☾ ※

"That's what?" Meren asks, her tone giving away the fact that she's still slightly nettled.

Lorkan isn't nettled.

Meren bets she could shout at him for half an hour, and his voice would remain as level as a still lake.

Goodness knows *she* has never had the guts to rant and rave, but every irritated word someone hurls at her is like a dry log on a fire; they build up and up, collecting in a heap of hot anger that smoulders away long after their torrent of abuse is finished. It makes her feel like a petulant teenager, her temper burnt—wan and thin—while Lorkan just lays there, serene and cool.

She considers pulling her limbs back towards her centre, straightening her spine and hurriedly scrambling to hide her exposed hair—

But he's staring at her with a gaze as sharp as a whetted blade, making it incredibly difficult to move.

"That pose. That's it, the one we've been looking for."

Bafflement scribbles itself all over Meren's face. "*This* pose?"

She gestures at herself in disgust; slumped like a bag of flour, legs kicked so wide she's thankful for the generous length of her skirt. If she were a young boy, she'd be rapped on the knuckles for insolence. If she were a young girl she'd—well, she doesn't know what would happen—she's never known anyone who dared to test it.

"You know I was going for arrogant indifference, right?" She sputters. "We were *arguing*."

"Yes, and it was very amusing," his lip curls, and she's tempted to stick her tongue out at him. "But we don't seem to be very good at it, do we? After all, arguments are supposed to *cause* problems, not solve them."

In a tone laced with heavy disbelief:

"But *this* pose?"

He tips his head to the side, dark eyebrows meeting over his nose. "What's wrong with it? Is it uncomfortable to hold?"

"No, it's the *opposite*, that's my point. It's *too* comfortable, it's—it's almost vulgar. I look like—"

"A princess."

"What?"

WHAT LORKAN IS

"You look like a princess," Lorkan elaborates. "Relaxed yet assertive; like you know you can do what you want."

Meren stares at him, his demeanour having shifted from laid-back to interested.

He's sitting up now, and swung his legs down to plant his bare feet on the floor, one pale hand curled before his mouth. Thoughtfully, he runs his thumbnail over the thin line of his bottom lip.

"I understand the window," Meren spells out, still thinking him to be slightly deranged.

Has he become desperate, so he just...settled? *Pretended* to have been hit by a bolt of inspiration, just so they won't have to go through the whole tedious charade of searching for a pose again?

No, she doesn't think so. She doubts he'd be able to fake that look; the glazed-over, critical stare of someone carrying out mental calculations.

His pupils, swelled wells of ink, outline her, flicking about and lingering on her dress, the sky over her shoulder, her hands—probably mentally estimating the ratios of pigments he'll need to create those same colours on canvas.

"I admit, the window makes a good frame," she continues, "it adds some nice light, a bit of contrasting colour—"

Lorkan's stare clears, his attention settling back on the present. Listening carefully, he absorbs her words.

"—but the pose itself? It's..." She trails off, the sentence petering out. It's not that she doesn't have a word to stick on the end of it, it's that she has too many. It's *brassy* and *brash* and *audacious* and makes her look...

Like a princess.

Lorkan is right because, when she'd shoved herself into a nonchalant slouch, she'd been mirroring his own relaxed, sprawling attitude. She's soaked up, collected, and noted—all by accident—his little mannerisms, coy smirks, his general Lorkan-ness, and thrown it all back at him.

"It's perfect," he assures.

There's that look again.

That one Meren can't read.

"You look like you own these chambers and everything in them."

22

THISTLE'S QUILLS & 'COAL

Meren waits while Lorkan darts off to fetch his easel and painting materials from the studio, and allows herself a private little blush while she's alone. Tentatively, her fingers reach up to touch her hair and, self-consciously, she sneaks a look at the doorway.

No one is there.

No one is ever there.

That persistent tugging sensation slowly ebbing from her scalp, she sighs, allowing her every muscle to melt into the gentle curve of the window seat, each bone to softening like melted snow.

'*Lorkan feels this way all the time*', she muses absently, watching a kittiwake preen its flight feathers, its webbed feet such a bright yellow against the limestone battlements. No wonder his features spend most of their days hanging in an easy-natured, amicable smirk.

Lorkan seems to have the ability to dominate a space just by simply being in it, and she has never understood how. She understands now; it's the way he sits, the way he stands, the way he holds himself.

If she could sit like this all the time, Meren would be constantly smirking too, she thinks bitterly.

※ ☾ ※

Lorkan returns, art supplies bundled into his long arms, and sets about propping the easel upon its spindly legs and arranging trays of pigments and pots of brushes over all the flat surfaces in his immediate vicinity.

Meren watches him with amused fascination, admittedly glad he has something other than her to occupy his gaze. With every passing second, self-consciousness digs its claws a little deeper, the temptation to correct her posture and wrangle her hair back into its usual bun growing ever stronger.

Pushing it away, she turns her attention back to The Prince, now setting down three jars of water on the floor by his feet.

He'd been holding them precariously in one hand, hooking a narrow finger under their rims, but they look even more vulnerable on the ground.

Meren opens her mouth to caution him about knocking them over, but closes it, knowing he'll just laugh at her. Instead, she asks curiously:

"Do you always paint in your rooms?"

"No, sometimes I go out into the woods or the gardens, but not often."

"How do you take all this outside?"

Lorkan perches on the lip of the chaise lounge, then lifts himself again so he can drag it forward by a fraction of an inch.

"I load a pallet with paint before I leave, and rest the canvas on my legs. Sometimes the weather isn't my friend so I add a lot of details from memory once I get back here. I could do that with this painting, if you like, so you don't have to pose for so long."

WHAT LORKAN IS

He meets Meren's eyes, his dark hair falling like two curtains either side of his face. "I'm so familiar with your features I could just about manage from memory."

She raises one eyebrow. "Is my face becoming tedious?"

She can't see Lorkan's answering smile because, seemingly content with the nest he's assembled for himself, he takes his place behind the white rectangle of canvas. She hears his chuckle, though.

"Quite the contrary." One of his pale hands plucks a slim stick of charcoal from the table by his left knee, and the satisfying, abrasive sound of rough sketching fills the room. "I feel that, with you as my muse, this will be one of my most impressive works."

"Very funny."

His head pokes out from one side, his brow knitted. "I wasn't trying to be."

Disappearing again, the scraping starts back up.

Meren can just about see the nub of his charcoal moving about the canvas, the nub of it creating a slight, tiny indent.

Not knowing how to reply, she simply says nothing, and turns back to concentrating on holding her pose; a feat that proves to be more difficult than she'd previously anticipated.

What had drawn Lorkan to this position, in particular, was its nonchalant, carefree nature, so she knows that—ideally—she must keep her muscles slack and her expression insouciant.

However, she's quickly finding it very tricky to *remain* insouciant and nonchalant whilst his crystalline eyes peek out to trace her body every couple of seconds. Each time she feels herself finally settling, he glances at her again —at the angle of her elbow, or the curve of her cheek—and her stomach curls up like an autumn leaf.

"By the way..." Lorkan's voice drifts out from behind the canvas, the scuff of his sketching ceasing. He leans to the left, so Meren can see his soft smile. "I'm flattered that you feel comfortable enough with me to let your hair down. Both figuratively and literally."

A heat dribbles down her neck and pools around her exposed collarbones.
She has been waiting for him to bring that up.

Every time the breeze from the window brushes a strand against her face, she's reminded that she's—in a way—somewhat naked.

Meren had thought the first man to see her with her hair down—besides her dear father, of course—would be her future spouse.

Some small section of her mind has been half hoping Lorkan isn't aware of the significance; after all, it is customary for *upper*-class women to wear their hair down, so maybe he'll think nothing of it.

But he's too sharp *not* to know.

"If you ever feel uncomfortable, you can put it back up."

Meren finds her head shaking, her hair brushing about her shoulders. "If it's all right with you...I'd rather leave it down."

※ ☾ ※

And so, once again, Meren's life enters a new tier of comfort.

Each morning she strolls down to the market for Lorkan's pigments, sits with him in the studio while they prepare them, and then poses for the rest of the day, taking breaks for snacks and to stretch her legs.

Since Lorkan had offered her the privileges of his lavatory, she hadn't taken him up on it but does so now, so she doesn't have to keep struggling out of her dress and into her uniform every time she needs to scurry down the hall.

Posing by the window is quickly becoming Meren's favourite time of day —his eyes resting on her like sunbeams, the wet dab of the brush, their easy conversations—and she misses it sorely on Sundays when she's not required to work.

The hours she spends in Lorkan's plush, cushy chambers have begun to have the rather irritating effect of highlighting just how drab the hours spent *away* from them really are.

WHAT LORKAN IS

Descending the stairs to the servant's quarters has started to make her feel like some kind of rodent; snuffling about dank tunnels into the soil so deep even the sun can't find her. They're busier than she remembers, alive and churning like a rat's nest, always humming with conversation and the constant, tapping sound of boots against stone.

Never before has she been susceptible to bouts of claustrophobia, and yet —in recent weeks—she's had to escape for air on several occasions.

She'll be spooning supper into her mouth or changing her bedsheets, and suddenly feel overwhelmingly suffocated by the heft of Aldercliff over head, slowly crushing the bowed ceiling. Her body craving the sky like a flower swamped in shade, she'll burst out into the courtyard and gulp a few deep breaths of chilled, northern wind.

There's always a gaggle of servants mingling outside, indulging in their smoke leaf habit, and they'll turn away from their rolling and puffing to give her a questioning look.

When Meren does nothing but tuck her arms close to her body and prop herself up against the brickwork, they turn back once more, disinterested, to huddling under their coats.

Awkwardly, she'll stand for a few minutes, shivering and watching their fumes mingle with the stars. Then, taking a deep breath, she'll force her feet back down, into the palace's great, toothless mouth.

Her free time has also sprouted a new challenge—one she never would have anticipated: amusing herself when she's not working.

The week used to leave her bones withered and aching like trees exposed to harsh winds. She'd happily spend Sunday in a coma-like state of dream-riddled recovery, rebuilding the parts of her that have been splintered and ground and worn into a fine powder.

Now, the hardest labour she experiences is climbing sixteen floors and, today, she finds herself slipping into consciousness feeling pleasingly refreshed.

Usually, the slitted window above her bed offer nothing but narrow bars of something weak and watery and awfully close to shadow. Today, however, what trickles onto her grey sheets stains them a clean, crisp white.

She sits up with a languid stretch.

The marketplace will be humid with rich scents, the colours vibrant and illuminated by beams of wintry sun. Lorkan's chambers will be bright too, each sweeping window displaying panoramic views of the kingdom as they pass lazy words back and forth, their hands paint-stained and clothes pigment-scuffed.

But then the realisation hits Meren like a hefty slap on the cheek.

It's Sunday.

Disgruntled, she flops back onto the mattress with a frown, and tries to catch the tail-end of her dream as it disappearing in the distance—but she's not tired.

She hasn't been tired for a long time.

Frustrated, she swings her legs out of bed, her bare feet landing on the cool, prickly jute rug. Instead of plucking up another brown, linen, uniform dress, she digs to the bottom of her trunk for her brown, linen, day dress, and shrugs it on.

As a child, she'd happily spend hours exploring the fields and marshlands around her parents' cottage, searching for bird nests and collecting critters with amusing little legs.

But her peers probably wouldn't appreciate her easing up the flagstones in search of woodlice, and she's *definitely* not permitted to rootle around Queen Lophia's roses for robins.

Even reading has lost its charm, she has realised disappointedly. The castles in Lorkan's books are nowhere near as decadent as his chambers, and the blonde princes and strapping knights seem to have somewhat lost their appeal.

What does one *do* with a day off?

Having a feeling no one at ground level will know the answer, Meren poses this question to Lorkan as she sits sprawled in the window seat on Monday.

"Most of your life is a day off," she says. "What do you do when I'm not here?"

"Hobbies," he replies simply. "Find things you enjoy and pursue them."

She blows a little laugh through her nose. "What? Like playing the lute?"

Lorkan tilts his head—not that she can see from behind the canvas. "Do you *enjoy* playing the lute?"

"I can't *afford* a lute. I don't think I've ever *touched* an instrument."

"Not all hobbies are expensive, Meren," he says, ignoring her tone.

He's leaning out to stare fixedly at her left arm, seemingly unable to get the curve of her wrist right. He's been staring at it, sketching, and then staring again for the past nine minutes.

"Most of the art I create is with charcoal sticks; you can get a whole box for a copper at the market."

Meren dismisses the idea with a wave of her hand. "I can't draw."

The corner of his lip twitches with amusement. "No one is *born* with the ability to draw, you have to teach yourself."

"But what if I'm *never* any good?"

"But what if you are? What if, one day, you make something beautiful? Something you can be proud of and hold in her hands?" His attention once again narrows to that one line of her forearm.

She holds it still for him, and turns his words over in her head.

☀ ☾ ☀

The next Sunday, Meren leaves for the market intending to pick up some art supplies. She counts out her earnings first and calculates that—with the loose change building up in her pocket—she can afford a few charcoal sticks and a substantial wad of cheap parchment.

There's no specific stall for artists, she discovers after an embarrassing amount of time spent searching for one.

For some reason, in her mind, she'd built up a table set out like a miniature version of Lorkan's studio; pots of brushes, feathery quills, thick notebooks bound in heavy leather stacked in towers—

In reality, artists seem to need to visit several different stalls to get the paraphernalia they require.

The first she comes across is a man selling sketchbooks, but they aren't piled up in disorganised stacks like Lorkan's. This man keeps them on shelves in tight rows, their spines lined up like the neat hairs of his trim little moustache.

Meren's gaze slides longingly over the more high-end, soft covers sandwiching thick, tidy pages—but she knows they're nowhere near suitable for her first attempts. No doubt she'll be tearing out the majority of the them before she manages to produce anything worthy of keeping, and the pretty little book would be bald and ruined.

Disappointedly, she drags her eyes down to the cheapest in the row; several hundred sheets glued roughly with resin at one end. They're tatty, but cost so little she buys two, just to be safe.

Charcoal sticks turn out to be much more complicated than she had anticipated.

"They're graded, you see," the store owner explains, probably noticing Meren's baffled expression. Her stall has its own ornate fabric banner reading in sloped letters:

Thistle's Quills & 'Coal

The stall's owner, who Meren assumes to be Thistle, is a willowy, stretched-out sort of woman with long, matted hair and dusty black smudges littering her heavily freckled skin. The only thing standing between her and a life of nomadic bohemianism, Meren thinks, is time.

"The higher the number, the softer the mark. If it ends in a 'B' it'll be fairly soft, and if it ends in 'H' it'll be quite hard."

Meren's eyebrows remain several millimetres below her hairline.

The stall is covered in rows and rows of charcoal sticks, some so thin it's a wonder they haven't snapped like a brittle bone, and others so thick they looked more like the lumps of ordinary coal one would use to line a fireplace. Many are close to identical in breadth, and yet Meren has a sneaking suspicion they differ greatly in some way.

"The softer the mark, the blacker it is. See?" Thistle takes up one of the sticks from a section labelled '9B' and draws it carelessly across a piece of test parchment.

The trail is so condensed it looks almost fluffy; like a long, wiggly caterpillar. It is cute, but not at all what Meren is looking for; every page of her sketch pad will end up coated in nothing but a haze of amorphous black dust.

"Which one do you need for just…you know—" she makes a gesture, miming the motion of drawing a little doodle over her palm, "—*normal* sketching?"

Thistle rubs her jaw with one hand, leaving a graze of grey on her chin like a low little thundercloud. "It depends on what you want to sketch."

Eventually, Meren leaves the stall with a packet that has a big number 'FIVE' on the lid, and the letter B, which is apparently somewhere in the middle of the charcoal-stick rainbow of softness.

If she ever feels inclined to do some shading, she is apparently '*very welcome to come back and try out number* EIGHT' but Meren doesn't think she'll be ready for anything above a 'SIX' any time soon.

✴ ☾ ✴

When Meren arrives at Lorkan's quarters, he immediately notices the additional, foreign bulges in her tote, and guesses it contains more than the usual boxes of pigment and scrumptious cakes. When she places it on the table, he hovers around it like a cat sniffing about grocery bags for food.

"You bought something." He plucks at the cotton with one finger.

Meren had disappeared into the washroom to change into her dress, already eager to feel the comforting grip of its velvety material. She misses it when she's not wearing it, the loss aching like the stump of a lost limb.

"You're very astute," she teases delicately through the door, knowing he's smiling on the other side.

"I was under the impression you were morally against buying things."

"Quite the contrary." The set of Meren's shoulders loosens as she slips her arms into her gown's delicate mesh sleeves. "I love buying things, I just can't usually afford them."

She leaves the washroom and Lorkan steps behind her automatically, his slender fingers gravitating to fasten the back of her dress with well-practised dexterity.

"So what did you buy? If you don't mind me asking." As he loops and knots the ribbons, Meren reaches up to take the pins from her bun.

Lorkan still watches her hair fall about her shoulders with curious fascination, despite having witnessed it many times before.

He releases her, and she stows the pins in her tote, bringing out the blocks of parchment and packet of charcoal sticks shyly.

Holding them out to him, she suddenly feels—for some reason—like a little child.

He has spent his entire life honing his craft, and she's here suddenly deciding—on a bored whim, no less—to give it a try.

She feels like she's insulting him and everything he stands for. Maybe she should have dropped her new art supplies off at the servant's quarters first, she wonders, chewing her lip.

However, the lower half of Lorkan's face has broadened into an unmistakable smile as he puts two and two together. "You're going to draw?"

"I'm going to try to. I'm taking your advice about getting a hobby. You were right, the charcoal sticks barely cost anything, and the parchment wasn't so bad."

Lorkan's face falls. "Does passion not at least play a little part?"

Surprised, Meren's cheeks heat.

WHAT LORKAN IS

Passion plays a larger part than he'll ever know. He's inspired her with his talent and prowess in so many ways and now, like a daughter dressing up in her mother's clothes, she's trying to mimic him.

"Yes. I want to be able to do what you do; drawing what I see, turning thoughts into physical matter." She can't help rubbing one of her bare feet against her ankle as though she's being chastised. "It feels wrong, though, trying to copy you. Like I'm insulting you by ever thinking I'll ever be—"

"If you say '*that good*' I'm going to tip another bucket of water all over these nice clean floors," he warns, straying purposefully to a nearby table. He sits down in one of the chairs, and kicks the other out for Meren to sit at.

For once catching a hint squarely with both hands, she obediently takes a seat. "Aren't we going to the studio?"

Lorkan had wanted to start painting the walls into her portrait today, which requires a special gold pigment. The dusty nuggets look what can only be described as 'magical', and she is eager to watch its metamorphosis into paint.

"Later."

Curious, she watches as he takes her sketchbook and sets it in front of her, the front page blank and wide and daunting.

"As I said, no one is born with the ability to produce art, which means it takes practice. However, it also means that *anyone* can learn if they're dedicated enough."

"I am dedicated," she says quickly, feeling more and more like a child by the minute. Sitting up a little straighter, she shuffles her chair with a grating of oak and marble closer to Lorkan's side.

He looks sideways at her through the corner of his eyes, a faint smile playing on his narrow lips. "I believe you. However, you must understand that even after years and years you will still make mistakes."

That sentiment is true for many things, Meren thinks as he begins freeing a charcoal stick from the box elegantly printed with *Thistle's Quills & 'Coal*. He peels off the wax seal with the nail of his thumb, then tips one of the slender black rods out into his hand. Star-like dust flecks his palm like an inverted sky.

"Art is not like theatrics or music. There aren't notes you have to find on strings, or words you have to remember already written out for you. There's no right or wrong, there's just...whatever you want there to be."

She mulls this over as he transfers the charcoal to her hand.

Its soft powder gets into the creases of her fingerprints.

"But how will I know if a sketch is finished, if there's no right or wrong?"

Lorkan shrugs. "It depends on what you want to sketch."

Meren huffs. "I wish people would stop saying that."

※ ☾ ※

Lorkan spends several hours introducing Meren to the basics of drawing, showing her how to hold her hand just above the parchment so she doesn't smudge her work, how to keep circles neat and even, and how to construct *larger* shapes from those circles.

Rarely needing to write, let alone draw, Meren's first attempts are clumsy and juvenile at best, her lines shaky as if the charcoal is painfully squeezing marks from itself rather than being dragged across the page.

Lorkan explains, patiently, that it will take time to build up the required muscles, watching her struggle with amusement as she muddles through several pages, determined not to let her limited skill get the better of her.

Every metaphorical block they run into, he slides the parchment to his side of the table and demonstrates how to bypass it, Meren's eyes following his slick strokes, the smooth competence having an almost soporific effect on her psyche.

Only when her hand begins to ache and their palms are stained as black as the night do they move on to their usual agender. The gold pigment proves to be as wonderful as Meren had imagined it to be, the finished paint like someone has taken King Cade's crown and turned it to liquid. When it is prepared, they progress to the lounge where she hops into her usual position on the window seat, and Lorkan arranges himself behind his canvas.

As they converse, his voice flows from behind it, now growing thick with paint and muffling his silken words, the only parts of him visible being the long column of his legs and the occasional a hand, reloading a brush with paint. Infrequently, he'll lean out to give her some sort of expression—usually, that trademark curling of lip—but mercifully, the colourful art supplies piled on the table, floor, and his own lap dampens the effect.

It's easier for Meren to pose for him when he looks like a painter and not a man.

Most of the time he's a painter; his eyes clear and calculating, features drawn together in poignant contemplation or a thoughtful frown as he estimates distance, figures out colour ratios, etcetera.

However, there are some moments when he looks like a man, and they make the nonchalant mask she pulls over herself slip metaphorically sideways. His face softens and his eyes glaze like he's staring at a sunset, or admiring the ocean in the moonlight. Sometimes he'll smile.

He'll look at her, and she won't know what he's thinking.

She just knows it's not about paint.

It's not that Meren doesn't like Lorkan looking at her like that. In fact, it's rather pleasant—even Arne hasn't looked at her like that. However, it does make her blush an awful lot so, to fight off the waves of pink his gentle smile pools in her cheeks, she asks questions.

These seem to act like little droplets of water being flicked in his face because his eyes will return to their sharp, crystalline self, and he'll quickly go back to dabbing the canvas, clearing his throat.

Thankfully, he doesn't seem to mind Meren interrupting his stupors, and never appears to grow tired of her inquisitive probing. He answers each query with amiable patience, perhaps even relishing in her attention.

"How long does it take to dry?"

"Several hours, usually. It depends on how thick the layer is."

"Can you paint over it when it's wet, or will the colours mix?"

"They'll mix but, sometimes, that's what I want them to do."

"Does the charcoal show through the paint?"

"Yes, at first, but you need to use a few layers anyway to keep the colours vibrant, so they get covered up after a while."

There's one question Meren keeps meaning to ask him, and today she finally does. Not whilst she's posing, but afterwards, as she strays over to take a customary look at the progress he's made.

"Do you always leave the face until last?"

23

CRYSTAL STALLION

Lorkan's brush strokes had stretched across the golden, russet, months of late autumn, and into the hushed, prickly heart of winter. Snow rarely touches Tawny's tiled rooftops but, recently, crystals of ice clink against the window pane at Meren she sits for him, the glass clouded over with frost.

As the town's people had celebrated Harvest in the streets below, she and Lorkan roasted corn on the cob over the fire and nibbled slices of pumpkin pie.

When Winter Festival rolled around, Lorkan gifted Meren some new charcoal sticks, a pair of wool socks, and a book wrapped carefully in star-patterned linen, and Meren meekly presented him with a wonky little deer she'd clumsily stitched onto a handkerchief.

"To clean your brushes with," she'd explained.

As New Year's Day becomes a memory, the majority of the stretched, cotton canvas has been smothered under at least several layers of paint—besides the little patch representing Meren's face.

Her skin tone has been set down, a simple block of colour, and then left; the rest of the image building up in increasing detail while that little section north of her neck remains naked and plain.

One day, Meren pokes her head around the easel, and Lorkan must catch her expression.

"Don't you like it?" he asks, and she shakes her head quickly.

"Of course I do, it's *beautiful*. It's just...unsettling seeing myself without a face. Or seeing myself at all."

The experience of seeing herself *at all* is still somewhat disconcerting, she thinks, especially in her new, decadent gown. For the majority of her life, her own reflection had only ever stared back at her from puddles, raindrops pocking her cheeks, ripples stretching her smile.

In recent years, she's become used to regarding her reflection in the tarnished mirrors nailed up in servant's washroom—and, of course, the burnished gold floors of the palace do have a habit of throwing her image back at her wherever she goes. It makes her look like a face on a coin, and the cheap glass in the washroom flecks her features with ugly smudges.

Somehow, she prefers *those* reflections to the one Lorkan's washroom. She'll peek sideways into the expensive looking glass only to turn away, not liking the red spot on her chin, the little points of her breasts, or the fluffy hairs above her lip.

Lorkan swirls his brush around a cup of water. "Do you like seeing yourself?"

Meren thinks about it while the water turns green. "I like seeing myself the way *you* see me." She gestures at the elegantly placed sweeps and dabs of paint, the colours, bold and bright as chlorophyll, blood, coral, petals, feathers.

They're soft and hazy—like a memory of a sun-dappled summer's day.

"But it doesn't look like what I see in the mirror."

"Mirrors are deceptive," Lorkan shrugs, gently wiping his new handkerchief over his brush.

Coming to stand at his side, both of them stare thoughtfully at his painting—as they often do once his supplies have been cleaned and stored for tomorrow.

Their eyes rest on the patch of bare paint where Meren's profile should be. It's framed by her hair, each strand catching and throwing back light from the window behind, its vibrancy and intricacy only heightening the simplicity of that bland block of colour.

Lorkan says nothing, just rubs his chin with his index finger. It leaves a scuff of lime-green paint across the angular line of his jaw and, without thinking, Meren reaches out.

His face is cool under her touch, as if he's been walking through the silver, wintery dusk.

She grazes the pad of her thumb over the pigment, collecting it up, and wipes it onto a messy rag on the table.

Pulling himself from his rivery, he turns his head to give her a soft smile. If he minded that she'd touched him so intimately, he doesn't show it.

"No, not usually," he says after clearing his throat. "I'm just not sure about the expression."

For a second, Meren had forgotten she'd asked him a question.

She'd like to touch his face again.

He's clean-shaven, but there's still that slight hint of masculine stubble somewhere below his skin; gritty grains of sand caught between two pages in a book.

"I did have an expression in mind...but it's difficult to fake."

"What do you mean?" she asks, although she knows what he meant, and it made her feel like she'd missed a step while walking down a set of stairs.

Posing lazily while he paints her is one thing.

Holding a specific expression, though—arranging her mouth and nose and eyes in a particular way and then keeping them there—is something else altogether.

"I mean, I know which expression the picture should have, I know what I *want*...I just don't know how we could..." he trails off, his elbow returning to his knee to defeatedly prop up his chin.

"You could tell me what you want me to do and I'll try to do it, but I've never been very good at acting. I broke a plate once in the kitchens, and opened my mouth to lie that it had been that way when I got there, but Yllva took one look at me and I confessed almost immediately."

Lorkan chuckles. "Well, Yllva *is* scary, I think even Father would quake under her interrogation. Unfortunately, though, I don't think this look *can* be faked."

"Well, what look is it?"

"Remember when you were cleaning and you found one of my drawings?"

"Back when I used to work for a living?" She quips snideley, and Lorkan elects to ignore it.

"It's that look you had then, before you noticed I was watching. You did it again when you first tried jam, and then again when you looked through the telescope." He pauses, riffling through his mind for the right words, waving a slender hang vaguely as if it might help summon them. Then he says slowly, like he's pulling them out of a box one by one:

"You looked so...alive. Your cheeks were flushed, but I can paint that in. It was your eyes...there was something about your eyes."

Meren presses her lips together. "That's very specific."

"Do you think you could replicate it?" He looked up at her, and she thinks it very bizarre indeed, seeing the top of his head. Few people have, probably. His hair is smoothed back over his skull like the breast of a crow.

Dragging her mind back to the task at hand, she tries to picture what she must have looked like, unfolding the parchment, the charcoal deer unfurling in her hands like a flower—and attempts to tug her features into the same exclamation of awe, hauling her eyebrows up her forehead and spreading her mouth into a smile.

Naturally, she looks ridiculous, and any progress she *had* made dissolves into peels of self-conscious giggles.

WHAT LORKAN IS

"Told you," Lorkan says, biting his lip to keep from chuckling.

He probably thought it cruel to make fun of her efforts, but Meren would rather he laugh, even if it was at her own expense; he doesn't laugh as much as he used to, his default demeanour almost sombre since Queen Lophia's visit months ago.

Sometimes it's easy for Meren to forget that the kingdom is teetering on the cusp of war but, as Cade's son, the topic must buzz about Lorkan's family conversations like an irritating fly.

"It can't be faked."

Meren rubs *her* jaw this time, catching the inside of her cheek between her teeth and chewing pensively. Suddenly, her spine straightens proudly, an idea popping into her head:

"Shock me again."

"What?"

"Shock me. I looked that way because I'd never *seen* art or jam or a telescope before. There must be more things around here you can bewilder me with."

✴ ☾ ✴

Meren waits on the window seat while Lorkan fudges about his chambers for things he hopes might spark that desired expression. Several minutes pass, one of her hands straying to fiddle with the hem of her dress, rubbing the velvety material between finger and thumb. She'd reminded herself of the worries that gnaw at her nerves at night—war, the alliance, her and Lorkan's futures—and is now endeavouring to wriggle loose from their tenacious jaws.

Lorkan must be struggling to find things she hadn't seen yet because she has—by this time—seen almost everything.

After months of dutifully cleaning each item, and then several more months on top of that just whiling away the hours in these chambers, Meren has become pretty accustomed to all of his little gadgets.

He'd even introduced her to several himself, when they'd cleaned together, proud of his treasures and pleased to have someone to show them off to.

Eventually, he returns and tugs a coffee table over with his foot and, curious, Meren perches on the lip of the window seat, watching him set various things down on its flat surface.

Most are new to her; things that had no doubt resided within cupboards and chests; and others are things she *has* seen before but not understood.

"I don't have anything quite as titillating as jam or a telescope, I'm afraid," Lorkan apologises, joining her on the window seat. "Most of these are desk toys."

"What's a desk toy?"

He checks her face and finds that she is serious. The corner of his lip twitches. "They're things you keep around your workspace to amuse you. Like this." He plucks up the machine closest to him and holds it out flat on his palm.

It's composed of a slim metal disk suspended upright like a wheel over a glass chamber. There's another disk inside that one, lying flat on the bottom. It really does look more like a machine rather than a toy, despite the name. It appears no fun to play with either, and if someone were to attempt to play with it, Meren guesses it would probably shatter.

She eyes it sceptically. "What does it do?"

It's pretty, yes, but utterly stationary, rather like some sort of obscure miniature work of art.

"It won't work for me. Here." Lorkan takes Meren's wrist gently and directs it palm-up, placing the machine in its centre.

They wait.

Nothing happens for a second, then, suddenly, the disk in the glass chamber lifts of its own accord, pushing against a few wires attached to the gold wheel.

WHAT LORKAN IS

Meren nearly drops it as it starts turning. "What's it doing?"

Lorkan's lips have curved into a soft smile, and she can feel his eyes on the side of her face—but, for once, she pays them no mind.

The little wheel has sped up, churning away happily to itself as the disk in the chamber rises and falls rhythmically, pushing on the pins holding it in place. That's all it seems to do; go around and around, making a satisfying little clicking noise as it spins.

"It's not *doing* anything. This is a heat engine. Well, a tiny one. The warmth from your hand makes it turn."

Still watching the delicate machine twirl away:

"Why didn't it work for you?"

"It's never worked for me. I'm too cold."

Meren feels sorry for him then, and she isn't sure why.

"Maybe it just doesn't like you," she points out, and is pleased when it makes him laugh.

They watch it turn around and around, then she asks, quietly:

"What's it for? I mean, why does it exist?"

"I told you; amusement," Lorkan states simply, plucking it off her hand and setting it back on the table.

Without the warmth of her skin, its momentum putters out and it falls still.

"It's a desk *toy,* remember?"

"Does King Cade keep toys on his desk?"

A towering, stoic man with power beyond the capabilities of her imagination, she tries to picture the ruler of Velôr balancing a little gold trinket in the middle of his vast, calloused palm. It probably wouldn't be able to sit flat, for all the battle scars crisscrossing his skin, each raised swell of flesh a symbol of a life he's extinguished.

When Cade passes away—

Which will, one day, happen, no matter how unlikely it seems—

And if Sol too meets his demise before his time—

Assuming he has no children to follow in his footsteps—

And if Lorkan does not wed the Calpurzia princess—
The throne will fall to him.
Meren hadn't really thought about that before.

Perhaps because Lorkan is not the type of person that comes to mind when imagining the ruler of Velôr.

She'd expect such a person to be broad—a heap of muscles bound tight in armour as thick as a dinner plate—not a lithe, marble statue of a man, all sharp angles and deep, thoughtful eyes.

That's not to say he does not look like *a* king.

The way he carries himself, Meren sometimes forgets he isn't one already.

She wonders if Cade is proud of his youngest son. Their core values obviously differ greatly. Lorkan is sharp, whetted wit, his methods for keeping peace with other realms most likely involving slick negotiation and quick, clever bartering. Cade, however, is famed for destroying any being that poses a possible threat. His armies are probably stationed somewhere right now, squashing some rival faction under the foot of his unyielding wrath.

"No, I don't think Father has anything like this," Lorkan says in a way that makes Meren wonder if he's ever been inside his chambers at all.

What is Cade like as a father? Hopefully, he doesn't approach the challenge of parenting with the same attitude he uses for stifling invasions and rucking up the land with war.

No, treating his sons with detached indifference seems more likely, which is, in many ways, slightly more tragic.

Meren's parents are coarse, hard-working people, and yet their poverty means they understand the importance of compassion and community. They'd set her peeling potatoes before she was barely old enough to grasp a blade in her pudgy fist—and yet, should she cut herself, she could always rely on the comforting embrace of her mother's arms, and her father's broad hands to cleanse the wound with tender endearment.

She tries to conceive what growing up without the loving attention of both parents might do to a person.

She doesn't need to; the result is right next to her.

WHAT LORKAN IS

"He has vast collections of artefacts though," he's saying.

Meren really must try harder to pay attention, even though speculating about Lorkan's past has an addicting, mysterious sort of allure to it.

"I'll show you one day, if you like."

To this, she agrees eagerly, although she has little interest in Cade's hoard of stolen battle memorabilia. She likes the idea of a walk with Lorkan—of spending time with him somewhere other than his chambers.

Would that even be possible?

What would she say if they were discovered?

'Don't mind me, I'm just bunking off work to fraternize with a member of The Royal Family'?

Before she can look into the idea any further, Lorkan has moved on to the next item.

✳ ☾ ✳

One by one Lorkan walks Meren through the items on the table, some of which include:

A model of the universe, each star a glowing speck of light, each planet a spinning marble, the whole thing suspended in an orb of glass.

A bronze, engraved microscope which they used to peer at a biscuit crumb, scribble of charcoal, and some fluff from under the settee.

A tiny spider made from metal cogs and slender wires, and a wide peg protruding from its thorax, which, if turned clockwise, makes the arachnid crawl across the table.

A tube that Lorkan claims can predict the weather; a few fluffy, moon-drenched clouds bobbing about like fish in a bowl.

Meren enjoys each but, when the desk toys fail to bring out that expression he wants, he moves on to self-consciously presenting some of his artwork.

He keeps most of it in sketchbooks—some huge and wide as the table, others small enough to fit in a pocket—but there's canvases too, stacked like crates, and snippets of parchment scribbled with charcoal. There's detailed sketches, rough sketches, doodles torn from books, pallid watercolours, and textured slabs of acrylic an inch thick.

Each and every picture is showered with praise and adoration but, halfway through the pile, Meren sighs.

"They're all breathtaking."

His colour high from her flattery, he shuffles closer to her side. "But?"

"But, when I saw your picture of the deer, I wasn't *expecting* it—that's why my face did that thing. Now, even though these are *excellent,* they're not surprising. I *know* you're an amazing artist—"

Lorkan glows with shy pride.

"—but, honestly, I'd be more surprised if you produced something ugly."

"Well, I don't have anything like that, I'm afraid," he chuckles, shaking his head. His hand moves to close the sketchbook, but Meren snatches it out of his reach.

"No, wait. I want to see them all."

"You don't have to say that."

"I know. I meant it."

Flushing, he lets her settle the book between them once more, and watches quietly as she marvels over brush strokes and arching, smooth lines.

When they reach the end, she pulls an uneven wad of mismatched parchment towards her, the whole thing bound together with twine.

"What's in this one?"

"These are all portraits," he explains, and she flips the first page over with a rustling like moth's wings.

Meren has often wondered how he taught himself to sketch people—seeing as he doesn't seem to meet many—and this book finally answers that question.

Every page is filled with servants.

WHAT LORKAN IS

Most face away from him, absorbed in their work, so he'd had to concentrate on perfecting the creases of their clothes, the movement of their bodies, their proportions and posture. He has managed to catch a *few* faces though:

Chimneysweeps smudged with coal.

Hall boys sneaking a quick chat between chores, their grins gap-toothed and cheeky.

Maids with furrowed foreheads hunched over a rug, trying to work stubborn boot polish from the weave.

Meren doesn't need to ask if they'd known they were being sketched.

They pass an old man stooped over a fire, the embers so convincing she can almost feel their warmth and, quietly, Lorkan says:

"I don't like looking through these."

She blinks, realising his face has fallen. "You don't?"

"Not these pictures. I'm not involved in what's going on in *any* of them."

She regards the dashes and strokes, the fuzzy black lines. There's a distance to each scene, a void where emotion would usually reside within the flecks of charcoal.

He probably doesn't even know these people's names.

"The majority of my memories seem to be of other people and what *they* were doing, rather than what *I* was doing. I didn't use to *do* anything. I'd go unnoticed for days, sometimes. Sometimes I'd worry I'd grow old and, when laying on my deathbed, I'd look back at my life and just see a patchwork quilt of other people's lives rather than my own."

He places a handful of loose sketches back on the table, and they settle like heavy leaves. "I used to feel like I was haunting the palace—a spirit of a prince that died long ago."

Meren places a hand on his broad back.

His shoulder hardens as if he hadn't been expecting it— then slackens. He gives her a small, grateful smile.

"I felt like that too. When I was working in the kitchens not so much, because it's hard to get philosophical when an angry six-foot woman is yelling at you to chop potatoes faster."

A watery smile quirks his lip.

"But afterwards, when I had to clean the steps—that's how I felt. I did the same thing every day, with no one around to see it, and I often wondered, if I stopped...would anyone notice? Sometimes I would forget I'm a person."

"If it's any consolation," his grip cool and gentle, Lorkan takes her hand from his back and gives it a squeeze. That smile has gone, and sadness ghosts his angular face, softening it, "you're a person to me."

* ☾ *

Artwork and trinkets pushed aside, Lorkan chews his bottom lip, and Meren reaches out and frees it with the pad of her thumb.

He rolls his eyes at her. "You do it all the time."

"That doesn't mean *you* should."

They sit in silence, him deep in thought, and her watching the little metal spider toy tap its way across the table. Eventually, he perks up, his spine straightening:

"...What if I show you a spell?"

Her eyebrows disappear into her hair. "I know your parents—and your brother...but I didn't know you could."

"Mother taught me as a child, then I moved onto my own studies as I got older."

"All this time...why didn't you tell me?" she asks, hurt, and he shrugs his wide shoulders stiffly.

"I thought it would be in poor taste."

"Why?"

WHAT LORKAN IS

"My ancestors are the ones that *banned* the use of magic by common people, Wren."

She gives him a long look, and his cheekbones heat.

"*And* I'm not very good—yet. It takes years of practice. I wanted to wait until I could show you something really amazing."

Meren shakes her head. "You could magic up an ant and I'd find it amazing; I've never met anyone who so much as dabbles in witchcraft."

He smirks. "Besides Aasta."

"Very funny." She gives him a hard nudge with her elbow, and he lets himself be pushed sideways, chuckling.

She waits for him to right himself, then nudges him again, encouragingly, this time. "Come on. Try me."

"I am."

Before Meren can frown in confusion, Lorkan reaches across the gap between them to curl a finger under her chin. Softly, he tilts her head up.

A wren is fluttering over her head.

The tip of one neat little wing almost clips her ear and she ducks—although she didn't need to, she realises with embarrassing slowness. It's just a projection; the only giveaway to its fictional nature is the faint light radiating from its stubby brown feathers—like a reflection in a pane of glass.

It circles soundlessly several times and, fascinated, Meren reaches out to touch it.

Her fingertips slip through its breast and, like the remnants of a dream, it vanishes.

"Sorry," Lorkan apologises. "Keeping the illusion solid enough to interact with is a little too much for my rudimentary sorcery skills."

"Are you joshing? It was beautiful!" she insists, shuffling closer until she can feel the strong muscle of his thigh against hers. Regretfully:

"I feel bad for breaking it."

"Don't be." He doesn't seem to mind. He's smiling at her.

"Does it hurt? To make it appear so life-like?"

"No, it just takes a lot of concentration." He runs a hand over his head like he's nursing a strained muscle.

Meren guesses, in a way, he is.

"Summoning illusions feels like trying to multiply large numbers without writing them down. Unless it's ice; that's easy for some reason." With a nonchalant flick of his wrist, a shard of solid water crystallises on his upturned palm, and he tossed it into the air for Meren to catch.

She does, both hands closing around the brittle little icicle.

The cold immediately bites hard into her skin, and she nearly drops what she expects to be a simple, amorphous chunk of frozen water. It doesn't feel like that, though. It's rounded and smooth.

Peeling open her fingers, she finds a tiny figurine of a horse standing on her upturned palm, as intricate as though it had been carved with a miniature chisel.

It's barely five centimetres in length and yet, if Meren narrows her eyes, she can just about make out bulging veins running down its shins, the scuffs and chips in its hooves. Its jaw is parted, teeth exposed, like it has been galloping with full force then solidified mid-step, wisps of frost smoke leaking from its muzzle like breath.

"You nearly did it then," Lorkan points out from her side. His voice has turned low and gentle, as though he doesn't want to scare away a butterfly that had landed on his arm.

With Meren's breath gracing the horse's flank, it's begun to melt, a single droplet of water building above its stifle like a tear of sweat.

She watches it roll down the narrow column of its hind leg and pool at its hoof, leaking into the lines of her hand.

"Hm?" she hums, just a distracted single syllable.

She's forgotten what it was they were doing.

How can Lorkan make this with just a fleeting thought? How can he just summon it, create such beauty without even trying? His father and brother are so prone—their bodies *honed*—to destroy, and yet Lorkan only ever uses his to *build*—

WHAT LORKAN IS

And why ice? It seems to come naturally to him, as though his body keeps a little blizzard somewhere within his veins—a private supply—to draw on whenever he wants.

"Meren," he says, and she realises he's moved to kneel in front of her.

She raises her head, reluctant to take her eyes off the tiny creature in her palm in case it should melt.

It's soon forgotten, though, with Lorkan's eyes level with hers. She meets them, feeling his gaze bore into her skull.

It keeps going until it touches her soul, caressing it; but tentatively, as though he's asking permission just to look at her.

"Wren, I have an idea."

She waits for him to elaborate, but he doesn't.

Gently, she prompts:

"Okay."

"Would you mind if I did something incredibly stupid?"

Meren shakes her head, even though she doesn't know what she's agreeing to. She'd probably agree to *anything* Lorkan suggests, some distant corner of her mind realises, absently.

He'd rather take his own life than cause her any kind of discomfort—she can tell.

She can tell by the way he's looking at her.

Lorkan's hand finds the bony knots of her knees. Smoothly, he pushes them apart enough to get between her legs.

She lets him.

And then his lips are on hers.

24

MILK AND HONEY

Lorkan's lips are warm.

Or maybe they're cool, and it's *Meren's* that are warm, heating his skin, her energy mixing and mingling with his atoms.

He's just pressing their mouths together softly, almost stiffly—but he loosens when Meren responds, tilting her head—

—and then it's over.

He eases away, but he's still cupping her jaw, the smooth curve of it cradled in his broad palm. His breath is quick, each exhale ghosting her face, setting it tingling. He drags his brilliant eyes open to gauge her reaction, his other hand still at her leg, almost hovering over it like she's something delicate he doesn't want to break.

His cheeks are pink. It's a light pink, delicate and barely visible—but it *is* there—and his pupils are swallowing up each iris, swamping them, drowning green with black. They're staring at Meren's lips as if he can't drag them away.

He must feel her pulse fluttering like frantic wings where his thumb is settled against her throat.

The width of a blade of grass is all that stands between their foreheads.

WHAT LORKAN IS

Lorkan still hasn't moved away, and Meren doesn't want him to—she's scared that he will, and her free hand reaches out of its own accord, finding the back of his head.

His hair is soft under Meren's palms. Softer than she imagined it would be. Shakily, she does the opposite of a sigh, sort of sucking air in and not being able to let it out again. Before she's even realised she's done it, her fingers have submerged themselves in his curls, the strands like scuffs of charcoal scribbled across the backs of her hands.

Lorkan lets her, his eyes slipping closed.

Encouraged, she clutches the thick coils, over-conscious of hurting him—

But she needn't have worried.

A small, low noise breaks in his chest.

It grates roughly against her core like a wet stone over a rock. Without thinking, just calling upon some instinct, some deeply rooted knowledge she didn't know she possessed, Meren tugs his lips back against her own.

Because she wants more of those unintentional little sounds.

And he's letting her touch him.

And what if she never gets to do that again?

Lorkan's palm finally closes over her leg, steadying himself as he falls into her embrace willingly, *eagerly*.

It's hard to keep her mouth politely closed, to keep a respectable distance; although that ship has long since left the metaphorical harbour.

Lorkan isn't even trying—to keep his distance *or* to keep his mouth shut. With the pad of his thumb at her chin, he eases open her jaw, swallowing the shaky edge of her moan as though it's sweet honey.

Encouraged, his hands bundle her closer, and Meren lets herself collapse against him, her body meeting the solid strength of his chest. It's steady and unmovable and reassuring; firm like the trunk of a tree.

She knows she should shove him away.

She's trying to grab those feelings he brings out of her, and stuff them back, deep down where they've been festering like weeds—but it's difficult when he's moving his jaw like that.

Her grip on his hair tightens, urging him nearer, and Lorkan falls against her with a pained sound, his hand at her knee hunting out the dip of her waist, grasping it. He's still kneeling on the ground, and pushes his body further into the space between her thighs, his heart hammering quickly against the bodice of her dress.

The tiny ice horse is liquifying in Meren's tightly clenched palm, the sharp points of its ears, muzzle and legs rounding into dulled nubs. Its transparent blood has begun to leak from the cracks between her fingers and she lets it go, the amorphous lump falling to the ground with a tinkling, metallic ring.

Had Lorkan been any other man, Meren would have hesitated before taking his jawline with that hand, numb and slick with cold. She would have wiped it on her dress first; given it a little shake to restore some heat and blood to the chilled skin.

But Lorkan doesn't even flinch. He just leans into it, giving the full curve of her bottom lip a little tug as if trying to show her he likes it.

* ☾ *

Meren is the one to ease away—tear herself away, *drag* herself away.

Because her chest is burning. She needs to breathe, and it's taken her an embarrassingly long time to realise that; her own survival just a sloppy afterthought, an irritating little voice poking the back of her brain.

Lungs replenished, she leans in again, expecting to find Lorkan's mouth waiting, hungry and responsive—

But it's not there, the place it had occupied—that humid space just in front of her own—now cold and vacant and empty.

Confused, her eyes flutter open.

He's just watching her. Yes, he's pulled back, his mouth curved in a smile.

He must catch Meren's brows come together like a tightly-pulled stitch, but gives me no explanation. He just says, simply:

WHAT LORKAN IS

"Perfect."

What's perfect?

Their kiss?

That *had* been perfect—

So why isn't he letting her do it again?

"Meren?" He'd asked something, something she'd missed.

Blinking, she grapples for firm footing on reality, but finds none. Her thoughts keep sliding sideways, falling back to Lorkan's *hair*, his *hands,* his *lips*—

They aren't so narrow now. They're not their usual pastel pink either, but a vibrant raspberry, the colour spilling out across his cheekbones.

"Yes?" The syllable wobbles limply off her tongue, just as weak as her knees. Every muscle she owns seems to have crumbled like cake.

It's wonderful.

But then Lorkan lets go of her waist.

"I said, do you think you can hold that look?"

The word '*look*' sparks some half-buried memory, and then a few more crop up like ugly fungi in a damp corner:

The painting.

Realisation slots into place, painfully, like a dislocated limb forced back into its joint. Shoving a nibbling sense of disappointment heavily to one side, Meren gives a nod.

"I think so."

And then her hands are empty.

Her eyes follow The Prince's triangular back as it crosses quickly over to his canvas.

✶ ☾ ✶

It's been a little while since anyone has said anything.

There is no sound to fill the silence; the area Lorkan is focused on is much too small for his brush to sweep and dab, although he *is* painting quickly. Every so often he glances at Meren fleetingly, then ducks back behind the easel, the point of his elbow dipping to the palette to retrieve more peony pink for her cheeks, more chestnut brown for the smattering of freckles over her nose.

Her kiss-dazed expression is time-sensitive, and she can feel it draining from her face already.

"I was going to offer my apologies for pouncing on you like that," His voice neatly slices the silence in two. It comes to Meren softened and almost fuzzy; like a line drawn by a 9B charcoal stick.

She's not sure if it is fondness, or the layers of paint filtering it, sifting each word smooth like a sieve.

He leans to the right, just enough to flash her a smile. It's all white teeth and smirky dashes of black eyebrow, and it makes her blush to the roots of her hair.

"But I don't think you minded, did you?"

"Nor did you, by the sound of it," she hurls back, puffing up her chest like a small animal trying to deter a much larger animal from eating it. "I'm pretty sure a prince shouldn't make noises like that."

That *noise*. She can still feel it humming against her lips.

He dips back behind the stretched rectangle of cotton. "Well, a respectable woman shouldn't be able to kiss like *that.*"

Heat pours from the crown of Meren's head to the base of her neck again, but this time for a whole different reason. Defensively:

"I was just copying *you.*"

"You shouldn't have—I didn't really know what I was doing."

Meren blinks, her humiliation momentarily forgotten. "What do you mean?"

"I mean: I haven't had any practice."

Unable to mask her obvious surprise, she blurts:

"But look at you."

WHAT LORKAN IS

Lorkan's elbow comes to an abrupt halt.

Even though she can't see his expression, she knows it's curled with a pleased grin.

Righting himself, his arm resumes its carefully dabbing. "Wren, I'm a prince. I don't get to meet many people, and even if I *did* find someone I wanted to...do *that* with, I can't have lovers traipsing through the palace to and from my bedroom, can I? People would notice."

"So? You're a prince, no one would be surprised, even if you had concubines." She nearly adds '*They already think you* do, *and that I'm one of them*' but manages to bite her tongue. She knows he won't let her come up to his chamber anymore if he believes it's harming her reputation in any way, no matter how many times she assures him she doesn't mind the teasing.

A chuckle drifts over to her place by the window, a velvet curl of amusement. "The public expects me to grossly misuse my power?"

"That's not what I meant."

"I know. And I know that's what people expect, but—regardless of the rumours—my family prefers to conduct itself with a bit more decorum. Father always told me that a ruler's reputation is like a cliff face. If it gets waterlogged with doubt and mistrust, it will become weak and will crumble."

Lorkan leans to the side and says in a measured tone:

"The royal family is supposed to *run* the kingdom, after all, not have their every need served by it." He says it firmly, pressing it to Meren's memory like something he hopes will stick—although she's not sure why.

"Plus," he's squints at her mouth, but as a painter, not a man, taking in the rhythm of the line, "I wouldn't want to share my bed with strangers."

Meren is grateful when he disappears back behind the canvas again. She wriggles, for the first time a little uncomfortable as she lounges across the hard wedge of window sill. "I'm sorry, I didn't mean to imply—"

"Imply all you like," he shrugs, taking some more paint; a pleasant hazel sort of colour. He applies it so finely, he appears still as a stone for several seconds, then swishes his brush around the jar of water at his feet.

Meren watches the paint curl away and dissolve—then something occurs to her.

"Lorkan?"

"Hm?"

"...Was that your first kiss?"

His brush doesn't stop, but his feet rearrange themselves on the rug. "Yes."

She had thought he'd stay hidden, preferring to admit something so personal to the picture of her rather than the real thing—but he leans out and meets her eyes—as a man now, not a painter.

He's smiling. "Thank you for that, by the way."

Meren moistens her lips. They still taste of him, and she becomes a little overwhelmed by the strong, insistent desire to approach the chaise lounge and capture his mouth again.

Would he mind if she suddenly stood up, padded across the cold floor and closed the space between them? If she cradled the angular cut of his jaw, would he distractedly drop his brush and palette? If she pulled his hair in that way he seemed to like, would he grab her waist and drag her onto his lap?

Not for the painting, but for the sensation of it, for the taste, the feeling, for nothing?

Instead, she says:

"Don't mention it." She'd meant it as a turn of phrase—a response picked hastily because Lorkan's sincerity had caught her off-guard—but regrets it almost instantly.

He takes her advice and doesn't mention it for the rest of the evening.

✵ ☾ ✵

As night begins seeping into the sky like ink spilt on parchment, Lorkan walks Meren to the door of his chambers. He stops before reaching out for the handle, and she wonders if he's going to bend down and kiss her goodbye.

He doesn't—because of course he doesn't.

Taking a scrap of parchment from a nearby chest of drawers, he scribbles something onto it in his steady, looping hand, and transfers it to Meren's palm.

They say their usual goodbyes, and she hears the soft click of the lock behind her, echoing about the vast, empty hallway. Squinting at the parchment in the gloom, she finds a short list of pigments.

✷ ☾ ✷

That night, Meren snatches little sleep. Her skull is fizzing away to itself like someone has filled it with ale and given it a thorough shaking.

Earlier, when she'd edged over to peek at the portrait's progress, Lorkan had stepped swiftly in front of it, shielding her view with his wide shoulders. "Not yet."

"But you always let me see," she'd protested, and he shook his head smugly.

Placing a hand low on her back, he guided her gently away from the easel. "I want it to be a surprise."

She'd pleaded with him, claiming to be fascinated by the process and pained to miss even a second of it—but of course, that wasn't the real reason, and something about the upward quirk of his lip suggested Lorkan knew that.

She wanted to see if he's managed to complete her face.

If he hasn't, he'll need to kiss her again.

If he does, will she mind?

And, will she let him?

Earlier, when he'd been painting, every look—every darting glance—threw Meren's senses into disarray. His eyes all glittery, his lips—still flushed from her touch, sent an electric tension filling her body and prickling each hungry nerve cell.

She had both delighted in it and feared it.

Why hadn't she tried to stop herself? Why hadn't she done anything about it? When that shy little sapling started to sprout deep within her heart, why hadn't she crushed it underfoot?

Selfishness, that's why, she realises with disgust. And curiosity. And because it's *Lorkan*. She couldn't pinpoint the exact moment it happened. Maybe there wasn't one. She'd visualised that crux in her life as a sort of hole that she'd suddenly trip into—she'd catch sight of a strapping male as he does whatever it is strapping males do—and that would be it.

But that is not how it had transpired. There had been no sudden transition from girl to woman, no awakening like a hefty slap in the face. No, instead, it seemed to happen secretly, somewhere at the back of her mind in a dusty corner she never explores; like an acorn left in a coat pocket and forgotten about.

Each smile he gave her, every curling laugh, fed the little sapling, The Prince inadvertently nourishing it with his general Lorkan-ness until, one day, Meren knew that if he leant down for a kiss, she probably wouldn't shove him away.

She couldn't bring himself to kill that feeling. Tranquillise it with denial, yes, but kill it altogether? Uproot it?

It's festered; that one stupid, tiny sapling has grown and multiplied and expanded and now, with his kiss fresh on her skin, it's become an entire garden—blossoms blooming in her lungs, her heart tangled with ivy the colour of his eyes, and vines winding in and out of ribs like a trellis.

Of all the people to fall for, why does it have to be him? Lorkan Aldrin, soon to be engaged; whisked away to another kingdom—a *prince*.

Would things have gone differently is he was just a man? Perhaps...an inventor, or an author, probably. Or a scholar. If they had met then—bumped into each other at the bookseller's wagon in the market—would he have kissed her much sooner? And for much longer?

WHAT LORKAN IS

Frustrated, and knowing sleep will evade her for many hours to come, Meren pushes off her bed covers. Slowly, as not to wake the woman in the cot next to hers, she takes her pad of parchment, charcoal, and a wax stick from her bedside table, and finds her way to the mess hall in the dark.

It's pleasingly empty, and Meren brushes a hand over the surface of a nearby bench, ridding it of a few leftover flecks of pastry. Holding the wax stick on its side, she allows some grease to leak onto the table and presses the end of the stick into it.

While she waits for the wax to harden enough to support its weight, she thumbs through her parchment pad for a fresh page, and contemplates what to draw.

Lorkan has printed a neat list of things she should have a go at—ascending in difficulty—and, so far, she's reached the seventh bullet point; a bird. He'd said it would give her a *'vital understanding of anatomy and movement'*, but Meren doesn't feel like drawing something that moves at the moment.

What she would *really* like to draw is the ice figurine he'd tossed to her all those hours ago, the tiny stallion that had melted with the heat of his kiss.

She knows it will be a challenge—bringing a memory into reality—and yet, letting such beauty go undocumented feels like more of a crime than misrepresenting it.

Once she feels the wax stick is stable, Meren releases it and pushes her notepad closer to the flame's feeble, flickering light.

As the kingdom sleeps, she sets to work.

✳ ☾ ✳

Just before the wax stick burns out, Meren pries it from the table and uses the nub to find her way back to her quarters, parchment and a (much shorter) rod of charcoal clutched in one hand.

Her sketchbook now holds a drawing of an ice horse, and it's actually rather good.

✶ ☾ ✶

The next morning, Meren wakes earlier than usual, so early she manages to join the hoard of servants filing into the mess hall for breakfast. After a quick, salty bowl of porridge, she sets out for the market, her pace subconsciously and unnecessarily brisk.

The sky is bright but brisk and, all before noon, she collects the pigments Lorkan has requested, hastily purchases two boxes of red velvet cake from Aasta, and arrives back at Aldercliff's gates with time to spare.

She'd spent most of last night turning over the conundrum of Lorkan's kiss in her head, and concluded that she *will* let him do it again, should he need to.

For the painting.

It would be a shame to deny the picture—the most elegant and sophisticated thing she has ever been involved in—the complimenting expression it deserves. If her expression had been anything like *Lorkan's* when they'd broken apart and taken a look at each other's faces, the portrait will be even more stunning than she had ever imagined.

She's stuffed the other reason in a dark, forgotten corner of her mind as though it is a hideous piece of furniture she's rather ashamed of.

As Meren's feet draw to a halt—the first time they've been stationary since sleep—outside Lorkan's chambers, she wonders about waiting for the bell to signify twelve o'clock before knocking at his door. However, after thirty seconds of dithering in the hallway, alone with her thoughts, she decides against it. They're buzzing like a hive of trapped bees, and the pressure of their multitudinous, vibrating wings is getting to her.

Thankfully, when she gives a tentative knock, Lorkan answers with bright eyes and steps aside, sweeping her into the room.

"Sorry, I'm early."

WHAT LORKAN IS

"Meren, you never need to apologise for blessing me with your company."

Instinctively, she glances at that corner of his lip; the one that usually quirks up like a string's attached to it whenever he's teasing her.

But it's merely curved in a genuine smile.

※ ☾ ※

They spend a few hours preparing the pigments Meren had bought, the movement a rhythm her hand can now carry out on its own, without her brain's interference.

Now that winter skulks about the palace, Lorkan has shut all his windows, for Meren's sake, and purchased several new rugs, creating a chain of warmth for her new socks to follow from the entrance hall to the studio. For the first time since his occupancy, the fireplace has been lit in the study, and it purrs away as they kneel by the low wooden table, their well-oiled conversations chugging through the rest of the morning and into the afternoon.

As usual, Lorkan inquires after Meren's day, and she inquires after his evening.

He asks her how her sketching is coming along, and she asks after the novel he's been devouring.

He asks after her family, so she asks after his.

"I received a raven letter from Sol this morning," he says, dripping some yellow oil into his bowl of ground ochre. With the end of a paintbrush, he gives it a stir.

"How is his training going?"

The oil beads and rolls like marbles over sand.

"He barely wrote of it," he chuckles disapprovingly. "They're teaching him combat magic at the moment, but all he goes on about are his friends and the women he meets in the taverns."

"It's understandable for him to have a little fun," Meren shrugs, and catches him rolling his eyes. "What?"

"Everyone defends him. He could commit *arson,* and the victims would insist he was just trying to warm their home."

"You talk about him as if he's a rogue."

"He's a spoiled, impulsive pleasure seeker but, because he's blonde with pretty blue eyes, everyone worships the ground he walks on."

"Oh, hello. Do I detect a hint of *jealousy?*" Meren gives him a light elbow in the ribs. "That's not like you."

He colours, abashed. "No! Not at all. It's just annoying."

"They worship you too, you know."

A brittle wind rattles the windows in their panes, and Meren shivers.

Standing, Lorkan disappears into the other room, calling through the open door:

"Not in the same way. Everyone is in love with Sol, but they look at me differently."

"With respect, probably."

He returns with a green patchwork quilt, and draws it around her shoulders, tying it carefully under her chin, wrapping her like a present.

She settles into the quilt's embrace gratefully, the fabric thick and heavy with embroidery.

Lorkan is watching her, probably amused, his eyes soft. "More like fear. People have been suspicious of me ever since they got a glance at my hair."

"What's wrong with it?"

"It's not gold like the sun, it's black like midnight."

"So?"

"So, people are scared of the dark."

"They're scared of house spiders too, but they never did anyone any harm."

Lorkan gives her a sideways smile. "I'm just bitter because Sol has never had to work hard for anything in his life." He settles back at the table, his legs crossed over his paint-stained pillow.

"Your parents met while His Majesty was training at Black Castle, didn't they? Has Sol met our future queen yet?"

"He's met *many* possible queens, and a few kings, by the sound of it. However, knowing my brother as I do, I doubt they're the sort of people Father would invite to dinner."

"So, Prince Sol can't marry who he likes either?"

Lorkan meets her eyes properly, for the first time since he'd peeked at her from behind his easel. "No, Wren, he can't."

When the paints are prepared, Meren helps him transport the multitudinous little bowls to his nest of art supplies, all waiting patiently for his arrival just as he had left them the night before. However, when she moves to arrange herself in the window seat, he takes her wrist softly, and gestures to the fireplace.

"Why don't we have a drink first? I feel guilty, making you sit on a stone sill for hours like a decorative vase."

Touched, Meren concedes, and Lorkan starts stacking kindling in the cold ashes of the hearth. He gratefully allows her to take the matches from him before he can light the pyramid of sticks, and she waits until he's safely perched on the long sofa before striking the match.

The wood catches at once and begins dancing happily across the kindling, splintering loudly now and again, hiccuping between mouthfuls of tree bark and sap.

Having poured some milk into his copper kettle, he hands it to her to place over the flames. Whilst she's setting it on its hook, careful to sweep her dress away from the hearth, he says quietly:

"By the way, I haven't finished painting your face yet."

Meren moves to take a seat, but Lorkan pats the space at his side. Moving over to him, she watches as he fills a mug with cold milk for himself, then ladles a heaped teaspoon of honey from a jar.

"Okay."

"Would you mind if I repeated the method I used yesterday?" His tone has softened with something she doesn't recognise, and a small smile twitches her lip.

"The *method* you used?"

The sharp ridges of his cheekbones colour. "Kissing you. I'd like to kiss you again, if you wouldn't mind." He's watching the honey ooze from the spoon, elongating into a rod of transparent amber before finally breaking the surface of the milk. When he brings his eyes up to meet hers, every shade of green is flickering like the fire. "That expression was wonderful."

"I think, yesterday, you described it as '*perfect.*'"

"Don't flatter yourself," he quips.

But he's smirking.

* ☾ *

Meren arranges her body in its usual pose upon the window seat, finding her limbs uncooperative and stiff with exhilaration.

Lorkan kneels before her again.

He takes her waist again.

Hums when she slips her fingers into his hair again.

And, when, he pulls away, he says again:

"Perfect."

His mouth had tasted of milk and honey.

25

AN ARGUMENT IN THE MESS HALL

Every session starts like that from then on.

Lorkan bends down, taking a knee as though to propose, sometimes cupping the line of Meren's jaw, or curling a finger under her chin. He will ease her face close to his own as if to kiss her—but he never does. Every time, as if bumping into an invisible barrier, he comes to a halt, his cool breath grazing her skin through parted lips.

At first, she'd thought he was teasingly withholding his touch, knowing she's aching for it. Savouring the moment, revelling in her torment—

But a few kisses later, it dawns on her that his hesitation might be down to something else. The way he catches himself before claiming her mouth—it's almost as if he's waiting for her to push him away.

Surely, he must know she wants him? All of him; his pointy, curling smile when he's particularly pleased with himself, his slick, witty personality, his skin pale as freshly fallen snow.

Perhaps it's a gentlemanly act of courtesy—waiting there for her to eliminate those final few millimetres between their mouths? He doesn't want to overwhelm her, to appear too forward, too ravenous, too hungry.

But he seems *ravenous*—as soon as Meren initiates the kiss, it's like she's opened a floodgate. He bundles her up against the solidness of his chest like he *needs* her there, clutches her waist like he *wants* her there, tilts his head like he's aching for the taste of her—whatever had been holding him back before completely forgotten.

So why does he never kiss her first?

Maybe he's giving her a chance to change her mind? After all, their kisses are not as simple as two people who love each other sharing a tender touch. Every squeeze of Lorkan's hands, every flick of his pointy tongue, every press of his lips has been due to, because of, and for…

A painting.

So why does he never kiss her first?

It prods at her like a stone in her shoe.

※ ☾ ※

"Ah, Hansen, there you are."

Meren raises her head from her roast pork to find a heap of neatly folded washing making its way carefully across the mess hall. She watches as it picks a path through the remaining diners before finally coming to a stop, Alfdis' little face popping out from one side.

"I've been meaning to talk to you about something." The little old lady's tone is light, but there's something apologetic behind her eyes that makes Meren nervous.

All the same, she swallows her mouthful of what Yllva had advertised as stewed vegetables, and pulls on what she hopes is a welcoming smile. "Good news, I hope?"

The lines surrounding Alfdis' mouth shift with the ghost of a frown as she brushes a few crumbs from the table and sets her pile of laundry down with a sigh. "I don't think it is, I'm afraid." She takes a second to catch her breath, and Meren realises it is not the burdensome pile of linen that's draining her.

Quickly, she pours her a glass of water, and Alfdis takes it gratefully, perching on the bench like a tired carrier raven finally come to roost.

'Someone must have died,' Meren thinks grimly, and angles herself towards the older woman.

She's cupping her glass in her lap in both hands as if it's a warm mug of tea, and moistens the thin dash of her upper lip. "You see, we should really start talking about what you will do when Lorkan moves to Calpurzia."

Meren blinks at her.

She feels as though something has been flung across the room and hit her squarely in the face.

On a matter of sympathetic principle, she has avoided asking Lorkan about the alliance, which he seemed to appreciate. Together, they'd reached an unspoken understanding—a pact formed entirely from deluded optimism—that his proposed wedding would just go away if they buried it far back enough in their consciousness. Meren did not want to needlessly toy with his wounds, and she trusted that, should there be news, he would share it with her.

But had something changed whilst she'd made the trek from his chambers to the servant's quarters? Has an announcement been declared whilst she'd been queuing for her meal, or visiting the privy?

The bench she's sitting on—and the whole world—seems to be slanting to the left. Taking up her own glass of water, she drags a few long sips to force an annoying knot of broccoli down her throat. It has a long way to go, because her stomach seems to have fallen wetly to the floor. "I thought nothing had been decided yet?"

The competent old bones in Alfdis' hand shift as though she's going to place a comforting palm on Meren's arm, but decides not to. "Nothing is set in stone yet, but it will be, one day. An alliance with the Calpurzian will benefit trade, prevent wars—it will do wonders for the kingdom, Hansen, do you understand that?"

Slightly stunned, she nods. When she finally finds some words, they're thin and taught and more feeble than she would have liked. "How did you know about the wedding? I thought it was supposed to be a secret?"

Alfdis raises an eyebrow and parries with:

"How do *you* know about it?"

"Rumours." A lie, and Meren can tell the head housekeeper knows it.

She doesn't chastise her, though.

She just sighs.

She has more wrinkles when she exhales, as though her body is tissue paper, so light its shape is dictated by the shifting of air particles. "Rumours leak through walls like water. Everyone in the kingdom will know, given a few days, and then His Majesty will have to take back control by making a decision."

"I thought you said it was '*His Highness*' when referring to a prince?"

"Meren, it's *not* Lorkan's decision."

Her tawny accent curls his name up—'*Law-can*' instead of '*Law-kun*'.

On any other day, this would have made Meren smile.

"But—" she tries, unable to stifle her desperately, "Surely there are other ways to make an alliance?"

Alfdis blinks behind her thick glasses. "Well, yes, but His Majesty—"

Meren ploughs over her words, regret searing her conscience. She isn't angry at Alfdis, this sweet woman who treats her with the compassion of a mother—

—and yet, all of a sudden, syllables are flying from her mouth like bats startled from a cave.

"You know, some few, *lucky* people in this wretched kingdom manage to marry for *love,* and even that isn't strong enough to bind them together forever. Surely Cade knows a *wedding* is not strong enough to heal a several-thousand-year rift between two kingdoms—"

Alfdis' kindly expression hardens in a way that would have been disconcerting had Meren noticed. "And you're suddenly a diplomat, are you?"

She feels herself prickle. "Of course not, it just doesn't make any sense—"
"Well, not to someone of our stature, obviously—"
Placing her cutlery down on the table, her meal forgotten:
"I don't think I believe in stature anymore."
This actually makes the older woman laugh, and it slices Meren's legs off at the knees. Suddenly, she's nine years old again.

But only for a moment.

"People say we *'can't understand such things'*, and *'It's not our place'*, but *why?* Are poor people's minds formed differently? Do they lack something? Is there a piece missing that means they can't comprehend beautiful, complicated things like history or chemistry or art?"

Once, Meren might have believed that, but not anymore. With Lorkan, with Arne, with Frode, she has discussed all of those things.

She's learnt about the planets and the stars, massive celestial bodies and their paths across the sky.

She'd learnt of particles, of atoms and bonds, how materials interact and affect one another. She's learnt of fields and electrons, that invisible energies pass through everything—*that's* how Lorkan created the miniature ice horse and phantom birds.

Her vocabulary has swelled, her skills have broadened, her thoughts curious and richer. Despite her class and her poverty and her background, she'd *understood*.

"In a fantasy land, perhaps," Alfdis quips simply and, with a white-hot flare of rage, Meren hates her cheery disposition, just for a second.

"No, the way I see it," she fights back, hackles raised as she clutches her new knowledge protectively to her chest. "With access to proper education, anyone can understand anything. I bet even children know *forcing* two people to be together is a *shit* solution to any problem—"

A look of slight alarm flashes over Alfdis' features, her eyebrows pushing up her forehead like a duvet kicked to the end of a bed. "Meren! Bite your tongue!"

"Why? Because it's not my *place* to recognise our king is making a terrible mistake? Lorkan is his *son*, and he's sending him away! Why is it okay to force a person to have to give their whole life over to someone they don't even know? Why can't—"

"No, it is *not* your place to question such things!" Alfdis interrupts this time, her words cracking cleanly through Meren's rant in a tone she has not heard before.

The hairs on her arms stand erect.

She had always wondered how kindly, simple Alfdis managed to claim her position at the top of the pile of servants, and then managed to maintain it— unopposed—for so many years.

This must be how.

"Hansen, I am a *reasonable* woman, but I am also a practical, *traditional* woman, and your employer. I can sympathise with your rapidly shifting life, and possibly your loss of a good friendship—even if that friendship should technically not exist—but that sympathy is limited and easily drained.

I have neither the patience nor compassion for silly, fanciful plights, and I haven't dedicated my entire life to the Royal Family just to have an insolent youth disrespect them like this. You are barely a babe—what do you know about treaties or entente or concords between entire nations?"

Meren's mouth opens, but she can't summon any sound. Two of those terms are so alien she can't even begin to guess at their meaning. As if recognising its defeat, her adrenaline putters out and she yields, ashamed.

"We must trust in our king. He knows what is best for us and his kingdom," Alfdis continues, but she'd softened her tone, now. She's speaking in that careful, measured way she talks when she feels that what she's saying is some form of 'advice' that should be taken very seriously.

She's usually right.

"I too was young, once, if you will believe it. I understand how powerful it feels to finally begin to make sense of the world—but that is all you have done —*begun*. Perhaps hold *off* leading a revolution until your perception is wide enough to take in the whole picture?"

Meren just hums.

Where is the line between genuine correctness and deluded youth? And how can one tell which side of it one is standing? Is this—who she is now, a curious, passionate woman bubbling with interest and an unrelenting sense of right and wrong—something she'll just...grow out of? Will she one day become like Alfdis, or her parents, or Yllva; submissively taking a step back whenever opinion or deep thought is required?

Not noticing that Meren's spine has sunken into a defeated slouch, Alfdis continues, metaphorically dusting salt onto her wounds and rubbing it in:

"All jokes aside, you must realise that getting promoted from a cleaner to a housemaid does not qualify you to critique even my decisions, let alone a monarch's. And as for His Royal Highness, it is his duty to his kingdom—"

"You didn't call him '*Lorkan*', that time," Meren points out sullenly, as if it means something.

Alfdis just frowns, her shoulders wilting. "I knew the young prince before he could stumble around the nursery; sometimes his name slips out and, if it does, it is entirely accidental. He will always be '*His Royal Highness*' to me, and to you as well." Her eyes narrow and she says firmly, reminding Meren very much of her mother:

"Even if he has told you otherwise."

The back of her neck heats as though she's been caught stealing.

They both fall into silence, but it is anything but quiet. Meren can hear the smooth cogs of Alfdis' mind churning away, and she knows she's deciding how to proceed.

Meren should be punished, even she knows that, the question is how, and what for? This argument, obviously—insubordination to her employer is worth a thorough pay-docking—or even dismissal—and her disrespect to the crown counts as borderline treason.

But what else does Alfdis know about?

Does she know that she's never bowed to Lorkan, not even once? And that she stopped being his housemaid months ago, and now spends most of her time playing with him, laughing with him, chatting to him like they're old friends?

Does she know he's dedicated hours to painting her portrait? That he's designed a dress for her, instructed the placement of each stitch, hand-picked every stretch of material, thread, and ribbon?

Does she know he has cupped her face in his royal hands? Nudged her back against his frost-prickled window pane?

That Meren has grasped at his hair, tugged several very ungentlemanly moans from his lungs?

A decision apparently reached, Alfdis brushes some imaginary dust from her impeccably crisp uniform, like a cat licking itself down after a fight. "Well, I'm glad your little temper tantrum is over. This time, you have escaped unscathed, but you must learn to restrain that temper, missy. It flicks out like the pointed, sharp tongue of a snake and, one day, it will touch on the wrong person's nerves."

She nods solemnly and releases a breath she didn't know she's been holding in.

"Anyway, I did not come over here to have a political debate with you. What I wanted to talk to you about is the nature of your position once His Highness leaves. May we get back to that?"

Deflated, Meren says nothing, knowing she has no choice in the matter; if Alfdis wants to say something, she will. She may be small and as old as time, but she's plucky and will keep plodding along relentlessly well after everyone else is dead and gone.

'Like a tortoise,' Meren thinks impassively.

"Now, even though you are technically a housemaid, you aren't *actually* a housemaid. You have never received training, have no real experience with waiting on royalty, and have never been taught the proper customs for such a prestigious position."

'A mean tortoise.'

"Thanks."

Alfdis neatly sweeps her hurt feelings away with more words, her tone brisk and efficient. "I speak only the truth, dear. You are only in the position you are in now because His Highness requested for you specifically."

Meren's ears prick.

When they had met on the steps all those months ago, under the brittle dawn sun, she had taken an instant liking to The Prince.

She had never considered the fact that The Prince might have taken one to her.

Despite everything, her lips curve into a smile.

Alfdis' gaze flicks over it, but she doesn't comment.

"Because of this, once he leaves, I can't let you continue as a housemaid. You will have to go back to cleaning the front steps—or perhaps, if a position is available, you may have a place completing minor household chores in the servant's quarters. Like changing the bed linen, or stoking the fires." She says it as though passing her a present and, Meren knows—in a way—she is.

However, it doesn't feel like that.

It feels like she's been given an award, but someone is trying to take it back, saying a mistake has been made and she didn't deserve it after all.

Her jaw twinges uncomfortably, and she realises she's been unintentionally clenching it. "I have to go back to cleaning the steps?" Not really a question, not really a statement.

She brings her hands out from under the table. They'd been scrunched up like the balls of parchment littering Lorkan's chambers, but she spreads them now, letting her gaze slide solemnly over their palms.

They prickle with memories of the numb, bitter cold; of the damp, splintering wood of the mop, of the sky so thick and black she could drown in it. She will miss their new softness, the smooth, unbroken tenderness of their skin, their sense of touch.

This time, Alfdis does let her hand rest on Meren's arm.

She barely feels it, it's as light as a sparrow.

"Maybe not. As I said, there might be room for you on the dormitory team and, of course, His Highness may want you to continue tending to his chambers every now and again so they are suitable for his visits."

"His visits?"

"Yes, dear. You know; when he and his new wife come to stay at Aldercliff for a season or two."

Meren ignores the knot her stomach curls itself into at the word *'wife'*—she will *not* be one of those pathetic, jealous people who pine over things that aren't theirs. No, she shall be the kind of woman who is *pleased* for the Calpurzian princess, she decides. It won't matter to her who is giving Lorkan the attention he deserves. All that matters is he gets it.

"Why would they do that?"

The bony ridge of Alfdis' shoulders rise and fall in a disinterested shrug, as if it's all the same to her, but Meren can feel her pulse in her ears. "It's customary for couples whose marriage joins two kingdoms to spend equal time at each; to make the public feel they're not forgotten."

Meren turns back to her meal and picks at it with the prongs of her fork in a way she hopes is nonchalant. "So... he'll be coming back?"

A tightness pulls around Alfdis' jaw, and when she replies, she does so carefully. "Perhaps. Unless he or his new wife decides not to continue that tradition."

Meren wonders if Lorkan would—if he was given the choice.

Would he *want* to return to the place he had once called home after being torn from it? Or would he prefer to sever all ties once and for all, mentally and physically, so yearnings for his past life can no longer pull and tug at him like thorns catching loose threads? Would it be too painful to return for a season, knowing he only has to leave again, over and over?

She imagines dragging a mop back and forth while he sips tea with his wife on the settee, their easy, hushed, intimate conversation buzzing in the air like flies.

She imagines the ache in her chest, and pales.

Maybe going back to cleaning the steps isn't so bad after all.

PART THREE
The Monster

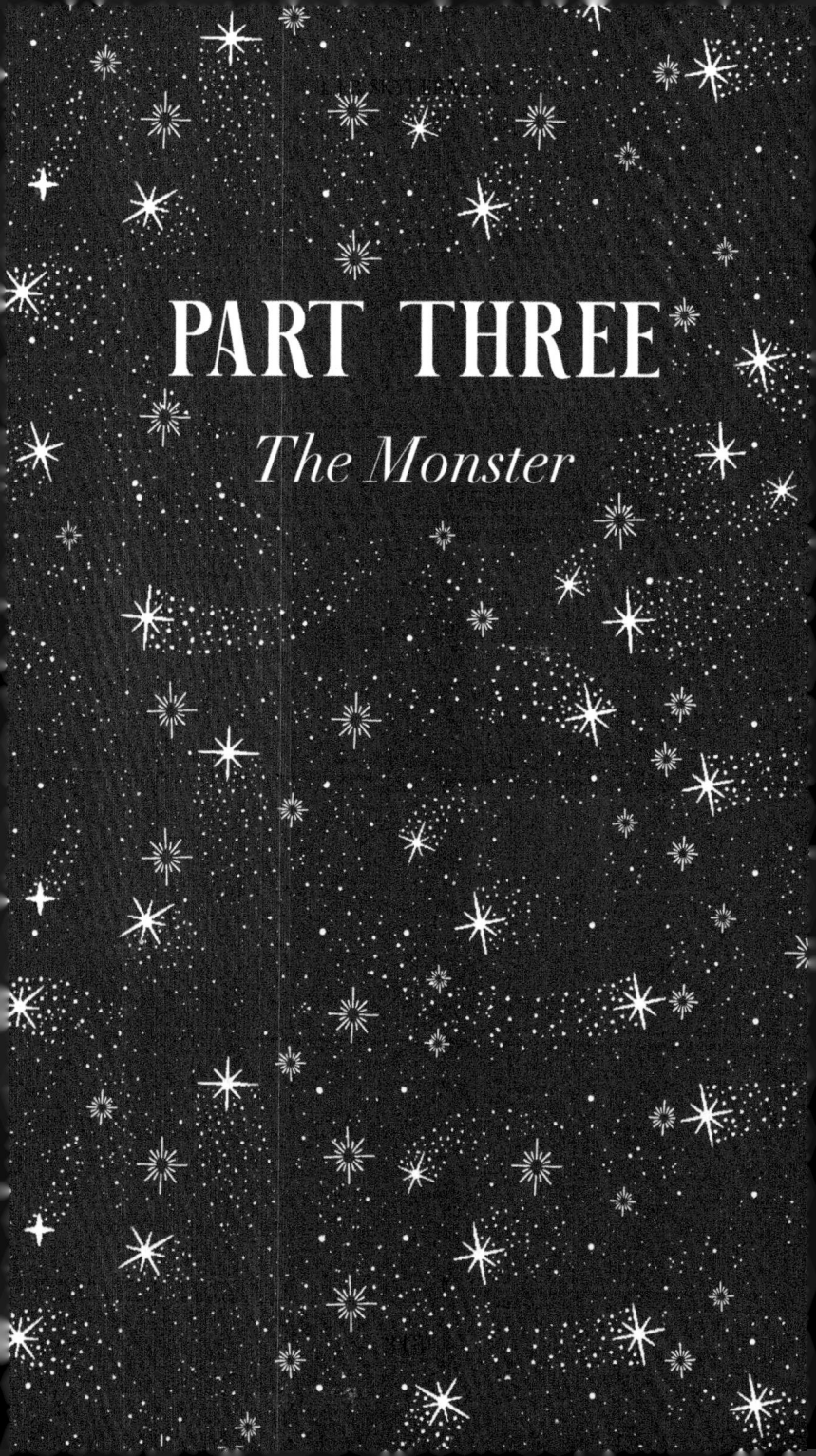

26

THE TIPSY DRAGON

Some hours later, the sting of Alfdis' little talk is finally beginning to wear off, fading until it's just a low, dull ache. It's still twinging as Meren clambers into bed, pestering her like a gammy tooth so, throwing off the covers in a huff, she heads once more to the mess hall where she sketches well into the night.

Her sketching is improving significantly, bringing truth to the phrase *'practice makes perfect'*— although, practising has not been her intention for several days.

She has noticed that Lorkan tends to draw as an expression of joy—to capture beauty and pleasant moments, whereas Meren has become rather fond of the opposite.

She does not note down the existing beauty she sees, she creates her own, and seeks refuge in it. She is soothed by the creamy span of the parchment, content within the minimalistic hug of fluffy black lines.

With every passing day, the fog of apprehension suffocating the sixteenth floor grows ever thicker. It seems to mar Lorkan's view, filling his head and getting in his eyes, snuffing out his artistic inclinations as beauty becomes more and more difficult to see. His chambers—usually riddled with balls of parchment like apples fallen from a tree—have become bare, as if that tree has suddenly ceased producing fruit.

Not for Meren, though. The uncertainty of her shifting, harsh reality, seems to have only fuelled her yearning for the dull, predictable parchment and gentle sweeps of charcoal. Things are simpler there, in her two-dimensional world of black and white, and—while Lorkan's enthusiasm for art appears to have trickled to a stop like a well run dry—Meren now spends most of her spare moments hunched over a sketchbook.

So far, she has worked steadily through four of them, despite—to conserve space—keeping every sketch huddled elbow to elbow.

Presently, sitting with clenched thoughts on the hard wooden bench, she has each book spread about her—for reference—huddled under the weak flame of a wax stick. It just about illuminates their smudged pages enough to make out the chaotic scramble of shapes. They look fuzzy in the soft light—half alive spectres or shadows with no source.

She is ashamed of many of them, embarrassed by their disfigurement, and the binding of each book has become fluffy with torn-away sheets she'd banished to the bin in frustration.

She's tempted to rip out the page she is working on and takes it in finger and thumb—but stops herself. Her sigh setting the wax stick's flame into a panicked frenzy, she turns the notepad around and begins the picture again.

She can see where she went gone wrong. The mistake sits strangely with the rest of the image, ugly and ill-fitting, like a mangled limb.

Her drawing is of the heavy-shouldered tomcat that keeps the servant's kitchen free of mice in exchange for the occasional chicken bone to gnaw on.

He turned up one day of his own volition, so he could be anywhere from a few months to several years old. Some of the staff have bet coppers on his age, but they won't know how they fared in their wager until the cat stops showing up, which Meren thinks is rather morbid. She had taken an instant liking to his wide, serious face, and the way his fur appears to be dappled with light even when he's in the shade.

WHAT LORKAN IS

She wants to do him justice, so tries to imagine what Lorkan would say if he were sitting beside her.

'He'd probably say the cat looks like Yllva,' Meren thinks, her quiet laughter bouncing about the mess hall.

Seriously, now, *'Then he'd advise me to plan the picture, and tease me when I complain that it's tedious.'*

She sometimes skips this step—setting out the '*skeleton*' of the image—because she lacks patience. This time, still to restless to head back to bed, she maps out each joint in the cat's legs with faint lines and circles; as Lorkan had shown her when they used to sketch together.

They still do, in a way.

Patiently, he'll sit by her side and watch as she muddles through wonky depictions of faces and crude little animals. Sometimes he'll even pluck up a stick of charcoal of his own—if Meren should need help with the rocky joints in a knuckle, or becomes stuck on the rose-like curve of an ear. He'll lean over, level with her sketchbook, his scent tickling her nose as he expertly fills in her gaps—but his own parchment remains void of creation, and has existed in that state for several days.

He appears reluctant to paint too, although it isn't clear whether the reason is down to unease gumming up his enthusiasm, or something else entirely.

He acts differently when he doesn't feel like painting to when he doesn't feel like drawing. When he doesn't want to draw, he just *won't*, preferring to contentedly follow Meren's hand with his eyes, occasionally offering advice or helpful comments. When he doesn't want to *paint,* he seems almost agitated—like a dog that can't find a comfortable place to rest.

Meren can't tell whether he has hit another inspiration block, or if he's simply not in the mood.

He won't let her see the portrait anymore, which makes it even more difficult to tell the precise nature of the snag he's encountering.

"You may see it when it is finished. Have patience, Wren, you are as restless as a child," he drawls lazily, lips turned up slightly in what could be considered a smile.

But Meren isn't the restless one.

With every passing day, his patience thins, his mood turning fickle and irritable as soon as he takes a seat before his easel. He'll select a paintbrush from the masses surrounding his temporary work surface, then—after a few swift dabs—suggest they move on to something else.

As Meren gently drags the tip of her charcoal stick over her page, her mind can't help turning back to Alfdis' earlier words.

Despite everything, Meren feels a smile curve the lower half of her face as she remembers the way Alfdis pronounces Lorkan's name. There's something endearing about it, and she makes a mental note to ask him more about the *younger* Alfdis next time she sees him.

The Alfdis who'd sneak him treats from the kitchen, and offer him snippets of attention between sweeps of her broom.

The Alfdis who watched the spindly boy with a crown too large for his head as he grew and blossomed into a man.

It's no wonder Alfdis fell in love with that spindly boy, Meren thinks.

That's probably how she knew Meren would too.

She had often suspected that the head housekeeper knew she loved Lorkan, but now she knows it to be true.

The question is: how? Can she see through walls? Is she a psychic?

Meren has seen psychics at the market; eccentric, bead-riddled women draped in lucky charms and strings, surrounded by trinkets and colourful rocks they claim aid them in their readings.

A chill dribbles down the back of her neck at the thought of Alfdis somehow being able to read her mind, although, as far as she can remember, she's never seen her wear so much as a pretty clasp in her hair, let alone a string of beads. And there doesn't appear to be any colourful rocks or trinkets in her office, apart from a few clumsy homemade gifts from nieces and nephews.

WHAT LORKAN IS

So how had she known? Meren mulls this over as she selects a finer charcoal stick from her pack. Not wanting to smudge anyone's uniform, her intuition warns her not to spill any black crumbs on the table.

Perhaps *that's* how Alfdis had known? She wouldn't be the first to spook Meren with unexpected intuition. Aasta, too, had been able to tell there was a man on Meren's mind, and—if Lorkan is correct—*she* possesses no magical qualities. Maybe Alfdis is just also abnormally astute?

After all, love does tend to cling to a person like sticky perfume.

Meren must reek of it.

※ ☾ ※

There are a few places to while away an evening in Tawny, and *The Tipsy Dragon* is as good as any.

A low, sturdy building mostly consisting of wood, flagstone, and stains, it appears to have forced its way up between a metalwork workshop and a butcher's like a tumour—although it predates them both by several hundred years.

On a good day, the air is soupy with not only hops, but the chewy beat of live music and, if you catch her in the right mood, the barkeep's stringy, decadent stories. They must be sipped rather than gulped down, and that is what many patrons prefer to do; drink away their few spare hours with easy chatter, a cheap ale, and a tapping foot.

Her shoes clinging to the floor and her mug glued to the tabletop, Meren had instantly warmed to the low-ceilinged little building. Since agreeing to remain friends after their somewhat awkward attempt at romance, Meren and Arne had become frequent patrons of *The Tipsy Dragon*, occupying the round table by the window two to three times a week.

Having spent another lazy, pleasant day on the sixteenth floor, Meren wraps her oilskin tighter about herself as she heads towards the glow of the inn's long, wide windows.

Several chunks have been replaced over the years—the roof patched over like a moth-bitten jacket, a wall knocked out and re-built, some woodworm beams collapsed and propped up—but, all the while, the glass remains. Thick and bubbled, it warps the sconces, making the building look like a giant, fizzing, full glass of cider.

Shards of northern wind slicing Meren's cheeks, she hurries inside like a cat escaping the rain, setting the bell frantically jangling.

The barkeep, a rowdy, dark-haired woman going by the name of Beca, has a brain for faces, and recognises her as soon as she flips her coat's oilskin's back with a sigh. She lost an eye in a way that varies with every telling of the story, and gives her a smile that sets her patch inching up her angular, dark cheekbone.

"The usual?"

Thanking her, Meren picks her way through the gaggle of already-tipsy men and women towards Arne, who greets her with a grin.

A deep tankard has already been delivered to his hand, and he raises it in welcome as Meren slides onto the bench amongst some stained, slightly limpid cushions.

Outside, a lightless dusk rolls in, slamming against the windows like a wave. It's forced the last weak, shaking sunlight from the horizon, pummelling the sky and leaving it streaked with bleeding purple bruises.

Turning away from it, Meren angles herself towards the steady onslaught of the fireplace's warmth, sliding her oilskin from her shoulders.

"It's busy tonight," she observes.

Indeed, there are more drinkers than the usual rosacea-flushed drunks, and they seemed to have emptied their tankards faster than usual, several already giggling between merry hiccups, leaning heavily on the bar, the backs of chairs, or on each other.

WHAT LORKAN IS

On the short, raised stage at the back of the room, a lute player plucks an upbeat tune while her companions strum a leesel, beat a tüge, and blow a pickanto, their heads ducked as not to bump them on the low ceiling.

Tables have been shoved aside to make way for those who wish to dance, their brown work clothes and uniforms swirling and jigging about like leaves picked up by the wind.

Arne shrugs, bringing his tankard to his mouth. "They're celebrating."

The ale's milk-coloured foam clings to the fluffy stubble on his top lip.

Preferring to sip music rather than drink, Meren knows it to be his first of the evening, even if he has been waiting for her for some time.

If he asks why she's late, she'll say Alfdis had her polishing silver—any lie sounds much more forgivable than the truth: that she and Lorkan had gotten so absorbed in a board game they didn't notice the sun sinking below the window sill.

"Celebrating what?"

A look of brief surprise pushes his pale eyebrows up toward his sun-stained fringe. "Haven't you heard?"

As Alfdis predicted, rumours had indeed leaked from Aldercliff and seeped into the surrounding lands, slick and fast as oil. Not nearly an hour after her talk with Meren in the mess hall, gossip of a supposed alliance had begun to sprout all over the kingdom, penetrating each conversation and creeping its way into every home like an outbreak of whooping cough.

Meren knows the conversation is marching swiftly into '*alliance*' territory and, curiously she feigns ignorance, edging closer to Arne's side of the table.

"That His Highness, Lorkan, is engaged to the princess of Calpurzia. Well, he will be. It's all just grainy speculation right now, but everyone knows about it, so there must be some truth to it."

That familiar tightening sensation begins to gently squeeze Meren's throat, and she raises her hand to loosen her scarf, only to find she isn't wearing one. "Ah, well, yes, that is worthy of a celebration. Will *you* be celebrating? Surely this will be great for apothecaries—all those new medicines and recipes once a trade is established."

Arne's hesitates. His eyebrows have fallen back down, furrowing into a slight frown—as if confronted with a maths problem he doesn't quite understand. "I'm not sure. You're right, the Calpurzians do have access to ingredients and knowledge that will benefit all professions greatly."

Meren waits for him to continue, but he doesn't.

"But?" She prompts.

He places his tankard down, a dollop of foam meeting the tabletop, adding another stain to the ever-growing collection. "Well...we've been suspended in a state of cold war with the Calpurzians for hundreds of years—for so long that no one can remember a time we ever got along. Maybe we never did." He casts a hurried look left and right. Finding no ears pricked in his direction, he utters, quietly:

"Does His Majesty really think a *wedding* will mend that rift?"

Meren has to catch herself quickly. Pulling her face into a thoughtful frown, she tries to look as though she's considering it for the first time.

"That's a good point. It's unlikely Cade is going to say, '*Oh, wait, I can't annex the Calpurzians' half of The Spice Trail because my daughter-in-law might get offended.*'"

At that moment, Beca brings Meren her usual. She blows a ringlet of hair away from her forehead as she throws her a knowing grin. It makes the corner of her one good eye crinkle.

"Are you two talking about the alliance?"

Arne is midway through another sip of ale, and sputters on it slightly, as though someone had just clapped him hard between the shoulder blades. He flushes under Beca's gaze, a shy smile twitching his lip. "Maybe."

Meren almost laughs at him; his blocky, sturdy body trying to shrink itself and getting nowhere.

He takes another drink from his tankard as if hoping to hide behind it, looking like a cart-horse trying to conceal itself behind the spindly trunk of a crabapple tree.

"It's all anyone talking about recently," Beca sighs, plucking a greasy rag from her apron pocket. She begins wiping their table with it, but the oily slip of material just shifts the stains around. "Honestly, I think it's all a bit strange. A wedding might be enough to unite two opposing kingdoms in fae tales but in reality?" She shakes her head, and Meren and Arne exchange a look.

Noticing, she furrows her brows at them. "What?"

"Nothing. It's just...we've never heard someone call His Majesty's choices '*strange*' before." He gives another fervent glance at the door as if expecting to find it darkened by a royal guard's silhouette.

Beca shrugs. "I hear all sorts in here. Gossip grows on the walls like mould."

"You mean you don't think it'll work?" Meren pipes up. As the rag makes its way to her side of the table for a second time, she lifts her apple tea by the handle, the mug huffing out steam like a fat, round dragon.

Beca mops below it, leaving the already-stained surface of the table dirtier than it had originally been. "Merchants are hungry for new trade, scholars and medics eager for new knowledge, and, who knows, maybe an alliance will bring that."

She shrugs, her shoulders disappearing into her hair. "But prevent wars? Bring us together? Put down our swords and take each other's hands? No way."

She gives a quick glance over her shoulder, as Arne had done, but her mass of curly hair occupies so much space she probably couldn't have seen anything, even if her tavern were to suddenly *fill* with The King's Royal Guards. "If bringing everyone together was that easy, why hasn't a treaty been arranged before?"

Meren and Arne say nothing, because the barkeep has a point.

"You have to ask yourselves; why now? Why this way? What is Cade's plan?"

Arne is the first to process Beca's words—or at least, *try* to process them. He still looks puzzled as he clarifies, placing the words down on the table:

"You think Our King has an ulterior motive?"

27

MONSTERS IN THE MOUNTAINS

Beca's lip twitches at one corner, and it occurs to Meren that she might be messing with them. "Do *you* think Our King has an ulterior motive?" she sends Arne's question back to him as though it's a ball she's deflected with a well-timed kick.

He's still taking the barkeep seriously; Meren can tell by the knot between his eyebrows—it bunches all his freckles into a galaxy. After a moment, he concludes thoughtfully, "It's a possibility, but I doubt it."

"Just because he's royalty, doesn't mean he's not capable of wickedness," Meren points out, hiding the bitter twist of her mouth with a sip of apple tea.

The heat pricks her tongue, but the sweetness tends to the burn like honey easing a sore throat.

"If he *is* up to something," Arne begins, his voice still low like an animal creeping tentatively from a hiding place, "what do you think it might be?"

Surprise flitters momentarily behind Beca's one good eye, and Meren rolls hers.

"She's joking, Arne," she says kindly, giving the broad back of his hand a little pat.

"Were you?" His cheeks colour, and Beca wilts a little, guiltily.

"Yeah. Sorry, pet. I've been surrounded by conspiracies all day; I thought I'd throw a few of my own into the mix."

"Oh."

"There's conspiracies?" Meren gestures at the growing group of dancers, their boots thumping the smooth flagstones.

The music players have taken up a fast-paced, energetic tune, every pair of hands clapping along to the leesel's joyful twang.

"I thought everyone loved the idea?"

She waves a hand. "More people are sceptical about it than you might think. The elderly, mostly. We may not remember wars with the Calpurzians, but they sure do. You never really outlive a war—it outlives you."

Beca's eyes barely crinkle with wrinkles, and her hair has only just started to streak with grey. Yet, looking up at her like this, Meren feels like a curious child begging for ghost stories. "What do they say?"

She shifts her weight onto her other hip and strokes a finger and thumb down the point of her chin, as though teasing a beard. "One man said he thinks His Majesty is trying to unite the kingdoms so he'll have more warriors—you know, in case the Hyluniens invade; the usual Ice Giant conspiracy nonsense," she adds, her light tone shedding some much-needed sunshine on Meren's mental state. "I asked, *Do you really think they'll try anything after last time?* And why would they invade, anyway?"

"They could want our land?" she suggests, but the barkeep shakes her head.

"They're *Ice* Giants. They wouldn't want our kingdom; it's too hot for them here."

Meren blinks. "It is?"

"Sure. Their realm is so cold that water can't flow, and if—by some miracle—a flower were to bloom, it would instantly turn brittle and shatter like thin glass," she recites as though it's a well-rehearsed poem. "Didn't your parents tell you stories about them when you were nippers?"

"Of course, but we'd rather *you* tell us about them." Arne gives her a smile, and she rolls her eye.

It's so dark the pupil and deep brown iris merge into one intelligent, twinkling black moon.

"I can't tell you much, but my pappy could, rest his soul."

"Surely, you've got *one* story?"

"You've *always* got a story."

"Of course, I've got one!" she snaps, as if offended by the very idea of her mental library running dry. "I've got loads."

Haughtily, she flings the end of her rag over her shoulder, and it disappears into her hair, probably never to be seen again. "I'll tell you one, but just quickly; I don't trust Egnor when he's sitting that close to the beer tap."

Arne chuckles as Beca inserts herself onto Meren's bench, scooting her along with a shimmying of her hips. When she's settled, she spreads her palms on the table as though opening a book.

"When I was a kid, we used to live up north-west in a small village close to the border—my mum, Pappy, and me. There were so few houses I could count them on my fingers, so we didn't have a proper market or anything. Instead, a supply wagon would come by once a fortnight, and most of the time, we had to hunt wolves for fur, and deer and game birds for meat.

When the meat ran out, Pappy would go into the forest with his traps and spears. He was a loving father but—at heart—a mountain man, and he was most content alone among the trees. Sometimes, he'd be gone for days. Sometimes a week.

One time, during a particularly bleak winter, he came back spattered in this blue stuff, all crusty and sticky. I remember it smelt of coins, like copper.

Mum didn't notice at first. She was angry because not only had he come home early, but he'd brought no meat.

WHAT LORKAN IS

'How am I mean to feed your baby girl?' she was saying, but he wasn't saying anything back—which wasn't like him. They were good at arguing, and they liked to do it."

Beca shrugs fondly. "It's how they showed love. Anyway, *I* noticed. His face was all grey, and he didn't bring his spear inside to sharpen. That was his ritual. He always did it after a hunt, while the food cooked and Mum sponged the animal blood from his clothes."

Arne shuffles forward on his seat. "What happened to him?"

"It took us ages to get it out of him," she continues, raising her voice over the band, which has picked up its pace, the dancers swinging each other back and forth in an erratic jig. "We gave him three fingers of whiskey and sat him in his chair by the fire. He took the bottle off me and drank right from it until Mum snatched it out of his hand. She wrapped a blanket around his shoulders, and finally, he told us that he'd seen a monster.

"He grew up in those mountains; he knew the land, but none of that matters in a blizzard. They set fast and thick, without warning—which happens a lot up there, especially around Winter Festival. He said it rolled in like a sea mist, blotting out the sun, and he wandered blindly, searching for familiar markers as the world disappeared around him."

Looking back, he thinks he must have crossed the border into Hylune, but he didn't know it at the time. It got so cold so, not knowing how long the storm would last, he did what he'd usually do: try to catch something small to keep him going, find shelter, and wait it out.

But hours went by. He went in circles, chasing shadows that twisted and vanished, his usually iron-clad senses confused by the swirling snow.

Finally, up ahead, a shape materialised. It was as large as a stag, easily enough meat to last him well into next week, and he aimed his spear as best he could—"

"It wasn't a stag, though, was it?" Arne asks, a childish grin twitching his lip, and Beca narrows her eyes at him.

"If you *listen*, I'll tell you what it was. Now, as my pappy tried to squint at this shape, it suddenly began to grow. It elongated and narrowed—more tall than it was wide—and he realised...it was a person.

He was worried about them, alone on a mountain in a blizzard, so he dragged his boots through the snow to reach them, calling out, but he got no answer.

The closer he got, the longer this person became, until they weren't a person at all. It was as tall as an elk, its limbs as thick and gnarled as the branches of an oak. He said it had hair as black as death, long and whipping in the wind, and it was barely clothed, its shame hidden by nothing but a slip of fur. Whatever it was, it was a male, its skin blue like a corpse.

It had been hunched over something, Pappy thought, but it was standing now. It had the body and face of a man but, when it turned to face him, its eyes glinted like a wolf's. They were the greenest thing he'd ever seen and they were looking at him.

Pappy threw his spear when it took a step closer. He hurled it so hard that he had to wear a sling for a week, but he got it, right through its heart. It must have had one because it dropped like a tree right in front of him, its blue blood dribbling all over the snow like spilt blueberry wine. He said it didn't melt the snow like ours would; it just beaded up like oil, the wind dragging it into wriggling trails."

"Did it die?" Arne mutters, his eyes wide and unblinking.

Beca shrugs. "Pappy didn't stick around long enough to find out. He left it there, his spear sticking up out of its body, pinning it to the mountain. We moved to Tawny soon after that. He said we'd be safer closer to our king's protection, and he's been right. Those giants haven't come anywhere near Aldercliff in hundreds of years."

Her lip quirks. "I like to think of the palace as a big mother hen, and we're all little chicks, safe and snug under her wing."

"So why did they invade last time?" Meren pipes up. "If it's too hot for them here, why did they invade?"

WHAT LORKAN IS

It takes Beca a moment to climb out of her story, and she shakes herself off like a dog dragging itself from a lake. She shrugs.

"I can't really remember. That war went on for so long, most of us have forgotten how it started."

"But you remember how it ended?"

"Barley!" She laughs. "We celebrated for weeks. I hadn't been that drunk since The Royal Wedding!"

"No," Meren corrects, "Do you remember how it *ended?* Was a treaty signed?"

"Well, look at you, little miss diplomat!" The barkeep must catch her lips flattening into a line because her smile fades. Thoughtfully, she twirls one of her ringlets around her index finger. "I don't think so. At the time, King Cade said his soldiers pushed the giants so hard they abandoned their villages, their homes—even their young—and fled further up north. I guess he trusted they were so scared they'd never return."

Arne is running his fingers through his stubble again. "Maybe the alliance isn't about an *Ice Giant* invasion but, you know...a different one."

"You sound like my friend Rosamind."

Meren's brow knits again. "Who does she think will do the invading? Us or the Calpurzians?"

"*Us* invading *them*, for land and resources and all that lark." Beca sighs, pushing herself to her feet. "But it's all just stuff an' nonsense, though, really."

"Would it work, though? Would having your son married to the enemy's princess give you a leg-up? Hypothetically."

The question sits on the table and they all stare at it for a bit.

Arne is the first to speak. "Maybe? The prince could relay messages, I guess, as a man on the inside. Or he'd be close enough to the enemy to... you know... murder." Then he continues, his hesitation hardening into confidence:

"But there's no need for that. If the wedding solidifies trade routes between the kingdoms, we'd have access to all their resources anyway, so there would be no need to claim their land."

Meren almost mutters '*Besides power*' into her apple tea. Instead, she turns back to Beca. "What do you think? Does your friend have a reason for suspicion, or is she just a sceptic?"

Beca laughs, bubbly like the fizz in the ale she sells. "Rosamind is more than just a sceptic, she is *the* sceptic. She got herself arrested once, for walking around telling everyone the world '*as we know it*' is going to end. Said it came to her in a vision. She had a rhyme about it…something about white fire and poison needles…I think a green woman was in there somewhere. The Palace Guards deemed her so bonkers they just let her go."

She and Arne chuckle, but when Meren doesn't, Beca turns to her, a troubled look shading her usually lucent face like a curtain drawn on the sky.

"Meren…do you *want* there to be an ulterior motive?"

✳ ☾ ✳

Meren turns that question over in her mind for the rest of the evening and for most of the night. It's sour in her mouth and she'd like to spit it out but can't; it sticks between her teeth like spoilt toffee, and she's still chewing it over on her way to the market the next morning.

The sky has warmed enough to drizzle, but she's shielded from the cold little droplets by the awnings and canopies spread over her head like a brightly-coloured, canvas jungle. Carefully, she slots two cake boxes into her tote and, since Lorkan hasn't requested any pigments, she's dripping on Aldercliff's steps by eight.

Yesterday, they had prepared a few light greens, several skin shades, and one shadowy black, but Lorkan spent such a short amount of time fidgeting before the easel that most of them remain unused.

He'd covered the bowls carefully with a damp slip of material, explaining as he did so:

WHAT LORKAN IS

"They won't be as smooth as they would have been fresh, but the areas I need them for are so small it won't really matter."

Meren watches as he uncovers the bowls now, and they both lean over to regard the contents.

They've acquired a glossy sheen; like the gummy film that forms over standing water.

"They'll be fine once I mix them a bit," Lorkan assures, probably catching her expression.

The colours appear dimmed like neglected, grubby stained glass windows, but if anyone can bring them back to life, it's Lorkan, Meren thinks. He has a way with colours, as if each scuff of paint is a living creature; bacteria or the plankton in the sea. They may not look like much at the moment, but, under proper conditions—if treated just right—they have the capacity to glow.

It has become instinct now—market, corridors, dress, pigment, kiss, pose—to such an extent that the little routine has grown a sense of immovable, unwavering permanence. Like a mountain, or a gully carved into the land.

For a moment, Meren forgets that with the completion of the portrait comes the end of their pre-painting kisses. Her heart is, for a second, filled only with the joy of the picture and the sweet promise of being able to see it again.

"Are these the last ones?" she asks hopefully as she gravitates toward the window seat. As usual, she tries to sneak a glance at the picture, but Lorkan doesn't let her; side-stepping in front of it and blocking it from view with his narrow waist.

He keeps a sheet draped over it each night—to keep the dust away, he says—but Meren knows it's so she doesn't get a peek at it before it's done.

She wishes she could somehow bring it to show her mother and father.

She imagines her boots sinking into the dirt track, turned to mud in winter, the marshes creeping ever closer to their garden gate. Even with the windows sealed shut, the chilly, clammy dampness seeps in through the cottage's foundations, pushing tufts of mould out from the walls. It's the only bright thing to be found in Holcombe, beside the breast of a robin and poisonous, bead-like holly berries; Mrs and Mrs Hansen's patterned green wallpaper.

Meren pictures herself turning up at their brown front door, in her brown uniform, against the brown backdrop of the fen, holding out her painting like an extraterrestrial presenting a gift from another world. She pictures her parents, squinting at the galaxy of greens and golds, their brows rumpling.

"*What is it?*" her father would ask, his question falling down onto his wife's head.

"*It's a picture,*" she'd reply, frowning at the glowing paint, the passionate brushstrokes, the foreign colours.

"*What's it of?*" he'd prompt, his grey eyes blinking dully, and his wife would shake her head.

"*I don't know. A woman.*"

"*It's me!*" Meren would pipe up. "*Look, Mother, there can be more to life than scrubbing! And look, Father! Some things aren't useful, but that doesn't mean they shouldn't exist! Look, both of you: there are more shades to life than greys and browns!'*

Lorkan waits until Meren has settled before delicately removing the cover. Slowly, his eyes slide down the portrait. His gaze is so intense, she worries he'll burn two holes right through the canvas. "I'm not sure."

There's another lengthy silence, but she's used to them by now, the air humming with his thoughts. She's sure she can feel them brushing her exposed skin; dandelion seeds travelling on a breeze.

Eventually, he says simply:

"We shall see."

"Well, *you* shall see," Meren huffs.

His lip only flickers with what could have been a smile, and he crosses over to her in a few long, soundless strides. Taking a knee, those sharp, jade-green eyes are suddenly level with her own. They glide up her bare neck, her parted lips, her pink-dusted cheeks—and her toes clench in her woollen socks.

She's used to that too—his pure, uncut attention; immunised to the concentration of it as one's skin darkens to bear the sun's rays. Excitedly, she moves forward on the window seat until she's perched stiffly on the lip of it, her body already buzzing with that familiar crackle, that energy.

When she takes the cool ridge of Lorkan's jawline, she can feel the weight of his head pushing into her palm, seeking it out.

He kisses her for a long time, for so long she wonders—half-heartedly—if she might drown in him.

She wouldn't mind.

It would feel like drowning in a serene, cool pool of water collected about the roots of a mountain.

She smiles as she pulls away.

His cheeks are pink, now.

"You had jam for breakfast."

"Pastry twists *with* jam, actually, but close. And you had…" The pink slip of his pointed tongue slides experimentally over his bottom lip as if trying to recall her taste.

The back of her neck heats.

"Kindling?"

"Grain."

His right hand moves the pads of its thumb and forefinger over one another as if imagining hard little kernels of corn rolling back and forth.

"You crush the grain up and bake it in a sheet," Meren clarifies, noting his puzzlement. "When it's dry you crunch it all up so it's little flakes. You have them with milk. I like to mush them all into it with the back of my spoon until they're soggy."

"That's disgusting. I'd be having words with Yllva if she wasn't so scary—and as tall as me."

Meren laughs, although she isn't one hundred per cent sure he's joking. "Surprisingly, they're kind of nice. She grinds salt up in them, and for once it actually improves the taste."

Returning to his easel, Lorkan's pale hand dismisses this comment as though it sends something crawling down the back of his shirt. "No, you shall breakfast with me from now on. I'll bring food up here from the kitchens—"

"And what about when you leave?" It cuts through his chambers like a plate shattering on the hard, golden floor.

He uses the easel to reflect the question, shielding himself behind it. The gauzy sleeves of his shirt are rolled up just past his elbows, one of which shifts slightly as he presses down the first dabs of paint.

Regret gnaws at the fringes of Meren's mind. They've frayed in recent weeks, becoming unravelled and matted like the seams of her stockings she's repeatedly darning. She opens her mouth to apologise, although she's not sure what for. Instead, she clears her throat.

"By the way, I was wondering...have you heard anything about a possible invasion? From Hylune?"

The acute angle of Lorkan's arm halts, and he leans to the side, giving her a questioning look.

She wonders if he had been alive for the most recent war with the Ice giants. If he was, he must have been only a babe.

"No. Why? Have you?"

She shakes her head, making sure to put it straight back where it had been; slightly tilted, the curve of her skull leaning nonchalantly against the wall. She doesn't *feel* nonchalant—but a sense of relief does wash over her body at Lorkan's words, loosening it.

"No. I was just wondering whether your father has a reason...for wanting to form an alliance after all these years."

He pieces her implications together with ease, and returns to the painting. "I think his reason is peace."

"Do you?"

Again, his arm falters. "Yes. An alliance with Calpurzia could prevent wars. It will benefit trade and medicine and—"

It's that same speech, that same string of words rattled off like a prayer. They're everywhere, tangling Velôr—and Meren—in tight knots.

"You're starting to sound like him," she quips, and bites her tongue, hard. She can feel his frown through the canvas, through the layers and layers of carefully placed paint. "Sorry. I didn't mean it."

"I know."

Without seeing them, Meren knows his shoulders have sagged. He reminds her of a tree bowing down to the wind.

"And I know why you said it, but I don't sound like my brutish, warlock father, I sound like my mother. She keeps pleading with me to find the situation's silver lining, but all I can see is an impending storm."

"You are struggling to find the good, and yet you let it go on?"

"There is no alternative."

The frustration simmering just below Meren's surface bubbles, white and scolding. "So they *are* forcing you?"

"No one can force me to do anything," Lorkan growls, as though making sure she remembers it.

Then his face falls back to that wrung-out look he wears when he thinks she isn't looking.

It causes a stinging sensation in the corners of her eyes—as if someone close by is slicing onions.

"But you must remember, Wren, that I am a son of Cade—even if I may not act like it."

She flushes, a memory from only moments ago igniting like the hot, tickling flame of a match; the passionate, ungentlemanly way he'd pulled her into his body, his soft, happy groans as she'd sucked his bottom lip.

One day that will stop, and the solid strength of his chest, the wings of his wide shoulders, the scent of his clothes will be nothing but a bittersweet memory.

"I have duties and responsibilities to tend to."

"Your duties lie here, with your kingdom."

"My duties lie wherever our king places them. Do you really want me to refuse the Calpurzian princess? Would you be willing to face the consequences?"

"They've had this argument dozens of times, and each one ends in several minutes of taut, prickling tension. Usually, Meren hunches over, lowering her eyes meekly to the floor, and waits patiently for it to pass, like a spell of bad weather—

But this time, she holds his gaze.

"Yes. A wedding isn't going to make any difference. If two kingdoms have spent centuries at war, a metal band isn't going to hold them together."

"Don't you think I've pointed that out to Father already?"

Meren blinks. A furrow rucks itself up between her brows like a crumpled handkerchief. "You're *submitting* to a betrothal to please your *father?*"

"Meren, I'm *submitting* to please *everyone.*"

28

THE ANNOUNCEMENT

By Friday, Lorkan still hasn't declared his painting complete.

He spends less and less time on it, his long, lean body restless and antsy, as if the divan he sits at is lumpy and uncomfortable; which Meren knows for a fact it is not. It is his mind that is uncomfortable, churning away inside his skull, stewing like a broth.

She almost wishes he'd start another painting, just so he'd have something fresh to cleanse his thoughts.

Due to his lack of ability to settle, the hours the two would usually spend crushing pigments, painting, and posing, are now empty—although they have yet to run out of things to fill them with.

They clean Lorkan's chambers, mainly, watering his plants and frightening away the shadows with playful laughter and raucous behaviour. He has tipped many buckets of water over the floor since the first time, some to clean it and others just to get on Meren's nerves.

He likes *getting* on her nerves, and she likes him *being* on her nerves. Even though he's trying to rile them up, his quips soothe them like ice pressed to a bruise.

She always gets her own back, anyway; purposely butchering words with her stubborn Holcombe accent, singing out of key, and refusing to take the coins he attempts to press into her palms when she leaves each evening.

"Please, let me pay you."

"For what? Eating cake and teasing you all day?"

"For making me smile."

"Lorkan, your smile is payment."

Often, they'll sketch together, consume the various treats Meren brings back from Aasta's stall, and make use of the amusing gadgets Lorkan has collected over the years. She remains fond of the telescope, and they've spent many hours spying on the unsuspecting people far below his bay windows or, on clear nights, mapping the stars.

Meren dislikes Saturday evenings and dreads them as most Velôrians dread the beginning of the week. They're the furthest point from her next trip to the sixteenth floor and, although she does manage to occupy herself over the weekend, she'd rather the familiar shape of Lorkan at her side.

She'd like to take him to all the places she knows he has not been or can not go. Places Lophiah has not permitted him to explore should he sully his shoes, or places Cade has not forbidden him to frequent should he sully his name.

Like *The Tipsy Dragon*. He'd look amusingly out of place there, his serene, refined features contrasting starkly with the grubby, general stickiness of the squat little building, his silken voice crisp amongst drunken mumblings. Meren thinks he'd like it there, at least for a little while, his feet tapping to the music. He'd ask Beca how she lost her eye, and she'd spin him a yarn that might be true, or might not.

Meren thinks he'd like the farms fringing the city, too; the cows with their broad, moist noses, the curious chickens, the endless patchwork quilt of swaying winter wheat. He'd probably see a beauty in the colours, and the texture of the grass.

She'd like to take him to the docks—her wrapped in her oilskin, him content in his gauzy shirt—unbothered by the iron grey wind and salty sea spray. She'd show him how to pick his way through the rivers of blood and scales until they get to the jetties leading out into the water. She'd buy him cockles for a few coppers, or potatoes that have been cut and fried, served in a parchment cone.

On this particular Saturday evening, Meren wonders about going down to the docks—to avoid whatever monstrosity Yllva has managed to concoct with the last of this week's store. She decides against it, however. With worries knotting her innards like a fist, she doubts she could stomach slurping little creatures from a shell, even if it is preferable to another steaming bowl of bubble and squeak.

Instead, tray in hand, she follows the scent of boiling mutton to the mess hall, and reluctantly joins the queue of hungry servants. She's moved barely three places before something like a bird seems to land on her shoulder. Turning, she comes face to face with Alfdis.

She's wearing an expression Meren doesn't recognise. "Hansen, there's someone to see you."

A few curious heads swivel in her direction, and Meren shrinks under their gaze self-consciously. "Who is it?"

Alfdis just makes a little '*follow me*' motion with one knobbly finger, and starts weaving her way towards the door.

Hurrying after her, Meren drops her empty tray back onto the pile. "Is it Arne?" She instantly brightens. "I mean Yllva no disrespect, but I wouldn't turn down a trip to *The Tipsy Dragon* right about now."

She had hoped to win a guilty chuckle, but Alfdis remains silent.

The head housekeeper is familiar—and perhaps a little irritated—with Arne's cheerful, round face ducking into the servant's courtyard in search of her company. Usually, she'll make him wait by the door while she fetches Meren with a weary sigh—

But today, she heads in the opposite direction, deeper into the ground and down a few more hallways, until they reach her office.

Meren stops in her tracks.

A tall man, dressed entirely in green, stands in the doorway, his china-cup skin and embroidered sleeves stark against the scuffed flagstone floor. The ceiling is barely an inch from being too low for him; his raven-black hair, tied up in a scruffy bun, just about brushes it.

"Lorkan?" Meren pads over to him quickly, a smile already blooming all over her face. "What are you doing down here?"

His lower lip is captured between the two, smooth ridges of his teeth, and her grin falters.

Gently, she reaches up and frees it.

It's pink and peeling like old paint.

She swallows. "What's wrong?"

Alfdis is watching their exchange carefully, but Lorkan doesn't push away from Meren's tender touch. Instead, one of his hands finds hers and, like a lost child, he links their fingers.

"Wren, I need to talk to you."

※ ☾ ※

Surprisingly, Alfdis allows them to use her office and closes the door respectfully as she takes leave without having to be asked.

Lorkan moves a few heaps of parchment delicately from her desk so he can perch on it. His long legs fill the cramped space, his polished shoes reaching the opposite wall, already scuffed with limestone dust. His irises—usually chips of jade—seem dull and wetted, as though they've been dropped in the ocean and rubbed down to smooth pebbles by the waves.

Taking his arm, Meren gives him a little shake. "Lorkan, you're scaring me."

He lets it oscillate through him.

"Wren, a date has been settled. I have until summer's last full moon."

Her hand on his forearm tightens into the soft green cloth.

WHAT LORKAN IS

It feels like water between her fingers.

"There will be a summons tomorrow morning. Everyone in the kingdom is invited to Aldercliff's courtyard to watch Father give a speech." He sniffs. "I wanted to deliver the news to you myself."

The last few words are muttered onto her head because she's fallen forward, seeking comfort in the solidness of his chest.

Pulling her between his thighs, Lorkan's arms wrap about her immediately, his nose finding the crook of her neck.

In the dark, cool privacy of his embrace, Meren lets herself weep.

✶ ☾ ✶

Meren whiles away the remainder of the Saturday sketching, and then whiles away the first few hours of Sunday sketching as well, using up three wax sticks before eventually falling into bed. Her stomach aches with an empty feeling that she knows has nothing to do with hunger, and she wakes early from a shallow sleep.

As promised, an announcement is given at breakfast, the words poured all over her porridge, turning it sour.

Like her, most of the servants take Sunday off, the mess hall teaming with late breakfasters, chatting cheerfully over fried eggs and rashers of bacon—a rare weekend treat.

The announcement is presented by Yllva, her voice—gritty from a dedicated smoke leaf habit—managing to grate against even the furthest corners of the room.

She reads from a crisp sheet of white parchment, a red wax seal weighing down the top edge. Several complicated words trip her up, and she stumbles a few times over the sloping, looping cursive, but no one laughs. All ears, young and old listen as she staggers her way through their king's message, all eyes fixed on her towering figure with unwavering seriousness.

She delivers the last line of the summons after what feels like hours, although it could only have been several seconds.

The message is clear and concise, simply inviting everyone in the kingdom to take a half-hour or so to watch King Cade give an address in the royal courtyard and, immediately, a tension charges the mess hall like impending lightning.

It's only when Yllva rolls up the parchment that anyone dares to utter a word. They creep from parted lips tentatively, then, when she disappears with Alfdis into the kitchen, conversations take flight, filling the air like a swarm of insects.

Meren continues to methodologically scoop porridge into her mouth.

* ☾ *

When Meren emerges, blinking, from the earth, she is greeted by a damp day dressed all in grey.

In the night, an unseasonally balmy breeze has risen up from the south, melting the prickly frost and bringing it back down onto the cobbled streets in the form of a steady, relentless drizzle. Heavy and listless, the sky and the trees sag under the weight of it, the air a haze of tiny, misty droplets.

As though sweeping lint with a broom, Alfdis herds the hoard of servants towards the royal courtyard in a tidy, efficient way, reminding Meren very much of a fire drill.

She's swept up in it too, although there really is no reason for her to attend. She knows what is to be said; hearing it again will just be a handful of salt rubbed into her gaping wound.

She hopes Lorkan will somehow feel that she's there in the crowd.

In their beige uniforms and cream aprons, moving as one wriggling, jostling mass, they shuffle through The Kitchen Garden, bumping together under oilskins stretched out like umbrellas.

WHAT LORKAN IS

On either side of the gravel path, hardy vegetables claw their way through the dark, sodden soil, their dripping leaves hanging miserably from their allotments like seasick sailors.

Its feathers dripping, a single, wet black bird scrapes a bare patch of dirt for worms.

"Can you imagine what sort of things come from somewhere like Calpurzia?" someone is saying and, the rain dribbling into her collar, Meren's ears prick with glum interest.

The woman talking is old Mrs Boyd, head of the infirmary, and the rest of the nursing staff cluck in agreement like a gaggle of hens.

"All those rainforests, they must have invented salves that can soothe even the roughest psoriasis."

"I need something like that for my bunions!" One pipes up, making them all nod in empathetic unison. "They don't half rub on these blasted canvas slippers."

"I heard they use wyvern blood to make this ointment that'll fix them right up," one says, which gets a disbelieving huff from Mrs Boyd.

"Realign bone? It could never!"

"It don't realign it, but it stops it smartin', so they say."

"I thought wyvern were extinct?"

To Meren's left, a bunch of kitchen maids are travelling as one, their arms linking them in a wonky chain. Their voices are hushed like little girls gossiping under duvet covers.

"I wonder what Calpurzian men look like," one of them hisses, which gets an overexcited giggle from her friends.

"They're all rugged jungle men, I bet. They probably have long, untamed hair and big, strong shoulders." Which gets a collective, dreamy sigh.

"Forget the men," a dish boy cuts in, made rowdy by the change in routine. He elbows one of his friends in the ribs. "Imagine the *women;* all sun-darkened skin as rich as cocoa—I heard they don't even wear clothes."

"'Course they do! They're not savages."

"How do *you* know?"

"I bet they have *better* clothes than us. All the best material comes from down south, don't it? So they probably have silk soft as a spider web, and cotton fluffy as sticking your hand into a cloud."

"What about the food? My dad lives right near the border, I'm going to ask him to go get me stuff from their markets when they start letting us lot in. They have this fruit that's red and spiky all over but, inside it's succulent and sugary as jam."

※ ☾ ※

Meren is one of the first few hundred people to take up a spot in the royal courtyard, and she watches as the general public files in like migrating geese coming to rest in a field.

Aldercliff's courtyard is like a field, Meren thinks—a vast stretch of nothingness, the ground flat, barren, and lifeless. It consists of many thick marble slabs pressed into the earth, and she claims one as close to the front as she can get, planting herself there like a stubborn acorn, growing roots between the cracks.

A spell has been cast over the towering walls, stretched like a membrane— every now and then, it glints, ballooning slightly as the courtyard takes a breath. The rain hits it with a pattering sound and dribbles away as though landing on a massive, invisible pane of glass. As they enter its shelter, people nudge each other, craning their necks up to watch the rivulets of water trickle harmlessly over their heads.

"That'll be Her Majesty Lophia's work," some are saying proudly, as though having identified the grape in a fine wine.

As the palace grounds become swelled with its subjects, Meren gets packed in, nudged and jostled from all angles, like a crate of apples on a cart, but she holds her place firmly. She doubts Lorkan will be able to find her face amongst the hundreds, but that's not why she stands her ground. She wants to get a good look at her king, this man who rules the kingdom from a golden tower, this man most have never seen.

Judging by the sun's position in the sky, she still has a while to wait before anything of interest happens, even though the walls are close to capacity, warm and teeming like a giant organism.

Meren doesn't feel as though she's a part of it; she's an outside party, an imposter. She's often used to being on the outside of things looking in—jokes, conversation, the loop, but this time she feels as though she's holding something special, something no one else around her has ever seen.

She has peeked behind the metaphorical curtain.

She has had the betrothed prince's tears stain her bodice.

Everyone is happy—but she knows he is not, and she wonders if anyone will notice when he walks out onto the stage.

Eventually, a door swings open, and a thick blanket of silence floods out like a burst dam.

The child to Meren's left ceases his fidgeting.

The group of boys to her right choke on their words, their conversation snuffed out, forgotten.

With the rustle of necks in fabric, every head turns to watch as a chain of royal guards flows out of the palace.

Marching upright, they arrange themselves to form a neat line along the entire length of the stage—like tin soldiers pouring from a toy chest. Their bodies are encased in sheets of gold and their faces are trapped inside heavy visors. They're cut with five slits—like the little potbelly stove in Alfdis' office—Meren thinks, and pointed like the long jaw of a wolf.

She can't tell if they're for protection or show. Perhaps both. They each proudly sport a Velôrian flag, the tips of every tall, ornate pole sharpened into a needle-thin spearhead.

Cade looks shorter in person than the king living in her mind, and she takes a moment to alter her perception.

She broadens the nose, dragging it down and out, hooking it like a buzzard's beak. She shortens his beard and pushes the eyes way back, shading them below a brow sticking out like a shelf. A patch cups one, and the other looks out, colourless and intense, from the ridge of a cheekbone. It's blistered with the gnarled rift of a scar.

The air bristles as he makes his way across the broad length of the stage. The couple in front of Meren clasp hands and, to her left, the boy's father silently lifts his son onto his shoulders. Somewhere towards the back, a child sneezes and is shushed. A woman coughs and it echoes off the walls.

The stage is formed of several wide, smooth wedges of gold-cloaked marble, their artificial sun-beam sheen thrown back up into the sky.

The temperature must double amongst their glaring reflections, and Meren wonders whether Cade is sweating, encased in his thick, armour shell.

'*Why wear armour to deliver good news?*' It makes him look as though he expects one of his subjects to spring forth and attack—or that they have some disease he doesn't want to contract.

Their king draws to a stop perfectly in line with the centre of the courtyard. The stage below him continues to gleam as if mocking him, but he does not narrow his eyes.

Keeping a respectful few steps between herself and his cloak, steps Lophia.

Lorkan's mother, of whom he speaks fondly, is fine-boned but not slim, her pampered, feminine figure the epitome of enviable beauty. Genetic. Unobtainable. Between two rouge-dusted cheeks and above a strong, aquiline nose, sit a set of deep, pool-like eyes, and they blink, saying nothing. Unlike her husband, she wears a gown rather than armour, the material a heavy maroon red, kissing her toes. She holds her hands—soft and rocky with rings—delicately behind her back, the Velôrian sigil embroidered across her heart on a golden sash.

Together, Cade and Lophia's outfits make the flag of the realm, Meren realises.

They smile.

There is a gap where Sol would be, had he had time to travel from Black Castle. The crowd watches the empty space move across the stage disappointedly, perhaps picturing his white-toothed grin.

WHAT LORKAN IS

As usual, Lorkan is dressed in gold and green.

He does not smile.

It has not crossed Meren's mind that Lorkan owns a suit of armour but—being a prince—he obviously does.

It covers most of him: moss-green cloth ending at his wrists and disappearing into the black leather of his boots. Like his father's, it's not designed for fighting; the slim, sparse sheets of metal slot together over his chest and arms like feathers.

An ivy-green, curtain-like cape patterned with stars hangs from two bulky shoulder pads.

'They're not bulky enough' Meren mutters in the safety of her own mind. *'They'll never be large enough to support the responsibility Cade is placing on them.'*

The royals stand for a moment, all in a line as if waiting for silence, although the hush in the air is already suffocatingly still. They seem to form some sort of gradient; Cade's hair as colourless as a phantom, Lophia's as gold as the stage they stand on, and Lorkan's; so dark it swallows light whole.

Everyone's eyes are tilted up towards Cade, hungry for his words. His wife and son fade into the background. They are not who they are here to see.

Meren has never heard the king himself give an address before and—despite the circumstances—she can not ignore her roused curiosity. She waits, expecting his sentences to roll out like thunder, to level the mountains, to grate like stone—

But, when he does speak, his tone is calculated and level, with a quietness that makes everyone lean forward on their toes.

"My people," he begins, and the courtyard erupts with adoring applause. He lets them continue for several beats, then raises both arms wide. His tiled armour snakes up them like scales, and they glint, stealing shades of grey from the sky.

As suddenly as they had began, the cheers cease.

✶ ☾ ✶

Meren listens as Cade pours out sentences, dozens of them, like pulling handkerchiefs from a hat.

He does not shy away from the past, addressing each war with Calpurzia and lamenting the fallen. He says he is painfully aware of the scepticism—the *mistrust* people hold for the neighbouring kingdom and those that inhabit it. He stresses that an alliance will finally heal those wounds. His sentences are so heavily peppered with the word *'peace'* that it begins to lose all meaning.

He speaks of a positive future—a brighter, more enlightened Velôr—and even Meren can almost feel that light on her cheeks.

"Our kingdom has war running through its veins," Cade is saying. "It's beating through our hearts, and etched into our genes.

It is time for a new generation. There will be children born this year who will never have to raise a sword. They will never taste the bitterness of resentment, nor the fear of invasion. There will be children born this year who—for the first time in centuries—will know peace."

This brings on another wave of applause, the crowd feeding it with their hands, fattening it, swelling it up until it overflows the courtyard's high walls.

It takes several seconds of patient silence for it to finally die, silence pouring in once more.

Cade waits until everyone is drowning in it before he continues. "We may always fear monsters, but we should not fear our fellow man. We should stand shoulder to shoulder. Arm in arm. We are stronger as one and, this autumn, that is what we shall become.

As the harvest moon rises in the sky, my youngest son will be handed over to the Calpurzians as a gift—a symbol of our trust and friendship. The wedding will be held in their royal palace; he will gain a wife, and we will gain trade, culture, and peace. All citizens from both kingdoms are welcome to attend—details will be posted as soon as they have been drawn up.

For those who cannot make the trip, I have arranged for Tawny's streets to come alive with food, drink and music. My son wishes you all to partake in the festivities—after all, this day marks a new chapter in our history.

As one final note, I ask you to be respectful of our new brother's and sister's customs. We may be rooted in logic and strength, but they are simple people. They still rely on magic, spirits and gods, and it is not our place to judge—but to educate. Teach the confused, be the light for the unenlightened, and give directions to those that are lost. We must set an example. We must show them what we are made of."

As their king gives a final bow of his head, the crowd flares up once more, the air crackling with applause like fire.

✳ ☾ ✳

Throughout it all, the glaring, unblinking gold, the words, the grinning faces, Lorkan had stood tall, and Meren feels a swell of pride for him.

It pains her she will have to wait until tomorrow to tell him so.

29

THE KISS

With the splashing sound of watery footsteps, faces all wrapped up in oilskins pour from the royal courtyard like grain from a sack. No longer sheltered below Lophia's blanket of a spell, they walk hunched against the rain, cheeks glistening and noses dripping.

Instead of returning to the servant's quarters, Meren lets the crowd sweep her along, dragging her deep into the city centre like a stick caught in a stream.

Overnight, silky red and gold banners seemed to have sprouted from everything a nail could be forced into, the kingdom's sigil rippling with winter's sodden coughs. Bunting weaves overhead, leaping from building to building and tying the city in ribbons, the Velôrian flag fluttering high and proud from awnings, brackets and sconces.

The palace-issued banners glint with gold thread, but the homemade flags that children wave on sticks and dangle from windows are simple and crude, featuring nothing but the king's yellow crown. They've darned it into bedsheets, pillowcases, and tablecloths, dyed with madder root to get that maroon red, and onion skins to mimic the regal gold.

WHAT LORKAN IS

A horse and trap rattles down the narrow road at quite some speed, and Meren leaps back to avoid it, her head becoming ensnared in a sheet of heavy, wet fabric. Sodden and dripping, it dangles from a pole protruding patriotically from a house's facade, and she peels it from her face, disgusted to find she'd accidentally kissed King Cade squarely on the lips.

The crowd's current dispatches her at the market, where she spends the rest of the day helping Arne man Frode's stall over the weekend shift. Arne appreciates the help and Meren appreciates the distraction but, even as she hands vials to customers and refills bottles with tonics, her mind can't help wandering to Lorkan.

She hopes that—once he'd turned to walk somberly back into the palace—he sought the company of Alfdis', or his mother, or anyone else that would bring him some source of comfort—

But she knows him well, and predicts that he had not.

Several times, Meren wonders about finding a way to sneak up to his chambers. She'd have an excuse ready, should she be stopped and questioned—

'His Royal Highness requested that I work a few hours on weekends.'

'I was given silver to polish and I've finished, so I'm returning it.'

'The Young Prince summoned me to clean up a spill of wine.'

—but each lie feels so flimsy in her head they'd probably fall to pieces under scrutiny.

Some small part of her is glad; she's almost scared to go up to his chambers when he isn't expecting her, just in case *has* been at the wine. She's never known him to drink but, if there was ever a time to start, it would be now.

To see him in such a state would break her heart.

✶ ☾ ✶

Eventually, a drab, colourless Monday dawns and—after a quick scrub in the washrooms and a breathless sprint to Aasta's stall—Meren grabs her bucket and mop from the storeroom.

The trek up to the sixteenth floor seems to take longer than usual; had she not known better, Meren would have accused the hallways of playing tricks on her—elongating and curling around and in on themselves just to watch her scurry down them like a ladybird over a child's hand.

The door to Lorkan's chambers opens as her hand reaches out to take the handle.

Framed by the ornate jamb, he stands bleary-eyed and dishevelled, his unusual features for once as grey and unsmiling as the portraits adorning the walls.

Wiping a hand quickly over her eyes, Meren snatches the beads of moisture from her lashes. They bloom on Lorkan's shirt as she reaches out and gently straightens his collar.

One pearly white button isn't looped through its hole, and his hair, usually so impeccable—like well-preened feathers—is unbrushed and flat on one side, wiry like scribbles.

"I didn't sleep well," he explains before she can ask, and her shoulders loosen thankfully.

At least he hasn't been drinking. Meren trusts his good sense and judgment, yet the possibility of him forming some kind of unhealthy vice still gnaws at her brain whenever she has to leave him alone for the night.

Lorkan must have noticed her obvious relief because he frowns as she steps into his chambers. "Thank you for the sympathy."

"No, I'm just glad that—" not wanting to give him any ideas, she bites the sentence off rather hurriedly. "Never mind."

His curiosity would usually have prompted him to enquire further, but he doesn't. He simply nudges the door shut with a bare foot and rubs at one eye with a bony knuckle.

Her eyes rove the rooms behind him, but find them to be more or less in order. In fact, they're more in order than usual; no dirty laundry waiting to be freshened, no balls of parchment strewn like snow, no ashes in the fire and no dirty pots sticky with breakfast.

She frowns. "What have you been doing for two days?"

He shrugs. "Nothing."

"Have you eaten?"

He shakes his head, his somewhat matted hair falling into his eyes, though he makes no movement towards brushing it away. It looks like it's in need of washing.

"Have you bathed?"

"No."

Taking his wide hand, Meren leads him to his washroom, her grip still a little slick with her salty tears.

He stumbles along behind her pliantly, letting her deposit him by the bath.

More of a swimming pool, it's pressed into the ground and, protruding from one side, smooth convex bumps form chairs so one can lounge back in the water and doze.

When Meren releases him, Lorkan just stands there, watching her until she sighs and crouches by the taps.

"Cold, right?" she clarifies, and he nods.

With the deep gurgling of pipes, water cascades into the bath, roaring as it slaps against the little tiles. A multitudinous array of glass bottles surrounds the bath, and Meren has to reach through the vines of a trailing ivy to peer at the ones at the back.

"How does this grow?" She prods the plant's dark, star-shaped little leaves. "There's no windows."

Lorkan shrugs. "Magic."

"I thought so."

Several of the bottles are labelled, and Meren selects a few, tipping a little of the contents into the water. Mounds of bubbles begin to form like summer clouds, the sweet scent of juniper berries filling the little room, and she stands, wiping chilly spray from her cheek with the back of her hand.

"You bathe, I'll get you some breakfast."

Lorkan blinks at her order but makes no great resistance. Taking the bottom of his moss-coloured shirt, he lifts it neatly over his head, letting it fall to the floor. "Thank you."

Cheeks searing, Meren tries to keep her eyes respectfully lowered to the gauzy fabric as she plucks it up. "Do you have any food here?" she asks, turning her back to him.

She can hear him unlacing the ties of his trousers, the smooth string sliding free from the soft cotton. She wonders if they are the same trousers he'd tugged on after his father's announcement yesterday.

"There's some shortbread rounds in the lounge."

"Biscuits aren't breakfast." She doesn't have to look at him to know his lips have ghosted with a smile. She can read him like a book, and he's quickly become one of her favourites. She's memorised paragraphs. She's kept notes in the margins. She is an expert on all things Lorkan, so she isn't surprised when he quips back:

"Agree to disagree."

There's another sound of light material hitting the floor, then bare feet on tiles as he crosses over the bath. It has filled quickly, the taps as thick as the branches of a birch tree, and he silences the flow with a squeak of the metal tap.

"You can look now, by the way," he says after a moment, and Meren turns to see he's submerged himself to his collarbones in the fragrant, frothy water. He'd dipped his head below the surface at some point, his wet hair hanging in a shiny, pitch-black sheet.

That water comes right off the mountains, Meren knows; a frigid smoothie of bitter snow and melted glacial ice funnelled directly into Aldercliff's veins. Despite this, Lorkan lowers himself further until his pointed chin caresses the bubbles.

"I'll go down to the kitchens and fetch you something. Will the palace cooks still be serving?"

"They serve whenever they are asked to serve."

WHAT LORKAN IS

Meren is about to leave but stops as she reaches the door.

Lorkan hasn't moved, his face suspended like a leaf on a still pond.

She narrows her eyes at him. "If I go and do that, will you actually wash your hair, or will you just sit there?"

He might have shrugged, but his shoulders are hidden below a layer of foam. Pale and glistening, he looks like a merperson trapped in a tub, yearning for the freedom of the ocean.

Signing, Meren kneels at the lip of the bath. "Come here."

Obeying, he moves over to her soundlessly, and looks up into her face, confused.

When she motions for him to turn around, understanding passes over his green eyes, and he does so willingly, presenting her with the back of his head.

To wet her hands, Meren dips them in the bathwater, wincing at the bite of the cold. It turns them pink as she gestures at the many bottles to her right. "Which one is for your hair?"

"Most of them."

Because he can't see her face, Meren lets her eyes roll, and picks a bottle at random. "This one?"

"Yes, but that's a conditioner."

"What's the difference?"

Lorkan doesn't reply, just reaches over his shoulder with one hand and passes her a vial.

The glass is tinted purple but, when Meren tips some of the substance onto her palm, it's bright blue. It oozes with the laziness of honey, and smells of citrus and cracked pepper.

"Are you just going to sulk all day?" She teases in an attempt to lighten his mood—although, by all means, he has a right to sullenness. When her parents sent her to Tawny in search of work, she'd spent several days in stony silence too.

Again, he says nothing.

"I've never used liquid soap before, least of all shampoo," she muses, rubbing the blue liquid curiously between her hands. It looks like it would be tasty, and she has to fight the urge to lick it.

"I'll buy you some."

She opens her mouth to say he doesn't have to, but she knows he will. Instead, she smiles. "Thank you, I'd like that very much."

Gently, she begins massaging the lather into Lorkan's hair. Her fingers are familiar with its softness from their countless kisses, but it's different now that it's wet—heavy and glossy as a horse's mane—and still manages to send tingles to her elbows.

"I was really proud of you yesterday," she says after some time. "I was there in the crowd." She expects a mere hum in answer, but is pleasantly surprised when Lorkan says instead, quietly:

"I know." He tips his head back a little as she begins working the foam into his scalp. His eyes have closed. "I couldn't look because I wasn't allowed to, but I did see you."

"How?" she laughs. "There were thousands of people."

"Thousands of insignificant people."

☾

Meren kneads the shampoo into Lorkan's hair until she runs out of foam to knead, then pushes herself up from the floor.

"You can manage the rest yourself, I gather?" she asks, her cheeks heating.

He smirks as though about to suggest something, then notices her hands rubbing her knees through her uniform, trying to ease the grooves left by the tiles. He nods. "Yes, thank you."

"I'll go get you some breakfast, then."

"Bring something for yourself too. One can not live off flakes of grain."

WHAT LORKAN IS

Leaving him to wash out the shampoo from his hair, Meren fetches a clean shirt and trousers from his dresser. It takes her a moment of pulling out and closing various drawers, but she eventually blushes as she locates his underwear, neatly folded into little squares. Placing them atop his fresh outfit, she leaves it by the washroom and slips out into the great, cavernous hallway.

Despite never having set foot in the royal kitchens, Meren has little trouble locating them—she just follows the rich scent of fried eggs, the lingering whiff of bacon, the tang of roasted bell peppers and a hundred other delicacies she can not place. The flavours tease her throat as she breathes them in, so thick she almost pokes out her tongue to taste the air.

She finds the dining hall first—a vast cavern of a room that is either plated in gold or possibly just made out of it—and stops.

A gargantuan stretch of table traces the centre of the room, and it's empty beside a bald, plump man, wrapped in purple silk as one would swaddle a babe. Surprisingly delicately, he holds a knife and fork between finger and thumb, and they look not unlike the sausage he's carefully severing into bite-sized chunks.

He has the room to himself, besides a few busy staff wiping down the other end of the table. They give him a wide berth, and Meren doesn't have to wonder why. She recognises his round, moon-like face from the circular glass of Lorkan's telescope—but it is not *him* that they cringe from.

Sure enough, his amphitere is curled not about his shoulders, but upon the table, its pin-prick eyes regarding his meal as though hoping for scraps. Unblinkingly, it uses the bone-coloured talon of a useless wing to scratch its transparent, fleshy head.

Invisible in her uniform, Meren expects to be ignored, but the man's face rises from his careful picking and prodding to regard her as she passes. He smiles, and it pushes his cheeks into little balls of dough, making him look even more like a babe than ever.

"You're not one of the kitchen staff," he says, and Meren can't tell if it's a question or not. However, his voice is kind and soft as cotton, so she offers a smile and a polite dip of her head.

"No, Sir, I'm a housemaid. His Highness sent me to fetch his morning meal."

"Ah." The man nods in a way she realises is pityingly. "The kitchen is through there."

He points towards a line of tapestries and, sure enough, a manservant emerges from the slit between the last two, having parted them like a curtain.

"Please take him something nice; the gods know he's earned it. He is fond of cheese, I believe."

Thanking the king's advisor, Meren treks across the hall, servants darting around her with bowls and rags and lemon polish.

If she works hard, will that be *her* duty, one day? Will it be Meren's job to dispose of Cade's leftovers, each pound of food she dumps into a bus box worth more than her weekly salary? When Lorkan is gone and she is a cleaner once more, should she even *bother* to work her way up the servant ladder? If Lorkan is not waiting at the top of it, what's the point?

Then again, what else could she do? Occasionally, she plays with the idea of finding a job in a local inn. It would be a step down—her parents would say—but she suspects she'd feel more at home in a lodging house packed with travellers and merchants than she would in Aldercliff.

It's ironic how the only thing in its stone walls that ever makes her feel warm is a prince too cold to make a heat engine turn.

When Meren reaches the tapestries, she pushes the thick material aside as the manservant had done, the scent of food so thick now she almost chokes on it.

Inside is a kitchen a lot like the one in the servant's quarters but larger, so much larger Meren can't see the other end of it. Everything is gleaming, crisp and clean, dozens of stoves and taps with real running water lining one wall, and dish racks stacked with crystal crockery.

'*What Yllva would do to work in this kitchen,*' she thinks.

WHAT LORKAN IS

The royal kitchen staff must be preparing for luncheon because they're flittering about like bees working together to build a humongous, complex hive. Not wanting to bother them—and slightly intimidated by their serious faces and sense of purpose—Meren decides to make Lorkan's meal herself.

She locates the storeroom—which is easy since it's so large—and bundles an armful of ingredients into a cotton net bag. Self-consciously, she keeps checking over her shoulder, expecting a hard wooden spoon to wrap suddenly across her knuckles—as Yllva had done when she'd caught Meren's finger submerged in the sugar jar.

However, no one stops her, or even appears to notice.

Taking more than a few things, Meren scurries back to Lorkan's chambers with her hoard, feeling slightly like she's gotten away with a minor crime.

✶ ☾ ✶

Once again locked safely away in the quiet privacy of Lorkan's chambers, Meren begins setting her spoils out in pots, and lights a fire in the hearth. She hangs them from a framework of poles, mixing what needs to be mixed and turning what needs to be turned. Accustomed to hiding himself away in his rooms for apparently days on end, Lorkan's cupboards are well stocked with crockery and seasonings, and—when he emerges from the washroom—she has a laden tray waiting for him.

Leaving his plate to cool, Meren has begun her meal and is almost finished as his bare feet pad over to the sofa.

He smiles and thanks her, looking less drawn out now that he's bathed—as though the cold water has washed away some of his wanness. He tucks a lick of wet hair behind his ear as he hungrily digs into his food.

"That's good," Meren comments, trying to stab a piece of egg with her fork.

Despite having only permitted herself what she couldn't fit onto Lorkan's plate, it's the best meal she's ever eaten.

"I thought I'd have to force-feed you."

"I could never refuse something so lovingly crafted." He smiles again, watching a globule of rich cheese stretch between his knife and a round of white toast. "Nor something so delicious."

Flattered, Meren reminds herself to thank her mother for her rigorous cooking lessons.

"I found oregano and thyme in your pantry. Do you dry your own herbs?"

He shrugs. "It gives me something to do."

※ ☾ ※

Meren lets the fire consume itself, the flames having long since petered out. The embers and hot coals keep the room warm, and Lorkan's hair soon dries. He appears to have merely scrubbed it with a towel because it's frizzed about his head, a chaotic scramble of black lines.

Meren excuses herself to fetch a boar hair brush from his room, and holds it out to him.

He bats it away as though it's paperwork he's putting off. "There's no need—I have no audiences until the celebration dinner on Wednesday."

"It'll get all matted."

"So I'll cut it off," he replies simply, and she almost growls at him.

"You wouldn't dare."

One of his dark brows arches. His plate is clear now, except for a wedge of honeycomb Meren had plopped onto his pancakes. He pops it into his mouth, licking the syrup from his pale fingers. A smile curves his words:

"Would I not?"

WHAT LORKAN IS

Electing to ignore that, she pushes herself up, wobbling as she sinks into the squashy cushions. Walking on her knees, she shuffles up behind him and lifts the brush to his head. Silently, she begins drawing it through his hair.

Lorkan stills, his spine straightening. "...What are you doing?"

"Fixing your hair."

As a babe, Meren's own hair was as light as dandelion tufts, and has grown little thicker—so she knows how to be gentle and start from the feathery ends, then work her way up.

Lorkan's hair is not as fine as hers, but she has to be gentle all the same. It's even more tousled up close; chaotic as though a fountain pen had scribbled narrow, erratic lines all over his head, spilling ink in the form of tight, matted knots. She has to stop every now and again to untangle bunches with her fingers.

"You must be very fond of it."

"I am. I like your long hair." Her cheeks heat as though the fire has blazed up suddenly, but it hasn't, the ashes still glowing only faintly. Before Lorkan can reply with something teasing and witty—as Meren knows he will—she asks:

"Have you eaten enough?"

"Enough for three lifetimes, thank you."

"You don't have to keep thanking me."

"When you stop doting on me, I'll stop thanking you."

"I'll never stop."

They fall silent, knowing that not to be true.

Come summer, she will have to stop.

Meren's other hand has been dangling superfluously by her side, unsure of what to do with itself, but it rises now and settles on his shoulder.

It loosens below her touch, so she leaves it there.

She wonders about telling him the other things she likes about him.

Like his smile—the old one, the one before all this, when he still liked to paint—cheeky and white and all teeth. She likes the jokes it spits, the way it curls more on one side than the other.

And his way with words—the way he delivers them, crafting pretty arrangements of syllables and sentences, playing with language like it's an instrument. He knows many things, and Meren wishes he had more time to teach them to her; she wants to collect them all—those facts and stories he spins like ribbons, pooling in her ears and curling up in her brain.

And she likes the feeling of him being there—near her. Brightening her life like a wax stick fighting against the darkness.

Meren carries on brushing and doesn't stop, even when Lorkan's hair is falling like a slick, velvety curtain just past his shoulders. Wordlessly, she just continues, hauling her hand up to the crown of his head, then pulling it smoothly down to the fluffy ends of his hair.

Across the vast expanse of the sixteenth floor, the only sound is the smooth whisper of boar hair bristles.

Lorkan lets her, apparently content—despite everything. Holding himself still, he's sat patiently, letting himself be tended to as if revelling in the attention.

Before the prince, Meren has never met a male with long hair, not up close. Just boys with floppy strands and cowlicks, and men sporting a run-of-the-mill cropped, choppy sort of style.

Lorkan's hair, though...it's long enough to twist into braids.

As a child, she had a friend back at Holcombe, and they used to sit together in the marshes—when it was dry enough to do so. They'd while away the summer winding daisies into each other's plaits; Meren's thin, stubby little things, Jenn's long and coarse as the bullrushes.

When caught up in a spell of childish impishness, Meren has often wondered if Lorkan might permit her to do such a thing, should she ask.

"What do you want to do today?" she ends the silence eventually. Unable to resist, she finally places the brush down, replacing it with her fingers.

She could have sworn a soft sound broke in his pale throat.

"Can't we just do this?"

A smile quirks at the corner of her lip. "All day?"

She collects a bundle of strands and draws them through the spaces between her fingers—a lick of black paint trickling over her skin.

Lorkan yawns before he replies, stifling it with the back of his hand. "Why not?"

She was joking, but he sounded serious. Her smile falls sideways. "Will you want to paint today? Surely it's nearly done now."

She wants to kiss him, even if it's just for the picture.

She's wanted to since yesterday—when he'd listened to his father give his life away before his kingdom.

She wants him to kiss her back. She doesn't care where. Her skin is open for it, waiting.

And she wants to see him paint, even if it means no more posing and window seat embraces.

His shoulder stiffens under Meren's palm. "Yes, it's almost complete."

"Shall we do that now?" she asks, already fizzing with excitement. "You could probably finish it before sundown."

A little of Lorkan's hair catches around one finger and, when she eases it free, he tips his head back as if he likes it.

"Hm."

She's not sure if it's a hum of dismissal or agreement.

Either way, neither of them move. A minute passes of Meren just fiddling; twisting braids and revelling in the fact that Lorkan is letting her. He's sagged tiredly, his shoulder blades a mere centimetre from her breasts. She wouldn't mind if he fell back to lean against her. She's tempted to prompt him; to ease him back until she's cradling his head in the crook of her neck, her body supporting his sleepy bones.

He's so tall that her eye-line only just brushes the crown of his head, even though she's kneeling. He's cross-legged, his back slumped like a pile of laundry.

She wonders about teasing him over his un-princely posture, but decides not to.

For the first time in a while, he is still.

Not physically; although the only movement that betrays he's not some sort of marble statue is the slight parting of his jaw to hum and gasp pleasurably every now and again.

He is still in the way that the ocean is still. It can not move without the tides to drag it, or the wind to whip it up into a swell. It can do nothing other than let powers beyond its control—his Father's will, the rigid laws of politics—do what they please.

There's no playful smirk tweaking his facial muscles. His jaw is slack. His eyebrows are relaxed; two dark lines resting in the centre of his forehead. Even that uneasy frown that's been haunting his expression in recent weeks has loosened, as if it's exhaling.

Like bullies bored with a victim, his troubles are finally permitting him a moment's rest. Later they shall return with full force—

But not yet.

※ ☾ ※

Some time later, Meren has completed a narrow fishtail plait down one side of Lorkan's head. It glistens, slick and shining like the scales of a real fish; blackened from night below the surface of a silent sea. Taking her own hair down, she uses the twine to tie it, and begins another one, collecting a few strands to do so, her nails acting like a rudimentary comb, scraping them together.

Lorkan definitely moans this time.

A soft sound, his head falling back enough for her to glimpse his narrow lips, white, rocky teeth, his pink tongue.

A memory of it curiously brushing her lips blossoms in her mind, strong and bright.

"Lor." She's never called him that before, but he doesn't seem to mind. It had slipped out before she could stop herself—because she *will* stop herself, if given enough time to mull this whim over, to marinade it in good judgment.

It is a stupid thing to say, a stupid thing to do.

She can not be in love with this man.

This man is a prince, royalty, second in line to the throne.

He's leaving forever for a far-off kingdom.

This man is engaged to someone else.

He replies with another distracted, single-syllable hum.

Meren should say something now, anything. The logical part of her brain is hurriedly hunted around for an excuse as to why she'd got his attention—but she can already feel herself leaning.

Gently.

Softly.

She presses her lips to his neck.

30

INSOMNIA FRECKLED

Meren lets her lips linger at Lorkan's neck, too long for it to be an accident, the pressure a little too much to be casual.

She hopes against hope that he won't mind.

She doesn't *think* he minds—he seems to like kissing, at least before he starts painting. And if there were ever a time he needed a kiss—someone to cradle his face, to caress and pamper him—it is now.

He's tensed up as though electrified.

Meren can feel it where she's still holding his shoulder—to support herself as she leans down—that knot of muscle hardening below her palm. She can't see his eyes, but she knows they've snapped open.

Besides that, he is not moving.

He continues to not move as she drags her lips a fraction to the left. She parts them this time, enough for him to feel the soft scrape of her teeth. His skin is sweet and cool against the wet heat of her tongue.

This *does* get a sound out of him.

A soft, broken groan.

It grates against Meren's core like a stone, low, deep, and delicious.

WHAT LORKAN IS

She's pulled noises from him before, but not like this.

Encouraged, she continues. She has to sweep his hair to one side to reach him, and it feathers against the curve of her cheek as she follows the muscle leading down into his pine-green shirt. He hasn't yet applied that scent he keeps on his dresser—that sharp, familiar tang, days old and faded. Instead, he smells of the bath he'd taken—of juniper berries, pepper, and citrus.

Carefully, Meren hunts out his individual nerves, caressing them with loving precision. She can feel his heartbeat in a few places, a quick pattering against her lips like summer rain landing on her face.

When she reaches a patch of skin just below his ear, his head tilts to grant her exploring mouth more room.

She smiles against him.

He likes it.

Her other hand is still in his hair and she pushes it deeper, the thick strands pouring into the gaps between her fingers like a black ocean filling a bay.

Even that gets a soft sound—something between a gasp and a shaky breath. Lorkan eases himself back, inch by inch to rest against Meren's front, the sweet, foreign pressure of his weight pushing her into the plump armrest of the settee.

Smiling, she slips an arm under his and loops it about his middle. He loosens, letting her support him, and the arm over his stomach rises and falls with his contented sigh. She only needs to turn her head slightly now to mouth at his neck, and he accepts it hungrily.

Lorkan's skin is fascinatingly pale. Part of Meren has always wondered whether he has blood at all, or if he's just full of meltwater and sleet. She decides to test it, and gives his neck a slow suck.

Another moan runs through him.

When she pulls away, his skin is flushed a tender, raspberry pink.

✺ ☾ ✺

"What are you doing?" Lorkan eventually mutters unevenly, his voice uncharacteristically breathy. His usually whetted tone is dulled like a blunt blade, and the pale column of his throat is now rosy and somewhat kiss-bruised.

He's melted limply into Meren's embrace, so it's easy for her to mouth the lobe of his ear. Apparently, it is a sensitive spot, because a weak groan pushes up from his chest. His hands have been gripping the knees of his trousers for several minutes, balling the light linen tightly in his pale fists.

She imagines them gripping *her,* and feels her confidence flare. "You only kiss me for the painting," she says, high on the weight of him, the taste, his sounds humming through her core.

This is one of those things she will not have the courage to say at any other time. It has to be now, while she's drunk on him, while his intense gaze isn't inadvertently sheering her confidence. While he's here, under her hands.

"But I just want you to know...you can kiss me whenever you want."

Lorkan's eyes remain closed, but he's stilled against Meren's chest as if alert. Had he been a deer, his ears would have pricked.

Nudging at his right one with the tip of her nose, Meren catches the helix delicately between her teeth.

"...I can?" The words are an exhale rather than a question.

"Yes. I want you to."

There's a pause in which she watches his Adam's apple bob up and then down his parchment-white throat.

Then, he reigns in his long legs stretched comfortably along the divan and sits up, turning to face her. A blush is ghosting the ridges of his cheekbones, turning them pink like a sunset cresting the snowy ridge of a mountain. He moistens his lips.

"What about...right now?" The green of his irises are alight as though a match has been struck behind them. It crackles and flares, looking stark and bright against his insomnia-freckled face.

Meren nods, and suddenly, he's kissing her mouth.

WHAT LORKAN IS

He's kissing her as though she's lemonade after days of thirst, cake after weeks of hunger, air after minutes of scrabbling below a wave.

The pad of his thumb finds her chin and drags it down enough to taste her.

She hums, and he swallows it whole.

When he releases her, a chuckle bubbles from his mouth, caressing Meren's lips like a breeze from a window.

She grins and her cheeks ache like hinges that need a good greasing. "What?" she asks, her fingers still clutching him, bunching his shirt, creasing it.

"Somehow, I knew I wouldn't be able to resist you." Lorkan tugs her back for another kiss, softer this time, catching the curve of her bottom lip between the stony line of his teeth.

Meren moans and she has to cling to the locks of his hair to steady herself, a few deep, dormant nerves igniting, bursting to life. Their flames lap excitedly around her belly, the underside of her ribs, up her chest. When she pulls back for a gulp of air:

"You were trying to resist me?"

"I had to." Another kiss. "We shouldn't."

Her hand finds his jawline. They're linked together like a chain—his hand against her cheek, hers against his. "No one has to know."

He pushes into her touch instinctually, butting his head into it. "It's more that I have never known love before, and I doubt I'll ever know it again—"

"You love me?"

This time he kisses her until she feels her back touch down against the soft swell of the settee. He's crouching over her like a dragon over its hoard, his broad back blocking the sun's glint from shining in her eyes. When he speaks, the words brush the shell of her ear, a rumble gritty enough to rival any dragon:

"Yes. So much so, that—when the time comes—I fear I won't be able to pull myself away."

'So don't,' Meren wants to say.

"I love you too."

So much.

It glows within her chest continuously, a constant, persistent fire that never dims. Even when those miles are wedged between them—even when a thousand millennia have passed and they're long since buried—that flame will still smoulder quietly away to itself amongst her bones and the soft soil.

The pad of Lorkan's finger touches to her lips as if to push the words back into her mouth. When he speaks, his voice is rough like a wheel forced over a badly-paved road. "Don't."

She bites the end of his finger lightly, making him withdraw it, and sends some words up into his face:

"I love you. I love you. I love you. I—"

He kisses her again to make her stop, and she feels him trying not to grin against her mouth. However, when he draws back, she can see his smile has turned brittle. Gently, he collects up both her wrists from his jawline and pins them either side of her head.

Something in the pit of her stomach stirs, the corners of her mouth twitching with a smirk—

But Lorkan isn't playing.

"Wren, darling, you can't."

"Because I'm poor?" she asks, knowing that's not why. "Because you're a prince and I'm a peasant girl from the west?"

She huffs, partly at him and partly because his hair is tickling her forehead like grass tickling bare toes. She can't sweep it away because he's still trapping her, his large hands still smothering her wrists.

Her pulse probably feels like a bird encapsulated in his palms, although she's not sure she *has* a pulse at the moment—her heart is crumbling like cake.

He laughs at her. "Do you really think so little of me?"

"Lorkan, I think the world of you."

The green of his irises turn pale and wet as sea glass. "Well, I think the *universe* of you—every sun and moon and star."

She sniffs. "Then why not?"

"Because," Lorkan explains, pressing a soft kiss to her closed eyes, her cheeks, her forehead, "after being warmed by your affection, excited by your touch, how will I tear myself away from you?" The words fall like dead autumn leaves onto her face. "I will have to leave, but how? How will I starve myself of your love once I've tasted it?"

Meren doesn't know what to say to that. Half of her expects to wake up any second to find Alfdis dragging the covers from her bed, telling her she's overslept.

She moistens her lips, Lorkan's gaze flicking down to watch.

When he returns his steady stare to her eyes, she wonders if he can tell they're prickling with tears. "Surely it is better to have a little bit of something than to have nothing?" she tries. The tips of her fingers ache for the masculine bone of his jaw, but he still isn't letting her touch him.

Only his eyes give away his intense desire to succumb to her pull—to let his body settle between her thighs.

For the second time in just a few days, Meren admires his strength.

"If you think you'll never feel love again, why deprive yourself of it while it's right here?"

His gaze sweeps her face as though looking longingly at it, that love that's right there.

Whatever her kisses at his neck had flushed his bloodstream with, it must have dribbled to a stop. His tiredness is back, his lack of sleep catching up with him, the heft of his responsibilities returning to his shoulders and weighing him down.

A floppy sort of smile comes to his lips as he releases her wrists.

Her hands gravitate to cradle his face, her legs winding about his slender middle. The unexpected touch makes him blush, and he lets himself fall to rest intimately against Meren's front.

He kisses her and it's sweet and slow like the syrup he'd spooned over his breakfast.

She returns it softly.

"Okay," he says when he eases away. His lips are flushed red and curling with a smile, but there's a sadness in his eyes that looks like it's there to stay. "But, come summer's last full moon, you'll have to be the one to tear me from your side. The gods know I won't be strong enough."

※ ☾ ※

They kiss until their lips are raw.

They aren't like the kisses for the painting. Those were urgent, desperate, almost a frantic scrabbling to grab as much as they can before the portrait reaches its completion. They have time, now—well, several months of it, at least.

Lorkan caresses Meren's face with almost glacial slowness, relishing her little gasps and grins. He's brighter now, his lips curved into a loose, almost drunken smile, as though each kiss is pushing summer a little further over the horizon.

He moves to nudge her neck with the point of his nose as if to kiss her— but he doesn't. He just seeks out the comforting space behind her ear and nestles there. Meren feels his contented sigh in her hair and runs her fingers through his, the same way she pets the tomcat that hangs around the servant's kitchens.

In her arms, it seems he can finally rest.

It doesn't take him long to fall asleep.

Dutifully, she holds him, comforted by his weight. It's a constant, steady sort of press, as though she's being snowed on and is just laying there, taking it, letting the flakes pile up. Like snow, Lorkan's presence—she knows—will be pitifully temporary.

But very beautiful while it lasts.

WHAT LORKAN IS

✷ ☾ ✷

When Meren wakes, the room is smudged with dusk, shadows sketched across the polished floor as though with thick chalk. She must have slept, although not for as long as her prince, who is still sprawled out over her like melted butter.

She doesn't want to disturb him. His slumber has been deep, as though void of dreams, his hand dangling from the lip of the divan tranquil and pale as stone. If the high position of the moon is anything to go by, he's grasped several decent hours of rest.

He stirs when she runs her fingers over his head, the touch easing him into consciousness. His hand draws in closer and comes to rest between her breasts, heavy against the ridge of her sternum. The touch is pure and entirely innocent; seeking out the beat of her heart.

She cuddles him closer. "You fell asleep," she points out through a smile, fully expecting a quip curled with amusement in answer.

Predictably, it comes, his voice gummed up and drowsy:

"Apparently so." Then, rather unpredictably:

"Sorry."

Her brow furrows like the creases now denting Lorkan's clothes. "Why?"

"I'm sure a nap is not what you had in mind when you started mouthing at my neck."

Meren feels her cheeks blossom with heat. "I don't know what I had in mind. Like you I'm...new. To all this. I just—how did you put it?" Her blush runs down her neck and pools around her collarbones. "Couldn't resist you."

Lorkan chuckles and it ripples through her, then the settee, probably only petering out when it meets the harsh slab of cold, gold flooring.

"Then I am forever indebted to your pitifully weak willpower."

Meren smirks. "What happened to *'we shouldn't'?*"

The fishtail braids she'd wound into his hair are still there. The twine clings better to his hair than hers—it's thicker, more wiry. She runs one little plait between finger and thumb absently, feeling the silken bumps of each knot. "Would you have ever given in if I hadn't touched you first?"

The moonlight is dripping onto his body from one of the tall windows. "Do you not remember my lecture about royalty abusing their power?"

"If I didn't want to be with you, I would have shoved you away, prince or no."

"You'd rather risk disobeying royalty than kiss someone you don't want to?"

"Yes. Cade could order me to kiss him and have every member of the royal guard point their spiky flagpoles at me, and I still wouldn't." Meren had forgotten to call their king '*His Majesty,*' but Lorkan doesn't seem to care.

He just laughs, and she feels it against her neck. "They're called a lance, but I take your point."

She doesn't have to see his face to know he's smiling.

They let a few minutes pass, blackness creeping silently around the window panes like frost.

"Alfdis will be sending search parties after you soon," Lorkan mutters eventually.

Meren replies with a hum.

"I don't want you to go."

"Is that an order, Your Highness?" She smiles, but it falls sideways as he pushes himself up.

If he made her, she would stay, and he knows that.

"No. I won't have you losing your position on my account—"

She opens her mouth.

"Even if you *are* willing to." He takes her hand and smoothly helps her up from the cushions.

Swaying a little after so long spent horizontal, Meren feels him take her hips, steadying her. As she blinks away purple dots, he presses a tender kiss to her forehead.

"I just meant that tomorrow feels too far away."

WHAT LORKAN IS

☾

As they reach the door, Lorkan places some coins into Meren's palm. There are a few more of the thick gold disks than usual, and she's about to refuse them when a smile twitches at his lips.

"Before you break out in hives, they're not extra wages. Here." He makes a few quick notes on a scrap of parchment.

She recognises them vaguely from Frode's stall. They're inscribed onto the tags tied about the jars lining the back shelf. Visibly, she lights up. "You're painting again?"

Lorkan's answering smile is strangely bashful. "It's nearly finished, I promise. I've just realised that something is missing."

31

SIGNIFICANT INSIGNIFICANT THINGS

By the time Meren steps into the hallway, the sconces have already been lit, their yellow, swaying light wriggling with dust. As he descends into the bowels of the palace, the fluff from tapestries and banners hardens into grit that flakes off the limestone walls, and the sweetness of beeswax sticks morphs into the inexpensive tang of burning fat.

Immune to their must, Meren's lips curve into a smile soft and bright as the sconces.

Lorkan's kisses still echo on her lips, his words still nestled close to her heart. She clutches them there, safe and secret, enclosed in the warm cradle of her palms.

He loves her. He loves her. He loves her.

It's a different sort of love to that of her parents, or Alfdis, or even Arne, and it feels different in the way it follows her about—unassuming, honest, and asking nothing in return. It keeps dutiful watch over her, his affection padding invisibly, loyally, silently at her heels.

It has been there the entire time, and she didn't even know.

WHAT LORKAN IS

As Meren loads some leftovers onto a plate and takes a seat in the almost abandoned mess hall, she self-consciously checks her reflection in the curved back of her soup spoon. Her bright expression shines back at her, her slightly kiss-bruised smile stretched into a grin. Hopefully, no one will notice.

※ ☾ ※

The glowing hasn't subsided, Meren discovers upon waking the next morning. She would have suspected it to be magic—some sort of mild spell she'd walked into by accident, like a spider's web—had she not known that to be near impossible. The only practitioner of magic she knows is Lorkan, and he of all people understands the importance of keeping their relationship a secret.

Once again, it's spitting with rain as she makes her usual walk to the market, the sloped road trickling with rivulets. It's a lazy sort of rain, falling in no particular hurry from a wet bundle of clouds that hide a limpid, hopeful sun. Meren seems to have contracted a case of uncontrollable smiling overnight, and she hopes the occasional cold dribble through her oilskin might help soothe her flare up.

However, she's still smiling as she reaches Aasta's stall and, nipping a fat wedge of cake with her metal tongs, the baker teases:

"Ooh, hello, someone's chipper this morning!" Shards of butter biscuit protrude jaggedly, yet Aasta manages to fit the rocky road neatly into a wood-pulp box and begins fastening it with twine. "You're glowing like a dog with two tails."

Once she's executed a deft, loopy little bow, Meren places it carefully at the bottom of her tote bag with the other. She shrugs with one shoulder, making sure not to shake up her cakes, and pushes down a blush. "I just like the rain."

"Of course you do." Aasta raises one round little eyebrow, and Meren retreats under the hood of her oilskin.

When she presses a few coppers into her hand, it's white with sugar and soft as the dough she rolls.

Her plump lips curve into a smile but, as Meren turns to leave she adds seriously:

"Just be careful, okay, sweety?"

Meren contemplates Aasta's words as she watches Arne fiddle about with some scales at the back of Frode's stall.

While he's distractedly tipping crumbly nuggets of gold powder onto the weighing dish, she makes a decision.

Suddenly feeling too hot in her oilskin—Meren leans over and whispers a few quick things into Frode's pink little mole-like ear.

She expects a judgmental, fatherly look or perhaps a lecture, but gets neither.

He just plucks a bottle from below the shelf. The label reads in big, serious letters:

SOLVEIG THOMPSON'S FAMILY PREVENTION TONIC

Below the title, in a proud, bold font, the promise *'INSTANT EFFECTS'* is scrawled, along with instructions, which are simply:

TAKE ONE DOSE AFTER

Feeling as though she's smearing a large stain on her honour, Meren embarrassedly slips the little bottle into her tote.

* ☾ *

As soon as Meren's knuckles ring a knock through the hallway, Lorkan's door opens and she is immediately tugged inside by a cool, strong hand.

Kicking the foot shut with a distracted foot, he pounces on her for a kiss, his grin bumping her lips.

Meren falls into it eagerly, letting herself drown in the soft satin of his shirt, the safe cage of his arms, the sweet scent of pine, books, and paint.

WHAT LORKAN IS

She's home.

Across the room, rain patters gently against the broad window panes, the sky still a heavy, moist grey—

But when Lorkan's grin falls down onto her face, it swamps the whole room in a warm fuzzy light.

"Hello," she says stupidly, getting the sense her cheeks are flowering with red roses. Will there ever be a day when his attention doesn't make her blush?

His beam twitches into a smirk. "I think we're a little past *'hello'*, don't you?"

One of his hands finds the bun atop her head and tenderly teases the pins free, letting her hair tumble about her shoulders. His pale eyes watch it with quiet satisfaction.

She knows the servant's dress code grates at him. If he had his way, Aldercliff probably wouldn't have servants at all. *'The man who forged my father's sword did so with one leg and one eye,'* he had once drawled with a twist to his mouth, *'yet our gallant king requires a man to help him with his socks.'*

Meren lets a laugh bubble in her chest and reaches up, taking the side of his face. She likes him being there, close enough to touch. She likes knowing he is safe and loved at her side, not off disappointing his father or shivering cold in the shadow of his brother.

He pushes eagerly into the touch—

Then something catches her eye.

"It's finished?"

A few links down in the chain of rooms, the easel stands where they'd left it—in the lounge facing the window. Surrounded by brushes and jars of water, the wooden tripod has become an honorary piece of furniture after all these weeks, and Meren has become accustomed to its almost ghostly appearance; the painting shrouded modestly in a white sheet.

But now the sheet is gone.

The block of canvas is bare and naked, sat heavily atop the easel's spindly legs, weighing them down with thick greens and vibrant golds.

Lorkan follows as Meren gravitates to it quickly, her slippered feet pattering from one room to the next.

Yes, it's complete, so perfect it's as though Lorkan has snipped a slice out of reality with darning scissors and plastered it there—Meren's own hazel eyes staring back at her as though through a looking glass—

Or a dream. The texture of the paint, the delicate dabs and subtle sweeps; they give it a fuzzy appearance, the colours dazzling, saturated, intense, more lavish than reality could ever hope of being.

"I actually finished your expression a while ago," he admits sheepishly. "I just wanted an excuse to kiss you again. I know I should have stopped, but you kept *letting* me—"

Meren turns to him, and he lowers his piercing eyes to his bare feet.

"I'm sorry."

The corner of her lip curls. "What have you been doing for all those hours while I thought you were painting my face?"

The broad line of his shoulders rises and falls in a shrug. His hair has grown over recent months, Meren notes absently, the loose waves swallowing his shirt collar. "Layering and shading, mostly—things I didn't really need you to pose for. Again, sorry."

"I don't mind. I didn't want you to finish it either because I thought I'd never get to kiss you again."

His muscles unfurl and she turns back to the canvas.

"But now...I can kiss you whenever I want." She gestures at the picture, at how he sees the world, so shrouded in colour and emotion and significance. "And I'm so glad I get to see it finished."

The painting is as luscious and alive as the palace gardens, freckled with little things Meren hadn't deemed important, things she would have left out —the thick volumes stacked on the little table to her left, their spines a deep, rich, caramel brown. The glint of a crystal vase sitting atop them like a transparent spirit, turning the wall to liquid. The bruises on the floor from spilt ink, the soles of shoes, chairs and end tables pushed about, making the picture look lived in like an old house—she almost expects the painting version of herself to blink, to yawn or stretch or blow her hair from her forehead.

She can see the beauty in them, through Lorkan's eyes; those insignificant things.

"It's breathtaking."

She feels him step up behind her wordlessly, his arms looping about her middle. The unexpected touch still sets her nerves tingling, and she lets her back fall against his chest.

His voice comes from above her head, bashful and hungry for her praise:

"You think?"

"Of course. Look at it."

They do, silently, for several minutes. It contrasts starkly against the window—the greens like summer grass, the sky puddle-grey. The rain goes on and on, masking the horizon in thick sheets, the city below blinking like lanterns through fog.

After a little while, Meren asks:

"So what's missing?"

"Your earrings don't match your dress."

Meren squints at the painting. "You didn't paint my earrings."

"Because they don't match."

She feels one of his hands rise to delicately cup her right earring, letting the little green stud roll over the pad of his finger. "These are silver. The painting is gold."

"You're really that particular?" she laughs.

He can probably feel it where his arm is encircling her stomach—and holds her closer. His nose replaces his finger at her ear, then his lips. He gives her lobe a playful little nip.

Heat dribbles down the back of her neck.

"I don't like this empty space here." His pale hand rises to gesture vaguely at the picture. "The lower half—with the dress's braiding is very gold-heavy. It makes the top half look empty."

"You could just use gold paint rather than silver."

"I have a better idea. Stay there." Drawing away, he slinks off to the next room and disappears around a corner.

"Lor?" Meren hopes he can sense her suspicion through the wall. It's playful—a teasing narrowing of eyes—and yet her heart has gently risen in her throat. She swallows to force it back down. "What have you done?"

He waits until he's returned to answer, a fabric-wrapped box in one hand. The size of an apple, it's dyed a clean, mint-leaf sort of colour, and she feels her chest tighten. "Now, I know you don't like it when I buy you things—"

She wants to shove him, but she's afraid to break whatever's in the box.

"—But I want you to know I bought these myself, with *my* money—that I *earned.*" He notices her mouth open to scold him and quickly adds:

"Not anything too strenuous, I promise. I just sold some old paintings."

Her voice cracks: "Your paintings—"

He presses a tender kiss to her forehead. "Nothing I wasn't fully prepared to part with, I assure you."

"But...your *paintings*—"

"You didn't care about the ones I sold for your dress!"

"You—? I didn't *know*—!"

His eyes roll. "Just open it."

She hesitates before taking the box, her hands clammy. She wipes them on her uniform first, the material scraping rather than drying.

Inside the box, resting atop a pillow much plusher than the one on Meren's own bed, lie two earrings. They consist of four parts: a wire hook, clean and fine as a hair; two pressed gold disks as light as foil; and, finally, a large hoop as wide as a gold coin. Suspended in the hoop, thin as the skin of an onion, hangs a sliced sliver of jade.

"*Lorkan.*"

His lip curls with a fond, teasing smile. "As much as I love it when you say my name, I *am* trying to give you a gift. Maybe you could try to sound a little less like I've asked you to clean a lavatory?"

She frowns up into his face, pushing the box back into his hands. "I *sound* like that because I don't *want* them." Crossly, she folds her arms tight—

But the earrings glint, green like his eyes.

She dithers. "Well, I *do* want them, of course I want them—but I shouldn't have them."

Her hand twitches in their direction, and he sighs.

"My gods, it's like trying to coax a squirrel to take an acorn from my hand." Holding them out a little further, he prompts:

"Go on. Take them. I'll be sad if you don't."

Pained, Meren's palms spread, but she stops. "Wait." Pulling a hankie from her pocket, she quickly draws her old earrings from her ears and wraps them in the little scrap of linen. Pushing them safe to the bottom of her pocket:

"Okay—but *you* put them in. Even my gaze feels too heavy. I'm scared I'll crack them just by looking."

That smile returning, Lorkan carefully lifts the new earrings from their cushion and deftly eases them into her ears.

Her bout of uncontrollable grinning has returned.

✶ ☾ ✶

Today, changing into her dress takes Meren longer than usual because she's spending a good deal of time tilting her head from side to side in the washroom mirror.

The earrings looked wonky whilst dangling above her starchy housemaid's collar. Not wonky as in off-centre, but wonky as in out of place, like something that had been sketched onto her person—and not very well.

But, slipping into her matching green dress, they settle into place immediately.

Lorkan bows as she eventually leaves the washroom, a shy smile curving her lips. "You look like a queen."

Her eyes widen with horror, her cheeks draining of colour. "You can't say that!"

Evidently, he does not share her panic. "Why not?"

"What do you mean *'why not?'* It's terribly disrespectful of Her Majesty Lophia—"

He waves off her concerns with one hand. "I don't see how."

"Because someone like me could never—should never—be compared to Our Lady—" she can see a frown furrowing that space between his dark eyebrows and cuts herself off.

'Housekeeping is what you do, but that doesn't mean you're a housekeeper,' he has often lectured, and Meren doesn't want to be lectured again. He can be a prince and an artist, and his brother can be an heir and a warrior—he doesn't seem to understand that all Meren can ever be is a servant. Her title clings to her like a limpet to the hull of a ship.

"—It's just...wrong." She sighs, smoothing the folds of her skirt self-consciously, feeling suddenly like she's stolen somebody else's skin. "You may treat me like royalty, but you mustn't forget that I'm not."

"You are to me."

Meren *does* shove him this time, and Lorkan lets her, his chuckles rolling like the clouds outside.

WHAT LORKAN IS

32

EMBERS AND GOLD

A damp essence of finality hangs in the air as Meren steps into Lorkan's studio. She doubts he'll start a new painting once this one is completed—not before he leaves for Calpurzia, anyway. Mentally, she tries to note the colourful scars bruising every surface, the view from the gaping windows, the sharp tang of dried paint; pressing the memories onto her brain in the hope that they'll stick.

The downward pull of her new earrings amounts to little less than a leaf, yet the lobes of her ears are extremely conscious of their weight.

What paintings did he sell? Whose walls are they now adorning? Do the new owners appreciate them? Do they know to frame them out of reach from children's sticky fingers? Far from the snarling sun that's eager to gobble up their vibrance?

Meren would utter a small prayer to King Cade—after the safety of their beauty—but suspects he would have few cares for such a matter.

She chews her lip.

Meanwhile, Lorkan has settled on one of the plump velvet cushions by the low table, his long legs folded like the neatly arranged sails of a frigate. He gave up trying to convince Meren that the earrings belong to her some time ago, pointing out that even if she did return them to him, it would not change the fact that his paintings are gone.

His paintings being gone doesn't seem to bother him. Presently, he's digging through her box-filled tote for whatever treat she's bought from Aasta.

Meren flops down next to him like a wet rag. "What if someone sees them?"

"Hm?"

She releases her tattered lip. "My earrings. Where will I say I got them?"

"You can keep them here with your dress," is the nonchalant reply, his nimble fingers working the twine bow keeping him from his cake. When it's sufficiently unravelled, Meren watches him ease open the wood pulp lid, a smile lighting up his pale, pointed face.

"What about when you leave?"

He shrugs. "Sell them. Use the money to buy a house. Put the dress in it."

Meren squeaks, horrified. "I'm not going to sell them!"

"Then *I'll* buy you a house. *You* put the earrings in it."

Meren pushes him, but it's like trying to playfully shove a deeply rooted tree. As if her assault had been little more than a gentle lap of the tide, he takes his wedge of cake in finger and thumb and bites into it with a hum.

"You'll do no such thing."

A blasé rise and fall of his broad shoulders. "There's nothing you can do to stop me."

"Are you *threatening* to buy me a house?"

Lorkan lifts his attention from his food to gauge her expression. "Would you not *like* a house?"

A scene sprouts and flowers in her mind before she can stop it—a cobbled bungalow nestled amongst a smattering of trees, a crunchy little path leading to a green painted door, a sitting room crammed with books—

She stamps the thought underfoot like a weed, and tries to mask her interest with a glare—

But she knows those chips of jade have already read the dreams printed all over her soul.

"You can't just buy someone a house, Lor."

"Why not?"

"Because it's not fair. Why should my peers have to work their whole lives for a pittance whilst I get things for nothing?"

Lorkan smiles. "Now you *sound* like a queen."

This time Meren sticks her tongue out at him, knowing he's probably only saying it to get her nettled. Moodily, she breaks into the other cake box and bites into her slice, the fragments of butter biscuit sharp on the roof of her mouth. Fluffy marshmallows soothe the hurt, sugar sweet on her tongue.

"Did you have breakfast today?" She asks, and his smile falls sideways.

"Yes." He dabs up some crumbs with the pad of his finger. "I dined with my family for the first time in a while. Mother looked like she might weep when she saw I'd finally left my rooms."

Come summer, Meren realises, she will not be the only person he is tearing himself from—a thought that makes it hard to swallow the thick knot of marshmallow in her mouth. He will miss his mother—the tutor of his spells and, sometimes it seems, his only ally—more than he can say.

He doesn't need to say.

She places a hand on his knee, and he gives the back of her palm a grateful squeeze.

"I was going to bring some food up for you, sorry," he apologised, and she shakes her head.

"You don't have to—"

"I'd like to. We'll have brunch later instead, or an early supper." His smirk returns, curving his lip. "And you're keeping the earrings, even if you won't let me buy you a house."

Meren's mouth opens to protest, but he pushes her lower jaw back up with one finger.

"Don't you know it's terribly rude to reject a present from a prince?"

✷ ☾ ✷

Their cake and all its pointy shards now consumed, Lorkan removes the other boxes from Meren's cotton bag and sets them about the low, colour-stained table.

She takes the mortar he hands her eagerly, tipping in the first colour, and sets into a comfortable, repetitive motion.

She had missed the work during his painting hiatus, finding her hours of lounging about and playing with him to be fun but wrong. Each week, she collects her wages from Alfdis with a taught smile, the knowledge that she had not earned them sitting like a rock in her stomach, the coins sitting, jagged, in her pocket. If the majority of them didn't go to her parents, she would have tossed them all into the upturned hat of a beggar.

Lorkan says very little as he kneels at her side, dripping various oils into a stained little bowl. Occasionally, he glances her way and offers a soft smile. The sadness from a few minutes ago has left his eyes, replaced with a quiet contentment.

Next to him, Meren dutifully crushes the first colour against the curved inside of the mortar. It's a bronzed sort of gold, as if tanned by the summer sun, and malleable. When it's fine enough, she passes it back so he can add the egg whites and oils and—while he mixes it into a fine paste—she empties the next colour into the mortar.

It takes her a little while to realise he's staring at her.

"What?"

"I was just thinking...you're gorgeous..."

Heat prickles the tips of her ears. It always will, every time—

But something in his tone makes her brow furrow.

"...But?"

"Something's still missing." Thoughtfully, he touches the tips of his fingers to the paint in his bowl. It clings to his pale skin like syrup, and he rubs it between finger and thumb as though to check the texture.

Meren expects him to say she has not ground the pigment fine enough, but he doesn't.

He just turns to her, eyes twinkling, and presses it to her face.

The skin below her nose chills as he drags the cool pad of his paint-covered finger sideways, above her lip. When he lifts it, he presses it back below her nose to give the left side equal treatment.

She can see the white of his teeth as he draws away to assess his handiwork. She doesn't have to use the reflective blade of a paint knife to know he'd rubbed an elegant golden moustache onto her face.

"That's funny," she says, selecting a bowl of her own. "I was just thinking the same thing about you. I mean, don't get me wrong, you are *breathtaking*—"

He is.

Especially now, eyes full of sparks, the thin line of his mouth turned up as he watches her submerge the tips of her fingers into a light bronze sort of colour. He knows what she's going to do but doesn't make any movement towards stopping her, even as she pushes herself up onto her knees.

What to draw on him?

A pair of bushy sideburns along those whetted cheekbones?

A third eye learning out from his alabaster forehead?

She remembers Frode, and how he keeps a little glass disk on a chain in his breast pocket. Sometimes he'll press it to one eye—squinting rather comically to hold it in place—and she has to hold in a giggle.

"—but you're right, you are...*lacking* something." Smiling, she circles Lorkan's right eye, the paint grazing the side of his nose and matting into his dark eyebrow.

The monocle looks lonely by itself, so she gives him a trim little beard that seems to be extremely popular among travelling merchants, and a beauty mark.

He gives her a broad, coy grin. "Am I handsome now?"

Returning his toothy smile, she laughs, giving a firm nod of her head. "The handsomest."

"As are you," he replies, his pale eyes sliding over the assortment of paints littering the table. "Or at least, you will be, once I'm finished with you."

Already shaking a little with half-swallowed chuckles, he pulls one finger across the length of her forehead, gifting her with a thick monobrow.

※ ☾ ※

By the time Lorkan declares that Meren meets his standards, she has gained spectacles, several overgrown, golden moles, and a pair of admirable sideburns.

"Now you *definitely* look like a queen," he drawls, one side of his lip curled with a smirk. It creases his monocle into a crescent moon.

"I *feel* like a queen," she agrees for once, and he leans forward in a graceful bow, the raven-feather tips of his hair brushing to the colour-stained floor.

"And what be your wishes, My Queen?"

Pressing the smile from her lips, she irons out her spine, giving her chin a regal jut. "My wish be that you kiss me, young prince."

Said prince raises one paint-caked eyebrow. "My queen lacks ambition."

When Meren shrugs her shoulders, she feels her new earrings touch them lightly. "Well, if you don't *want* to—"

She doesn't get to finish that sentence.

Lorkan leans forward as if to bow again but catches her lips instead, showing her that he very much *does* want to.

His kiss is greedy and starved—lips, tongue, teeth.

It is hard not to touch him, Meren's paint-coated hands longing to reach for the reassuring solidity of his body. She recognises the feeling—a familiar echo that's been ringing throughout the past year. It bounces off the walls of this room in particular—an ache for him. He's always so close and yet, simultaneously, so out of reach.

He breaks the kiss, his own arms tight at his sides. "There will never be a day when I do not want to," he breathes against her mouth, each word tasting of cocoa and butter biscuit and sugar.

WHAT LORKAN IS

She shuffles forward on her knees to catch his lips again, but he tilts his head, her kiss scuffing their sharp corner. They slide over his jawline, clean-shaven, smooth, soft—

His mouth falls open. "Kiss me like you did yesterday."

She knows which kisses he means—those long, lingering, curious ones she'd used to map out his wonderfully responsive neck.

Mouth widening into a nervous little grin, she presses a light, fleeting caress to his chin. "...Like this?"

Lorkan's elbow twitches as though about to take her face, her waist, to pull her little body against his—

But, with admirable control, he stifles the urge. He can't stifle his grin, though. "You know that's not what I meant."

"Do I?"

Velvet ribbons: "Don't toy with me, Wren, darling."

Smiling, she strays over the sharp dash of his cheekbones, down the column of his pale throat, all quick touches of her lips—butterflies landing and then leaving, startled. "These kisses?" she taunts, and he shakes his head—

But his breath *has* quickened.

Gold paint blemishes his skin like glittering bruises, smudging against Meren's mouth, the texture glossy, the taste chalky.

"How about these?" A little firmer, a chaste press to his collarbone, between the loose lapels of his shirt.

Lorkan makes a soft sound.

She had planned to play with him more.

He's always playing with *her*, trying to ruck up the space between her brows into that vexed frown he's so stupidly fond of.

She wants to get him back—

But how can she keep him from what he wants, when he makes noises like that?

Blood heating as though placed above a flame, Meren doubles back in search of that spot, her lips grazing and dragging, eager to draw out more little hisses and gasps. Each one grates against her core like a slice of flint, sparks bursting, igniting, glowing—embers flickering to life between her cells.

"Temptress," Lorkan hisses through a smirk as she kisses that hard line of bone again, just enough to make his breath catch, not enough to turn the little huff of air into a moan. "You and your glorious golden moustache."

A roll of giggles bubbles up from her lungs, and she lets them mingle with the kiss she's giving him; a caress of joy, tongue, and heat.

That seems to break him, as she feels him take her wrist, his grasp slick with gold. Pupils deep and black, he guides her hand to the collar of his shirt, pressing her paint-stained fingers to the buttons—yellow against green, like sunlight through leaves.

"You've ruined a perfectly good shirt," she chides through a smile. If he hadn't done it, she would have. She would have fervently wiped her hands on a matted cloth until they were clean-ish, and tugged down that tauntingly wide v-neck—

Lorkan finds her ear and nips it. "Worth it."

He's not on his plump velvet pillow anymore. He's managed to wriggle right off it to board Meren's like a pair of lovers sharing a hunk of a sinking ship.

33

THE LOW, WOODEN TABLE

The joints in Meren's fingers gum up with exhilaration as she clumsily eases the first of Lorkan's shirt buttons from its loop, then the second, then the third. It's hard to concentrate with the rough scrape of his teeth at her neck, his hair tickling her face—but she manages, and lets her eyes slide down the narrow column of skin she'd exposed, pale and mysterious as the moon.

She has seen shirtless men before; metalworkers glistening from the heat of their fires, burly and coal-blackened, farmers thick as oxen turning over fields, their backs peeled by the sun—

But Lorkan doesn't look like them.

As though drawing back curtains on something she's not allowed to see, Meren slips the material from his body.

"The handsomest," she says again, seriously this time, and feels him grin against her throat.

She doesn't know what she wants to touch first. The firm hills of his pectorals. The taught knots of his shoulders. She wants to touch all of him, have him against her, engulfing her, the sweet, hard weight of him pressing her into some kind of horizontal surface.

Anything will do. A bed. The table. The floor.

That foreign desire floods her all at once, and she swims in it for a second, wondering if Lorkan is feeling the same thing.

He probably is.

She can feel his heartbeat as she kisses his throat.

He's not touching her, but she'd like him to. Dripping with paint, he's holding his hands behind his back—like he'd done on the front steps—but, this time, Meren can see the tight muscles in his arms working to keep them there. Perhaps it's a blessing. She never would have managed to get his shirt open had they been allowed to roam.

Touching a palm to his chest, her hand tingles against his forbidden skin.

His kisses stumble at the contact, his heart quick beneath her palm. The rest of him stills as he adjusts to this new, intimate touch. When he resumes, his lips part, the wetness of his tongue startlingly hot.

Meren whimpers.

"That's my favourite sound," he growls, and she gives a shaky giggle.

Kissing Lorkan's neck feels different now. As her trail extends lower, she keeps expecting to touch the collar of his shirt, to hit a wall of gauzy fabric—

But, of course, there isn't one anymore. She can just keep going and does, clutching onto his hair, his waist, his shoulders to keep herself steady.

He exhales thickly as the tip of her nose brushes a bare nipple.

"Is this okay?" she asks, but it's a stupid question, and she watches his pale stomach contract with a laugh.

"More than." A small suck at her ear.

A small moan from her.

"I've been thinking about this since I saw you dragging that wretched mop over those blasted steps," he says, the words low and gritty.

Meren lets her hand slide to his belly, liking the catch of his breath and the slight, surprising softness. He's filled out since she'd met him, she realises—wider, bigger, stronger. He's grown into a man.

"Even though my lips were chapped from the cold?"

"Especially because your lips were chapped from the cold." His paint-stained hand delicately cups her chin.

Her body floods with signals to spread herself open to him.

"It took all my willpower not to scoop you up and tend to you myself."

She wants him to kiss her somewhere else, anywhere else, everywhere else.

For the first time, she curses her beautiful velvet dress.

"Tend to me now," she breathes.

A smirk curls his lips. "You know I want to," he mutters, "but I don't have any—"

"It's okay, I do." She assures, bundling him closer. "I'm taking something."

He blinks. "You are?"

A nod.

A beam.

A greedy, overwhelming kiss.

"Thank the gods!"

She laughs at him. "That's the happiest you've been for a while."

"That's what you do to me," his lips mumble against her cheek. Shaking his head in disbelief:

"Good Gods, look what you do to me."

His caresses tumble lower, her chin, her neck, then the collar of her dress settled around the base of her throat. His nose nudges under the tulle.

"Wren...if you took this off—"

Rather than words, he finishes that sentence with a kiss to her lips, so deep it whips up her blood like wind twisting fallen leaves.

He's showing her.

Showing her what he'd do if she did.

Legs structurally sound as suet, Meren pushes herself to her knees and collects up her heavy, curtain-like skirt. Her heart is in her mouth, she can feel its wild rhythm against her teeth.

What would her parents say?

No one has to know.

What would their king say?

He'll never find out.

Find out what? That his son is loved?

I've never known love before.

Why deprive yourself of it while it's right here?

With one smooth motion, she drags her gown over her head and tosses it onto the floor.

Lorkan swallows roughly.

She watches his jaw clench as her naked skin reacts to the brisk chill of the room, prickly gooseflesh rising in tight piques. She's bare besides a plain pair of knickers, and his eyes chew on them hungrily before sliding ravenously over her curves.

His pupils are so large they're engulfing his irises—black consuming green, a forest swamped in night. He looks like he's going to eat her.

She feels her delicate little breasts tighten under his gaze, and his eyes drop, watching.

"My queen," he mutters as he draws her to him, and Meren does not correct him.

She just lets his arms cage her up against his chest, his cool cells connecting with her warmth in a crack of lightning.

In his embrace, she *feels* like a queen.

His mouth finds hers and smothers it, her hands tangling in his hair, and she gets an approving growl. It rolls through her core like thunder, his arousal already nudging insistently against her hip.

Experimentally, she shifts against that building heat.

It must have shot a bolt of something through him, because Lorkan's body tenses up with a shuddering groan.

"Wren," he mutters unevenly, just to taste her name on his tongue. His paint-covered hand climbs her chest, sliding up to softly cup one of her breasts. The wide, firm spread of his palm dwarfs it, his skin surprisingly rough.

She sucks in a breath.

"Okay?" He prompts gently, the word an exhale.

"Yes." Her every cell is humming. "Don't stop."

He gives the slight softness a curious squeeze, and something deep in her stomach tightens. Against her mouth, Lorkan smirks, catching her bottom lip between his teeth.

She wants to tell him she likes what he's doing, but her words keep melting into heaps of letters. She clutches onto the wide stretch of his shoulders instead, fingers digging into the lean muscles and elegant bones.

The floor has fallen away beneath her knees— the colour-stained rugs, the hefty marble, everything— until there's only Lorkan: the masculine power of him, the salty taste of his skin.

The hand at her breast starts drawing delicate circles around her nipple. He's following the pinched, pink skin, closer and closer until the pads of his finger and thumb close over the flushed bud at its centre. Tender and defenceless below his touch, he rolls it like a jewel—lovingly, softly.

Meren mewls.

It must be his undoing, because Lorkan takes the swell of her hips, lifting her smoothly onto the table, pots and bowls scattering like a flock of hollow, wooden birds.

When he eases his trouser-covered waist between the warmth of her thighs, it sets that ache in her abdomen ablaze. Automatically, her legs wind around his waist, and she lets him nudge her down until her shoulders touch the scuffed wood of the table.

He gazes at her, gold paint smudged all over him like glistening bruises.

After a moment of staring, drinking her in, he draws back and takes her hand. His cheeks are flushed, lips parted to vent his heavy breaths but, when he speaks, it is pensive.

"When I first saw you..." He circles the base of Meren's third finger, the pads of his own still stained with pigment.

They leave a golden shadow.

"I dreamt of putting a ring here."

He's frowning, but she kisses it, and the creases smooth over like a bedsheet tugged at the corners.

It takes her a second to collect enough breath to answer.

"We may not be united here."

Leaving her own ghost of a wedding band about his finger, she scoops some more paint from a nearby bowl.

This gold is stronger than the last, lucent; the colour so plentiful it's overflowing.

With it, she draws a hoop over Lorkan's chest, encapsulating his heart. She can see her fingerprints in it, the marks like delicate, metal engravings.

"But we are here."

He presses his lips to her smile and says he loves her into her mouth.

Silky as ribbon in her throat, she swallows the syllables, thankful for the wide, sturdy table, the wood steady against her back.

"Wren...have you ever?"

She shakes her head.

"Me neither."

His kisses drop lower, swerving left to mouth at her nipple, letting it roll over his tongue. She clings to his hair, her stomach clenching, the sensation some sort of strange, blissful agony.

Unable to resist, his hand wanders down, exploring the softness of her belly, her thighs, tantalisingly close to that hunger between her legs, and she gasps.

"This okay?" he asks in a low voice. His lips are curled with a smirk at her sounds, but he pauses all the same, easing his thumb into the band of her knickers, setting her blood fizzing.

Pulse loud in her ears, she takes his wrist and pushes his hand down below the cotton. "More."

As he touches upon the wetness waiting for him, Lorkan's groan of satisfaction tumbles heavily onto her shoulder.

With the pad of a finger, he gives a soft, tentative stroke.

A shudder rolls along Meren's core.

"Good?"

WHAT LORKAN IS

Her answering moan is just a weak little breath amongst his ragged panting.

Spurred on by her response, he rubs her folds again, curiously exploring that bundle of nerves with one strong finger. Experimentally, he dips down to her entrance, then back up, relishing in her tormented whimper.

She needs something to hold onto, something to keep her tethered to reality as it disappears around her—the pigment-freckled walls, the cabinets, the paintbrushes—all replaced by heat and whiteness bursting on the insides of her eyelids.

"Lor," she begs, moving a hand up to grip his coal-black hair.

He makes a low sound, and slips his finger in a little deeper.

Liking the way that makes her buck against him, he takes up a leisurely pace, in and out, slow and hard, getting a desperate sob.

Meren's hips move with him, every nerve in her possession coiling tight as a spring. It doesn't take long for relief to barrel down her spine, a startling, throbbing, writhing few seconds of nothing but light.

She's lying on the sun, surrounded by lapping, licking tongues of fire.

Vaguely, as she comes down from it, she hears Lorkan groan with need at the sight of her, the feel of her pleasure clenching about his fingers. He's covered in colours—sky blues, apple pink, sunflower yellow—and, for a moment, Meren thinks they're the same lights from behind her eyes; but they're not—

The table below her is covered in pigment, and she'd transferred some to his china-cup skin as she'd clung to him.

Hard as granite, cheeks flushed, he draws his hand to his mouth and sucks at the sweetness there. When he speaks, Meren's sweetness sparkling on his flushed lips, his voice cracks, half-starved:

"Can I?"

"I've never wanted something more in my entire life."

She has never seen a man move so fast—all of him standing to his full height, a swift grappling with the tie at his trousers, the soft sound of clothes hitting the floor.

He's naked except for a grin, muscles creating small hills, bones making smooth angles, the two clean-cut lines at his pelvis dragging her eyes proudly downwards.

Her abdomen coils at the size of him, and Lorkan's eyes watch the bob of her throat, crinkling with a smile.

When he prowls back to her, he falls to his knees and, tenderly, strokes a hand over her hair. "I don't think I've ever *loved* something so much in my entire life."

Meren's face is cupped in the spread of his palms as he kisses her again. They've grown warm, all of him is warm, and she wonders if he minds.

Probably not. He doesn't seem to. It's as though he's trying to consume it —her heat—with his inquisitive, searching mouth and ravenous, eager hands, eating it up with his violently sensitive skin.

She wants him to feel what she'd felt—that great rippling spasm of something—that *magic*. The silken length of him is solid as against her belly, and she grates against it, Lorkan's answering cry crashing into her mouth.

She needs him.

Now, forever.

How will she ever let him go?

She tries to tug him deeper into the comfort of her thighs, but he breaks their kiss with a choked:

"Wait."

He sounds like he needs to clear his throat; the word a sooty whisper of smoke.

Before she can open her mouth, he stands back, scooping her up, and spins them both around, the backs of his legs pressing into the table.

"I want you to be on top."

Smiling, Meren takes his forearms, easing him down amongst the colours.

He lets her, the dip of his paint-stained stomach rising and falling with his quickened breaths. Taught with anticipation, he blinks up at her, his green eyes sparkling, as she arranges herself over his hips.

She hopes he feels loved.

She hopes having her astride him makes him feel wanted.

She hopes he knows she needs him.

The grin he's giving her is wide, and she can feel his delight like sunbeams on her face.

I've never known love before.

Why deprive yourself of it while it's right here?

She's ready, and pushes him into her, all of him, and Lorkan arches up, his groan loud enough to level the mountains.

Perhaps it *has* levelled the mountains, the way the very ground seemed to quiver.

Pausing, Meren settles herself as her rainbow-coloured prince pants below her, opening his closed eyes enough to give her a sloppy, love-sick grin.

With her weight, his fit is so deep the tip of him is grazing her soul, brushing against it.

Drunkenly, he reaches up with a paint-stained hand. The circle he draws over her heart matches his own.

Tentatively, she shifts her hips in a minute, grinding circle.

Thank the gods Lorkan has his own corner of the palace.

34

AN ADVENTURE

It is Lorkan who suggests they bathe, the words more tactile than audible, a deep rumbling of letters against Meren's throat.

Lazy and sated in his arms, she wonders how she'll manage to tease the paint from her hair in the washroom sink. Perhaps fill it, and tip her head forward? As if reading her thoughts, her prince adds:

"You'll bathe in the bath with me, of course."

※ ☾ ※

Meren stands on the lip of the bath as she watches a pool grow in the centre of it, crystalline water pouring from the heavy taps, distorting the delicate little tiles. She's still unclothed, and feels her skin tighten as spray leaps out to nips at it, sucking it into gooseflesh. She doesn't care. She wouldn't mind if shards of ice are mingled with the frigid water, so long as she gets to enter this glorious lido-like bath.

Lorkan had carried her to his washroom, placing her down gently by the colourful little bottles and climbing ivy. He'd fetched her dress from the studio, and fresh clothes for himself, then pulled a thick cord hung by the door.

Somewhere in the distance, Meren knew a bell had jingled. She pictured her peers back down in the bowels of the palace scurrying about, sparking fires under swelled boilers, redirecting the pipes. Guilt nibbles, turning her excitement an ugly colour and, quickly, she tries to think of something else.

It takes a few moments for the water to shift from crisp glacial runoff to seething liquid. It hisses as it meets the water already in the tub, mixing to form a comfortable temperature somewhere close to a good, hot meal.

Crouched by the taps, Lorkan scents it with oils as it gushes from the pipes. Steam begins to rise, moist and fragrant.

"You're making the bath warm," Meren worries, sort of a question, sort of not.

The hard blades of his shoulders shift about his back as he upturns another miniature bottle. It spits out little rocks, like chunks of table salt—but pink as blossom, and weighed down by the strong musk of rose oil.

"Of course."

"But won't it hurt you?"

Standing, he steps up behind her, looping his long arms about her middle. He's still half-hard, having never fully settled down to begin with, and becomes more so as his hips meet the soft curve of her back. He dips his head to mouth at her ear, a smirk curling his words.

"I'd walk through flames for you, my love."

Leaning back into him, cheeks red from his touch, his sentiment, and the humid air, Meren feels her lip twitch. "Well then, I'd brave blizzards for you, my prince."

A laugh rolls through him, and her lips widen with a grin.

There's something exciting about standing here, naked. She's not supposed to be naked here. She's not really supposed to be naked anywhere—even when showering in the servant's washroom, she scrubs a sponge over herself as quickly as possible, itching to retreat back into some form of decency.

She would be nervous about being naked here, now, but Lorkan is naked too and she likes the crackling sparks their nerves make as they touch. She couldn't feel it before, when she'd kissed him wearing her lovely green dress, or her stiff brown uniform.

And, if she thinks about it, she's not completely naked—not really. Paint still clings to her, cracked and drying, shrouding her like the finest, most delicate wisps of satin.

Lorkan rubs a gold scuff of it at the ridge of her hip bone, the nail of his thumb pushing away the flaking crumbs. They fall into the bathwater, eaten up by the swelling mounds of foam.

☾

When Meren eases herself into the bath, the sweet foam swallows her too, engulfing her bare shoulders. She melts into it—the clean, mellow embrace of the sweet water flecked with spice—letting the warmth come right up to tickle her chin.

'*I shouldn't be in here.*'

The thought throws itself up into her brain. She half wonders whether the bathwater will somehow know that—the oils merging to create greasy hands that'll tug her to the bottom and drown her like the imposter that she is—

But they don't. They run over her skin, slick and smooth, caressing it, soothing it like a lover.

As he joins her, Meren regards *her* lover carefully, checking for a wince of discomfort, a flinch of pain as the heat bites into him—

But, thankfully, Lorkan's expression remains serene and apparently untroubled.

He sinks below the surface momentarily, submerging himself right to the crown of his head. When he rises, the gold pigment matted into his hair has liquified, merging with the infinite darkness like comets streaking a night's sky.

"I was thinking..." he says, feeling for the protruding edge of the bath's wall.

It makes a simple seat and, when he finds it, he sprawls there, taking Meren's waist and easing her onto his lap.

Straddling the steady strength of his thighs, lets her shoulders ease back to settle into the curve of his lanky figure. A smile tugs the corner of her lip. "That's worrying."

His chuckle sends ripples out across the water, a physical manifestation of something usually invisible. "No, it's just curious how I can be so sad—and yet so *happy*—all at the same time."

Meren feels the pads of his lips press a kiss to the side of her neck.

It isn't even a kiss, really—he's just holding them against her, feeling her pulse thrum tiredly beneath his touch.

This is a new tired, a wonderful tired that has come from doing nothing really at all.

"I was thinking the same thing yesterday."

Rubbing slow patterns over her ribs, Lorkan starts climbing them, one, then the next, then the next. One hand cradles her breast while the other splays over her belly, and Meren can feel how much he's enjoying himself against her lower back.

Automatically, she spreads herself open to him, her head falling back to rest on his shoulder.

The hand on her stomach gives the softness there a small squeeze. "I'm obsessed with this," he purrs, setting her spine vibrating. "I used to worry that, if I touched you, you'd crumple like parchment."

She bites her tongue about how she and Alfdis used to have the same concerns about him. "I *felt* like crumpling, sometimes," she confesses.

When the hours were long and the mornings cold, and her breakfast was nothing but a dry round of rye, she'd often wondered whether a strong gust of wind would be enough to whip her out to sea. Perhaps it could—she had felt so light on the inside, between her ribs where her heart sits. There was nothing there, nothing keeping her weighed down to the ground.

She smiles. "I don't feel that way anymore, though."

"You shouldn't have had to feel that way at *all*." Lorkan growls, clearly nettled—yet his touch remains so gentle. "There's so much blasted gold in this fucking palace and yet its employees are living off grains."

He's sort of massaging her, sort of playing with her, teasing her, enjoying her, and she's finding it hard to catch his words through her contented haze.

"When I was a very small child, I tried to snap a finger off a gold statue of my great-grandfather."

Meren listens, his youth still such an oddity. She collects his stories like sea shells washed up on a beach.

If she were to tell him about her childhood, the word *'gold'* would not make an appearance at all—unless to describe swaying wheat and the sunsets that came in like the tide.

"I'd planned to give it to a maid I'd seen stoking the fire in my father's chambers. She was covered in soot, but I knew her hair was grey underneath it all. I'd hoped she could use it to retire comfortably, but I wasn't strong enough to break it."

"What happened to her?" Meren asks, trying to ignore his hands and their stroking. His description doesn't match anyone she's ever seen in the mess hall, and her heart sinks as he confirms her suspicions.

"I think she passed away. I swore that if ever the throne somehow fell to me —may the gods forbid it—I'd have all those useless trinkets melted down and handed around the kingdom." He kisses her neck properly this time, parting his jaw so his tongue can lap at a bruise he'd sucked earlier—a pink stamp in the shape of his mouth.

She hums distractedly. "You don't want to be king?"

"No. I don't want to be a prince either. I'm sick of niceties and duties and not being able to go into town or walk along the docks. I can't go where I please, when I please—*marry* whom I please. It's like living in a painting."

Having seen Lorkan's paintings, Meren doesn't think that sounds so bad. Although, who knows—perhaps being surrounded by vibrant colour would make one's eyes ache, after a while.

"If I *were* king, though," he muses absently, "I guess I could rule the kingdom my way. Get rid of some of the niceties, some of the gold. Like the walls. They're limestone, mostly, underneath it all. We could peel some off with a cheese grater and hand it around."

"We?"

"Well, yes. If the throne were mine, you would rule beside me." A rough scrape of his teeth at her throat, his hand thoroughly enjoying the softness of her breast. The palm at her belly slips down to play softly with that ache between her legs. "Or on top of me."

Meren pushes against his touch, and his voice is rough as he mutters:

"Or under me." He takes her hips as if to lift her, but she eases herself from his lap instead, moving next to him and slotting herself neatly under his arm.

"You've touched me already," she says, surprised at the low, sultry tone of her own voice.

He opens his mouth as if to object—

But closes it again submissively as her palm meets his chest.

"It's your turn."

He remains still as her hand wanders down, farther, following taught, coiled muscles until it meets with the impressive length of him.

Lorkan hisses at the touch. It tastes nice as she kisses him, finding his mouth already open, wide and desperate and ravenous.

In an attempt to push deeper into her grip, Meren feels him lift his hips, but she moves her hand with him, swallowing his tormented whine.

"How does your own medicine taste?" She asks, slipping the warm pad of her thumb teasingly over his silken skin. Her touch slips softly, barely a whisper.

He chuckles, but shakily, one of his hands desperately clutching the tiled lip of the bath.

She leans up to kiss him—because she can't seem to stop doing that—his lips plush and red. She takes the bottom one between her teeth and, when he moans, she swallows it like candy. "Do that again."

He has to bite off a chunk of air to reply with a flash of teeth. "Tighten your grip and I won't be able to help it."

Curiously, slowly—*tortuously* slowly—she strokes down to the base of him, then back up, right to his painfully sensitive tip.

Lorkan's smirk turns into a breathless little sob. "Wren...*please—*"

How can she resist that?

※ ☾ ※

Lorkan wriggles under Meren's assault, then, mustering all his strength with a pained growl, swaps them around, pressing her against the smooth edge of the bath. Instantly, he uses one hand to nudge her knees apart, and she lets him eagerly, clawing at his back to drag him in closer.

He takes her there in the frothy water, her name ricocheting off the curved walls.

Afterwards, Lorkan sponges the paint still scarring Meren's back with long, gentle strokes and, when he offers his shoulders to her, she lovingly rubs away each scuff of colour he'd gained when she'd ridden him on the table. He loosens as though it feels good, and hums shamelessly when she washes his hair, the blackness of it wound about her fingers as though she's kneading the night.

WHAT LORKAN IS

The bath has cooled by the time they're more or less clean, and he gives her a plush towel to dry herself with.

She can't help glancing at his lean, powerful form as he tends to his own dampness, his skin glistening white—besides a few remaining patches of cornflower blue.

They're light, as though shrouded—like the summer sky through a pale cloud.

No matter how many times Meren had run over them with the sea sponge, she hadn't managed to shift the stubborn pigment—but she guessed it didn't matter. If they hadn't come off in the water, she doubts they'd stain his clothing.

And, after all, they are quite pretty.

※ ☾ ※

That evening, Meren tucks her freshly washed hair up into the tightest bun she can muster, prodding in several more pins than necessary just to make sure the glossy strands—and the lingering scent of oils and spices—won't tumble free and give her away.

She has prepared a lie and keeps it ready, folded into quarters—something about the prince insisting she fragrance the water she uses to mop his floors—

But she doesn't need it.

No one asks.

They're all too busy with their own lives, wrapped up in endless to-do lists, racing towards the end so they may sleep, then do them all over again.

Once more, Meren will be one of them, come summer.

She elbows that thought aside.

※ ☾ ※

Several weeks slip by, and winter reluctantly eases into spring, although it's difficult to tell. The air warms a little, though the sun is often swamped by swollen clouds, and the trees are late to bud.

As Meren had predicted, Lorkan hadn't started a new painting, and now there is insufficient time for that to change. Little does it matter, though; they are mutually agreed that their new activities are far more amusing.

Each morning, he greets her with a long kiss, which sometimes leads to him scooping her up and carrying her to one corner of his chambers or another.

He's taken her on a chaise lounge, the sofas, the rugs—even the thick bearskin by the fireplace. Together, they'll spread out blankets and heap pillows like a nest on the hard floor, or tug the heavy curtains behind Meren's back so Lorkan can take her against the wall.

The only place he has not taken her is the bed.

"If we make love in a bed, Wren," he'd promised into her ear when she'd asked him about it. "I want it to be ours."

They draw together, they clean together, and they wash together. They tend Lorkan's plants, picking things from stems and roots to drop into pots bubbling and frying in the fireplace. When the light begins to drain from the sky, they light wax sticks and curl up in a chair so they can read to each other from the numerous leather-bound volumes lining each wall.

They may be contained in Lorkan's chambers, the key jammed into the lock, but each book takes them on adventures far beyond the borders.

Presently, Lorkan is reading aloud from a squat little pocketbook, the letters pinpricks of ink, the story large and sprawling as an ocean. Earlier, he'd made a hot drink of milk and cocoa, and Meren sips it happily, wrapped in his heavy arms and a throw blanket darned with moons.

After a little while, his sentence pitters out as though it's run out of momentum, and she draws the mug away from her lips.

"Why have you stopped?"

WHAT LORKAN IS

It takes a few moments for him to reply, his pale hand rubbing a sun-yellowed page through finger and thumb. His voice comes from just behind her head, the syllables getting caught in her hair. "What if we went somewhere else tomorrow?"

"You mean sit in the study rather than the lounge?" She thinks about it. "The chairs aren't big enough for the both of us, but I guess—"

"No," Lorkan interrupts gently. "I meant...why don't we go somewhere else in the palace?"

Meren's most recent gulp of cocoa rises a little in her throat, singeing her tonsils, the burn sickly sweet.

"Lor, you know why we can't do that. What if we're seen together? Best case scenario: I'll be dismissed—without a reference—due to misconduct. Worst case: imprisonment."

"I won't let any harm come to you or your position," he says it so firmly, pressing the words into her palm so resolutely, she almost believes he has the power to make them true.

Almost.

"What about yours?"

"I'm leaving soon—uniting two war-scarred kingdoms. I could probably light Father's beard on fire and get forgiveness within a week. People who used to think me not even half my brother are now treating me like a king."

Meren knows his brows have furrowed with a frown.

"It's almost unnerving."

"Even so, they wouldn't let us keep seeing each other, would they? You're engaged, and I'm—" She doesn't know how to finish that sentence.

She doesn't know what she is anymore. Her days are spent in luxury, surrounded by fresh, clear sky and the lavish affection of her prince—

And her nights are spent on a straw-stuffed mattress in a shared room, the air prickly with dust and breath.

Half of her life takes place below the world, and the other half high above it.

Why can't it be somewhere in the middle? *On* the world, amongst regular folks like Aasta, and Frode, and the strangers wriggling down the crowded market pathways like ants through a crack in a flagstone.

She's sure *their* sweethearts aren't being used to hold two unstable kingdoms together. And she doubts any of them have fobbed off work to repeatedly fuck one of the—very much engaged—royal sons. All they have to worry about is plain, ordinary things: selling produce before it spoils, and selling enough of it to keep food on the table.

"We could go somewhere where even the guards aren't allowed," Lorkan breaks Meren's stupor. "Father's relic room. I told you I'd show it to you, and I intend to keep my promise. It's not hugely interesting, but it's quiet and empty and could be a nice change of pace."

Placing her mug on a nearby cabinet and wriggling around in his arms, Meren pushes herself up enough to give his mouth a long kiss. "Am I failing to amuse you, my prince?" She smirks, and he returns it, licking up the cocoa she'd left on his lips.

"Quite the contrary." His cool finger loops under her chin and tugs her back, for so long that her lungs ignite. "I'm just sick of these blasted rooms. Surely you must be too? Every other lover in the kingdom is treating his beau to fine meals and walks under the sunset—what am I doing?"

Meren wants to reassure him, but she's not sure she has the heart to snap his rose-coloured glasses in half—real life isn't much like the stories he reads to her, but he is.

"Lorkan, you've already given me more than anyone else ever could. Plus we do all those things in here—well, some of them." She smiles, trying to smooth out his frown. "Tomorrow evening we could travel from the entryway to the study and *call* it a sunset walk, if you like. Goodness knows the distance is far enough to qualify as one."

His mouth curves with a single-syllable chuckle—

But he still waves a hand, brushing aside her suggestion. "I've been thinking about it a lot—the Relics Vault. It could work. We'd have to keep out of the guards' sight on the way, but once we're there, we'll be all by ourselves."

WHAT LORKAN IS

Admittedly, the idea of exploring more of Aldercliff is hard to resist, and Lorkan nudges her.

"Come on, you know you want to. Didn't you tell me once that Father's treasures are—how did you put it? '*The stuff of legend*?"

Flushing at her earlier naivety, "Well, aren't they?"

He shrugs. "I don't see how blood-stained weapons deserve any degree of reverence, but they do have some interesting stories. Let me show them to you. I've wanted to take you out since I met you."

"Lor, we *are* going out. I'm dating you. You seduced me. Well done."

Flatly, "You know what I meant."

Rolling her eyes, Meren dithers. She takes a long sip from her mug. "I guess I *do* like the idea of sneaking about and hunting out treasures. We'd be just like Otto." She gestures to the book dwarfed in Lorkan's hand, forgotten.

He reads her face like *she's* a book, her worries written all over her cheeks in big letters. "But...?"

"But people like Otto aren't *real*. If he's caught in a tough spot, we know he'll find a way to wriggle out of it. Every story in the series has ended happily, but I'm isn't sure that *our* story will."

Frustratingly, Lorkan's shoulders rise and fall in a shrug. "I promise you, we won't be disturbed. Aldercliff is so large I've gone days without seeing anyone, and only royalty is allowed in the Relics Vault." Softly, he pries Meren's bottom lip from between her teeth.

She hadn't even realised she was gnawing it.

"No one should disturb us. It's not a romantic walk under the colours of dusk, granted, but it's an adventure. Sort of."

A crease forms between Meren's brows. "Only royalty is allowed in?"

"So?"

"So, *I'm* not royalty."

"Wren, darling." Kissing the corner of her mouth, Lorkan says against her lips:

"If we'd been permitted to wed, you *would* be royalty."

✶ ☾ ✶

And so it is settled. The next day, Meren and Lorkan will wait until the soothing cloak of afternoon, then creep from his rooms and down to King Cade's Relics Vault.

Despite the risk, Meren is excited for the change of pace, so much so her fizzing nerves wake her unnecessarily early. She bolts her breakfast—sketching with one hand and spooning oats into her mouth with the other—and is following the hill down to the market before the sun has properly dragged itself into the sky. She purchases a clean sketchbook, and some fresh charcoals from '*Thistle's Quills & 'Coal'*, then collects her usual sweet treats from Aasta.

Back in Holcombe, a barn owl often used to roost below the Hansen's roof each year, its wide face watching Meren come and go from tucked below the eaves.

Aasta reminds her of that owl, she thinks, as she blinks up at her. Both she and the owl would look at her like they know things.

She is sure Aasta knows exactly what she's about to do, and could have sworn *'be careful'* is laced into the baker's otherwise good-natured:

"See you tomorrow, pet."

When Meren arrives at Lorkan's chambers, his hair is wiry from his slim fingers raking through it, and the smile he gives her is wobbly.

He makes sure the door is closed, then kisses her. "We don't have to go to the Relics Vault if you don't want to. Yesterday morning, I saw the forsythia blooming from the window and it reminded me how little time we have left and...it frightened me. I wanted to do something different so all my memories of our time together don't merge into one—but, actually, I don't *mind* if they do. They're all similar but they're *happy*."

WHAT LORKAN IS

He kisses her nose, and her cheeks crinkle, which makes him do it again. "So happy. It's a stupid, risky thing to do, so I don't *mind* if you—"

"I want to," Meren assures, nodding her head. She runs a hand through his hair, smoothing it, and he leans into the touch.

He's let her twist in a few more braids since the first one, each one fastened with a little coil of twine.

She wonders if Cade and Lophia have asked why he'd started wearing knots in his hair.

They probably haven't.

"My memories are happy too—the happiest I've ever been."

He beams.

"But...you were right when you said I'm scared to do things I shouldn't. I don't want to be like that anymore." She smiles a proper smile, much more sturdy than his own. "Come on. It'll be an adventure."

35

THE BASEMENT

Meren waits in the safety of Lorkan's rooms as he checks the hallways, looking left and then right for stray maids, wandering royalty, or very lost members of the king's court.

Evidently, he finds no one, because he eases one foot over the threshold.

He waits a moment as though expecting a booby trap to spring, then, when one doesn't, he turns back to Meren with a shrug of his wide shoulders.

"It's fine, no one's about." He appears nonchalant enough, one end of his mouth twitching up in his trademark smirk.

The same can not be said for Meren, her ribcage all alight with little licking flames of excitement—and she's not even out the door yet. Rubbing a centimetre of her crisp maid's dress anxiously between finger and thumb:

"Are you sure?" she asked stupidly and feels her cheeks dust pink as Lorkan laughs.

"Yes, I'm sure—unless someone's hiding in a cupboard. No one really comes around this part of the palace; that's why I picked it."

WHAT LORKAN IS

She knows he's right, and yet when she follows his lead—vacating the sanctuary of their private little patch of Velôr—she does so with cautious, tentative steps.

Lorkan waits patiently while she edges over to his side. When she's close enough, he touches a comforting hand to the small of her back.

It makes her jump several centimetres off the ground, and he stifles a chuckle. "Wren, we don't have to—"

"No, I want to," she presses, although she's still trying to even out her breathing.

Casting her a sideways look, he locks the door, dropping the key into his pocket.

It's gold, the metal twisted and knotted as though still molten, the bow shaped like a pointed leaf of ivy.

"*That's* your key?"

"Yes, I had it made. Why? What's wrong?"

"I always wondered what yours looked like. The one Alfdis gave me is so boring," Meren huffs, presenting her own drab slab of a thing from her apron.

"Well, of course mine's going to be better. I *live* there."

"I *know*. It's just nice, is all."

"Fine." Lorkan shrugs his wide shoulders, reaching back into his pocket. "Swap, if you're going to get all stroppy about it."

☀ ☾ ☀

Meren's joy is short-lived, her new and improved key quickly forgotten as they take up an easy walk. Like a child, she finds herself wanting to take Lorkan's hand—the long corridor suddenly bringing on a bout of vertigo— but thinks better of it. The hallways are clear now, but someone could round a corner at any moment. Their rehearsed lie will be easier to deliver *without* their fingers intertwined.

"We can turn back if you're scared," he assures kindly enough, although his lip is still doing that smirky thing, and she huffs at him—partly because she still can't grab a proper lungful of air.

"I'm not scared, I'm excited." She tries to match his long strides, and he notices, slowing enough to let her catch up.

"So," she challenges, gesturing to two sets of stairs, one spirals up into the heavens, sunlight pouring down it like a fountain, and the other buries downwards, the bottom glinting like pennies at the bottom of a well.

"Which way is it?"

Lorkan gestures to the set on the right: long, slender bars of gold pressed seamlessly into the palace floor. The sooty afternoon light dulls them, darkening them into teeth lining a huge, open maw.

"Down."

※ ☾ ※

Before each new corridor, Meren waits for Lorkan to give her the all-clear, then scurries to match his footsteps. His pale feet are silent, hers slippered and quick, like a rabbit racing for a burrow.

The palace, predictably empty, they encounter no one and brave a few small, quiet conversations—usually about statues or paintings they pass along the way. Many are of Lorkan's relatives—grizzled, war-scarred men as large and fierce as bears, and regal, powerful women whom Meren doubts even her mother would be able to boss around.

"I'll be up there one day," Lorkan points out. "I'll look quite out of place, won't I?"

WHAT LORKAN IS

They take every one of Lorkan's shortcuts and lesser-known passageways, but now and again, they still catch the occasional hum of conversation behind closed doors. Descending into Aldercliff's core, Meren wonders if they're going right down to the servant's quarters. However, as they near the bend where she would usually turn off to reach the entrance, Lorkan takes a right, leading them in the opposite direction.

Eventually, the windows fade into lit sconces, and the gold and marble gives way to gritty limestone. Meren struggles to drink in the size of the palace, trying to remember how many turns they'd taken, how many flights of stairs.

It must have been a lot because they're at the basement levels now, the air stuffy, eerily still, and sickly sweet with burning beeswax.

"How do you remember where you're going?" she asks quietly, the wax sticks bowing as they pass.

"Honestly? Smells, mostly," Lorkan admits with a small laugh. It bounces about the low ceiling, doubling over on itself.

Meren isn't sure if he's joking. After all, she herself had located the royal kitchens by following the lingering scent of breakfast, and could probably use the cheap tang of wax stick smoke to find the servants' quarters with her eyes closed.

"If my magic was more powerful, we wouldn't have to go this way," he apologises, frustrated. "I could have disguised us somehow."

Meren watches curiously as he holds out one hand, the light from the sconces staining it yellow.

His fingers flicker, his bony joints fading like a mirage. His nails disappear with a fuzzy shifting of particles and—even though Meren knows it to be magic—a bolt still zig-zags its way up her spinal column.

What if he slips up, metaphorically, and casts the wrong spell? What if he tears off those fingers she's so fond of, or accidentally rips his atoms apart one by one? What if his cells never come back?

But, of course, they do. They return as soon as he grows tired with the effort of shrouding them, and she flushes at her ignorance.

Lorkan doesn't seem to notice. "I guess we could have taken the way Father uses to reach his trophy room—it *is* much grander to look at—but we'd probably be seen."

"It's okay, I like this way," Meren assures, and means it.

The usually shining floor has a light fluffiness to it, flecks of dust having been given a chance to settle—a rare and somewhat comforting sight.

"I feel like a mole."

He gives her a puzzled look, and she squints at him in the low light.

"You don't know what a mole is?"

When he still looks confused, she cups her hands, miming holding a tiny bundle of brown fuzz.

"They're little soft creatures that live in the dirt."

Lorkan's cheekbones cast long shadows down his face. "As a prince, I have little experience with dirt."

Meren can not imagine such a travesty. "I'm guessing you didn't make mud pies as a child."

"You ate *mud?*" He exclaims, appalled, and she can't help cackling with laughter.

"You don't *eat* it, you just pretend." Noticing the disgusted expression still well and truly plastered to his face, she clarifies:

"For fun."

"Oh. Didn't you have… you know…" He flushes guiltily. "Toys?"

"Not really. I assume you did?"

"Yes."

"Tell me about them."

"Are you sure?"

"Lorkan, I do *know* you're rich—I have noticed."

His cheeks redden again, sheepishly, and she elbows him lightly.

"Hey, I'm teasing. Come on, I'm interested."

"Well…since you asked: I spent my youth in the nursery. It's a big room where your parents can dump you with a nanny while they go off to do important things. It was the only room where we could make a mess, shout, and throw things—you know—building blocks, balls, and tantrums."

Meren snickers at the mental image of a tiny Lorkan stamping his little feet, and he brightens, encouraged.

"It's full of toys and it always will be—it just sits there, waiting. I guess it's spooky now, how quiet it is—like it's sleeping. It was fun when I was a child, though. We had wooden horses big enough to ride, pretend swords painted with red blood, and boxes of robes and hats for dressing up. There's even a model of Aldercliff with doors that open, glass windows, miniature tables and chairs, and four-poster beds. It was built for my great-great-grandmother, and her doll still lives inside with a king and a queen and all her brothers."

"I would have loved that when I was younger," Meren interjects. "I used to tie my hair ribbons around Mother's wooden spoons and pretend they were people."

The corner of Lorkan's lip curves as he falls in love with her all over again. "I would have happily played a game of spoon-people with you—I wasn't so keen on the doll's house. The paint on the king's face had started to peel away, and the little platters of pretend food were all starting to look like they'd gone off, so Mother sent it away to be touched up."

"What's wrong with that?"

He shrugs. "The people came back all wrong. The king's friendly eyes had been dabbed over with soulless black dots, and the queen and princess's lips had been painted with these clownish, big red mouths. Sol and I stopped playing with them after that."

"*You* should have painted them," Meren points out, which sets Lorkan smiling again. "You would have done a much better job of it."

"That's what Sol said."

They descend another set of stairs, these ones bitten and chewed by the passing of time, their edges rounded and crumbling. A spider, perhaps decades ago, has tied a sconce in a feathery web, and Meren asks:

"Did you have any pets?"

"Ponies when I was young, horses when I was grown. Sol and I begged Father for a dog, but he said he wouldn't have any dirty mongrels pissing up his gold pillars, so we never got one."

Meren's lips purse as she forced herself to swallow a sharp word. "My mother is the same, so we didn't have any animals either—but we lived next door to a farm. The other kids and I used to chase the sheepdogs and bothered the hens. We used to see how close we could get to the geese without them hissing at us."

"You used to chase *geese,* and now you're scared of little old Alfdis?"

"Ah, but the geese didn't pay my salary."

Lorkan's green eyes roll, glinting like gems. "You know I'd set you up for life, if you asked me."

"I *do* know that, and that is why I do not ask."

✶ ☾ ✶

It is perhaps a good thing that Cade's Relics Vault is buried deep into the earth, because Meren and Lorkan's conversation has become excited and giggly by the time they near it.

Meren said that if they could have wed, she would have bought Lorkan a big, black, shaggy mutt, and they'd live in a squat little countryside cottage surrounded by molehills, perfect for mud pies.

Lorkan had added things—a pretty view for him to paint and Meren to draw, and a bed all of their own squashed tight into a too-small second room.

However, their laughter dribbles to a stop as the corridor widens out into a vast, cave-like hall.

Every surface rough grey stone, there's nothing to look at besides two dark slabs of marble.

They loom, high and heavy like sentries, and Meren half expects them to fall flat, crushing her bones into a fine powder against the flagstones.

WHAT LORKAN IS

Two ring pull handles hang like empty eye sockets, and they glower as she scuttles at Lorkan's side, so close the stiff cotton of her dress rubs against his satin shirt.

"Why aren't there any guards?" she realises aloud. "I thought the relics were worth stealing."

"They are. That's why Father never lets anyone down here, even staff."

"And you're *sure* this isn't the dungeons?" Straining her ears, she listens for the distant wailings of tortured souls. She's never seen a dungeon, but this place is the sort of thing that comes to mind when she pictures one. All that's missing are the rattling cries of anguish—although it is entirely possible the impenetrable walls are muffling them like a gag about the mouth.

It's a wonder there's enough air for the sconces to chew on.

Lorkan chuckles, taking hold of one of the door's gargantuan handles. It swamps both his hands, making him look as though he's been shrunk down to two feet tall.

The door heaves open with a great scraping of cold stone, a chink growing between it and its counterpart. Usually, chinks are bright, promising things—

But this one is dark and infinite and musty; a universe stuffed to the back of a cupboard and forgotten about.

Lorkan ceases pulling when the gap is just large enough for him to wriggle through.

Meren waits, her slipper pawing the ground. It's almost sandy, the limestone walls silently flaking off, atom by atom, slowly forming a desert. Behind them, layers of dirt sit dormant, ancient.

The silence becomes deafening.

Sheepishly, she peers over the edge of the universe. "Lor?"

A pale hand emerges, motioning for her to follow. "Aren't you coming?"

She dithers.

From inside, his voice sparks, burns, dies out like a match:

"I promise they're not dungeons."

Biting off a breath, Meren slips between the doors as quickly as she can, waiting for them to close, squatting her like a gnat between two palms.

When she turns around, though, they haven't moved. There is a chink now: a narrow strip of light.

Lorkan pulls them closed with a full thud, encapsulating them both inside like a tomb and, blindly, Meren finds the solid trunk of his waist and clings to it.

He chuckles, but a heavy, comforting hand presses to her back. "Hey, you okay?"

She gives a meek little squeak.

Cade's Relics Vault is just as dark and foreboding as its vestibule, although that could be because the only source of light is a small fire fluttering away in a deep bowl by the door. A charred-looking torch is propped up against the pillar supporting the bowl, and Meren lets Lorkan take her to it through the darkness.

"Here we go." He stoops to light the torch, and she watches as he touches it to a faint mark on the ground.

Coals jump to life, illuminating a streak of fire scored into the ground like a rain gutter.

"It's a lot more creepy in here than I remember," he muses absently as the room comes into focus.

The line of fire is still going, snaking off into the distance.

Meren briefly wonders if the room goes on forever.

It looks like it does, the marble walls rich and dark as tar. They're completely void of markings, carvings, paintings—and yet Meren still gets the sense she's being watched.

If he wasn't holding a lit stick of fire, she would have given Lorkan's arm a little tug. "Are you sure I'm allowed in here?" A furtive glance about for swinging battle axes or automated crossbows. "The room doesn't...*know* I'm not royalty, does it?"

He throws her an easy smile. "It's not cursed, if that's what you mean."

"Oh, good."

"It's guarded with a sentinel enchantment, but it's so old now my blue blood will mask you easily."

WHAT LORKAN IS

"Wait, what?"

"You'll be *fine.*" A smirk plays just behind his lips. "Probably."

"Lorkan," Meren growls, "that's not funny."

He shrugs, the light from his torch dancing with the movement. "It was a *little* funny. Your eyes went all big."

"Is it *really* cursed?"

"No, I specifically said it *wasn't* cursed."

"Okay, protected by magic, then." She hooks her fingers into air quotes, throwing rabbit ear shadows onto the walls.

"Oh, yes, that's definitely real."

"Why didn't you tell me that *before* I went through the massive scary doors?"

"Because you wouldn't have gone through them if I had."

"Exactly!" Meren scowls, but she does feel safer with his joy softening the still air—even if it is at her expense.

With the sconces lit, shapes begin to hove into view: waist-height blocks of stone placed in equal increments along both walls. They hold objects, just like the one supporting the bowl of fire that, now that Meren looks closer, she realises is burning without fuel.

"This fire is eating nothing but rocks," she points out, narrowing her eyes at it with suspicion. She had wondered whether it was fire at all, but when she reaches for it, its heat bites and snarls at her fingertips.

"That's The Infinite Flame," Lorkan says from behind her, making her jump, and this time she does give him a prod with one elbow. He just laughs. "It's been burning forever, but no one really knows how."

"I wish I could parcel some up and send it to my parents," she muses, half-joking. "They'd never have to pay for kindling again."

He hums in his throat. "A nice idea, but if it got out of hand, we wouldn't be able to put it out."

"Oh." Meren thinks for a second. "What if we had some...infinite water?"

His lip quirks. "Water that never dries up?"

"Exactly."

"Well, Father doesn't have any of that. He has got a rock that he says can summon monsters; do you want to see that instead?"

36

THE STORM IN THE JAR

As the yellow light of the sconces wriggle with dust, Lorkan leads Meren down the centre of the room, pointing out each treasure and explaining what they do—if he can remember.

If he can't, they try to make it up.

A hand made entirely out of gold that Lorkan says was probably someone's first go at making an oven glove.

An engraved tablet that Meren suggests translates into the first dick joke.

A pillaged statue with its head missing, which Lorkan jokes his grandfather left behind because it was ugly.

When they come across a helmet the size of a sink, he hefts it from its stand and slots it onto Meren's head, keeping hold of one thick horn to help her support its weight.

She giggles as it falls over her eyes, the sound echoing around the inside, bumping into her smile.

There are other things they can pick up too—heavy cloaks, rare elements, blood-encrusted weapons.

"I understand the appeal of keeping mementoes from battles," Meren muses as she watches Lorkan pluck up a rusted longsword experimentally. Brown blood seems to ooze from the weapon itself like sap from a tree. "But why keep the gore?"

He brandishes the blade in both hands, turning it this way and that. The slick metal should have flashed threateningly, but the light can't reach it through the matted, gunky chunks of residue.

"I know," he sighs, placing it back onto its stand with distaste. "My Father really is quite disgusting."

Meren has to try to stifle a laugh. "You shouldn't say that."

"Why not? He'll never know—and it's true, isn't it? Most of these things were made to kill, and the rest he stole like a petty thief." He raises one dark eyebrow at a rock tablet, a detailed diagram carved carefully into its delicate stone. "He probably doesn't even know what half of this does."

"To be fair," Meren quips, "nor do you."

"Ah, but you see, Wren, darling, they do not belong to me." He gestures about him, encompassing the entire palace in his arms. "None of this does, and Father seems to want to keep it that way."

"What do you mean?"

"As the youngest son, there is little chance the throne will fall to me—but there is a *chance*. You'd think I'd receive training for that eventuality, wouldn't you? No matter how slight."

"Of course. If, may the gods forbid, something were to happen to Sol, you would—"

"Exactly. But I am rarely trusted with the responsibility of running messages to his council, let alone taught how to run his kingdom."

Meren's forehead knits. Lorkan's mind is sharp and quick; surely his input would be useful for something better than couriering notes between bearded old men?

"Maybe it's best Father doesn't know how to use half of these things," he's saying, eyeing the row of objects they'd passed. Their ominous shadows stretch to climb up the walls, elongated and flickering as though awakened. "Who knows what he'd use them for."

She feels her lips press into a line.

Meren and Lorkan's moods had turned sullen, but they're soon laughing again; Meren finds the broken breastplate of a giantess warrior queen, and points out that it's large enough for her to use as a sledge. Lorkan watches her climb into it, then suddenly gives the edge a shove with one foot, sending her whizzing down the centre of the room.

Their smiles help to soften the hard walls, their laughter bringing some of the dead air to life.

Between their jesting, Meren takes a few quick moments to genuinely appreciate the treasures around her. When they get back to Lorkan's chambers, she'll search his bookshelves for information on the things they'd not understood, she decides.

"The Infinite Hard Candy?" He suggests as they reach a vaguely glowing green stone. "No matter how long you suck it, it doesn't get any smaller."

Meren snorts, although she'd been a little distracted.

The end of the room has appeared: a sheer block of obsidian rising out of the darkness like a gravestone. The ground rises in chunks to create a wide, low stage, where one pedestal remains—taller and grander than the rest. Framed by that final wall like a picture heavy with negative space sits a cylinder, roughly the size of a biscuit tin.

It's a curved jar of thick glass, clutched tightly between two jaws of metal at either end. Although too frosted to see inside, it clearly contains something blue—its colour throwing itself against the glass, writhing, stirring, churning like a restless storm. Perhaps there is a storm inside; Meren can feel its chill tickling the air, nibbling her fingers like winter.

'What's this? The Infinite Ice cube for Our King's lemonade?'

She'll turn around and present it to Lorkan as she says it—

No, she'll press it to him like a cold pack:

'Does Lophia hold this to Cade's forehead when he has a temperature?'

She has to tiptoe to climb the pedestal's slither of a stage and curiously pads closer to the cylinder, as though it's an animal she doesn't want to wake.

There's something familiar about the chill of it.

Meren's quips and jokes dribble absently from her mind as she reaches out a hand. Her fingers cool gently as she nears the glass's smooth surface, the cold like a playful breeze. Pressing the pad of a forefinger to it, she feels it wriggle into her skin, right through her bone marrow, like a tongue against ice cream.

It makes her smile.

Gingerly, unsure about what to expect in terms of its weight, she takes an end in each hand, the carved metal bowing into what could be considered handles.

Tendrils of light sway dreamily on the other side of the glass like sleeping snakes, but they twist as Meren eases the cylinder free of its stand.

It looks like a bottle left out on a cold winter's night: frost-prickled and heavy with ice.

It's heavy, but not too heavy to carry, and she turns, hefting it into the air. "Hey, Lor, do you think—"

"Meren!"

Before she can finish her joke—something about Cade using the cylinder as a nightlight—it's snatched from her in a scramble of limbs.

Lorkan's worried expression rakes over her bewildered frown. He looks almost ghostly in the low light, the faint blue glow of the mysterious cylinder reflecting off his snowy skin.

It takes Meren a moment to realise his eyes are hunting for something, roving her face.

She pales. "What's wrong?"

"I was always told not to touch this." He moistens his lips. "Are you alright?"

She thinks about it for a second, her pulse beating so hard she can almost hear it echoing off the inky black walls. "I think so. Why? What does it do?"

WHAT LORKAN IS

And then she sees it. As if the cylinder is answering her question, a pale blue tinge begins to blossom at Lorkan's knuckles.

At first, Meren had thought it was a reflection; his porcelain fingers throwing the glass's blue hue back at itself—
But it's growing now, those patches of blue, creeping up his arms and pooling at his elbows.
Her mouth opens, but her tongue is dry of words.
Lorkan follows her eyes.
All at once, he's overcome by a look of fear that she has never seen on him—on anyone. His whole body freezes up as though the cylinder of frigid air had opened and solidified him in place.
A swell of that blue begins to bud at his collarbone like mould, and Meren darts forward, wrenching the cylinder from his hands.
It had felt cool before, but it's almost freezing now, searing her palm, and she almost drops it back onto its pedestal.
It grates against the hard stone, and she wipes her hands frantically on her dress as though she's contaminated. She feels contaminated—and Lorkan—
Gods, *Lorkan*—
"Are you okay—?!" A stupid question, but an important one. One that should be shouted, hurled, caught and thrown back—
But it comes out as a little pitiful squeak. She reaches for him, to soothe his worried skin, but he jerks away as though her touch were fire.

"Don't!"

"I'm sorry!" She scrapes the words out, shaking her head, "I'm sorry, Lorkan, I didn't—"

"No, I mean don't come any closer," his eyes are shining and wide like a startled deer, and Meren feels her face crumple. "I might be cursed."

She tries to wet her sandy tongue. "Do you *feel* cursed?"

He's so still for a moment that she fears it's already taken effect—but then he shakes his head. "No. But—what does a curse feel like?" His voice has gone all shaky, stumbling over itself, bumping into his teeth.

Meren's eyes are wet and it makes him look fuzzy; all green and white and blue—*so much blue.*

"I don't know." She tries to get closer again but he's holding up his palms as if she's brandishing a blade. She drags a knuckle over her eyes. "We'll fix it," she promises, each word falling, shattering around her feet. "Whatever it is we'll fix it; we'll go to your father, he might know what it is—"

Suddenly, more panicked than before:

"No! No, we need to get Mother, she'll know—she's better at—"

The sky-blue tinge to his cells is starting to subside, Meren notices with a drunken sort of relief. It's collecting like droplets of oil, shrinking away, easing back like low tide.

She reaches to take his arm without thinking but stops herself. "Okay, you go to your rooms, I'll get Lophia. Lor, I'm so sorry, I didn't think—"

He hasn't moved yet, his bare feet still planted firmly to the floor as if they've grown firm little roots.

She wants to grab him, to pull him—somewhere, anywhere—away from *here*. Suddenly, the blocks of marble and gold above their heads seems to grow, the whole palace swelling up, becoming fat and bloated and stiflingly suffocating. Meren could swear the ceiling has sagged a few inches under its weight, the obsidian bowing—streaked with cracks like bursting blood vessels. She pictures the earth on either side of them—miles of it, too deep for worms, compact as rock—and grabs for Lorkan's shirt before he can stop her.

She gets a handful of it, the buttons digging into her flesh.

His heart thumps like a fist below her grasp.

With a hard yank, she begins to drag him.

"Lor, we have to go *now*, we don't know how long—" she can't bring herself to finish that sentence. She pulls him harder, all of him, with everything she has, until he stumbles slightly.

It seems to break his daze because he nods quickly.

"Come to my rooms with me, you touched it too, you might—" he chokes on the very thought. "Get a guard. They're everywhere, find someone and ask them to bring Mother. They'll be faster, they know where they're going."

431

WHAT LORKAN IS

Overcome with new urgency, he matches Meren's pace, his long legs quickly overtaking her. She doesn't want to let go of his shirt, she doesn't want to let him go at all, so she doesn't, not even when they're sprinting down the main corridor.

Only an hour ago they'd weaved up through these golden tunnels, laughing—

But now their giggles are shallow intakes of iron-tasting breath.

'It's hard to find any breath here,' Meren thinks as they run, the air too sweet, too silent, too thick.

Lorkan's feet are falling hard beside hers. "This was stupid of me," he apologises in five exhales—he's said it eleven times now and each one is like a swift punch to Meren's solar plexus. "I'm so sorry."

"Don't be, really, please, it's my fault—"

"But if I hadn't taken you down there—"

"I shouldn't have touched it." Her brows draw together, but not in anguish —in rage. "Why can't I just learn to leave things alone?"

"Don't say that; your curiosity is one of the things I love about you. It was me who—"

"Does the curse make you unbelievably stupid or something?" she gasps.

How long is this tunnel?

She hears a shaky laugh and, amongst the fear, finds a smile on Lorkan's face. "Seriously," she snaps. "None of this would have happened if I hadn't looked at that drawing you threw out. I should have just done my *job*— "

She's not talking about the curse anymore, she realises.

She trips on an uneven flagstone.

Lorkan yanks her up.

Without stopping, they carry on.

"Meren, it's me who should learn to leave things alone; if I hadn't have asked Alfdis to make you my housemaid—"

"Okay, okay, we're both stupid." Another sideways glance at his bare wrists, his pale throat. "The blue is gone, I think. Is that good?"

The hallways finally spits them out into a bright corridor, and Meren internally rejoices at the sight of muggy daylight. It's staining Lorkan white, bleaching him like a bedsheet.

"I don't know," he pants. "But Gods, I missed the sky."

37

A TALE OF FIRE AND SNOW

Spilling onto the sixteenth floor, Lorkan bolts himself in his chambers while Meren scrabbles for a member of the Royal Guard.

She finds one by following the rhythmic clanking of armour, each step hacking away at the silence. She's patrolling the corridor alone, her legs moving stiffly like a wind-up toy soldier, her eyes glazed over as though painted on. She blinks, somewhat startled, as Meren comes to a panting halt in front of her, her face wet and salty from sweat and tears.

She throws a bunch of words at her golden helmet—*urgent* and *Lorkan* and *Lophia*—and the guard sprints away like a box of symbols.

Meren's lungs smoulder as she forces herself back the other way and kicks her legs into a jog.

She has to use her new key to shove her way into Lorkan's rooms, the metal warm where it had sat against her thigh. She finds him in the lounge, perched on the edge of a sofa, pale and hollow as empty bones.

His narrow bottom lip is caught tight between his teeth, and she wants to kiss it free. She wants to pepper his rumpled forehead with affirmations, but she knows he'll just push her protectively away.

"How do you feel?"

"Okay. I think." He's looking up at her, his face like it's been wrung out. "How about you?"

"I'm fine. Don't worry about me." Her hand twitches, aching to at least settle on his back. "Your mother will be here soon. I should go hide in the study."

Lorkan's own fingers clench as though he wants to take her wrist. He's looking at her in a way she doesn't recognise. Quietly, he utters:
"You don't have to."

Despondently, she shakes her head. "Now isn't the time, Lor."

He sags.

"I'll be right behind the door."

"Okay, but if Mother brings bad news... you must come out. You'll need to be tended to. Promise me you'll be brave enough."

"I promise."

"Thank you. If anything were to happen to you—"

Meren kisses him, even though she knows she shouldn't. She uses it to push those words back down his throat, to ease the frown from between his eyes.

He forces himself from her grasp, but not right away. Not until that muscle by his jaw has slackened—until his hand has reached out and clasped her waist.

A knock rings through the room, and Meren wrenches herself away.

"Lophia will know what to do," she's saying, but the words are all breath. They have no weight to them, no substance.

Lorkan laps them up anyway.

He twists his mouth into a reassuring smile.

✺ ☾ ✺

WHAT LORKAN IS

Meren waits amongst great pillars of silence as Lorkan leaves to greet his mother.

Stowed safely in the study, she keeps the door ajar and tucks herself close to the gap. Thin as a hair, light from the window can barely suck in its stomach and enter. Sound, however—sound slithers through like smoke.

Meren inhales it, her ear pressed against the jamb.

She can't hear Lorkan's footfalls as he returns, but she can hear his hurried words and the soft pad of Lophia's satin slippers. Her skin prickles at her proximity.

She doesn't have to see Lophia to know she's a queen. Her grace swamps the room, almost choking it. How do her handmaidens manage to speak in her presence? To ask her which shawl she would like to wear, or how she would like them to fashion her waist-length hair? Meren is sure that, should she ever come face to face with Her Majesty, she wouldn't be able to say anything at all.

Lorkan doesn't seem to share her problem. She can hear him spinning a vague lie as they near the lounge—about how a book he'd been reading spiked a sudden wave of curiosity for one of his father's treasures, and he'd gone down to the relics room for a closer look. However, Meren knows he's being truly sincere as he says:

"I'm sorry. I know Father forbade me to touch it—although he never told me why. Maybe if he had, I would have feared it the way he wanted," he mutters, then sighs. "I don't know why I did it. It was just there, in the corner of my eye, and I got curious."

He must have fallen onto the settee because Lophia's gown rustles quietly as she lowers herself next to her son. Like Meren, she probably tries to touch him, only to have him shrink away.

"...Is it bad magic?" Lorkan asks.

For what feels like three days, Queen Lophia says nothing.

'*So?*' Meren wants to hurl the question like a snowball. '*Is it?*'

Has she not heard what has happened? Does she have nothing to say?

For a moment, Meren wonders if she's doing what her own mother would do when she misbehaved as a child; only replying with vague nods and uninterested hums until she begged for redemption.

"No, it's not bad magic," Lophia finally utters, her voice low and quiet. She doesn't sound angry, yet something grey and wan is laced in with her mother's love. "Even the most educated scholars couldn't figure out what it is. What we do know is, the thing you touched is technology from Hylune."

Meren guesses Lorkan's brow has risen in surprise.

"The Ice Giants have technology?" he sputters, and she almost sputters it with him. "How did we get it? During the invasion?"

Material rustles again as Lophia neatly folds one leg over the other.

Meren doesn't like this rustle.

Several years ago, her mother had sat her down at the kitchen table and asked her to seek work in Tawny. As she heavily pulled up a chair and placed a coarse hand over hers, her dress had rustled in the same way—though rougher, a detergent-scented scraping of linen and cotton.

"There was an invasion. But it wasn't the Hyluniens."

※ ☾ ※

Lophia tells a story, then.

For a while, Meren thinks it is a story; a real story; the sort of tales spun to get small children to eat their vegetables and wash behind their ears. But, as it goes on, it becomes startlingly real, like a dream solidifying into consciousness.

Lophia's story concerns The Hyluniens. Meren blinks when she hears their name; she hadn't been expecting them to make an appearance, although perhaps it makes sense: a cold cylinder from a cold land cursing you with skin so cold it turns blue.

"The Ice Giants did not always live in the North Mountains, and they didn't always look like giants," Lophia is saying. The words are slow and chosen deliberately, like she's picking her way down a woodland trail, being careful not to crush any wildflowers.

"They used to live everywhere, but when settlers came from across the seas, the Hyluniens found themselves nudged further and further North. Eventually, they were pushed right up onto the mountains, where they were forced to survive in lands too harsh even for elk, the cold too much for rivers and blood to bear. Somehow, though, they managed, and over time, like the finch evolved a wide beak to gnaw seeds from cones, their hair turned black to shield them from the wintry sun, and their skin fell pale as the snow they walked on."

Lorkan says nothing, but Meren wants to. She wants to ask why any of this matters.

"They became elusive and cautious, never venturing back down to these lands that used to be theirs, and keeping their walls tight against outsiders," Lophia's sombre tone continues. "We thought they'd remained primitive, perhaps falling even further, turning into feral beasts scrabbling for survival, but—"

"You were wrong," Lorkan interjects. His voice has grown tight as though his collar has been buttoned all the way, pinched under his Adam's apple.

Meren knows Lophia is giving a nod, her butter-coloured hair reflecting the mackerel-grey sky.

"They can't be primitive if they've figured out how to blow glass and forge metal. Whatever that thing is, they made it." He seems to realise something. "…Do they…want it back?"

"I'm getting to that. You see, the Hyluniens lost their land and their life here, even their bronze skin, but one thing they did not lose, it seems, was their knowledge."

"But the stories—"

There's that rustle again; a shake of a head.

"That's exactly what they are. Stories. Decades ago, King Willan The Third sent an expedition into their territory. He thought they'd all died off and he could claim the land—it would have turned Velôr into one of the largest kingdoms in the West. His men went up there expecting a barren land—or, at the least, thin, wretched souls scavenging deer carcasses to survive. They were expecting wolves, monsters—

You can imagine their surprise when they found life. Buildings. Apothecaries. Agriculture—somehow. The Ice Giants have found ways of harvesting the powers of nature, thriving, even, in their harsh environment. Some nights, when the sky is especially clear, their lights glow amongst the mountains.

They've confused Velôr's kings for centuries, but they *angered* your father. How could they survive where no living thing should ever be able to survive? How have they made fires so bright they manage to reach through the snow, over the mountains, to fleck his windows like smudges he can't wipe away?"

"But I've never seen those lights," Lorkan interjects.

"You have. You've mapped them. They're painted onto your ceiling. My Sweet, Vixer, Aetheris, and Caster aren't stars. They're villages."

"Villages?" he swallows. "But... our books list them as stars. When we studied Astronomy, Mrs. Berg told us they were stars."

"That was Willan's doing. When his men returned with stories of thriving settlements and, not only survivors of the mountains, but families—children, elders, pregnant mothers—he realised he couldn't claim the land like he'd wanted; it was already occupied."

"That never stopped Father," Lorkan mutters.

By the sound of it, his head has turned to squint at the mountains. The sun is setting, and they appear to blush.

Lophia gracefully ignores his jab.

He must have turned back to her as he asks, shuffling closer on the settee's plush cushions:

"But why are you telling me all this? Why are they mapped as stars? Why does everyone think they're monsters—?"

There's another rustle—a clinking of glass beads—as Lophia raises a hand. "I never said they weren't monsters. Just because they're intelligent, doesn't mean they aren't capable of evil."

"But are they evil?" he implores, sounding frustrated.

She merely shrugs her slim, sloping shoulders. "Perhaps. They've certainly done evil things to us—but we've done the same to them. They distrust us, Lorkan. Our people aren't welcome there. The public believe them to be monsters, and your ancestors didn't correct them because they thought that would be better."

"Better than what?"

"Better than our people marching off into the mountains to get a look for themselves. Better than travelling merchants and apothecaries wandering off into Giant's villages looking for trade. They could be killed, captured—it is a parent's duty to protect their children, and the easiest way to warn them of danger is through stories. I told you of Little Red Riding Hood when you were little, didn't I?"

"Yes, and I was terrified of the woods for weeks."

"Exactly."

"But... the invasion. You said the Giants weren't the ones invading."

Lophia sighs; a tired deflating of lungs.

"Your Father used to look at those villages twinkling away. They'd glow while our people fell to poverty, ill health, or simply worked themselves until they couldn't work anymore. No one has the time to create, to invent, to improve—no one has the time to educate themselves enough to do so.

Cade swore that when he finally became king, he'd lead some men up to Hylune and find out how they're doing it—finding light in the darkest dark, warmth in the coldest cold.

So, when his father died and the throne fell to him, that was the first thing he did. He gathered an army, and they stormed the Hyluniens."

Meren had heard this story before—the war with the Ice Giants—but she had never heard it told this way around. In Lophia's version, the Hyluniens hadn't come charging down the mountain, threatening the kingdom with daggers of ice—it had gone the other way, with Cade charging North, not in pursuit of attackers, but with intent of theft.

"When your father returned, he said very little about what happened on the mountains, but his men told tales of tall fires and destruction, and victory."

Every time Meren had heard this story, she'd pictured King Cade returning to his kingdom with a sense of nationalistic pride. She'd pictured their horses' strong hooves kicking up snow as they marched, blue bloodstains freezing on blunted swords.

This time, as she pictures it, the background is in focus while Cade's bearded face is fuzzy and unimportant. She sees what they're walking away from; tongues of fire lapping up the snow, ropes of smog curling, twisting, choking the air. She pictures little houses pressed into the cliff faces and nestled in gullies like puffins sheltering from the wind, their red beaks the flames, their black feathers the smoke.

"He didn't tell his men *why* they were storming the Hyluniens. Instead, he gave them vague sentences about quelling an uprising—having grown up on a diet of Ice Giant propaganda, they swallowed the lie like honey.

His armies charged into the villages like bulls, waving swords and spears. While they quelled an attack that wasn't there, your father sifted the wreckage for what he sought.

You see, the Hyluniens have buildings like your library—whole houses built only for words— and that's where Cade began his search. He wanted information to bring back, things to help our crops grow, to cure our sick and to improve our lives. He was looking for information."

"Did he find it?" Lorkan asks.

"Not really. Every book was written in a language we didn't understand, and his soldiers had done a better job at pillaging than he'd wanted because it wasn't long before everything was up in flames—but that's not the point,

Lorkan. He may not have found what he was looking for, but he did find something else."

"The cylinder?"

"Well, yes. But I was going to say a baby."

38

LOPHIA'S SPELL

A silence stretches two miles wide.

In the studio, Meren eats her own breath. It bumps into the door and she gasps it back in, hot, fast, deafening silence.

Lophia had told her story eloquently enough. She'd recounted it deftly, patiently, and tied it up in a neat bow—

But Lorkan replies as though she'd dumped a tangled knot of ugly twine in his lap.

"But I look nothing like an Ice Giant. The legends say they're as tall and thick as trees, with skin just as twisted," he's gasping the words, clinging to them like a rope. "I have no tusks, no horns, no gnarled limbs."

Meren can hear the rush of her own blood.

For years, Aldercliff's servants have found amusement in speculating why the youngest prince keeps himself privately stowed away in his chambers.

She had paid them no mind, waving off their suggestions as though they were nothing more than the ramblings of imaginative children.

But she thinks of them now.

'He keeps a hideous monster locked up there—'

'No, he is the hideous monster.'
'The locks aren't to keep others out, they're there to keep him in.'

"No, you do not," Lophia says. "But, then again, nor do they." There's a pause in which she takes her son's hand in her own. It sets her bracelets jingling with a rain-like clink of pearls and gold. "Lorkan."

He does not draw it away.

Meren has a feeling he's gripping it tight, Her Majesty's dainty palms swamped by his much larger ones, his knuckles white, pointed bones.

"When you touched the thing in the basement, my spell was overpowered—"

Weakly, "Spell?"

"We don't know what the cylinder is, but it seems to contain some kind of magic. Being so close to it must have been too much of a strain on my enchantment, and it weakened."

"But," Lorkan stutters, actually stutters, tripping over those three letters, his question staggered like he's falling down some stairs. "What did Father's men think of him taking me? Surely they wouldn't have allowed a Giant to enter their kingdom—"

"They didn't know. They had so much Hylunien blood on their palms, Cade was scared yours would join it, so he kept you hidden."

"But—how?"

"Luck. A miracle. A blessing. As king, your father walked farther ahead than his men, so they never heard the few times you cried. You were a quiet baby, although, I guess you've always been quiet. He said it was easy to stow you in his wagon. He wrapped you in his clothes, and his jars of preserves passed as baby food. For weeks, you lived off apple sauce and jam." She sounds like she's smiling a little—a watery sort of curve to her lower face, turning her words soft and fond.

"On his return, my dear husband brought you to me, and I loved you instantly. We feared that others would not, however, so, to keep you safe, I studied the old magic until I could shroud your true colours with a spell."

Swelled with clouds, the grey sky has split at the seams, streaks of peach and lemon leaking out and mixing in with the salt of the sea.

Meren has slid down to flop on the ground, hunched against the door like a cloth hurled against a wall. Temple leaning against the jamb, she watches as each colour drips, maturing into ochre, orange, red, violet.

"I...*was* going to tell you of your true heritage, my sweet," Lophia tries, quietly. "Once you were powerful enough to maintain the illusion yourself—when the time felt right."

Lorkan says nothing, and Meren's eyes fill slowly with fat, overwhelmed tears. His studio blurs, the pigment stains merging until all she can see are colours, billions of them.

"Despite your blood, Lorkan, you are Velôrian," Lophia says firmly, plonking the fact down on his lap. "You are Cade's child, Sol's brother, and my son."

"But I'm not though, am I?"

At first, Meren isn't sure it had been her prince who had spoken.

He'd sounded so small, a child with a bottom lip wobbling with the promise of a tantrum.

"Why did Cade take me?"

"He rescued you."

"He stole me!"

Then something seems to occur to him, because his tone finds new purpose. His bare feet smack the ground as he stands quickly. "He knows what I am, yet he's still sending me to Calpurzia? They'll be expecting a Velôrian prince, and I'll turn up on their doorstep, with blue blood, yes, but the wrong shade—"

"If we are careful, the Calpurzians will never learn of your secret. I shall continue to shroud you, and you must promise me you'll prepare yourself for the day when I no longer can."

Hearing Queen Lophia plead with her son makes something cold and squirming draw a finger down Meren's back.

Lorkan must have felt it too because his reply isn't with anger.

"If they find out, they will kill me," he mutters quietly. "What if the princess wants children? Is that even possible?"

"I don't know, but—"

"She's expecting a Velôrian, not a whole different *species—*"

"You're not *that* different—"

"Cade's plan is s*uicide—"*

"*We must trust trust your father.*"

"He's not my father!"

"He raised you, Lorkan—"

"No, I don't mean it like that. A father doesn't sell his son, even for a promise of peace. A father doesn't choose favourites, doting on one child whilst the other withers in his shadow." The words are falling thick and fast, each one grating his throat, cracking like brittle dead leaves forced over his tongue. "At least now I know why he did it—why he's getting rid of me—because I'm one of them. He could never have an Ice Giant for a son, he could never—"

Meren stifles a little sob with the back of her hand.

"He loves you, Lorkan!" Lophia's words split her son's rant in two. It slices the end clean away, and it falls, limply, to the floor. "If you don't believe me, you can go and ask him yourself! He didn't plan to take anything from that war besides solutions to his kingdom's problems. He didn't expect to find a wee babe, alone in the snow—he came across you and felt sorry for you and took you home because he was scared no one else would."

Meren knows Lorkan has stopped pacing back and forth, probably in front of the fireplace, the great, gaping mouth of it swallowing him whole. She wishes she had the power to cast spells; to see through this stupid door, to squeeze an invisible hand about his own.

No.

She wishes she wouldn't have to cower behind a door at all. She wishes to be worthy of his mother's approval, a respectable, high-class maiden Lophia would be proud to call her daughter-in-law. She'd be at Lorkan's side, a hand on his back, a promise of devotion on her lips.

Would she?

He's an Ice Giant.

A very kind one.

But he's still an Ice Giant.

Does it matter?

He's cool where he should be warm, with blue skin and black hair and ice in his blood—

And he's Lorkan.

He's always just been her Lorkan.

"But he's selling me to the Calpurzians," he says, bringing Meren back from her stupor, and she aches to run to him.

Perhaps she could grab his hand and drag him, out of his chambers, out of Aldercliff, out of Tawny, out of Velôr—

To where?

"He loves you," Lophia is saying, and Meren wonders whether Lorkan believes her. "But he also loves his kingdom. You and Sol are his sons, but Velôr is his baby." Her dress rustles like felled leaves, and Meren knows she had stood and taken both his hands in hers.

She pictures them; Lophia's so small yet self-assured, Lorkan's hesitant and restrained; both pairs delicate as twigs from a willow.

They are not related but they could be. Cade's lie must have been easy to keep.

"You do want your kingdom to be safe, don't you?" she asks, so soft her words barely make it to the studio door.

Meren fears for a horrible moment Lorkan will deny that Velôr is his kingdom.

But he doesn't.

"Of course I do, Mother. We have spells, yes, but what if they falter? I'm not strong enough. If the Calpurzians find out Father is deceiving them...there would be a war so great it could end both realms."

WHAT LORKAN IS

Lophia sighs with a tiredness she usually keeps flattened under a regal smile. There's a gentle sound as she presses a kiss to his forehead. "You must trust your father, and your king."

Silence settles like a mist, for a while.

Although she hasn't heard the soft pad of Her Majesty's slippers, Meren thinks Lophia might have left.

Prying her ear from the door, she nudges it open tentatively, an inch at a time—

But she's holding her son tight in an embrace. She has to stand on the toes of her pretty slippers to reach her arms around his neck, even though he's stooped down to tuck his face into his mother's hair.

Meren feels a strong pang for her own parents; the hard prickle of her father's stubble, the soft smell of her mother; lard and pastry and clean linens. Smiling a sad smile, she retreats quickly before she can be seen, her heart warm. It's a shame she isn't a high-class maiden—Lophia is someone she would have liked to get to know.

Lorkan gives a sniff as his mother eases out of their cuddle. Meren longs to wipe away his tears, but it's okay because his mother is there to do it for her.

"Am I dangerous?" he asks quietly.

Her sleeves swish as she reaches up to slide a thumb over his cheek.

"You are whatever you choose to be."

☀ ☾ ☀

Lophia asks Lorkan if he will be joining his family for their evening meal, but he refuses, saying he'd prefer to be alone for a while. He accepts another kiss on the forehead and, finally, Meren hears the sound of his mother's slippered feet receding as she heeds his wishes. She must be close to the door of the lounge when she comes to a stop.

"Who is this?"

All at once, Meren's throat tightens as though a noose has been pulled around it. They'd forgotten to cover her portrait. She waits. The door will swing open, the chink of light growing, thick as a blade, slicing her in two—

"Who?" Lorkan asks.

Lophia stares directly at Meren's face for a few moments—her painted face, the one spread over the canvas—but she feels just as vulnerable as though her queen were assessing the very real flesh of her naked body.

"This one. The woman in your painting."

"Oh." Smooth and apathetic. Thank the gods his tears haven't rusted his silver tongue.

"I wanted to practise painting faces, so I asked someone to pose for me."

"Are you in love with her?"

The question clobbers Meren in the back. Does she... know? What a stupid question. Of course, she knows. Anyone who ever looks at the painting will know. It's written in the brushstrokes; they're pressed on as though he'd been fondly caressing Meren's curves, dabbed like kisses. There's love in that painting. It's given texture to the ink and injected colour into the pigment.

'Deny it,' she silently begs. She pictures little strings of thoughts wiggling through the air and into Lorkan's brain, burrowing into his ears, right down to his skull.

'Lor, she'll never let me see you again.'

He doesn't say anything, and she feels her shoulders tighten like screws driven too deep.

"It's a beautiful painting," remarks Lophia.

"Wait," he stops her, so quiet it's a wonder his mother can hear him. She can, though.

"Your spell. The one that keeps me..." He struggles for a word, and Meren's heart twists, "...like this."

What does he really look like? She hasn't dared to wonder. It doesn't matter, not really—she just can't bear the thought of looking at him—the real him—only to cringe away. It would crush him.

WHAT LORKAN IS

What are Ice Giants, really? Are the tales true? Is Lophia's spell constantly straining to contain the grizzled, frost-bitten body of a nine-foot monster?

"Could you leave it off for a bit? Please. I need to..."

Meren knows he means *'get used to himself,'* and she wonders with a sick feeling whether he ever will. After years of stories—tales of evil creatures that lurk in the dark lands—how do you accept that you are one of them?

39

BLUE

There is no sound as Lophia lifts her spell.

For some reason, Meren had been expecting... something. Perhaps a flash of light or a crackle of power, like lightning tearing up the sky.

But there is nothing—only silence—then the distant sound a few minutes later as the door to Lorkan's chambers slides shut.

Meren doesn't leave the studio right away. Partly because she wants to make sure they are well and truly alone, but mostly because she doesn't know what she'll find on the other side of the door.

When she does emerge, slowly, with tentative steps, what she finds is...
Lorkan.

Just her Lorkan, with his pointed nose, his sharp chin, his black hair. Everything is the same—

Except his skin is the colour of the sky.

And he looks wretched. He's slumped on the sofa, hunched over as though sheltering from grey, slush-filled rain.

He doesn't look up as Meren approaches, but she can sense that he's coiled, waiting. Waiting for what she'll say next, what she'll do.

WHAT LORKAN IS

She doesn't really know what to... look at. Her eyes keep finding places to rest, then retreating again, like an animal that can't get comfortable. She doesn't want to stare—but it's hard not to stare.

He doesn't look like the ugly monsters history has told of.

Not at all.

If this is a monster, they're unexpectedly beautiful.

She's found somewhere to look now. The closer she gets, the more she's seeing. His skin varies in blueness. Some parts are lighter, soft swirling sort of patterns—like cirrus clouds—over his white bones, then darker over knots of muscle—

And he has patterns.

Meren has seen tattoos before; on burly men and mysterious, spiritual women—living, walking picture books. Their art can never be taken from them, not by a good scrubbing with carbolic soap—or even by death's prying fingernails.

Lorkan's patterns look like tattoos. Simple, minimalistic ones, softer blue than the rest of him. They're brushed onto him in delicate lines like with a brush, arcing over his brow, disappearing into his shirt and circling a few of his fingers like fine rings.

"I love you," Meren says, meaning it—meaning it so much it's a wonder he can't see it, that flame in her chest burning just for him, always.

She doesn't really know what else to say. She wants to tell him he's pretty, but she doesn't know if he'll believe her.

Not yet.

"Sorry, I should have left. I didn't mean to eavesdrop. Especially in a conversation so personal."

It feels wrong to talk; her words like butterflies with big beating wings, kicking up all the silence like dust.

"I didn't mind you listening." He still hasn't lifted his head, as if it's too heavy to do so. He's probably supposed to be more blue, Meren reckons, but he isn't because he's sad—like paint drained of its pigment.

"I would have had to tell you at some point anyway."

Right in front of him now, she takes the sides of his face in both hands. She expects him to pull away, but he doesn't, and when she tilts his head up a little, he lets her.

He has more of those patterns—the slender lines like rivulets—running over his cheekbone, and she traces one with the pad of her thumb. It's raised slightly, a tiny ridge, smooth mountains.

Slightly—ever so slightly—he pushes into her hand.

"Do you really want to be alone?"

"No... but I'd understand if you wanted to leave."

Her brow furrows, and she frowns down at him. "Why would I want to do that?"

He raises one eyebrow. It's that expression people give her when she doesn't know something she should.

The corner of her lip twitches with a smile, and she presses a kiss to his forehead, over his closed eyes. "Don't look at me like I'm stupid; *you're* stupid for thinking it matters. I wouldn't care if you had vampiric fangs, twisting horns, or a scaly, flicking tail. I'd love them because they'd be *yours.*"

Lorkan shakes slightly, but she isn't sure whether it's with a sob or a laugh. Before she can find out, he's taken her hips and pulled her onto his lap, holding her so close her knees are stabbing the backrest of the sofa.

"If it doesn't matter, then why are you crying?"

"They're happy tears!"

Cradling his head, she wraps her arms around him so tight it's a wonder he can breathe, her grin burrowed in his hair.

"You're not cursed."

"Am I not?" he asks bitterly from where he's tucked below her chin.

"Why, out of all the kingdoms, did it have to be Hylune? Why not—I don't know—Calpurzia? At least they *look* Velôrian."

Meren can't help laughing, just a little giggle, his head on her sternum rising and falling with the tumbling syllables.

"Being an Ice Giant isn't that bad."

"Oh, really?" He raises his head to meet her eyes, the stare a harsh challenge.

WHAT LORKAN IS

They're still chips of jade green, but the whites have been rubbed a raw pink.

She gives him a genuine smile and a long kiss.

He's still at first, still as though it's the first time he's been kissed.

For one horrible second, Meren worries he won't kiss back—

But when she coaxes his lips apart, he melts, clutching her tight.

As she eases away for breath, she keeps her mouth close to his, their noses bumping.

"No, it's not. You might be an Ice Giant, but you're also you. And anyway," she says, finding his hand and bringing it to her lips, giving the ridge of his knuckles a kiss.

"Blue is one of my favourite colours."

✶ ☾ ✶

It takes a while to get Lorkan to... well, anything. He doesn't seem to want to move. Meren doesn't blame him, but she's been sitting on his lap for so long that she starts to wonder whether enough blood is getting to his toes.

What gets him to move is a knock upon the door. It startles him into a standing position, and he rises with Meren in his arms so fast that her head spins. Stretching out a leg, her toes find the floor and she clambers back down onto the marble.

While she leaves to greet their visitor, Lorkan cowers, as though he thinks they'll force themselves into his chambers and—

Scream and run for the guards?

Shout his secret from the battlements?

Chain him up in the dungeons?

Whilst Meren turns the key in the lock, she wonders what would happen if someone did find out that there's an Ice Giant inside—the very monster from their fairy tales—hidden away in the heart of Aldercliff like a stolen relic. She readies herself, bracing one arm against the door in case she needs to shove it closed again, her hand hovering over the key.

A maid stands boredly on the other side, a wide tray at her feet. She hefts it up embarrassedly as she's exposed, muttering a sheepish, "Sorry, it was heavy," as she hands it over.

Meren's sagging shoulders get a raised brow, but the maid doesn't have time to comment. Shoving the hefty slab of wood with her foot, Meren locks it again, sealing the world back out once more.

As promised, Lophia has had Lorkan's supper sent up to his rooms.

The meal consists of mutton and roasted vegetables, with crisp potatoes, batter puddings, and soft ice cream for dessert. Even when he's shared it out between two plates, there is still more than he could have eaten alone. Cross-legged on a bear-skin rug, he and Meren dine by the window, looking out at the night-cloaked kingdom.

"I think Mother knows about us," Lorkan says after some time.

She pierces a hot potato with her knife. Steam billows from its fluffy innards, and she stifles it with a wedge of butter, watching the sunny yellow cube liquify, making the steam smell sweet. "Do you think we should... do anything about it?"

"What? You mean silence her?" The corner of his blue lip twitches up into a smile, despite himself.

"No! Of course not. I meant... I don't know. Should we explain ourselves? Or promise that it won't affect the alliance—or you moving to Calpurzia?"

He appears pensive as he methodically dissects a batter pudding. "I don't think we have to do anything. If she cared, she would have done something about it, don't you think?"

"I guess so."

"Either way, let's not worry about it. I just want to enjoy what little time we have left."

As if to illustrate his point, the clouds jostle with one another, moving aside to let a wedge of moon move to the front.

A chunk of its silver light falls onto her plate, and the soft potato in Meren's mouth hardens.

She doesn't know what to say next. She doesn't really want to talk about summer either; she wants the opposite.

She wants to ask what it feels like, spending years shrouded by a spell only to have it ripped off.

Does he feel naked, now, without it?

Can he remember Hylune at all, even just the sting of the cold or the darkness of the sky?

Is he curious about his true parentage, just a little bit?

However, every time Meren opens her mouth, the words shrivel and die.

If he wanted to talk about it, he would.

✳ ☾ ✳

As he asked, Lophia has also left Lorkan naked of her spell, the moonlight turning him a silver blue, like a night-cloaked ocean.

Eventually, Meren's shift ends and, reluctantly, she stands to leave—

But he reaches for her with a "Wait."

He doesn't reach for her hand or her wrist or her waist. Just her, any part of her he can get.

It happens to be her elbow, but that seems to be enough because he doesn't let go.

"...Could you stay?"

Her mouth curves with a teasing smile. "What happened to wanting our first night to be in a bed we share, without the secrecy, all romantic and—"

"I know, I know." He swallows, releasing her arm. "I don't care about that now. It was stupid... I thought I'd be able to wriggle out of the engagement somehow, so we could actually have that, but... now it's not looking like I can." He cups her cheek with a broad palm, almost dragging her closer. "Please stay. I don't want to be by myself."

She blinks at him. She'd thought he was joshing. She'd thought this was just like every other evening, where they'd fantasise about a shared night together, plan it out in detail—

But only fantasise.

Only plan.

But today hasn't been an ordinary day.

When Meren turns her head to kiss his palm, the blue of his skin contrasts with the warmth of hers. "Alfdis will know I'm missing."

He pulls away and stands quickly. Bent over a desk with a quill in his hand, he scribbles something onto a scrap of parchment and presses it into her palm. "You won't be missing, you'll be running an errand for me."

She reads the note; an eloquent excuse in his eloquent script. A ragged lip between her teeth, her feet waver, one pointed towards the door, the other towards her prince.

She sighs.

"It's risky, Lor. She'll probably know it's a lie. What about your honour?"

He gestures at himself, a bitter twist to his mouth. "My honour is already royally fucked."

* ☾ *

A guard stationed close to Lorkan's rooms takes his note down to the servant's quarters.

Meren tries not to imagine Alfdis' little bird-claw hands unfurling it, her wrinkled eyes squinting to decipher the looping ink.

"I don't think our note is fooling anyone," she sighs, joining Lorkan in his bedroom. "Time has not marinated Alfdis' mind as it does most elderly people. She's still as sharp as a blackbird's beak, and I'd bet three crescents she knows about us. Hopefully, she loves you enough not to tattle."

Lorkan's bed is very large and very grand. With its canopy and velvet drapes, it's almost like a room within a room, Meren has often thought whilst she plumped the pillows and rubbed varnish into its carved posts. She and Lorkan often change the sheets together — holding a corner each and stuffing the duvet down into its depths — but she has never let herself so much as lean on the mattress to spread out the linen, let alone get on top of it.

It's not that she's not allowed to. Had she asked, she knows Lorkan would have encouraged her to climb aboard and explore all she likes —

—and yet, even now, she dithers awkwardly, her feet kneading the rug.

Lorkan had lent her a sponge and some toothpowder so she could wash, and joining him in his bedroom, she'd found him rummaging through his chest of drawers.

"I don't mind sleeping with nothing on, truly," she assures once more.

Ignoring her, he holds up something green and made of cotton. "How about this shirt?"

"Surely you'd rather me naked?"

"Or this?" Something else green, but this one is embroidered with little pheasants pecking up and down the sleeves.

He'd wrapped her in a silk robe too — so she wouldn't get cold trekking from the washroom to the bedroom — and she fingers the knot about her waist.

"...Lor?"

It falls open like a curtain, the night air flooding in.

His eyes tumble down the exposed column of her skin as it tightens with the chill, his Adam's apple bobbing up and down his pale throat. He moistens his lips, his cheeks turning a sort of blueberry colour.

Meren guesses that's the Ice Giant version of a blush.

"Of course I would."

But he holds the shirt out to her all the same.

She sneers at it — even though the fat little pheasants make her smile. "Then why do I have to wear that?"

"Do you not like it? I have more."

"No, it's fine, this isn't about the shirt." Hurt: "Why do you suddenly want to cover me up?"

He hesitates, running a thumb over one of the pheasant's colourful backs. "Because I'm scared I'll make you cold."

Meren feels her brows come together in a puzzled frown. "We've cuddled hundreds of times before, and that hasn't happened."

"Yes, but not for this long."

It's hard to keep her eyes from rolling. "You're not going to sap the life out of me, Lorkan."

"You don't know that."

She sighs, but he looks so forlorn she takes the shirt from him all the same.

Lorkan watches as she slips it over her head, then stands, bare feet sinking into the shaggy rug. His shirt reaches down past her knees. Despite everything, his lip twitches, just a bit. "I doubt it will keep you very warm, but it's the best I can do."

"It's okay." Meren shrugs, trying to find her hands among the seemingly endless sleeves. "I guess an Ice Giant isn't the best person to go to if you're looking for snuggly pyjamas," she quips, and his smile falters. She notices and places a hand on his arm.

"Sorry. I guess you're not ready for that yet, huh?"

His lips press together as he shrugs off her apology.

She's still standing there, dithering awkwardly by the bed, and he gestures to it.

"You *can* get in, you know."

Meren feels her cheeks heat, but she's not sure why.

Gingerly, she clambers onto the vast mattress as though boarding a ship (which she has never done before, but assumes that, if she did, she'd go about it with similar tentative excitement). Her weight seems to tip below her —

WHAT LORKAN IS

exactly like a boat on the sea — as though the down-stuffed mattress is mouthing friendlily at her hands and knees.

Wriggling under the covers, she hesitantly reclines back against the mound of pillows. For a terrifying second, she thinks she'll just keep on reclining, back and back until the cushions swallow her, tassels and gold lacing filling her lungs—

But she doesn't.

The pillows appear to have accepted her as one of their own.

"Good?" Lorkan asks, and she grins, although he probably can't see it through the jungle of velvet and satin.

"Good? I'm going to spend the rest of my days lounging here like a seal sprawled on a hot rock."

There's that smile again, faint and watery—

But it's there.

Swimming her way out of the heap of pillows, Meren pushes herself up into a sitting position and crosses her legs, settling back against the headboard.

The window is cracked to the night, and she watches with sleepy amusement as, methodically, Lorkan draws the curtains on it, extinguishes the wax sticks, and folds his clothes over the back of a chair.

When he slips from his dressing gown, her breath catches in her throat.

It's the same body she knows so well, the same body she's mapped out hundreds of times before like stars in the sky, rivers on a map—

But it's different — just a bit.

A different shade.

With the faint glow of feeble flames, the sky-blue hue of it has mellowed into a rich teal.

There are more of those tattoo-like lines, she notices. They arc over his sharp shoulder blades, run between the muscles of his back, then trickle down to pool at his thighs like glacial run-off.

She hopes he'll leave them bare.

She wants to kiss them when he joins her in the bed.

As he hangs the dressing gown on the back of the door, she plans the trail she'll take; sweep his hair aside so she can begin at the very top of his spine—

He notices her staring, and tugs some nightclothes on quickly.

From the bed, she frowns, but he doesn't see; he'd turned to take a brush from the dresser.

When he begins dragging it through his hair, Meren says:

"Let me."

He smiles a little as he boards the mattress, much more gracefully than she had done. Sitting before her, he crosses his legs neatly, holding the brush over a wide shoulder.

At the end of each day, Meren's mother would sit with her before the dying embers of the fire, and give her hair one hundred strokes.

Whenever Meren brushes Lorkan's hair — which she does a lot — she does the same, counting each one in her head.

Around stroke eighty-six, she says gently,

"If I had just found out I don't look how I always thought I looked... I'd spend much longer gazing in the mirror."

Lorkan says nothing.

Perhaps because his new appearance isn't something he wants to look at.

Or maybe because, when someone is touching his hair, he struggles to pay attention to much else.

Perhaps both.

"You barely looked at all."

Stroke ninety-one.

The boar hair bristles catch on a stray knot, and Meren teases it carefully until it comes loose.

"Why don't you like it, Lorkan?"

He knows what she means. His eyes are closed, but she can feel his muscles coil up. He's been doing that all evening — unwinding, then tensing as soon as he catches a glimpse of his reflection in the window or the back of a spoon. As if he's seen a ghoul or a stranger staring back through the curved metal.

It makes her heart twist every time.

WHAT LORKAN IS

"Am I *supposed* to like it?"

"Ideally. But if you can't do that, at least try not to hate it. It's who you are."

"That's *why* I hate it."

Deciding to complete the last few brush strokes with her fingers, she gives the back of his head a little soft scratch.

His shoulders loosen again. They'll stay like that until he next sees himself, in the looking glass across the room or in the shiny curve of a candelabra.

At this moment, facing away from her, his hands clasped in his lap, she can't really tell he looks different.

Slowly, as she'd planned to do, she sweeps his raven-feather hair aside, exposing a flash of blue. A smile steals across her face.

"Well, I love it."

Lorkan actually laughs, a bitter bark. "No, you don't."

She wants to give him a shove. She usually would, under normal circumstances. If this had been any other day, she would have shoved him right off the bed.

Instead, she bends her head and kisses his neck, parting her jaw enough to give him a playful little nip.

"Yes, I do."

He still feels the same against her mouth; that refreshing coolness. He still tastes the same; male, salty, with that tang of cracked pepper and citrusy soaps.

She doesn't pull away. She just continues mouthing at his throat.

Lorkan's shoulders loosen gradually, an atom's width at a time. Eventually, he moistens his lips before replying, breathing in a shaky breath.

"No, you don't."

There's one of those tattoo-like lines over his cheek. Meren can remember the flow of them, and she moves around to find it, following it over his face like a little carriage being drawn down a winding country road.

It deposits her mouth over his, and she pushes herself up onto her knees so she can reach his lips.

Kissing him is still the same.

Still heavenly, overwhelming, and perfect.

"Yes. I do."

"You're just saying that." But the corner of his mouth is twitching with what could be a smile — if he were to let it.

"No, I'm not."

He unfurls shyly as Meren's kiss deepens... but he still hitches as she fingers a button at his collar.

"I promise I do. Let me show you how much." She prompts him encouragingly. She pauses to let him push her away—

But he doesn't stop her as she eases the little pearly button free.

"...Are you sure that's wise?"

"I told you, I don't care what you are."

"Wren, you wouldn't put your hand in a wolf's mouth, would you?"

She shrugs. "Depends on the wolf."

His palm has found her hip, the other burying itself safe in her hair. "Even still... I'd understand if you don't want—"

He never finishes that sentence.

Meren kisses it away, swallowing it.

Lorkan is so much bigger, so much stronger, but he lets himself be nudged down onto the bed as if she's dipping him in a dance.

She can feel him watching her carefully as she unfastens the rest of his nightshirt.

He expects her to cringe, or something like that.

He's cringing; his eyes running from her reaction.

"You're in love with colours." Meren sighs. "So how could you not like this?" She gestures at him, the subtle shifts of blue, the vibrancy, the clusters of freckles; pin-pricked navy stars.

There's more of those delicate little lines running down his chest, and her lips follow them over his belly.

He shifts below her with a soft noise.

She's sure he can feel her toothy smirk against his skin. "That's new."

"Hm."

She hadn't realised how quick his breath had become. She'd been so distracted by her own curiosity that she hadn't noticed that he's revelling in it, his toes curling amoungst the sheets.

"Where was it?" She asks, her voice low. Pressing another kiss, just a little higher than the band of his pyjama trousers:

"Here?"

He squirms. "Yes."

Thoughtfully, she traces the tattoo-like line with her finger, feeling it flow up and down with ridges of rib, hills of muscle, slight swells of softness. "I think these are sensitive."

The line continues into his trousers, lining up prettily with the chiselled V at his pelvis.

"... There's more of them," Lorkan says.

Meren has rarely heard him shy—rarely seen him so hesitant. A grin plays around the lower half of her face.

"Is there really?" Replacing her finger with her tongue, she draws a hot trail along that beautifully responsive little line.

Lorkan's back arches. He has to gasp for a little while before he has enough breath to speak. "...Yes. I saw them when I got changed. But you don't...only if you want to."

"Lor, how many times do I have to say it?"

The tie of his pyjama bottoms is tricky to undo—as though he'd knotted it tight to keep her gaze out.

Or to keep his blue skin in.

Either way, she gets it undone, and he even helps tug them off his hips— well, tries to. His hands shake every time her fingers 'accidentally' brush him.

"I love you," Meren states as he lies all spread out below her.

She states it like a fact, because it is a fact, she loves him no matter what colour he is, no matter what patterns he has, where he comes from or what runs through his veins.

He's her Lorkan.

He's always just been her Lorkan.
"All of you."

※ ☾ ※

For a little while, Meren is convinced Lorkan is asleep behind her. They'd blown out the wax sticks some time ago; they'd been lit so long they'd halved in length, overflowing their little dish and pooling on his bedside table. The room is cloaked in darkness, their entwined bodies cloaked in bed linen.

Lorkan's breaths are deep and slow, ruffling Meren's hair. She's tucked tight against his chest, her body bundled in his arms as though she's a rag doll. The bare skin of her back is pressed to the bare skin of his front—but she's not cold. She doubts she will be, even when morning rolls around.

Lorkan had thought he'd draw the heat from her hungrily—slowly draining her of life as the hours went by—but that's not what's happening at all. He's almost reflecting it, Meren's heat, his cells processing it, deciding they don't like it, and sending it back, his body curled around her like a muffling, insulating snowdrift.

'I'd be happy to lie like this until the ground claims us,' she thinks absently. Maybe they could find a comfy patch of moss in the woodlands, curl up together, let the lichens, the ivy, and the funny mushrooms have their jumbled-up bones.

Inch by inch, she feels her mind sliding sideways into dreams of sweet forests and curious deer tiptoeing about their sleeping bodies. Then Lorkan says, quietly:

"When Mother asked if I love you, I was going to say something."

His hand smothering Meren's belly moves around and slides up to cup one of her breasts. He runs his thumb over her skin gently, and she imagines what it must look like: the icy blue of him and pink, kiss-bruised hue of her.

"I worried you might, for a second."

WHAT LORKAN IS

"I wanted to. I know I shouldn't, but, honestly, I want to tell anyone who'll listen. I want to shout about you from the battlements. I want to proudly introduce you to my father. I want to catch the look of jealousy on my brother's face as he sees me holding your hand."

"I know." Finding his arm, Meren cradles it. She rubs a thumb over his fingers; the one a ring would encircle if they were allowed to marry. It's bare, besides his patterns, sketched on like ink. As she brushes one, she feels his heartbeat quicken tiredly against her shoulderblade.

"I want that too. Sometimes I imagine bringing you home to my parents. You'd have to duck under the low little door, and the cottage would be much too small for you—but it would be warm and smell of grass and laundry and freshly baked pie. Father would welcome you to the family with a chuffed clap on the back, and Mother would drag you down to kiss your cheeks."

Lorkan's nose nuzzles against the back of her neck. "I came so close to telling Mother. I almost did it, but then…I thought I could hear you. You were telling me not to, and I realised you were right—so I didn't."

Meren presses her lips together. "I think you made the right choice."

"Yes. But that's not what I meant. I could *hear your voice*—as if you were talking to me."

Her sleepy chuckle falls from her mouth and onto the pillow.

"Have I become your conscience, my prince?" she teases, and feels him give her a playful squeeze.

"Never mind. It was probably my imagination. It just shocked me, how clear it was. I thought you'd come out of the studio, tugged on my sleeve, and begged me to deny it. I was so surprised I couldn't say anything at all."

Something occurs to Meren then; she had been mentally pleading with him. She'd been so terrified they'd be discovered and separated—

But that's nonsense. She hadn't said any of it out loud, and if she had, surely Lophia would have heard—then prized the studio door open to see what sort of eavesdropping little minx had been spying on her and her son.

And of course, there's no way he could have heard her thoughts, that's ridiculous.

She yawns, slotting her fingers between his. "You probably just know me really well."

Lorkan presses a kiss to the back of her neck, that place that sends a tingling sensation right down to her toes.

"True."

40

THE LAST FULL MOON OF SUMMER

Lorkan had said he wanted to enjoy his last few weeks before summer's last full moon, yet Cade and the rulers of the Calpurzian Kingdom seemed to have other ideas. He's been sent several parcels, all bound tight with twine and sweet-smelling wrappings. When Meren arrives at his chambers one morning, she finds him sitting cross-legged upon the rug in his study, the contents of the parcels spread about him like maps on a sea captain's desk.

"What are you doing?" Lowering herself to sit at his side, she greets him with a kiss.

"You seem awfully chipper."

"It's hard not to be chipper when there's books around."

By now, Meren has thumbed her way through much of Lorkan's library—slipped easily through the thin little paperbacks and waded through heavy hardbacks. She doesn't recognise these books, though. Even their dusty smell is different to those on the shelves... almost... spicy. She takes a closer look, easing a heavy cover open, and blinks, confused. The words are all in wriggly little symbols she doesn't understand. She half expects the letters to writhe about before her eyes as though they're real little black inky worms.

Lorkan is drowning in them, a deep rift wedged between his dark brows. Once again shrouded by his mother's spell, his pale skin has dulled as the days slipped through his fingers, turning to a damp shade of grey.

"What's the matter?"

"The Calpurzians have sent me papers to help me adjust to their ways of life."

Meren's ears metaphorically prick up. "These are from the Calpurzia Kingdom?" Taking some of the parcel's wrappings to her nose, she sniffs. Yes, definitely spicy. Like summer flowers and the colourful herbs mixed into flatbread.

Lorkan doesn't seem as impressed. He has a sheet of parchment in one hand and keeps looking between it and the book by his left knee, that frown getting deeper.

"Do you understand this?" she gestures at the page that is clearly puzzling him. It, too, is covered in those tight little squiggles. They even seem to go the wrong way—from right to left instead of left to right.

"No," Lorkan sighs. He waves the parchment in his hand frustratedly, like a white flag of surrender. "They gave me this to help me learn the language—but it's all nonsense. You don't pronounce half the letters, and if they make a certain sound, they group them together to make another letter. Their alphabet is almost twice the length of ours, and they don't use full stops."

He almost growls the last few words, and Meren presses her lips together to keep in a guilty little laugh, pulling him into a cuddle. He falls against her gratefully, her hand gravitating automatically to his hair.

"You'll pick it up in time," she soothes, although it'll probably be a very long time, judging by the complexity of the page he'd been deciphering—*trying* to decipher.

One of the other books catches her eye.

"This one's in Velôrian." Gently nudging Lorkan upright again, she pulls it closer. In block capitals, the title reads simply:

'*COMMON CALPURZIAN PRACTICES*'

WHAT LORKAN IS

No wonder it hadn't caught her attention before now; there are no pretty patterns pressed into the binding, no carefully painted covers, and—when she flicks through the pages—the diagrams are merely two-dimensional, hurried sketches.

"Because it was written by a Velôrian," Lorkan states flatly.

"Really?" Meren's page-flicking comes to rest at a crude drawing of two men in headscarves doing a sort of bowing motion at each other. A thick paragraph rests below, explaining the greeting in detail.

"How would they know all this?"

"He lives there."

Her eyebrows touch her hairline. "What?"

Lorkan shrugs. "He lives there. These books were from my father. The author sends them to him directly once he finishes writing them—as a sort of... man from the inside."

That explains the crude drawings. And the ink stains, the plain, almost shoddy cover. Meren knows how books are made; large printing presses stamp words onto lots of pages at once—but this book doesn't look printed. Not like that, anyway. It looks typed as though on a machine; like the rickety little typewriter on Alfdis' desk she uses to do the expenses.

This book is a first edition.

"There's Velôrians inside the Calpurzia Kingdom?"

"Just one." With one pale hand, Lorkan angles the cover enough to read the name inscribed along the bottom. "Anthony Merlmon."

Bewildered: "Is he still there?"

"I assume so." He notes Meren's surprise. "Yes, I thought our knowledge of Calpurzia was limited as well. Father only told me about his stash of encyclopaedias this morning. Apparently, Anthony did something very bad, so Father gave him the choice; be executed, or live out his life there, sending information back like a spy." He sneers at that word, 'spy', then shrugs.

"It's very low of Father to get someone to tattle on the enemy for him like that, but I guess I shouldn't complain; thanks to Anthony I won't be starting my new life empty-handed."

"You've got these," Meren teases, referring to the (what seem like) untranslatable books, and Lorkan gives her a push in the ribs with his elbow.

"Big help they'll be. Big help any of it will be." He gestures at the mess surrounding him with both arms as if he'd like to scoop everything up in them and dump it out the window.

"Life there seems so different. They're spiritual. Religious. So much more so than here. Here we joke about the old gods, only mentioning them in times of shock—or pleasure," he gives a smirk, and her cheeks flush. "But the Calpurzians take them seriously. Very seriously."

"How so?"

"Well, for a start, they think the sun is alive, and they say death is the doing of a malevolent bird spirit."

"And that... angers you?"

"Of course! Doesn't it you?"

"Well, yes. It's illogical, fantastical, naive... but a good story, don't you think? I'm imagining a smoky figure pecking away at any life it can find like a crow, hiding in dark corners and slipping through crowds on wispy wings."

Lorkan rolls his eyes. "I don't have the time for nonsense and irrational phobias."

"You're scared of spiders."

He decides to ignore that, and Meren turns a few pages of the book close to her foot. It's labelled:

'RELIGIOUS LAW: BOOK ONE'

She'd hoped for an illustration of the death spirit, but there were no drawings in this book; just lots of names and what appeared to be recipes.

"How do they get anything done if they're all hiding from evil ghosts all day?"

WHAT LORKAN IS

"Apparently, they ward them off with charms and symbols and things like that. Well, they think they do. I mean, look at this magic." His lip curls, and he hefts a book onto his lap, its full wingspan so wide Meren has to stretch her legs out flat so it can spill over from his thighs onto her own.

Excitement prickles her skin into gooseflesh at the mention of magic.

Lorkan finds the page he's looking for and runs a slender finger down the lines of text. It clearly appals him, but Meren doesn't understand any of it.

"They cut corners almost lazily," he explains, probably sensing her confusion. "Magic is manipulating the energy of atoms around you; using them to your advantage. It takes years of practice, effort, and patience—but look."

Meren leans over the wide old book to see what he's pointing at; an index listing what appears to be ordinary, somewhat random, items and movements:

WALKING STICKS

HERBS AND COOKING

DANCE

CHARCOAL STICKS

SONG AND CHANTED WORDS

GLYPHS AND SYMBOLS

The list goes on, each subject housing pages of information. She's figured, by now, that each thing is a way of using magic, but Lorkan's way—his mind—isn't mentioned.

"It's like they're doing it with a crutch," he says, noticing her puzzlement. "They lean very heavily on objects to do it for them, but it doesn't work that way."

Meren just nods, because she doesn't really know what to say. Her knowledge of magic and how it's executed is about as large as a squirrel's know-how when it comes to shortcrust pastry. Clearly, the Calpurzia's use of such power bothers Lorkan, though, so she lets him rant next to her, occasionally thrusting passages and pages under her nose that particularly annoy him.

She partly understands his concern; if magic means tampering with atoms themselves, it can't be... safe to do it wrong, can it?

So often she's worried he'll hurt himself while she watches him practise; fearing his masked fingers will never return, or the ice figurines he can form with a wave of his hand will burst all of a sudden, freezing everything in the room.

Meren wouldn't trust that power with—what had the index said? Herbs? A walking stick? She imagines a carved cane and a sprig of rosemary trying to alter matter itself, and feels herself frown. "Do many Calpurzians do magic?"

"By the looks of it, their daily life is weaved with spells and sorcery. Mother said that'll make me feel at home, but, honestly, it just makes me feel more out of place." He holds out a palm, a small mirage appearing in the centre.

Meren watches it form, Lorkan's concentration charging the air, almost setting it crackling. It buzzes about, she can almost feel it, atoms rushing to the spot, coming together to form the illusion, just as he'd said. They became a glass marble—just a simple shape—

Yet, when he closes his hand on it, it vanishes, barely powerful enough to withstand a brush of his pale fingertips.

"I doubt my little tricks will be enough to impress my soon-to-be-mother-in-law."

Meren lets her head lean against his arm. She'll miss it; that knot of muscle, the steadiness of his body at her side. "You're Velôrian; they probably aren't expecting you to have magical abilities at all."

WHAT LORKAN IS

∗ ☾ ∗

Lorkan continues to study for another few hours, fear driving his need for knowledge more than curiosity. It's alien sight, him puzzled, his forehead creased as he tries to understand what's before him. It makes him look older, his troubles all mingling in his face, weighing it down.

Leafing through the materials surrounding them, Meren remains at his side, both interested in and despising the place that will soon be absorbing her Lorkan.

She tries having a go at translating the Calpurzian text as well, using the (now rather worn and dog-eared) key Lorkan had been given – but she barely manages three words before her head starts to spin.

She likes the books by Anthony Merlmon.

He isn't a good writer; his sentences are rough and cut short like a bad hair cut, but that makes them easy to digest; although the subject matter often goes over her head.

After some time, Meren realises Lorkan is watching her. His smile is lazy and mellow, but his eyes are sad, the lids heavy.

The finger she's been tracking her place with comes to a halt as she turns to him."What?"

His mouth twitches at one corner. "Nothing. I'm just...looking at you."

When she flushes, he eases himself down onto the carpet, stretching out on his back like a cat in the sun. His spine clicks in a few places; he must have been studying long before Meren came up to his chambers.

"You don't have to study with me. Go do something fun."

"This *is* fun. Well, maybe not fun, but interesting."

He turns onto his side to face her. "In that case, read to me?" He smiles like a dog begging for scraps. "I might absorb it better if the words are coming from the woman I love."

Feeling her lip twitch, Meren presses it down into a pretend frown. "Flattery will get you nowhere, Lorkan."

But she backtracks by a few pages all the same, and starts the chapter again.

* ☾ *

Meren has always admired summer: the overwhelming colours of it, the sweet-smelling honeysuckle with their sunny petals, the busy birds with beaks full of fat caterpillars—
Her mop felt less heavy, and the palace steps less long when the hopeful summer sun was out to warm her face.

But now, for the first time, she's finding herself thinking the bright flowers mocking, and the nesting birds irritatingly smug.

The last few weeks whipped by so rapidly they felt like a strange dream. There were no distinctive landmarks to help segregate each day; each one became a useless blur—a soup of vague activities: drawing together, reading together, playing together.

Because they hadn't dared to leave Lorkan's chambers, their last precious moments together could be nothing more than that: fast, fuzzy memories like scenery speeding by a racing carriage.

Lorkan appears to have accepted his fate with depressed submission, right until his final night when realisation seemed to hit him all at once like a hard punch to the stomach.

He did not sleep, his breaths coming too quickly, his heart thrumming too fast.

WHAT LORKAN IS

    Meren didn't sleep either; she stayed with him that night, stooped over him like a deer protecting its fawn. She'd tried to smooth his rumpled feathers with affirmations and soft words, her tears falling silently onto his hair.

    She never used to be much one for crying, but she seems to do it often now, as if her body is trying to drain something out of it in the form of salty little tears.

    She doesn't think it's working.

    She feels as though she's about to lose a limb.

    Lorkan told her once that he has never left the kingdom before and rarely leaves Aldercliff's high walls. A prince's life is plush and comfortable but terribly unformed. Meren hasn't voiced her concerns, but she fears he'll feel so naked and vulnerable out in the big, wide world, like a baby bird forced too early from the nest—

    And so unwelcome, unwanted; the Calpurzia Kingdom has kept its gates closed to Velôrian blood for as long as anyone can remember.

    But he isn't Velôrian, she realises, even though the skin she presses her lips to is pale as a wax stick. What if Lophia's spell slips or falters?

    She doesn't dare let herself fathom it and whips those worries hard before they can advance any closer. They're always there now, those anxieties, in a dark little corner of her mind she never lets herself go. She tries to keep them chained up like shadowy beasts, far away so they can't snap at her with their snarling jaws.

    Lorkan has these worries too, but there's no way he can chain them up; Meren is pretty sure they're prowling about his mind freely, gnawing, chewing, biting. Stalking between his everyday thoughts like wolves through trees.

✶ ☾ ✶

Morning comes through the curtains on the dreaded day, and Meren blinks at the light as if confused about where it had come from. Yesterday evening had been a few minutes ago—she could have sworn it—and yet, when she rises from the bed, her limbs creak from hours curled tight about Lorkan's shoulders.

There's so much she wants to say, but none of it will come. The sentences knot in her throat, a thick ball of tangled yarn, choking her whenever she opens her mouth.

They dress in silence, then methodically collect the few items Lorkan has been permitted to bring with him: a few articles of clothing for the journey and a small case of his prized possessions.

He packs them into a leather trunk: a little hand-printed novel from his mother, a sleeve of charcoals from his brother—but his heart doesn't seem to be in it. When he picks up a slender letter knife given by his father, he hesitates.

Meren takes it from him and places it amongst his green shirts and black trousers. "You should take it. You'll regret it if you don't."

She had wanted to give him a gift as well—a ring to keep on his finger, or a band of prettily knotted twine to tie about his wrist—but feared his new bride might notice the nature of these items and suspect a secret beau.

In the end, she settled on one of her sketchbooks: a matted wad of scruffy parchment, every inch layered thick with even scruffier doodles.

It was not her first, or even her second; it was probably the fifth or sixth. It's not good, per se, but she likes it because it marks a turning point in her art—when everything started to finally take shape. The first few pages feature slightly wonky drawings of cats, shopfronts, Aasta's cakes, faces—

But by the end, each picture is clear and skilled, the lines almost confident, the strokes more purposeful.

Lorkan's eyes turn moist as she hands it to him, and he tucks it carefully into his case as though swaddling a baby.

Although neither of them feel like breakfast, Meren prepares some oats over the fire and drizzles them with sweet honey. Neither of them knows exactly how long the journey from Velôr to Calpurzia will be, but strength will be required to get through the day. When Lorkan pushes his bowl away, she nudges it back until he's cleared it.

His case looks so small by the door.

"Surely you can bring some more clothes?" she asks, thinking of his fondness for gauzy green button-up shirts and the loose mossy trousers that swish about his bony ankles. "You should be able to wear what you want; they don't own you."

"But they do, Meren," Lorkan says gently. "I'm a gift."

He gives her a kiss on the corner of her mouth before she can argue with him—as she's done countless times; angry rants about injustice, her face red, her every cell prickling with rage. Sometimes they'd make Lorkan smile, her wilfulness annoyingly amusing; she knows her feet have a tendency to stomp angrily like a petulant child.

He's not smiling now.

"Take this," he says as he eases away, and Meren realises he's pressed something into her hands.

Her jaw parts to refuse because it's gold. She can feel hard, flat disks of it in her palm.

"Take it," he says more firmly, almost gruff, his voice a tired wave grinding against a damp beach.

She lets him close her fingers over the coins, and they're cold like his clammy hands.

"I need to know you'll be okay."

"How can I be okay when you're so far away from me?" Her voice cracks like a tree pushed over too far by the wind, and Lorkan's face blurs.

"I want you to forget me, Wren," he says, and she blinks.

When he comes into focus, she finds his cheekbones slick too, the stupid summer sun reflecting off their sheen.

Shaking her head: "You know I can't do that, Lor."

"Then at least try to love again. Anyone. Anything. Everything." He sniffs and gives her a sad smile, taking the sides of her face in his hands.

They're so large, she realises for the millionth time, so broad, so wide, they can cup her whole skull.

So important he is—so significant in the grand scheme of things—and so fleeting is she, so unimportant, so small.

His marriage will set history on a new path.

And she will scrub floors.

"I've sent money to your parents," his voice comes to her, and she blinks up at him. "Not enough to make them feel guilty about taking it, but from now on they can always put food on their table, and coals on their fire."

Meren finds herself crying for a whole new reason. She wants to tell him he shouldn't have, but all that comes out of her mouth is:

"Thank you."

It makes his lips twitch at one corner. "Meren, do you like being a maid?"

Why lie?

It makes her hands cracked and hard, her bones heavy and tired, her eyes droop, and her spine sag.

And is it really an insult anymore, to disrespect a palace that is no longer his?

"No."

"Then be something else. Be an artist." He gestures at his case, standing waiting at his feet.

Meren pictures his belongings inside, all jumbled up because it's standing the wrong way; little items marking turning points in his youth, his whole life trussed up in a box light enough to carry.

"Your sketchbook—it's really good. You're good. You've gotten so good." He sounds so proud, a watery beam brightening his whole face. "The kingdom has little use for portraits and likenesses, but you could design. Find a master seeking an apprentice; invent clothes or furniture or buildings."

Her head spins as she pictures it, an entirely different life—with nothing sharp besides the point of a charcoal stick, and nothing rough besides white parchment—and it scares her.

WHAT LORKAN IS

But she nods, not wanting to disappoint him.

He needs to know she'll be okay—that his kingdom will be okay.

That he's leaving for a reason.

"Your reading is good too. You're so curious; please keep the books—the ones about Calpurzia. I can't take them with me."

"Won't Cade need them back?"

"Not anymore. I'll become his next spy, nestled deeper into their kingdom than old Antony could ever manage to get. Father never really cared about how the commoners say hello, or what gods they pray to anyway."

"What if someone asks where I got them?"

"Say they were given to you by a friend."

"Lor." Meren sniffs. "It's not *fair*. You were like a shooting star—you lit up my whole life—and now you're just... *disappearing?*"

His face crumples and, with a strong thumb, he wipes away her tears.

She can't stand it anymore and drags him down to her lips.

They kiss.

He tells her he loves her into her mouth, and she mutters it onto his cheek.

They say it again and again, as if they'll never stop.

But they do stop, they have to, because his mother is calling through the door:

"Lorkan, it's time to go."

WILL MEREN AND LORKAN EVER SEE EACH OTHER AGAIN?

BOOK TWO IN THE
BLUE BLOOD
TRILOGY

WHAT MEREN BECAME

SHE'S A THIEF,
A FUGITIVE...
HIS KNIGHT IN
SHINING
ARMOUR?

LJR SKYLERMAN

BOOK TWO IN THE BLUE BLOOD TRILOGY
COMING SOON

Acknowledgements

When it comes to thanking those whose support brought this book to life, I find myself indebted not to just one person, but to thousands.

I started planning this story at eighteen years old, but it wasn't complete until I turned twenty, and not perfected until three years—and four drafts—later.

Failing to find the sort of stories I wanted to read on the shelves, and then failing to find them online, I decided to start writing my own. Beginning with fanfiction, I published my nonsense on *Archive of Our Own* and *Wattpad* in the off chance that someone might stumble upon it—and perhaps even like it. You can imagine my surprise when my audience started racking up in the hundreds a day.

By my late teens, I had gained enough popularity in my niche corner of the internet for readers to start requesting plot lines, and it was here that this story was born.

What began as the ramblings of a teenager knocking out a 3,500-word chapter of fanfiction each week soon grew into its own universe, complete with unique characters, lore, and even the occasional fanart shyly emailed to me by one of my readers. Finally, after some persistent pestering, I decided to adapt it into a fully fledged, original work—and here we are.

I've fantasised about holding my own novel in my hands, smelling the pages, and slotting it onto my shelf since I was a little girl. You, my dear readers made this possible. Your kind comments, support, and persistent prodding to post another chapter (even though I'd *just* posted one!) helped me achieve a dream much earlier than I ever thought possible. To you, I raise a glass of apple tea and give my wholehearted thanks.

I hope you will continue this journey with me to the second book in the trilogy, which I guess I should start editing now. I sincerely apologise for the desperately sad ending of *this* book and—given how many of online readers complained that I made them cry—I hope this copy came with a complementary box of tissues.

Although I edited, illustrated, formatted, and wrote this book all on my lonesome, I would like to thank my friends and family who tried to help me come up with a cover design (and put up with my rants when LibreOffice wouldn't behave the way I wanted it to).

Thank you to my sister Katie, who I paid to clean up the stray pixels from my cover's line art—you did a great job.

Thank you to Maria for our brainstorming and art sessions. We may not have ended up chatting about a cover design, but we did chat about everything else.

Finally, I would especially like to thank my mum, Bridget, for her continuous support of my silly literary fantasies. I never let you read my online nonsense—through sheer embarrassment—but you were so proud of me all the same. The best thing about receiving positive feedback from my audience and passing 10,000, 100,000, and 1,000,000 reads was getting to share those moments with you. I hope seeing your name in a book can make you feel at least a fraction as special as your praise made me feel.

PRONUNCIATION GUIDE & GLOSSARY

CHARACTERS

Meren: Meh-ren
Lorkan: Law-kun
Alfdis: Alf-dis
Yllva: Ill-va
Arne: Arn-ee
Aasta: Ast-ah
Cade: Cade
Lophia: Low-fee-ah
Beca: Beck-ah
Bazyll: Baz-ill
Sol: Sol
Hectate: Heck-tate

PLACES

Velôr: Vel-oar
Calpurzia: Cal-purr-zee-ah
Hylune: High-lune
Tawny: Tor-ne
Holcombe: Hol-comb

OTHER

Amphiptere: A smaller, much more common, legless, flightless relative of dragons.

Wax sticks: Candles, often made of animal fat or beeswax.

Reems, Halvings, and Crescents: Units of Velôrian currency

Printed in Great Britain
by Amazon